SHE HAD TO KNOW WHAT IT WAS TO BE A WOMAN—WHATEVER THE COST. . . .

Afraid that any movement of denial would break the spell, she lingered motionless, eyes locked with Robert's. Then his eyes moved slowly to her throat, her breast. Her body responded to the touch of his glance. He lifted her gently in his arms and placed her on the bed. Esmeralda felt his growing excitement. It increased the rapture generated by his hands and his lips. There was a swelling, answering thrill in her own body.

"Wife," he murmured. "Lovely wife." He groaned with pleasure. She cried out, but the pounding of his blood urged him on. And beyond those pleasures she sensed another desire, deep and hidden—the desire to claim her, to make her forever his own.

D0047022

Other books by
Roberta Gellis

ALINOR
BOND OF BLOOD
THE CORNISH HEIRESS
THE DRAGON AND THE ROSE
THE ENGLISH HEIRESS
GILLIANE
JOANNA
THE KENT HEIRESS
KNIGHT'S HONOR
RHIANNON
ROSELYNDE
THE SWORD AND THE SWAN
SIREN SONG
WINTER SONG

FORTUNE'S BRIDE

Roberta Gellis

A DELL BOOK

™ Created by the producers of
**Inheritors of the Storm, The
Heiress,** and the **Wagons West** series.

Executive Producer: Lyle Kenyon Engel

Published by
Dell Publishing Co., Inc.
1 Dag Hammarskjold Plaza
New York, New York 10017

Produced by Book Creations, Inc.
Lyle Kenyon Engel, Executive Producer

Dell ® TM 681510, Dell Publishing Co., Inc.

ISBN: 0-440-12685-1

Printed in the United States of America
First printing—December 1983

*This book is dedicated to the memory of
Edwin J. Newman, who, with the greatest kindness
and generosity, gave me invaluable source material
and assisted me in the historical research upon
which this novel is based.*

CORUNNA   *Asturias*   SANTANDER

LUGO

Galicia   VILLA FRANCA   SAHAGUN

VIGO   ASTORGA   MAYORGA   BURGOS

BENAVENTE

Atlantic Ocean

Leon

Douro River   VALLADOLID

Tras Os Montes

Douro River   Tormes R.   ALAEJOS

SALAMANCA

OPORTO

OLIVEIRA

ÁGUEDA   ALMEIDA   CIUDAD   BÉJAR   *Old Castile*
RODRIGO

COIMBRA

FIGUEIRA   *Mondego*   MADRID
DA FOZ   *River*

Beira   *S P A I*

CALDAS

LAVOS

BRILOS   LEIRIA

PENICHE   LUGAR   *Tagus River*   TOLEDO

ALCOBAÇA

ÓBIDOS   *New Casti*

ROLIÇA

VIMEIRO   SANTARÉM   *Estremadura*   *La manch*

TÔRRES
VEDRAS

LISBON   ELVAS

BADAJOZ

P O R T U G A L

Alentejo   BAYLEN

Guadiana River   CORDOVA

Guadalquivir River

Algarve   SEVILLE   GRANA

Andalusia

MALAGA

0 10 20 40 60 80 100 120   CADIZ

Miles

RON TOELKE '82   GIBRALTAR

Strait of Gibraltar

THE PENINSULA
Spain and Portugal
1808~09

TOULOUSE

BAYONNE

France

UNA

rre

River

SARAGOSA

Catalonia

Mediterranean

Sea

agon

Valencia

Murcia

Officer, Fourteenth
Light Dragoons
1808

XIV
LD

© BOOK CREATIONS INC. 1982

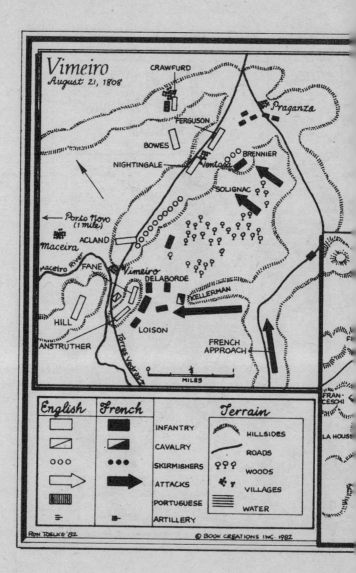

Vimeiro
August 21, 1808

CRAWFURD
Praganza
FERGUSON
BOWES
BRENNIER
NIGHTINGALE
Ventoza
SOLIGNAC
Porto Novo
(1 mile)
Maceira
ACLAND
Maceiro River
FANE
Vimeiro
DELABORDE
KELLERMAN
HILL
LOISON
ANSTRUTHER
Torres Vedras
FRENCH
APPROACH

MILES

English	French		Terrain	
☐	■	INFANTRY	hillsides	HILLSIDES
▱	◣	CAVALRY	⌇	ROADS
ooo	●●●	SKIRMISHERS	♀♀♀	WOODS
⇨	➡	ATTACKS	✿	VILLAGES
▤		PORTUGUESE	☰	WATER
⊟	■▬	ARTILLERY		

RON TOELKE '82   © BOOK CREATIONS INC. 1982

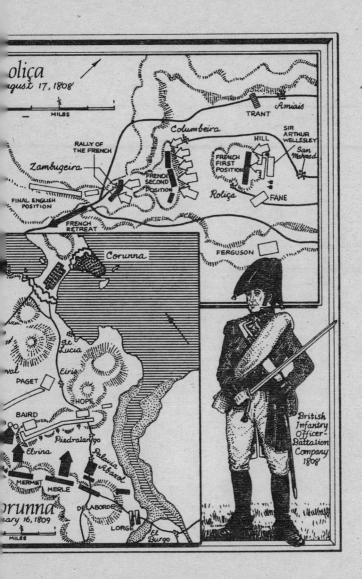

Roliça
August 17, 1808

MILES

RALLY OF THE FRENCH

Columbeira

TRANT — Amiais

SIR ARTHUR WELLESLEY
San Mamed

HILL

Zambugeira

FRENCH FIRST POSITION

FRENCH SECOND POSITION

Roliça — FANE

FINAL ENGLISH POSITION

FRENCH RETREAT

FERGUSON

Corunna
January 16, 1809

St. Lucia

Eiris

PAGET

HOPE

BAIRD

Piedralongo

Elvina

Palavia Abaxol

MERMET

MERLE

DE LABORDE

LORGE

El Burgo

MILES

*British
Infantry
Officer—
Battalion
Company
1808*

FORTUNE'S BRIDE

Chapter 1

Captain the Honorable Robert Francis Edward Moreton strode along Harley Street in London quite unmindful of the attention he was receiving. He was accustomed to creating a stir when he appeared in the full dress uniform of the Fourteenth Light Dragoons, the regiment in which he held his regular commission. Dragoon uniforms were always dressy, and the Fourteenth, its blue coat trimmed with orange facings, silver lace, and topped with a fur-edged pelisse, was brighter than most.

Robert had, in fact, never served in the regiment, having been a staff officer from the beginning of his military career, but he liked the uniform, especially the Tarleton helmet, which he thought much more sensible than the busby or the shako. It was one of the reasons he was still only a captain, for he could well afford to buy a promotion. However, Robert did not wish to change regiments, and no vacancy had occurred in the Fourteenth that would permit him to purchase a higher rank. He did not mind that. Since he did not serve in the regiment, he was not subject to the occasionally erratic orders of its superior officers. Nor did he need the increased stipend of a higher rank, having a very generous allowance from his father, the Earl of Moreton, and being a relatively sober young man, free of the vices of excessive drink and gambling to which so many of his peers were addicted.

In fact, Robert's character would have been as perfect as his features, which were better fitted for a Greek god or an idealized painting than for a young English gentleman, had it not been for an obsession deplored even by his affectionate family—his fixation on a military career. Nothing his worried father could offer had been sufficient to blunt this passion, and, in 1798, when Robert was seventeen, Lord Moreton, fearing that his son would join a line regiment as a volunteer or even be so desperate as to join the ranks, had agreed to purchase a subaltern's commission if his son would agree to serve on Sir John Moore's staff.

Robert had not been very happy about that. He had been very eager to fling himself into the war against revolutionary France, but Sir John was stationed in Ireland. On considering the alternatives, Robert had accepted the compromise and soon was delighted with his decision. Sir John was an active and brilliant officer and by 1799 was engaged in a more thrilling campaign in Holland. In 1800 and 1801 he was in the fighting in the Mediterranean and Egypt. Robert was delighted, though his family was not, and he came through both disastrous campaigns in which Moore was wounded five times, twice quite severely, with no worse damage than a saber cut and a crease from a spent ball.

Neither these minor wounds nor the dreadful mismanagement of the campaigns by the government and high command had the smallest dampening effect on Robert's military ardor. Actually, he developed so strong a taste for action and for tropical climates that when the Peace of Amiens was signed in 1801 and Sir John went on inactive status, Robert requested and obtained a recommendation to transfer to Sir Arthur Wellesley's staff in India. He did not inform his family of what he had done until after he was safely aboard ship.

Letters, alternately furious and pleading, followed him, but Robert ignored them, aside from writing soothing—and often quite false—reassurances about his health and safety. It had turned out that he need not have transferred, as Sir John was back on active service the next year. Nonetheless, Robert never regretted his choice. He succumbed neither to the weird diseases of the East nor to the desperate battle of Assaye or those that followed, and he enjoyed the strange culture and developed a deep admiration for his commanding officer.

Robert had been genuinely sorry when Sir Arthur, who was not well owing to the climate and some professional disappointments, had decided to return to England. Being a member of General Wellesley's personal staff, Robert had accompanied his commanding officer home. He had given some thought to requesting yet another transfer, but decided he would not want to serve under any of the senior officers remaining in India. However, general officers and staff officers with specific assignments, such as quartermaster general, were not so fortunate. Their posting was controlled by the Horse Guards, which was what everyone called the bureaucracy, including the Duke of York, who was commander in chief, and his staff, who together issued the orders that ran the army.

Actually, Robert was thinking about the Horse Guards as he walked away from General Sir Arthur Wellesley's house at 11 Harley Street. He was so lost in thought that he was quite unaware of several parties who were forced to step right off the walk to avoid him. Sir Arthur had just told Robert that he had new instructions from the government. The plans to invade South America were to be abandoned, and the force assembled at Cork was to be sent instead to Spain.

On a personal level the new orders were welcome. Robert had already been the recipient of a tearful lecture from his mother and an admonitory one from his eldest sister, both alarmed by the huge losses, largely from disease, that previous expeditions to South America had suffered. How they had heard of the proposed, supposedly "secret" invasion, Robert did not bother to wonder; in Robert's opinion any spy with a modicum of sense would attend ton tea parties rather than skulk around military installations.

His father, who also certainly knew through government sources about the plans for a new invasion of South America, had made no remarks, having doubtless come to the conclusion that argument was useless and that Robert, at twenty-seven, was old enough to manage his own life. But it was clear that the earl was also worried sick. Thus, Robert, who was as fond of his family as they were of him, was pleased that his parents and siblings would have less cause for concern.

He was less pleased about the insecurity of Arthur Wellesley's position as his commanding officer. The conservative and elderly officers of the Horse Guards who surrounded the Duke of York— equally elderly and conservative—did not like the brash and brilliant Arthur Wellesley. Sir Arthur had won his knighthood and his promotion, becoming the youngest lieutenant general in the army, by the brilliance and success of his campaigns in India. But he had won as much animosity for his stubborn honesty, his protection of the natives from the rapacity of the Indian and the English governments, and his fierce, unconcealed ambition. The response of the Horse Guards was to appoint one of their own favorites, who had seniority, to command over Sir Arthur's head.

Robert was sure that it was only because Lord Castlereagh, an old
friend and great admirer of Sir Arthur, was now Minister of War that
Sir Arthur had grudgingly been given the appointment to command
the expedition to South America—and then only because no senior
general was willing to go. But Spain was a different kettle of fish.
Most of the doddering half-wits on the Duke of York's staff would
love an appointment to a command in Europe. Castlereagh had
managed to get Sir Arthur the command temporarily on the grounds
that only he and his troops were ready to leave immediately; however,
could that last? With good winds, a fast ship could arrive at Corunna
or Vigo in only five to eight days bringing a new, and probably
incapable, commander.

Robert's lips compressed. He had no very good opinion of any of
the older generals—except Sir John Moore, and Sir John was not
much older than Sir Arthur. Moreover, Sir John was already abroad
with an expedition intended to defend the Swedish against the French
and Russians. It had been impossible for Robert to voice his concern
to Sir Arthur, partly because there had been no time, partly because he
did not wish to add any worries to those Sir Arthur already had, and
partly because he knew little beyond the bare fact that they would be
going to Spain rather than to South America.

There was no use going to the Horse Guards for information. Those
willing to speak to him about the probability that Sir Arthur would be
superseded by a senior general would not really know anything. His
father was also unlikely to be able to obtain any reliable information
on the intention of the Horse Guards because he was involved mostly
with domestic issues of trade and agriculture. Robert frowned, but a
moment later his brow cleared. His older brother, Perce, probably
could find out through his betrothed's foster father.* Roger St. Eyre
always seemed to know everything.

At the next crossing, Robert turned in the direction of the Stour
mansion. Technically Perce was living in Moreton House, but actually
he was seldom to be found there. All of his free time was spent with
Sabrina. Robert smiled involuntarily. He liked his future sister-in-law,
who was as sensible as she was beautiful. Come to think of it, Sabrina
was the widow of a high-level diplomat, William, Lord Elvan, and
had carefully maintained her own connections with the diplomatic

* See *The Kent Heiress.*

community because Perce was also interested in entering the diplomatic service. She might know as much as Perce or St. Eyre about the reason for this change in plans and whether it was a lost cause that the senior generals would choose to avoid. If that was the case, Robert wasn't worried; Sir Arthur had turned more than one forlorn hope into a resounding victory.

At Stour mansion Robert found his brother and Sabrina in what was to be their sitting room, studying swatches of wallpaper and cloth. Both looked up and smiled, and Perce lifted his fair brows as he remarked, "I see there's been some change of plans."

"Have you heard already?" Robert asked, astonished.

"No, I haven't heard anything," Perce replied, "but I can't imagine that you'd be out walking in full regimentals in this heat if you weren't running errands for Sir Arthur, or that you wouldn't have changed before you came here unless there was something urgent you wanted to talk about."

"We aren't going to South America," Robert said.

"Thank God for that!" Sabrina exclaimed.

Robert looked at her in some surprise. She hadn't previously voiced any concern about the expedition or about him, and neither had Perce. "I didn't know you didn't like the idea."

Both of them laughed. "Don't be so thick," Perce commented. "How could we like you going into that hell? We've lost eighty thousand men there, as many from fever as from action."

"There was no sense in nagging at you," Sabrina said with a slight shudder. "It was your duty."

Robert felt surprised again. His mother and sisters, although quick enough to point out such duties as escorting them to balls, never seemed to associate his military work with duty. They understood that he was required to obey the orders of his commanding officer, but they seemed to feel he should sell his commission and leave the service any time such an order was dangerous or disagreeable. Sabrina was the first woman of his acquaintance who had recognized his army career as a patriotic duty, not a form of amusement.

Perhaps, he thought, if there were more women like Sabrina, marriage would not be utterly impossible for him. But in the next moment he dismissed the idea. Marriage would still be impossible. One could not drag a woman through the hardships of a campaign, and to leave her behind was to condemn her to constant loneliness and anxiety or, far more likely, to invite unfaithfulness. These fleeting and not very serious thoughts were scattered by his brother's voice.

"Besides," Perce was saying, "Mama and Mary were at it hammer and tongs, and Fa was walking around with a face like a corpse. I thought you were getting enough objections from them without me adding any, but I'm damned glad it's off. I knew Wellesley didn't really approve of the objectives of the South American mission, and he approved even less of that Venezuelan general, Miranda. Who are they sending instead? Another old fool like—"

"No, I'm pretty sure that campaign won't be undertaken," Robert interrupted. "Sir Arthur told me we will be ordered to Spain instead, but—"

"Spain!" Perce stood up. "You mean there's been confirmation of the uprisings against the French?"

"Yes, but that's about all I *do* know," Robert said. "I was supposed to leave for Cork tomorrow with instructions, and Sir Arthur sent for me to tell me to return to the Horse Guards the papers I was to carry, but he didn't have time to say much else. You may be glad South America is off, but if there's too good a chance of making headway in Spain, Sir Arthur will be superseded, and I'm not so sure I like that."

"Take off your helmet and sit down," Sabrina suggested. "Would you like something to drink?"

Robert nodded in reply to her question and not only took off his helmet but unhooked his pelisse, threw it on a chair, and unbuttoned the top of his dolman. The removal of the helmet exposed a head of bright gold curls, flattened and darkened by perspiration, but detracting nothing from his exceptional good looks. His brow was broad and well shaped; his eyes were large, and their bright blue was only intensified by the tanning of his naturally fair skin. A straight nose set over exquisitely curved lips, which lifted just a trifle at the corners as if always ready to smile, and a rounded but determined chin made for a countenance that was totally ravishing.

Nor did removal of the pelisse, which for some men disguised narrow or sloping shoulders, prove in the least detrimental to Robert's figure. He was not as tall as his elder brother, but the strong neck exposed by the loosened dolman and the way the cloth fitted his shoulders without need for padding hinted at considerable power. If confirmation were needed, it could be found in the muscular thighs, well exposed by the molding of the tight breeches.

As Sabrina rose to ring the bell and to hang Robert's pelisse more neatly, she suppressed a sigh. It was not that she desired her dear Perce to look like his brother—to her, Perce was utterly perfect just as he was—but Robert's total indifference to women was such a waste. Any girl he chose would be a devoted slave for life, would fit herself to any pattern he desired. That sounded dreadful, but it would not be a bad thing because Robert was the kindest creature. He seemed completely unaware of how handsome he was and always picked out the unlovely and neglected girls at any social affair as if he expected to be rejected by the beautiful, sought-after belles.

Sabrina had once talked to him about his preference for wallflowers—timidly, for she did not know whether he would be angry—but he had only smiled and said it was unimportant because he would never marry anyway. That had frightened her enough to ask Perce if Robert was "different." It was as near as she could come to asking if he preferred men—or boys—but Perce had assured her his brother was quite normal and satisfied his sexual urges regularly, as her foster brother Philip had done for many years before he married Megaera.* Robert, Perce explained, confined himself to light-skirts because he did not think a soldier had a right to marry. A military man could spend so little time with a wife and his children that he soon became a stranger to them.

There was some truth in that, of course. Sabrina agreed that children must not be exposed to the dangers of a war zone. A wife was another matter. Sabrina heartily concurred with Robert's notion that there was no sense in marriage if one's husband would be at home only a few months, weeks, or not at all for years at a time. However, the right woman would think nothing of accompanying her husband, no matter what the danger. Sabrina knew of several such women, and she herself had been in situations of considerable peril owing to her late husband's diplomatic posts. She had never minded the danger; in fact, it had exhilarated her. It was William's personal doings that had caused her to accept his death with so little grief.

As for any children Robert might have, something could easily be managed. Even if the wife Robert chose did not have a mother, or he

* See *The Cornish Heiress.*

did not like her, Lady Moreton would gladly oversee the children.
Like her son, Lady Moreton was kindness itself. Or if Robert felt his
mother would be too indulgent, Sabrina would be glad to care for her
brother-in-law's children—only she might not be in England. But that
would not matter, for Leonie* would watch over them as Leonie
would watch over her own children if God would only allow her to
have them.

"Brina?"

The anxious note in Perce's voice woke Sabrina to the fact that she
was standing with her hand on the bell pull and staring blankly at the
wall behind it. She started slightly and pulled the delicate tapestry
ribbon that would ring a bell in the servants' quarters below. Then she
turned and smiled.

"I was thinking," she said not quite truthfully, "that if Spain really
has rebelled against Bonaparte, it might be important to us, too,
Perce. If you were to be sent there, or to Portugal, or if we had the
expectation of such an appointment, even if it did not come through,
that would be a good reason to set our marriage ahead."

Perce's expression cleared, but before he could answer Sabrina,
Robert said, "There will have to be a government not at war with
England before any diplomats are likely to be appointed. And I tell
you right now that if they replace Sir Arthur with one of those old
fools from the Horse Guards, Spain and Portugal will have to win
against Boney on their own. Do you think Castlereagh can hold out
against them?"

"No," Perce replied, "not indefinitely, anyway, because the Duke
of York has too much influence, but they might not push the matter
too hard until they see whether Sir Arthur makes any headway. In any
case, Sir Arthur may be more fortunate to be relieved of his command
than to keep it. I know the government presently believes Spain only
needs a little help to push out Bonaparte, but I don't think the Spanish
emissaries who are here are representing the political situation
accurately. I'm afraid—"

"I don't care about Spain's political situation. All I want to know is
whether Sir Arthur will keep his command."

Perce sighed with gentle resignation. Robert's obsession with
military matters did not yet include the recognition that political

* See The English Heiress.

maneuvering all too frequently was concluded on the battlefield. Robert was not unintelligent. He was an ardent student of the art of war, ancient and modern. He read every book on military history and military tactics he could obtain, and he remembered everything he had heard from Sir John and Sir Arthur about the battles they had directed. However, he was still young enough to regard the subjects of where and why one fought as irrelevant. In a sense he had the perfect military mind; he was quite willing to obey orders without ever requesting an explanation.

"But the politics in Spain may make it very hard for Sir Arthur to accomplish anything," Sabrina pointed out gently. "And I'm terribly afraid that this may be our last chance to fight Bonaparte outside of England."

"The navy will keep him off," Robert said, more to comfort Sabrina than because he had any doubts about the success of any campaign Sir Arthur led.

"For a while." Perce's voice was so grim that Robert looked at him in surprise. "The whole problem is tied up with Boney's fixed idea that he has to beat Britain and his realization in 1805 that he couldn't build enough ships to make an invasion possible."

"You can't mean that he fought Austria, Prussia, and Russia to beat us," Robert protested.

"No, of course not. I'm sure Bonaparte intended to be emperor of all Europe from the beginning, but he wanted to put us down first. Since he couldn't do it, part of every victory has been to pick up another weapon to use against us. Every treaty he's made includes stoppage of trade with Britain because he hopes to ruin us so completely that we can't fight him or encourage others to fight him."

"That's true," Sabrina put in. "There were a number of reasons why Tsar Alexander went to war, but one of them was the subsidy that Pitt offered to pay—a quarter of a million pounds for every hundred thousand men."

Perce nodded agreement and continued, "Another part of Boney's plan was to grab a ready-built navy. He didn't dare demand too much from Russia or Austria, and Prussia doesn't have a navy worth the name. But he insists that the small countries that can't resist give up their navies to the French. If he had succeeded in grabbing the Danish and Portuguese fleets as well as the Dutch and Spanish, he would have had about two ships to every one of ours. I know our men and officers are better, but at two to one, he might have managed so great a concentration of vessels as to pull off an invasion."

"We would have beaten him," Robert said.

"Yes." Perce closed his eyes for a moment, and when he opened them his face was bleak. "We would have beaten him because the farmers would have fought in the fields with pitchforks and the cobblers in the streets with hammers, but what it would have cost in lives . . ."

They were all silent for a moment, and Sabrina shuddered, remembering Perce's physical condition after the battle of Eylau. "That's what must be happening in Spain now," she whispered.

"Yes," Robert said briskly, "and if the Spanish are that determined, surely they'll cooperate right down the line, especially once Sir Arthur shows them he can beat the French."

"I wish it were that simple." Perce sighed.

Robert looked a bit rebellious, but he said nothing.

"The trouble is," Sabrina said, "that the Spanish probably don't realize what they're up against. They've never fought the French. Remember that Boney didn't conquer Spain. He took it by a trick. And it's useless to say that the Spanish should understand that if Boney beat Austria and Russia—" She stopped abruptly as the door opened and a footman stepped in.

Sabrina began to order drinks and then realized it was past noon. She asked Robert if he was free and he assured her he had no duties until that evening, when he was due to appear at a dinner-dance with Sir Arthur. One of the attractions of serving General Wellesley was that he was a most social person and expected the young officers of his "family" to attend functions with him and make themselves agreeable. It had been said, perhaps only half in jest, that the general chose his staff for their ability and indefatigability on the dance floor.

However, when this unkind remark came to the general's ears—for the truth was that Sir Arthur's staff was mostly forced upon him by "recommendations" he could not reject, as Robert originally had been—he uttered his typical, loud whooping "haw, haw" laugh and said it was an excellent notion. He pointed out, smiling, that grace in dancing indicated good timing, coordination, and balance, which were also the marks of a fine horseman; ability to deal with ladies showed courage and high spirit; and any man who had the strength to stand up to a full night's cavorting on the dance floor would certainly be strong enough for army service.

Robert's face had lighted as he mentioned the engagement. He loved to dance and enjoyed social functions as much as Sir Arthur, particularly when he attended as a member of the general's staff. Such attendance could arouse no speculations in any young lady or her matchmaking mama. When he was with Sir Arthur, any attentions he bestowed must be taken as merely his duty, since the general's opinion on the behavior of his young staff officers was already known.

Sabrina suppressed another urge to sigh over her brother-in-law's fitness for married life and instead merely instructed the footman to serve luncheon in the small breakfast parlor. On the way down to eat, Perce reminded Robert that since Bonaparte had beaten Prussia, Austria, and Russia, the only ports that were still officially open to British goods were those of Portugal, and he pointed out that because the French navy was still inadequate, the only way for Boney to close off Portugal was to invade by land. But that meant marching through Spain.

"I can't imagine Boney is worried about the Spanish after wiping up the Russians," Robert remarked as they seated themselves.

"No, but whatever else Boney is, he's no fool. Why should he waste men fighting his way through the Pyrenees when he could trick the Spanish into welcoming him? The Spanish have always resented the fact that Portugal defeated them back in the seventeenth century and has managed to remain independent ever since. Boney got the Spanish to let in his army by promising to hand Portugal back to Spain."

"And he didn't. The more fools they were to think Boney would keep a promise."

"They were worse fools than that," Perce remarked. "I'm not going to go into the crosscurrents in the Spanish government—"

"Thank God for that," Robert muttered.

Perce gave him a sardonic look but continued without comment, "—but because they all hated each other and thought they were smarter than an 'upstart Corsican,' the king—although you can't blame him, poor thing, he's nearly an idiot—the queen, her chief minister—who's probably her lover—and the crown prince all walked right into a trap Bonaparte laid and were forced to abdicate. Then

Boney thought the way was clear to establish another puppet throne with his brother Joseph on it."

"It wasn't unreasonable," Sabrina commented. "It had worked in Holland and Italy and other places."

"But Boney had beaten the Dutch and Italians first," Perce reminded her. "He hadn't beaten the Spanish. He had tricked them. Apparently as soon as news of the abdication spread, rioting broke out spontaneously all over the country. By the end of May, Sir Hew Dalrymple, the governor of Gibraltar, had received an appeal for money and arms from the revolutionary junta of Seville. But the point is, they seem to think they can beat the French on their own—and in my book that means trouble for Sir Arthur or whoever else commands the expeditionary force."

"If they think they can beat Boney when the Austrians, Prussians, and Russians couldn't," Robert remarked, "they're plain mad. But don't worry about Sir Arthur. He's used to native allies with swollen heads."

"I hope so." Perce looked worried. "The trouble is . . ." He allowed the sentence to hang in the air for a moment, then went on, "Canning at the Foreign Office is a clever devil, but I can't say I like him much, and he does have a tendency to jump at opportunities without investigating them sufficiently."

"You can't investigate military opportunities too closely or for too long, or they disappear," Robert pointed out.

Perce shrugged, but his voice was bitter when he spoke. "It's true, but it works both ways. Maybe if General Bennigsen had taken the time to investigate a little more closely what he thought was an opportunity, there wouldn't have been that bloodbath at Friedland. Maybe Russia would still have been in the war against Boney. Maybe the Russians could even have defeated the French. They came damned close a couple of times."

Robert glanced at his brother with considerable sympathy. He, too, had been in bloody, hopeless battles, but he had always felt he was tougher than Perce and that his elder brother should be shielded from such horrors and employ his considerable brains in seeing that the government supported the army properly. All he said, however, was "Castlereagh wouldn't jump just because Canning did, and Castlereagh is no fool."

"No, no, he isn't," Perce agreed, "but the whole government is

getting pretty desperate for a victory of some kind. The pressure on
Castlereagh at the War Office must be very high. Between trade being
badly hit by the blockade so that the cloth manufactories are closing or
turning away workers, and the bad harvests, which have nearly
doubled the price of wheat, the Midlands are in an uproar. There were
riots in Manchester—"

"They'll get their victory if they'll give Sir Arthur a free hand."
Robert stared at his brother. "That's what I've been asking you all
along. What are the chances of his keeping the command? They
couldn't have gotten at him in South America, but in Spain . . . The
damned Horse Guards can be sending messages every week, and he's
way down the list. . . ."

"What do you want me to say?" Perce asked, his voice sharpened
by frustration. "You know the situation as well as I do. Castlereagh
got the appointment for South America for Sir Arthur because no one
else wanted it. Europe is another matter. Castlereagh will fight for Sir
Arthur. They're old friends. They served together in the Irish
Parliament, and Castlereagh has a real appreciation for Wellesley's
abilities. He understands what Sir Arthur accomplished in India. But
there's a limit to what Castlereagh can do. Oh, I'll ask around, but the
best you can hope for is that so *many* favorites will be trying to get the
appointment that there will be some delay in deciding where to drop
the plum."

Chapter 2

A good deal of information flowed from the official embassy in Spain to England during the month of June. There were, indeed, popular uprisings all over the country. Although the riot in Madrid had been put down at the cost of more than three hundred Spanish lives, Cartagena rose against the French at the end of May. During the next few days, Valencia declared they would accept no king but Ferdinand, and the district of Asturias declared war on Napoleon, as did Seville and Santander. Granada, Corunna, and Badajoz took up arms. In Valencia every Frenchman seen on the streets was killed, and in Valladolid a gibbet was erected in front of the residence of the governor of Léon, who was given the choice of rejecting the French or being hanged.

At Cádiz and Vigo the French warships in the harbor were seized. The Spanish who had been besieging Gibraltar marched away to confront the French at Madrid, and the Spanish troops, which had made up two thirds of the army with which the French general Junot was holding Portugal, deserted to return and defend their own country against their erstwhile allies. Then, when the Portuguese also rose, the beleaguered Junot withdrew his remaining troops to a limited area around Lisbon.

The news arrived in England and was believed. However, in the primitive countryside of Portugal, the rumors that the French had been driven out did not drift into the small villages until July, and they roused uneasiness rather than rejoicing. It was not that the Portuguese people had any fondness for the French. Indeed, they hated them with more reason than the Spanish because Portugal was considered a conquered country. Thus, the French soldiers had been authorized to seize food and animals for transport, and their officers made no attempt to prevent them from taking anything else that appealed to them as well. Nor had the officers objected to the misuse of anyone who protested. What the people of the tiny rural hamlets feared was that the French would return, more ferocious than before owing to the opposition they had met.

In a small fishing village about fifteen miles north of Oporto, a young woman was trying clumsily, and somewhat inattentively, to spin. All the other girls in the village, practiced in twisting the carded wool into yarn from earliest childhood, did not need to think about what they were doing to produce perfect results. But Esmeralda had only recently learned. Of course, the village girls rarely had thoughts as frightening or as painful as Esmeralda's were that afternoon in July. News of the French retreat had raised hopes and fears in everyone. For Esmeralda the news had also presented an agonizing opportunity to make a choice.

Esmeralda had not been born in the village and had no intention of dying there. She had been born in Bombay, India, but she was no more a native of that land than of Portugal. She was an English gentlewoman; her father, Henry Bryan Talbot, was a distant relation, through a collateral Irish branch, of the earls of Shrewsbury, Talbot, and Waterford. It was an ancient and honorable family, but unfortunately Henry had not been one of its shining lights. Actually, he had been so unsatisfactory a young man that after an attempt to improve him by marriage had failed, he and his poor wife—guiltless but condemned by association—had been shipped off to India.

In a sense the exile had been of the greatest advantage to Henry. It had not made him more pleasant or honest, but it had given him great satisfaction by making him very, very rich. Nonetheless, he had never forgiven his family nor that of his wife, Mary Louisa. The Connors had done their best to induce their daughter to stay with them and let Henry be sent off alone. They even suggested that hopefully the climate would kill him. But Mary, though gentle and yielding of manner and sweet of disposition, had a strong and rigid sense of duty. She had sworn to take Henry for better or for worse until death did them part, and she kept her oath.

Despite the unpleasant aspects of his character, Henry had not been unappreciative of his wife's loyalty. He was neither generous nor affectionate, but he never mistreated Mary, either. His only real

unkindness was related to his obsessive spite; he would not permit her
to communicate with her family in Ireland, not even to announce the
births—or, sadly, the deaths—of her children.

This spite increased rather than faded with Henry's acquisition of
wealth, as did his parsimony. He intended, when he was rich enough,
to return to his native land, to ruin and then buy out all those who had
earlier scorned him. To forward this purpose, everything beyond what
was necessary to run his various ventures and live with great
simplicity was sent back to England to be safely invested. But to a
man of Henry's temperament it is impossible to become "rich
enough."

The years passed, and the climate and diseases of India took their
toll. Of the eight children born to Henry and Mary, seven died. Worn
out with grief and with labor—for as well as being housewife,
hostess, and mother, Mary had often been pressed into acting as clerk,
bookkeeper, and secretary to her husband—she, too, succumbed. All
that remained to Henry was a thirteen-year-old daughter, Esmeralda
Mary Louisa Talbot.

Until her mother's death, Esmeralda had lived a pleasant life. One
advantage of Henry's niggardliness was that no one in the English
community in Bombay had any idea how rich he was. Thus, no spite
or envy was directed against Merry—as she was called by her friends
for the liveliness of her disposition and the quickness of her wit.
Unfortunately, her vitality and humor were not valued by her father,
although they did testify to Esmeralda's considerable intelligence—a
characteristic he noted just as he took note of any asset that might hold
value in the future.

That future became the present soon after Esmeralda's mother died,
for her childhood ended as soon as those who came to offer sympathy
were gone. Henry immediately began to teach Esmeralda to take her
mother's place, attending to the many aspects of his business that he
would not trust to native clerks. The sudden change produced
rebellion; rebellion produced retribution. Henry was not a sadist, but
he could be cruel in order to get his way.

To facilitate the grooming of his daughter, Henry moved from
Bombay to Goa, the Portuguese community in India. The move was
temporarily convenient for his business, but Henry's main purpose
was to isolate Esmeralda, for in Bombay the families of her many
friends offered an easy escape when her father was otherwise

occupied. Besides, he did not want her complaining to others of his
unkindness or, more important to him, exposing his business dealings
by accident or for spite.

Esmeralda soon learned to obey her father, at least overtly, but
fortunately this was not because Henry had succeeded in breaking her
spirit. Once the initial shock of grief and change was past—and really
she had no time to grieve—she found the tasks her father was asking
her to do quite fascinating. Her willing application soon satisfied
Henry, who was clever about money but not about people and did not
realize that, young as she was, his daughter had already discovered
how to circumvent him.

By the time they moved back to Bombay, however, Merry was long
buried under the outer shell of Miss Esmeralda Talbot, a quiet, insipid
girl, whose rather unsuccessful father could not afford a proper
carriage for her, so that she rode everywhere on a small, ugly, but very
sturdy, mare. This constant exposure to the Indian sun wreaked havoc
with her complexion, which was much darkened, and with her hair,
which was dulled and bleached. What might have been her saving
graces, a pair of enormous, beautiful, dark-blue eyes and a perfectly
enchanting smile, were rarely in evidence. She kept the lovely eyes
lowered, and in her father's presence she did not smile.

But Esmeralda knew she had only to wait, and not for very long.
She was her father's heiress, and Henry was not the man he had been.
Although she did not like her father, she suggested more than once
that the climate was growing too much for him and that they should
retire to England. In Henry's own opinion, however, he was not yet
"rich enough." Then, in 1806, he had a violent seizure and very
nearly died. Esmeralda nursed him carefully. She did not lie to
herself: She hoped he *would* die, but she had her mother's strong sense
of honor and duty and she could not live with the knowledge that she
had not done everything in her power to save another human being, no
matter how unlikable.

In the long run, it was her father's illness that had brought
Esmeralda to this Portuguese village and to the unaccustomed task of
spinning. Not that making her spin was an act of unkindness on the
part of the villagers; it was an attempt to conceal from the French
Esmeralda's difference from the other girls. Henry might have been
greedy and might have lacked perception about people, but he had not
been stupid. When he had recovered from the seizure enough to get

about, he had sold his business and possessions in India, transferred all his assets to England, and booked passage for "home."

But Henry's luck had run out. Although they had waited until April when they had the best chance of good weather and a swift passage, everything possible had gone wrong with the voyage. And at last, off the coast of Portugal, the overstrained vessel had met one storm too many and had begun to sink. Esmeralda remembered very little of the terror-filled hours that followed. She was not unacquainted with danger. Because of Henry's reluctance to spend an extra penny, she had occasionally been exposed to bandits and to mob violence, but never had she felt so helpless, so utterly afraid.

She did remember being placed in one of the few small boats with her father, and she remembered bailing water from that fragile craft while it tossed and pitched. But when she saw the huge breakers, the wildly flung spume, the pitiless rocks and cliffs of the inhospitable shore, she gave herself up for dead and her memory held no more. When she finally regained consciousness, she found herself in a hut in the Portuguese fishing village where she now lived. How she had come there and what had happened to the sailors who had been in the boat with her father and herself she had never discovered.

Perhaps Esmeralda could have obtained more information had she asked at once, but at first she was too exhausted and too busy caring for her father. Surprisingly, Henry had survived the actual shipwreck, but he did not survive for long. The strain had been too much. Another seizure and the hard, primitive life killed him, in spite of all the villagers could do. By the time, several weeks later, Esmeralda had asked what had happened to the sailors, the headman of the village shrugged and shook his head. They had gone south, he said, toward Oporto—but the French were there.

Still, the villagers were kind. Although they knew that all British citizens were supposed to be given up to the French, they buried Henry with all the dignity so small a place could muster, and they hid Esmeralda when the troops came to forage. They did their best to make her indistinguishable from their own girls, but they were afraid. If it was discovered that they had been concealing an enemy, they would be harshly punished.

Esmeralda was aware of this fear, although no one spoke of it openly. It was an important consideration in the dangerous decision she must soon make. If the French returned, someone from the village might become frightened enough to betray her. Or Pedro, the headman's son, whose advances she had rejected several times, might do it for spite. Or, even more likely, one of the village girls to whom Pedro had previously paid attention might wish to be rid of her. Esmeralda's lips tightened as she thought of Pedro. The first time he had approached her, before her Portuguese had become as fluent as it now was, she had gone out of the village with him, not quite understanding what he wanted and thinking that perhaps one of the sailors had returned or that the French were coming and she was to be hidden.

She had soon discovered her mistake. Fortunately, because Pedro had thought she was willing and had not been prepared for her violent reaction, she had been able to fight her way free. But Pedro was not discouraged. He took her resistance for coyness and explained that his intentions were strictly honorable. Esmeralda did not believe this. Courtship was a very formal matter among the Portuguese. She guessed that he had heard tales of the immoral behavior of the British heretics and had expected her to welcome any man who offered. His profession of honorable intentions was no surprise; it saved face for both of them, and her unwillingness gave him an easy excuse to withdraw.

However, rather surprisingly, Pedro did not withdraw but pursued her in a more formal fashion. Esmeralda was considerably puzzled by his persistence. Surely, she thought, he could not really wish to marry her. It was ridiculous. Setting aside her own unwillingness, she would be utterly useless to him as a wife. She had none of the skills necessary to village life. She could not spin or weave; she had no idea how to wash clothes; cooking, beyond the boiling of eggs, was a mystery to her. In fact, she was learning a bit of all these skills, for she did not want to be a greater burden than necessary to her hosts, but it must be plain to everyone that it would be many, many years before she could become proficient. A man with so inept a wife would be very uncomfortable.

If she had been very beautiful, Pedro's interest might have been more reasonable. Some men did think beauty made up for other deficiencies. But Esmeralda knew she was not an especially attractive girl. Even in Bombay, where there were so many more Englishmen than Englishwomen that no girl ever lacked a partner at a dance, she had always been the last to be asked. Suddenly Esmeralda's hands, which had continued, no matter how clumsily, to twist the wool she was spinning, became still. It was not true that she had *always* been last. Twice, in India, several months apart, her ball card had been solicited as soon as that of the reigning belle—and by the most handsome man any of the women in that room had ever seen.

Captain Robert Moreton—it was a name to be cherished in the very depths of her soul, but that was all. Esmeralda had guessed what had drawn Captain Moreton to her for the first dance of the evening. She was the worst dressed and one of the plainest girls in the room. No one could really think he favored her. He asked her to dance first both as an act of kindness and to make clear that no invitation marked any serious intentions toward the partners he chose. No girl could misconstrue a request to dance after he had invited the unlikely Esmeralda Talbot.

Perhaps some girls would have been angry at being used that way. In fact, Esmeralda *had* been piqued at first and had nearly refused to give him her card, but his smile was so sweet and the furious, envious glances cast at her had been so amusing that she could not resist. Still, it had not been Captain Moreton's beautiful face or strong body that etched his image indelibly in her mind. She had looked on those rather as one looks at an exquisite portrait—a beautiful thing but with little human reality.

It had been Captain Moreton's kindness that fixed him in her memory. He had used her, but not callously as some highborn young blood might have done, showing his boredom and contempt while they danced. Captain Moreton had done his best to prove that he enjoyed the company he had solicited and to give her pleasure, too. He had talked to her and done his best to make her talk also.

Esmeralda sighed. It had not been possible for her to respond as she knew she could. If her father had heard of lively conversation and laughter—and he would have heard, for he kept close watch either by himself or through others on what his daughter did—she might not have been allowed to attend another social function for months. Henry had not wanted Esmeralda to attract men. He had no intention of allowing her to marry, thereby losing his confidential secretary-bookkeeper. In fact, Henry had disapproved violently of any strong relationship for Esmeralda. Love or friendship might induce her to speak of his affairs.

Thus, it had been impossible for Esmeralda to offer anything

beyond the normal insipidities on the weather, the decoration of the
ballroom, and the food and drink provided for the delectation of the
guests. Plainly, although he struggled to hide the fact, Captain
Moreton had been very bored before the dance was over. Still, he had
not "forgotten" that his name was on her card for two other dances.
He had been at her side as soon as the music began and, each time,
had lingered until the correct moment at which he was expected to
seek his new partner. That was truly kind and beyond what many of
the young men in Bombay were willing to do.

"Ah, perhaps it is better that you sit and do nothing than that you
make such a tangle."

Esmeralda jumped as the voice of the elderly widow with whom
she was living broke into her thoughts. "I am so sorry," she said,
laughing in response to the amused resignation of her hostess. "I'm
afraid I've made a worse mess than usual, Tia Maria. I was
thinking. . . ."

The courtesy title of *tia*, or "aunt," had been decided on as the
safest. An orphaned niece could conceivably appear in a village where
no one had ever seen her before. If, later, it was discovered by
someone outside the village that she was not, after all, a relative, it
would not be the villagers' fault that they had accepted her. Custom
and charity would have obliged them to do that, and there was no
reason why they should suspect any deception.

"Of Pedro?" the old woman asked, her voice now neutral.

"No!" Esmeralda exclaimed rather mendaciously, for she had been
thinking about him. Nonetheless, it was not really a lie. To answer yes
to Tia Maria's question would have implied something far different
from her actual thoughts. "Why do you ask me that?" she asked,
suddenly suspicious.

"It seems he thinks of you."

"But that is crazy. I am no fit wife for him." Esmeralda then
repeated aloud her earlier thoughts about her lack of wifely skills.
"What I was wondering," she finished, "was, if it is true that the
French are gone, whether I should try to go to Oporto. I know that
there were many English there before the French came. Perhaps some
of them are still there."

"Why do you not think of accepting young Pedro? Then you would
truly be of the village, and it would not matter if the French came
again."

Esmeralda was shocked. The one reason she had found for Pedro to be attracted to her, despite her lack of obvious charms, was that she was different. After all, he had known all the other girls in the village since they were babies. Whatever value novelty might have for a young man, it had never occurred to Esmeralda that anyone else could possibly approve of such an impractical arrangement. Her eyes went to Tia Maria's hands, swiftly making firm, smooth yarn out of the irregular, lumpy rope Esmeralda had produced. She pointed to what the woman was doing.

"Is that not reason enough, Tia Maria?" she asked. "Pedro is a fine man. All of the people in this village are good people, but I do not fit here. My life was very different. I do not know the things I would need to know to make Pedro a good wife. In the beginning, perhaps he would not care, but later he would grow tired of bad food, ill-knotted fishnets, and clothes that fell apart because I could not weave them properly. He would be unhappy. I also would be unhappy when I saw that my husband was not satisfied and that others laughed at him because I was not a good wife."

Of course, Esmeralda would no more have considered marrying Pedro than cutting off her nose. To her he was a common creature, outside her class, totally unacceptable even if he had been as beautiful and as kind as Captain Moreton. However, if Tia Maria was speaking of marriage, apparently the villagers had not, as she had believed, noticed the difference in class—or they did not care. To speak of it, then, or of her personal preference would be useless, so she tried to put the rejection in terms that Tia Maria could understand.

"But with the money, that would not come about," Tia Maria said. "You are rich. You could build a big house on the hill and hire others to cook your husband's food and weave the cloth for his clothes."

"Money! What money?" Esmeralda's heart leapt into her mouth.

She knew that her father had investments in England worth well over half a million pounds, investments that brought in more than twenty thousand pounds a year in interest, and that did not include the huge sum that had been sent off just before they left India. The income would permit her to live like a queen—if she could ever get to England and establish who she was. However, no one besides her father and herself, and, of course, her father's English bankers, knew what Henry Talbot had made and salted away. Why should Tia Maria speak of her riches?

"You mean you do not know?" the old woman asked. "Your father told old Pedro that he would pay well if we kept him safe from the French. Did he lie?"

So that was it. Esmeralda was relieved. She had feared that her father might have raved of his wealth in a delirious moment when someone other than she had been attending him. That would have been dangerous, but it was reasonable that he had offered to pay for sanctuary. Now she understood why the villagers had braved the dangers of hiding her from the French; it also lightened to a considerable degree Esmeralda's sense of obligation.

"No, he did not lie," Esmeralda said.

She was more than willing to fulfill Henry's promise, whatever it was, being certain that it was far less generous than it should have been, considering the service rendered. As she spoke she realized that she probably no longer needed to worry about being betrayed to the French out of spite should they return. Since Pedro's attentions had been paid in the hopes of winning a rich wife . . . Esmeralda's mind checked. A new danger had reared its head.

Pedro and his father might try to force her into marrying him in an effort to obtain her entire fortune rather than whatever sum her father had promised to pay them. Of course, no one in the village could even conceive of how rich she really was, nor would they believe her if she tried to explain that it would not be possible for Pedro to use her money as other village husbands used their wives' dowries of linens, sheep, or land.

These simple people would not understand that Esmeralda would retain control of her fortune after she married. The usual situation, in England as well as in Portugal, was that a woman's husband legally used her money and property as if it were his own, doling out, if he were generous, a pittance that she was free to spend as she liked. Many did not even give their wives that much freedom, insisting on having all bills sent to them so that any tendency toward extravagance in their women could be checked by argument or blows.

However, special arrangements could be made, and Esmeralda had long ago consulted several solicitors, selected the plan that suited her best, and induced her father to make the settlement she desired. Henry proved cooperative. He could see no reason, aside from what she might be expected to inherit, that would induce any man to marry his daughter. Thus, the fact that Esmeralda's husband could not benefit from her income, except as she wished to distribute it, should, Henry believed, serve to keep her single even after his death. He thought he was playing a nasty joke on her, but Esmeralda did not care what he thought as long as she achieved her purpose.

"But, Tia Maria," Esmeralda protested, "although my father did not lie and I will gladly pay—if I can—whatever he promised, the money is not here in Portugal. What little we had with us to pay our traveling expenses is most likely at the bottom of the sea. To obtain more I must go to England."

"And how will you do that without money?" the old woman asked sharply.

"That was why I was hoping there were still some English people in Oporto," Esmeralda answered. "It might be that my father had done business with one of them—he bought wine from Oporto, I know. If so, perhaps that person would send me to England or lend me enough to pay my passage. . . ."

"But then, if you had to pay back that debt, you might not have enough to pay old Pedro what your father promised."

Esmeralda bit her lips to prevent herself from laughing. A few hundred escudos was a large fortune to these poor people. Even if Henry had promised them a conto—a thousand escudos—that would come to less than £250. The cost of her passage and payment of the obligation to the village were the very least of Esmeralda's worries. Far more terrifying was the problem of identifying herself to her father's bankers—if she could ever get to England.

Tia Maria, however, took the bitten lip to be concern about the size of the debt. "You could write a letter," she suggested.

Esmeralda shook her head. "Would you send out so much money just because a letter said you should? And think: The letter would not be from my father. The money is mine now that he is dead, that is true, but how would he who receives the letter know that to be the truth just from a letter? When I am there before his eyes and he knows that if I lie it will soon be discovered, then he will give me what is mine."

On those last words, Esmeralda's voice trembled. It was so easy to say, and if the sum involved were small, perhaps that would indeed have been all that was necessary. But bankers do not hand over huge estates just because a strange girl comes and says Henry Bryan Talbot is dead, and I am his daughter, Esmeralda Mary Louisa. How was she to prove who she was?

"It is true that he who holds the money might not be willing to part with it if there is only a letter, and from a woman, too." Tia Maria, who had been watching Esmeralda, was aware of her uncertainty. "It would be even better," she said, "if you had a husband who could speak for you."

At the thought of Pedro in the offices of her father's bankers speaking for his wife, Esmeralda choked. It was true she had never seen those offices, but she was sure her father had chosen the oldest, most reliable, most august banking house in London. Henry did not speculate with the money sent to England. He ordered his bankers to invest it in the soundest of securities. Nonetheless, the situation was not funny. It seemed as if her fear that pressure would be applied to her to make her marry Pedro might be true.

"But that would mean the payment of two passages to England," Esmeralda protested, saying the first thing that came into her mind.

"Perhaps not," Tia Maria remarked, smiling slyly. "We in this village have no boat large enough to sail so far, but one might be found."

Esmeralda was growing frightened. "No," she said. "I do not wish to marry Pedro. I am English. I wish to live in my own country among my own people. You have all been very kind to me, but I am homesick."

"Ah, and so was I when I came from my village to this one, but it passes quickly. A strong, young husband and a few babies, and one thinks no more of such things. Besides, all the English are rich. There you will be nothing. Here you will be a great lady."

"No!" Esmeralda exclaimed. "No! I will not marry Pedro!"

"No? But I tell you, no one will help you get to Oporto. And even if you should be mad enough to try to go alone, without money or a man to speak for you, you will starve in the street. Think it over. It will be good for you to be married. You should be glad Pedro will take you, even with the money, for you are not so young or so pretty that many would offer. Pedro will do his duty by you, for he has the interest of the village at heart. Think it over."

Chapter 3

In the small boat being rowed out to the berth of the fast cruiser *Crocodile* in the harbor of Corunna, Robert Moreton and Fitzroy Somerset sat still and silent. Usually Sir Arthur's relations with the young men of his staff were very friendly, but Wellesley, who was sitting across from them, had a ferocious temper, which had been severely tried by the gentlemen of the revolutionary junta. Under the circumstances, Robert and his fellow aide-de-camp neither spoke nor fidgeted, either being likely to bring down on his head the wrath of his superior officer.

Sir Arthur was not particularly generous with information, but the young men had easily discovered for themselves that, although British money and supplies were welcome to the Spanish, the British army was not. The elaborate welcome Sir Arthur had received did not include an offer of a landing site for the troops following in slower transports. In fact, nothing beyond high-sounding phrases had been provided, and the sincerity of those was becoming rapidly more questionable as facts were wrenched with considerable difficulty from the officials of the junta.

The Spanish officials had, for example, initially told Sir Arthur that their General Blake had gained a great victory over the French, although he had failed to complete the work by destroying the enemy. But Robert and another ADC, John Fane, Lord Burghersh, had picked up rumors around the city that hinted at a different story. Robert could not be entirely sure of what he had heard. He knew a little Portuguese, which he had learned in India during the treaty negotiations in Bassein, but Portuguese and Spanish were not the same.

Nonetheless, he had mentioned the less favorable rumors to Sir Arthur, who in turn had pressed the Spanish for more information.

They had continued to insist that Blake had been victorious, but then admitted that the general had thought it wiser to withdraw. Alerted by the inconsistency, Wellesley asked more questions, whereupon it appeared that "perhaps" Blake had really suffered a slight check. Worse yet, no junta officials to whom Wellesley spoke seemed to have the slightest idea about what was going on in the rest of the country or, at least, none would tell Sir Arthur.

"We will try Portugal," Sir Arthur said suddenly to his ADCs in the boat, without a hint of anger in his voice.

"I hope they are more welcoming, and more truthful," Somerset remarked.

Sir Arthur smiled without amusement. "One should not expect truth from native allies. I learned that lesson in India." He paused, then went on dispassionately, "But I must confess that I was somewhat disappointed to learn it to be equally true of European allies."

"Do you think the Spanish were lying about anything else, sir?" Robert asked. "I don't think the people in the town know any more, but surely the officials have better sources?"

"It's very hard to say," Sir Arthur replied. "If the unrest in the country is as great as reported, there may be confusion about who *is* an official. In addition, the French move very fast. And then, there is always the possibility of interregional jealousies. In that case, they wouldn't tell each other the truth any more than they would tell it to us."

"Then all we have done is waste two days," Somerset commented angrily.

"No, I wouldn't say that." Sir Arthur smiled again. "There is considerable value in having learned that we cannot rely too firmly on any intelligence supplied by the Spanish or, at least, not on that supplied by official sources." He looked out past Somerset in the direction of the *Crocodile,* but he was not seeing the ship. "Knowing what *not* to do is worthwhile."

The *Crocodile* made quick work of the sail around the northwest coast of Spain and on July 24 landed in Oporto, Portugal. Here the situation was somewhat more hopeful. Antonio José de Castro, Bishop of Oporto, head of the local insurgent junta, had convinced a few hundred ragged Portuguese regulars and a crowd of peasants armed with pitchforks to drive out the French. Moreover, the information that the whole country north of the Tagus River was free of French and that General Andoche Junot and what was left of his army were confined to the area around Lisbon seemed to be true.

Neither the bishop nor General Bernadim Freire, who was in charge of the remnants of the Portuguese army in Oporto, voiced any active objection to a British landing, but Sir Arthur knew that it was not practical to bring troops ashore so far from the enemy. It would be best to land somewhere along the Tagus estuary; however, there was little possibility of that. Junot was said to have about 26,000 men, and even if that was an exaggeration, the French marshal was far too experienced to leave the sea gate to Lisbon open to the British.

The most hopeful site for a landing was at Figueira da Foz at the mouth of the Mondego River. However, Figueira was still more than one hundred miles from Lisbon, making necessary overland transport for food, guns, ammunition, and the other endless materiel of war. A discussion—some of it acrimonious—about the alternatives ensued among Sir Arthur, the junta, the bishop, and General Freire. However, the Portuguese were truly enraged by the robbery, sacrilege, and oppression the French had visited on them and were, at least marginally, more interested in driving out General Junot and his army than in personal glory or aggrandizement. In addition, owing to an avid taste for port wine and long-standing business dealings, the British were relatively well liked and trusted at Oporto. Thus, Sir Arthur was able to carry nearly all of his points.

If it was possible for the fort at Figueira da Foz, which had been taken from the French by a heroic troop of students from Coimbra, to be secured by British marines, Sir Arthur would order the troop transports to Mondego Bay, which was just north of the fort. Wellesley himself would sail south in the *Crocodile* to consult with Sir Charles Cotton, the admiral in charge of the ships blockading Lisbon. If Sir Charles agreed with Sir Arthur that it would be impossible to make a landing nearer Lisbon, the troops would be brought ashore at Figueira. Meanwhile, the bishop would undertake the task of gathering up the hundreds of oxen and pack mules necessary for transport, and General Freire would march those troops he could supply south along the road to Leiria.

However, although Sir Arthur obtained the agreement of Bishop

Antonio and General Freire, he did not feel any very strong conviction that the promises they had made would be fulfilled. He hoped, because the agreement had been relatively voluntary, that at least part of the assistance offered would actually be provided, but he was much too wise to rest the success of a military action on the promises of men he could not control.

Sir Arthur felt he could accomplish his purpose even if the bishop and the general did nothing at all, but he must at least know that no help would be forthcoming from them. Thus, he assigned Colonel Trant to act as liaison officer between General Freire and the British forces and left Robert, who could speak some Portuguese, to assist the bishop. Sir Arthur provided Robert with a sum of money to be judiciously used for bribery or minimal but tempting payment to the muleteers and ox drivers. Robert's instructions were to scour the countryside himself for transport animals if the bishop grew indifferent or was too busy.

Neither of Sir Arthur's fears about Bishop Antonio was true, but it was obviously not possible for the bishop to go about from village to village personally. He preached about the coming of the British in Oporto and instructed his aides and the other members of the junta to spread the word to the priests and to the *regadors* of the towns to urge compliance. However, with harvest coming and the countryside already ravaged by the foraging of the French, it was a bad time to collect draft animals.

On July 25, Sir Arthur left and Robert spent the day arranging for the quartering and victualing of the animals and drivers that were collected. With the support of Bishop Antonio and the other members of the junta, this was easily settled, and there was nothing more Robert could do in Oporto until the transport animals began to come in. Considering the circumstances, it seemed wise to him to spend the time out in the countryside himself, assuring the owners of the oxen and mules that they would be paid for their time and the use of their animals.

Bishop Antonio agreed heartily to this proposal, saying that word of actual payment would spread from hamlet to hamlet and do much good, and he offered a young priest as a guide. Although he was relatively certain of the genuine goodwill of the bishop, Robert did not propose to go far from the city, since he was eager to start the

animals south toward Figueira da Foz within the six days stipulated by
Sir Arthur. However, he decided he could range out about twenty
miles from Oporto, starting west early in the morning, going as far as
he could until noon, and making his way back eastward by a different
road, stopping at each town and large village to solicit help and offer
payment. The next day, he would go north.

There had been more than one unpleasant interview between
Esmeralda and the elder and younger Pedro in the weeks that followed
Tia Maria's first suggestion that Esmeralda marry the headman's son.
Inducements were offered and then threats, but neither Pedro nor his
father had Henry Talbot's strength of character. Esmeralda had learned
in a hard school how to resist without infuriating, and she pointed out
many difficulties that stood in the way, even had she been willing: She
was not a Catholic, was not willing to convert, and she would tell that
to any priest, who would then certainly refuse to marry them. Even
more important, Esmeralda said most untruthfully, was the fact that
she did not know what arrangements her father had made. He might
have appointed guardians for her, who were directed to arrange her
marriage and who might be able to cut her off without a penny if she
disobeyed them. The last argument was particularly telling. It was
most reasonable to both Pedros that no woman should be allowed to
pick her own husband.

In addition, the younger Pedro was growing less and less willing to
take to his bosom a woman with so sharp a tongue, which was not
even compensated for by beauty, when he knew he could have his
pick of the village maidens or, if he wanted a better dowry, of girls
from nearby villages. How did they know, he asked his father,
whether Esmeralda really had any money? The old man had been very
sick and very frightened. Perhaps he had offered most of what he had,
or more than he had, in order to buy safety. The refugees' clothing,
young Pedro pointed out, was not like that of great ones. A fine
situation he would be in, he complained, if the girl's father had lied
and he was trapped in a marriage with a wife who could not perform
the simplest household duties.

Because he was not the one who would have to live with the plain,
sharp-tongued wife, the elder Pedro was unwilling to give up so
easily. He tried repeatedly to pry information from Esmeralda about

her late father's business and fortune, but she was more than a match for him, partly because of his total ignorance of the world outside his own immediate surroundings and partly because he *expected* her to be ignorant of the very facts he was seeking. Esmeralda did not even have to lie; old Pedro asked her such things as whether her jewels and fine clothes had been lost, and she could say, quite truthfully, that she had no jewels except for the gold locket containing a miniature of her mother, which she was still wearing, and that her finest clothes had been two party dresses, which were several years old.

By July 26, when Robert and his guide approached the village, the headman was almost as sick of Esmeralda as she was of him. Despite his greed, old Pedro was not bad at heart. Thus, when a shepherd rushed down from the grazing grounds to give warning that there were riders on the road and one of them wore a blue coat and a cocked hat, Esmeralda was hustled into the darkest corner of the hut in which she lived. Robert's staff uniform, much plainer and more serviceable than the gaudy full dress of the Fourteenth Light Dragoons, had been mistaken for that of a French soldier. And, threats or no threats, old Pedro did not intend to give Esmeralda up to the French.

The young priest rapidly cleared up the misunderstanding and explained that the English had come to help them drive out the French for good but that draft and pack animals were needed. Instantly old Pedro began to shake his head. In his fear that a new wave of foraging would denude the hamlet of what few animals they had managed to hide from the French, he completely forgot his other "English problem." But Robert was accustomed to this reaction; he had met it in almost every foreign country in which he had served. Before the headman could maintain that they had no such animals and then perhaps be afraid to admit later that he had lied, Robert spoke his carefully rehearsed lines stating that he would buy the animals or hire them and any driver who would come to Oporto with cart and oxen and serve the British army. Then he took silver from his pouch, being careful to expose the long-nosed pistols he carried at the same time.

"We are a small, poor village," old Pedro said. "If we do not have oxen for the harvest, we will starve. And much has been stolen from us already. The few animals we have are worth a great deal to us."

Although Robert's Portuguese was not very fluent, he understood more than he spoke and made out enough of what old Pedro was saying to recognize a standard gambit for bargaining. Nevertheless, it was plain to him that what old Pedro had said was true. At most, such a place could supply no more than one or two mules and one yoke of oxen. He had already arranged for a dozen mules and four yoke of oxen in somewhat larger villages and did not think it worth his while to spend an hour bargaining for so small a return. He shook his head and made another prepared speech.

"It is the Bishop of Oporto who has set the price." This was not actually a lie; Bishop Antonio's secretary had discussed with Robert what he would be likely to have to pay for the purchase or hire of mules and oxen. Robert recognized, of course, that it would cost the British army more than the Church—if the Church paid at all—and he continued with his set lines. "Naturally, there will be extra pay for serving a foreign army. If you have animals to sell or hire out to us, bring them to the field opposite the Church of Santa da Lapa. They must be fit for work, not lame or starved or too old."

"But how can we know—" old Pedro began.

Young Pedro, like every other villager who was not out fishing, had come into the open area near old Pedro's house as soon as the priest had established Robert's bona fides. But young Pedro was not listening to his father. Unburdened by any responsibility for the welfare of the village, he did not allow himself to be distracted by talk of mules and oxen. The foreigner was English—and he had money. Here was his opportunity, young Pedro thought, to get what had been promised to them and also to rid himself of the threat of a plain, sharp-tongued wife, who said openly she did not want to marry him and thus would grow uglier and sharper tongued with every year.

Quietly young Pedro eased himself through the group of men and women who were listening intently and made his way to Tia Maria's hut. There he grasped Esmeralda by the wrist and began to pull her out. He did not explain. Although he, no more than his father, would have given Esmeralda up to the French, she had hurt his pride, and he was spiteful enough to wish to give her a good fright.

He succeeded completely in this purpose. Esmeralda struggled violently, believing that she had gone too far and convinced father and son that she would not be able even to pay what Henry had promised them and that they were thus about to rid themselves of the danger her presence posed to the village. However, this time her struggles were ineffective, since Pedro knew she would resist and was prepared. The only thing he feared was that she would scream, for he did not want the Englishman who had the ear of the Bishop of Oporto to think that he or anyone in the village had harmed a countrywoman of his. But, frightened as she was, Esmeralda did not make a sound. To scream would only attract the attention she was fighting to avoid.

Having dragged her out of the hut and had his little revenge, Pedro tried to tell Esmeralda that the visitor to the village was English, not French. By then, however, she was so terrified, knowing how the French troops would use an Englishwoman who had no proof of her identity and thus no claim to honorable treatment, that she could not take in what he said. Now young Pedro regretted his petty revenge. He certainly did not wish to drag a struggling, disheveled girl before a man of wealth and influence. It would make it very difficult to claim that they were her saviors and had been good to her and that, therefore, the Englishman should pay her debt to them.

Young Pedro paused behind one of the houses and shook Esmeralda until her neck nearly snapped. "You fool!" he snarled. "It is your countryman to whom I bring you. Listen! The man is English, not French."

Esmeralda heard, but she did not believe him. She thought he was saying it only to trick her into going willingly. Of course, there was no sense in that, but she was too much afraid to think clearly. She made one last effort to wrench herself free, managing to kick young Pedro most painfully on the shin and sink her teeth into his hand. He howled, as much with shock and surprise as with pain, and Esmeralda managed to gain her freedom.

She did not know what to do with it, however. She darted away behind another building, but there she paused. She could hear young Pedro cursing as he trotted back toward his father's house. If the headman had already betrayed her, she realized, there was no sense in running. The Frenchman was on horseback and could easily catch her. The only hope Esmeralda had was to convince him she was a lady and that there would be serious repercussions from his officers if she was molested. Thus, she fought back her tears, smoothed her hair quickly, and came out into the open.

The very first thing she saw was Robert, who had just remounted his horse. For a moment, Esmeralda believed that terror had unhinged her mind. In the next instant, she remembered that young Pedro had insisted the visitor was an Englishman.

"Captain Moreton," she gasped, but shock froze her voice and the words came out scarcely louder than a whisper.

Robert, who had said his good-byes, lifted his reins. Again Esmeralda tried to cry his name, but this time no sound at all came from her throat.

Chapter 4

Young Pedro, who saw his release from a shrewish wife about to disappear, gave up his low-voiced argument with his father, and as Robert's mount began to move, turned and cried out, "There is an Englishwoman here who owes us money."

He spoke quickly in his haste, so that the only words Robert caught were those for "English" and "money." He did not rein in because he did not wish to waste any more time, and he thought the young man was asking another question about whether the English could be trusted to pay. However, the priest understood. He was puzzled by Robert's indifference and asked, "An Englishwoman? How did she come here?"

And almost simultaneously, Esmeralda found her voice and called, "Captain Moreton! Wait!"

The feminine voice drew Robert's eyes, and he frowned. Esmeralda, freed from the paralysis caused by fear followed too quickly by relief, hurried forward. "Captain Moreton," she cried, "do you not remember me? I am Esmeralda Talbot. We met in India, in Bombay."

For a moment, Robert just stared. The face and voice were only vaguely familiar. His own appearance was notable. Very few people who had seen him, male or female, forgot those perfect features. To Robert, however, Esmeralda Talbot had been only one of many plain, uninteresting girls. Nonetheless, the accent was that of an English gentlewoman. Robert dismounted again and went to meet her.

"Miss Talbot?"

Esmeralda picked up the uncertainty in his voice. "You must remember me," she gasped, beginning to tremble. "You must! Please! Oh, please!"

"Of course I remember you," Robert assured her soothingly,

taking her hand. It was not exactly the truth. Robert did know that he
had met this young woman before, but where and when had faded into
the general blur of innumerable dull, dutiful parts of otherwise
enjoyable social engagements.

"Thank God," Esmeralda breathed, clutching his hand as if it were
a lifeline. "You must help me, Captain Moreton."

"I will if I can, Miss Talbot," Robert said cautiously, "but I am on
duty, and—"

"You cannot leave me here," Esmeralda cried, her voice rising
hysterically. "The old man wants to force me to marry his son because
he thinks I am rich."

"Good God!" Robert exclaimed, realizing for the first time that
Esmeralda was not in the village of her own free will.

He had assumed, when she said she had met him in India, that her
family had moved to Portugal for some business reasons. Robert had
left India in 1805, two years before the French had invaded Portugal.
There had been a reasonably large colony of British in and around
Oporto involved in the wine trade. It was conceivable that some had
not believed in the seriousness of the French threat and had not wished
to abandon their businesses and return to England in 1807. For that
kind of greed, Robert—whose family was rich and therefore could
afford to be contemptuous about money—had little sympathy.
However, if this young woman was alone and unprotected, Robert's
duty was clear to him; he was not happy about it, but he would not
shirk it.

"No, of course, that cannot be permitted," he added hastily,
fearing Esmeralda was about to dissolve into tears. "Something will
have to be done. Please try to be calm, Miss Talbot," he concluded
desperately.

Esmeralda drew a long, shuddering breath. "I am very sorry," she
said more steadily. "If you will listen to my problem and advise me, I
promise I will not afflict you with vapors."

"That's the dandy," Robert remarked with hearty encouragement
and an enormous sense of relief.

When his sisters started to cry, he had found that they also seemed
to lose the ability to make sense, so that it was nearly impossible to
discover what had caused the distress in the first place and stop the
waterfall. He began to feel more kindly toward Miss Talbot. As his
alarmed concentration on her diminished, however, he became aware

of a babble of excited voices behind him. He turned slightly and noted that the headman was alternately shouting at a younger man close to him and whining at the priest. Both the young man and the priest were replying, and owing to the medley of voices, Robert could not make out a word.

Robert began to feel worried again. If the villagers wanted to hold the girl, there could be trouble, and Sir Arthur had given strict instructions that everything was to be done to conciliate the people. Nonetheless, Robert could not permit the forced marriage of an English gentlewoman to a common peasant. He cast a glance at Esmeralda, but although she, too, was now looking at the three vociferous speakers, she showed no signs of becoming tearful again. He assumed that was because she could not understand what was being said.

"I do not wish to alarm you," Robert said, "but perhaps it would be better to explain later. I would prefer that we leave before there is any trouble. That young man—"

As he spoke, he had watched Esmeralda anxiously, but instead of looking frightened a very faint smile appeared on her lips, and when he said "we leave" she relaxed the tight grip she had kept on his hand. Robert then gently disengaged his fingers altogether and felt even better pleased when Esmeralda showed no sign of objecting.

"Young Pedro will not try to keep me," she said. "His father—old Pedro is the headman—is angry because young Pedro is the one who told me there was an Englishman in the village." Now that she saw salvation within her grasp, Esmeralda was more than willing to forgive young Pedro for the fright he had given her and certainly did not wish to make any more trouble for him than he was in already. "You see," she continued, "young Pedro is the one who would have had to marry me, and he didn't like the idea any more than I did. I am afraid my putative riches did not make up for—for my other lacks."

"The more fool he," Robert said automatically. He was not, of course, thinking of the "putative riches" Esmeralda had mentioned but only saying the polite thing to a girl who was obviously too aware of her plainness. "If you have kept your head in such a difficult situation, you cannot lack much," he added, seeking to make the compliment he had paid a little less empty. Then, to avoid having to find another compliment that was not obviously a lie, he asked, "Do you understand them?"

"Oh, yes," Esmeralda replied. "You need not worry about old Pedro making trouble. The reason he is so angry is because he thinks that the villagers have lost all chance of obtaining what he feels is owed to them, as well as personally having lost the chance of snaring a rich daughter-in-law. But, really, if it is at all possible I would like to explain part of the problem now. You see, I . . . I do feel I owe the villagers a debt, and I have no way to pay it until I get to England." Her voice began to tremble on the final words, and she stopped and swallowed hard.

"Now, now," Robert soothed, "there is no need to worry about money. Something can be arranged, I am sure. How much is this debt?"

Esmeralda uttered a rather tremulous chuckle. "I am not quite sure. You see, when we were shipwrecked—"

"Shipwrecked!" Robert exclaimed. "You have had a rather rough time, I'm afraid. Perhaps you would like to sit down."

A more natural laugh was drawn from Esmeralda. "It was more than a month ago, and I am quite recovered from the exertions involved," she said primly but with twinkling eyes. However, she sobered immediately and added, "But Papa did not recover. We had left India, you see, because his heart was weakened and he could no longer tolerate the climate. Although he did survive the shipwreck itself, the shock was too much for him. And he could not stop worrying. Papa was terrified of being taken by the French. He offered to 'pay well' if the villagers would hide us. But I don't know whether he ever offered a particular sum, and old Pedro has never mentioned any specific amount, either. However, that may be because Papa offered more when the French were foraging in the area and then reduced the amount again when they were gone."

Robert had only been listening with half an ear. As soon as Esmeralda began to talk about "Papa," the name Talbot had finally rung a bell in his mind. He still could not recall distinctly where and when he had met Esmeralda, although now he was certain he had danced with her at some ball or other, but Bombay and Talbot had come together to produce a clear memory. He did remember meeting Henry Talbot and not finding the experience a pleasant one. The man had tried to interest him in investing in some very dubious enterprises. Realizing suddenly that he had made no response at all to

Esmeralda's mention of her father's demise, Robert said hastily, "I am
very sorry to hear of Mr. Talbot's death."

There was a slight pause during which Esmeralda stood absolutely
still with lowered eyes. She knew what was proper, what was
expected of her. Every daughter was supposed to grieve over a father's
death, but Esmeralda was envisioning the tens, perhaps hundreds, of
times she would have to mouth falsehoods and pretend emotions she
did not feel. What was more, she had sensed the coolness and reserve
in Robert's tone when he spoke the formal regret for her father's death
that politeness required. Impulsively she spoke the truth.

"You do not need to offer me sympathy over Papa's death. He was
not a very nice person and not kind to me. I have nothing to regret. I
did my duty as a daughter, but Papa did not love me and did not wish
that I love him, so there was little in his death to cause me grief."

Robert had been cursing himself, thinking he had precipitated a
new emotional crisis. He had been casting wildly around for some
sympathetic phrase that would not make matters worse, when
Esmeralda had raised her eyes to his and spoken. In that moment of
relief, Robert thought them the most beautiful eyes he had ever seen.
Further, he was so delighted that he would not need to wade through a
bog of bathos that he found her candor far more refreshing than
shocking. However, he had not the faintest notion of what to say in
reply to such a statement.

Fortunately, there was no need to say anything because at that
moment the diatribe old Pedro had been delivering to his son and the
priest flooded over onto them. Pointing his finger at Esmeralda, old
Pedro accused her of ingratitude and heartlessness, reminding her of
the shelter, food, and clothing that had been bestowed upon her. Then
he turned to Robert.

"She is lying to you," he declaimed passionately. "She is saying
we were cruel to her and that she owes us nothing—"

"Quiet!" Robert ordered, having remembered that one appropriate
word from his limited Portuguese vocabulary. He then said to the
priest, "Father, would you be good enough to translate what the
headman said? He speaks too quickly when he is so excited for me to
understand. And would you also translate what I say? It would take
me too long to find the right words in your language."

The priest repeated what Pedro had said. Robert flicked a glance at

Esmeralda, and she nodded, smiling slightly, indicating that the
translation was accurate.

"You are quite wrong," Robert then replied. "Miss Talbot has not
been accusing you of unkindness at all. She has, in fact, told me that
her father promised you a recompense for what their keep has cost you
and for your good faith in protecting them from the French. We
English are honest people. We do not wish to cheat you." At least,
Robert thought, he had been able to get in a useful conciliatory
statement.

While the priest translated, Robert made a rapid calculation of the
amount of money he had with him. He knew that there could now be
no question of riding farther to seek animals for transport. Sir Arthur,
he was sure, would have agreed, had he been present, that Robert's
first duty was to get Miss Talbot to Oporto and make what
arrangements he could for her safety. How to get her there, however,
presented a problem. He asked the priest to stop translating for a
minute while he consulted Esmeralda.

"I will walk if necessary," she said gratefully, "but I could easily
ride a mule or an ass. I was accustomed in India to riding long
distances."

"I am glad to hear it," Robert replied, "but there is a problem. I
am sure there will be no lady's saddle in this village—if they have
saddles at all."

."Dear Captain Moreton"—Esmeralda laughed while she blinked
back tears—"you are very considerate, but this is no time for
delicacy. I would be happy to leave here draped over the back of an
ass like a sack of wheat. I will not object to riding astride on a blanket,
I assure you."

A most reasonable girl, Robert thought. He wondered why he could
not remember her more clearly. She was no beauty, certainly, but she
had fine eyes and a good spirit. Usually he did remember young
women who made interesting conversation.

"Tell the headman that I will give him two hundred escudos," he
said, "but that must not only clear Miss Talbot's debt completely but
include a mule and some kind of saddle for the animal."

Robert then resigned himself to the endless haggling that followed.
First there was a violent protest that a mule was not necessary;
women, old Pedro claimed heatedly, only rode pillion behind a man.
Robert quelled that quickly enough by saying coldly that he had no

intention of tiring his fine mount by making the horse carry double for that distance. And when the headman protested that she would only fall off and be hurt, Robert stated even more coldly that Miss Talbot was no common Portuguese peasant girl but an English gentlewoman, who knew well how to ride and was not accustomed to being bumped about on a horse's croup like a faggot of sticks.

Meanwhile, Esmeralda had been thinking over Robert's offer, comparing it with what she knew of the amount of money circulating in the village. Considering the fleeting expression she had noted on old Pedro's face, she soon came to the conclusion that far from feeling cheated, the headman was afraid that Robert would later think he had overpaid and come back to reclaim his money if the offer was accepted too eagerly. Thus, she was not surprised when the first mule presented should long ago have been retired, and the second had a wheeze that could be heard across the whole square.

Robert was not unaware that he had been generous. As soon as he had been made responsible for the transport animals, he had begun to acquaint himself not only with their value but with the cost of forage and the wages a driver might expect. He knew that two hundred escudos was about the equivalent of what all thirty or so villagers would earn in a year. Information did spread from village to village, and Robert wished to be generous, to underline the value of preserving the life and honor of any British citizens who might be exposed to future dangers in the area.

Nonetheless, Robert scornfully rejected the two wrecks offered him. He did not actually care, so long as the animal could survive carrying Esmeralda to Oporto, but he did not wish to leave the impression that the English were not only honest and generous but also stupid. Thus, he displayed not only an assumed indignation but his thorough knowledge of beasts of burden, and the third animal that was offered was quite serviceable.

Then the argument about a saddle began. Robert was less certain of his ground here, not because of any concern over the value of the saddle but because he did not know what might be available in a small village. To his surprise, Esmeralda said nothing, although when old Pedro began to lament that there was only one saddle and giving it up would cause great hardship, she shook her head and winked. Partly because of that warning and partly because their pace would be too slow if Esmeralda had only a blanket to ride on, Robert persisted.

At last, the saddle was brought forth, the mule was readied, Esmeralda mounted with casual confidence—which caused gasps of surprise from the villagers, who had not really believed Robert when he said she could ride—and they turned south toward Oporto.

"Captain Moreton," Esmeralda said in a slightly unsteady voice as soon as they were past the last houses, "I do not know how to thank you for what you have done."

"Don't have to thank me," Robert replied a trifle brusquely. "You are a British citizen in distress. I've done no more than my duty to you. And any officer would have done the same. I just hope I didn't take the one sound mule the French left them. I thought you would say something one way or the other about that."

"Oh, no. I would have found a way to warn you if you were really hurting them, but they can buy ten mules with what you gave them—not that they need them. Most of their income comes from fishing. I couldn't *say* anything, however." Esmeralda smiled at him. "That would have lowered your status. Only henpecked husbands allow their wives to speak even a word when men talk business." She chuckled. "It wasn't only that I wasn't as pretty as some of the village girls that made young Pedro decide he didn't want to marry me no matter how rich I was. It was the fact that I dared to argue with his father."

This logical reply to what Robert had considered a somewhat unfeeling attitude toward people who had, despite an uncomprehending greediness, protected Esmeralda from a real danger made him laugh heartily. "I didn't think of that," he admitted. "Well, thank you for saving the honor of the British army." He had turned to look at her while he spoke and added doubtfully, "I'm afraid you are not very comfortable."

"No, I am not," Esmeralda replied forthrightly, but she tempered her statement with a brilliant smile. "I am not used to riding astride, of course, but even riding sidesaddle I am sure the gait of this animal would have nothing to recommend it. However, I am not repining," she assured Robert merrily. "I prefer this mule infinitely to the one I left back in the village."

Robert laughed heartily before he realized that no delicate young woman could possibly have meant what he was thinking. Then he hastily smothered his mirth and examined Esmeralda's expression, wondering whether she had intended the double meaning or whether he had shocked her into recognizing it by his burst of laughter. Girls, Robert knew, were never as ignorant as their mothers or governesses would like one to believe. But what the devil could Miss Talbot have meant if she had not been comparing young Pedro's sexual gaits with those of the mule she was riding? Still, he did not know how to respond.

Breaking the moment of awkward silence that ensued, Esmeralda said blandly, "The old man was so stubborn. No matter how many difficulties I pointed out, among which was the fact that his son was unwilling, he would not move from the position that marriage would be best for both of us."

It was, of course, the perfect answer to the question Robert had asked himself, but he remained somewhat uneasy. Had there been a wicked glint in Miss Talbot's eyes for the brief instant they had met his? Robert faced forward to watch the road and once again wondered how he could have so completely forgotten so clever a girl.

By the time they reached Oporto, he admired her courage, steady good sense, and good humor, too. It was plain that she was suffering considerable discomfort, not only from her unaccustomed position and the awkward gait of the animal she rode, but also from the necessity, despite the excessive heat, to cover her legs with a blanket to preserve the decencies. Still, not a word of complaint did she utter, nor did she propose that they stop and rest every few minutes. To add to those remarkable qualities, she did not chatter compulsively, only answering cheerfully any conversation addressed to her.

During the ride, Robert learned the facts about the shipwreck and Esmeralda's sojourn in the village. He could see that, although she was greatly relieved to have been rescued from that situation, there was something else troubling her. However, she did not seem to wish to speak about whatever it was, and Robert really had no desire to inquire too particularly. If she presented a problem to him, he was bound to try to help; but he had no intention of looking for trouble.

Chapter 5

Trouble came soon enough without being sought. Having established Esmeralda in the best hotel in Oporto and arranged for a dressmaker to visit her at once so that she would be able to appear in public, Robert began to investigate means of getting her back to England or, if that failed, of providing her with sufficient money to live decently until passage could be arranged. Both avenues were blocked. There was, at present, no ship leaving for England nor any expectation that one would be leaving in the near future. And as for money, Robert found to his horror that he could not obtain personal credit—not even from the Bishop of Oporto. The refusal was couched in diplomatic terms, but it was definite.

Moreover, though Robert had brought with him a substantial sum, knowing from previous periods of service in war zones that at best his pay would be irregular and might under certain conditions become nonexistent, his personal funds were now rendered almost useless. Robert would have been perfectly willing to expend every penny to get Esmeralda safely off his hands, but he had naturally carried pound notes rather than gold, and no one in Oporto was willing to exchange more than one or two pounds for Portuguese money.

Robert was certain that Portugal would be cleared of the French, normal trade with England would resume, and British pounds would retain their value; Portuguese bankers and merchants, however, did not share his confidence. If the British were driven out instead of the French, pound notes would be little more than worthless paper. They were willing to change relatively small sums to pacify and please their allies, but nothing near the amount Robert felt to be necessary could be obtained.

Of course, there was the money that Sir Arthur had left with him to pay for the transport animals and their keep. The two hundred escudos Robert had given old Pedro had, in fact, come from this purse, but Robert had intended from the beginning to make up the sum from his private resources. However sympathetic Sir Arthur might be to the need to rescue Miss Talbot, Robert knew the government would take a dim view of such an expenditure. And even if the payment were condoned owing to the emergency, further expenditures for clothing and accommodations were not likely to be acceptable, particularly if that meant there would be fewer mules and oxen to carry supplies.

Remembering that he had set no limit on Esmeralda's orders to the dressmaker, Robert hurried back to the hotel, wondering how he was going to explain these unpalatable facts to her. Thus, he was considerably relieved when, as soon as he entered the sitting room the hotel had provided, she said calmly, "I see that something has gone wrong, Captain Moreton. Please sit down and explain to me what has happened."

"I am afraid," Robert began, "that I was too sanguine when I spoke of arranging your passage to England. It seems that no ships are going there, at least not from Oporto."

To his surprise, instead of crying out, *What am I to do?* Esmeralda smiled faintly.

"I know you will think I am quite mad," she said, "but I must admit your news is the greatest relief to me."

"Relief?" Robert echoed. "What the devil— Oh, I beg your pardon. What do you mean?"

"You need not bother to beg my pardon for a most natural expression of irritation," Esmeralda remarked. "Papa used the most unsuitable language before me. I am quite unshockable. But I am sure you are more interested in why I do not wish to go to England." She paused and sighed. "I know I am a most unwelcome burden, Captain Moreton, and I had resolved not to add my troubles to the ones you already have, but—but really I am in the most dreadful situation."

Robert's lips tightened. He remembered Henry Talbot's seedy appearance, and he thought he knew what was coming. Probably Talbot had been carrying with him whatever small fortune he had realized when he had sold his house and whatever other holdings he had in India—and that had gone down with the ship. His daughter was thus penniless. Well, Robert told himself angrily, it was no business of his. He would not, of course, expect her to return the money he had paid old Pedro or the dressmaker's fees, but he was damned if he would get in any deeper.

"I assure you," he said, "that there is no need to repay—"

"Oh, no!" Esmeralda interrupted. "My problem is not any lack of money." She blushed painfully and then continued with obvious discomfort. "We were not—not so badly off as Papa liked to pretend. That was just—just his way. I can well afford . . . That is, I will have a—a comfortable competence if—if . . . My problem, Captain Moreton, will be in proving who I am."

"What?"

"You see," she went on hurriedly, "Papa quarreled with his family and with Mama's also. He was not of a forgiving disposition, and he forbade all communications." She hesitated again and blinked back tears. "He even forbade Mama to speak of his family or hers and—and she was afraid to disobey him. I do not know exactly where my relatives live, other than that Papa and Mama originally came from Ireland and that Papa was very distantly related to the Earl of Shrewsbury. He spoke of that because it was useful to him, but obviously I cannot presume on such a relationship, and I have no idea whether any of my grandparents or aunts or uncles—if I have any— are alive. Nor do they know that I am alive. What is worse, all Papa's papers went down with the ship, and no one in England has ever seen me."

"Good God." At the moment, Robert could think of nothing more useful to say.

"It is not quite hopeless," Esmeralda began again. "I wrote most of Papa's letters to his bankers. Do you think they would recognize my handwriting and accept that as an identification? Or, perhaps"— her voice was growing unsteady because she was more and more frightened by Robert's frozen expression, but she continued valiantly—"I could write to India. Many people know me there. If someone who knew me in India was now in England, one of my friends could tell me and that person could identify me, or . . . or . . ." She fumbled at her neck and drew out the locket. "I have this," she said desperately. "It has Mama's picture. . . ."

"But you don't know anyone in England who would recognize the picture, and it would take months for a letter to get to India," Robert said somewhat absently.

He had been growing more and more appalled as he listened,

wondering if he had been trapped in some elaborate coney-catching scheme, but the locket Esmeralda held had finally jogged his memory. He remembered seeing it, the one pretty item in a rather drab costume that had endured a few too many wearings. It was the locket that had attracted Robert and decided him to ask Miss Talbot to dance first. He breathed a sigh of relief. Of course her manner was different now. Three years ago she had been barely out of the schoolroom, too shy to speak up, but he remembered her eyes, too, even though she had only raised them once or twice.

"Yes, I know," Esmeralda breathed, clasping her hands and fighting helplessly against the tears that were now coursing down her cheeks. "And how am I to live until then? And where? Oh, do forgive me, Captain Moreton. This is not your problem. You have already done more—"

"I know you," Robert said.

His voice was strong and so redolent of relief and satisfaction that Esmeralda's tears checked. She stared at him for a moment and then started to laugh, hiccuping between sobs and giggles.

Poor Robert thought she was hysterical and rose to his feet making inarticulate noises he thought were soothing and looking anxiously at the door. Should he try to find the landlord's wife or some other woman to help? But how could he ever explain what had driven her into this state? God knew what would be thought. The idea of trying to express what was necessary to be said in Portuguese was far more frightening to Robert than riding through an artillery barrage.

However, such desperate measures were not needed. Before Robert could force himself to the door, Esmeralda had caught her breath and gasped. "You are the kindest person! You did not really recognize me, did you?" As she spoke she sniffed and wiped the tears from her face with the heel of her hand. Delicate cambric handkerchiefs were no part of Portuguese peasant costume.

Robert gravely presented his own handkerchief, and Esmeralda used it. "I did and I didn't," he confessed. "That is, I knew I'd seen you before, but couldn't remember where or when." He did not mention his brief and passing suspicion that she had been setting him up for a skinning; he felt very guilty about that. "But I know you now," he went on heartily. "Remember your locket and remember signing your card, thinking what a pretty name Esmeralda was."

Robert stopped abruptly again. He had almost added that he had also thought it was a pity the girl wasn't as pretty as the name. Happy in his escape from one faux pas, he did not realize that what he *had* said was almost as cruel as what he had not. Internally Esmeralda winced, but she took no offense at the implication that her face was not memorable. The hurt only drew a few more tears, which she wiped away surreptitiously. She knew Robert had never had any special interest in her and the strong attraction she felt for him had been most unintentionally engendered.

"Ghastly hot it was at that ball," he went on reminiscently as he sat down again, hoping that recalling a pleasant occasion would cheer her up.

"Yes, indeed, it was," Esmeralda replied, smiling. She understood Robert's intention and responded gallantly, knowing that he meant well and was doing his best in an impossible situation. "But Governor Duncan's balls always are. After all, one cannot refuse the governor's invitation, so his balls are always the greatest crush."

"Were you ever tempted to refuse?" Robert asked curiously. He had often wondered whether plain girls, who knew they would not receive the same attention as the pretty ones, exposed themselves voluntarily or were forced by their parents to do so.

"No, certainly not," Esmeralda said. "I love to dance, and in India where there were so few English girls, I was assured of a partner. I am not so sure I would be equally eager in England where I might be . . . Well, but we are talking great nonsense. We are not likely to be troubled by balls here, and there are worse problems than those of finding a partner for me."

"Don't be so sure of a lack of balls. Wherever Sir Arthur sets up headquarters, there are bound to be . . ."

Robert's voice drifted into silence. His mention of Sir Arthur had reminded him that it would be necessary for him to leave Oporto in a day or two at most. The two satisfactory parts of his interview with the bishop's secretary had been the report that a surprisingly large number of animals had come in already and that more were on the way. The combination of French atrocities and the offer of coined silver had worked a miracle and produced a good crop of oxen, mules, and horses from a seemingly barren countryside.

Had he been able to obtain sufficient funds to rent a house for Esmeralda, provide her with servants, and leave her money enough to live on for a month or two, he would have done so and dismissed her

from his mind, except for reporting her presence to the proper
authorities. Since this was impossible, he had to make other
arrangements. He cleared his throat uncomfortably and explained this
to Esmeralda.

"I would not have wished to remain in Oporto anyway," she said
quietly, "unless there were some English family with whom I could
stay. . . ."

The indefinite ending and lift of her voice made the statement into a
question. Robert shook his head. "I am very much afraid," he said
slowly, "that you will have to come south with me. Unfortunately, I
can get no information about the roads—except that they are
dreadfully bad. I am not sure a carriage could get over them, even if I
could convince someone to sell me one for pounds. I am very sorry,
Miss Talbot, but—"

"Good heavens," Esmeralda exclaimed, her smile lighting her
face, and her eyes shining with joy. "Please do not apologize. That is
just what I would have wanted, but I did not dare ask. You have
already done so much, I *could* not think of imposing myself on you
still longer. But if you are willing to take me—oh, I will be so grateful
to you."

"Yes, but you know it is a good distance, over one hundred miles,
and the weather . . ."

Esmeralda laughed like a bird singing. "But my dear Captain
Moreton, I am quite accustomed to a hot climate, and I am equally
accustomed to riding. Oh, dear, I never thought I would be grateful to
Papa for his meanness, but I am. He would never buy a carriage, and
quite often we had to ride from Bombay to Goa."

She thought she would burst with joy. That invitation to ride south
was her salvation. Once Robert had brought her to a place where there
were other British people and introduced her as Esmeralda Talbot, her
identity would be established. Very likely Sir Arthur would send her
back to England on one of the ships that carried dispatches. Esmeralda
was almost certain that, if Robert and Sir Arthur requested him to do
so, the commander of the ship would be willing to escort her to her
father's bankers and confirm her explanation of the shipwreck, her
father's death, and the loss of all his documents. Then her handwriting
and her knowledge of her father's affairs should settle the matter.

All that was an enormous relief, but the real source of Esmeralda's
well of joy was the knowledge that she would have several days more

of Robert's company. It was no use telling herself that such thoughts were futile and unhealthy. She knew perfectly well that she was nothing but a duty—and a worrisome duty at that—to Robert. But just to look at him was a precious delight to her. And with the thought she hastily lowered her eyes, fearing that there had been an adoration in them that had made him uneasy, for he was frowning.

But Robert's frown had nothing whatsoever to do with Esmeralda's expression. Although he was looking at her, he had noticed nothing beyond her obvious relief at the proposal he had made and the confidence with which she had assured him that she would not mind the hardships of travel. Fortunately he had the evidence of her behavior on the ride from the village to Oporto to support her statement, and he could believe her. What was more, he was sure that he would be able to obtain a proper saddle and a mare or gelding with a less jarring gait so that, although the distance would be greater, the discomfort would be less.

What had brought the creases to Robert's fair brow was a very delicate matter. He and Miss Talbot would be four or five days on the road, and their only company would be a few dozen Portuguese muleteers and ox drivers—scarcely acceptable chaperones for a young lady of breeding. It was all very well to say that they were in Portugal and it was an emergency; the whole thing was still highly improper, and Robert was afraid that there would be no way to keep it a secret.

His fellow aides-de-camp were from the best families; Burghersh was the Earl of Westmoreland's heir, and Lord Fitzroy Somerset was the youngest son of the Duke of Beaufort. They were the best of fellows, but it would be too much to expect them to keep so good a story to themselves. Robert could just hear them: *It's just like Moreton's luck,* they would say. *You'd think it was enough that he has the prettiest face in the whole army, but he goes out to pick up asses and oxen and instead finds a shipwrecked damsel in distress.* Of course, they would mean no harm. They would tell the story in the strictest confidence, only intending to poke fun at him, not to make difficulties for Miss Talbot, but it was sure to get out.

Unfortunately, too, Miss Talbot had no friends or family who would support her. With a story like that going around, she would not have a chance to establish herself. Under other circumstances she doubtless could have obtained introductions to the families of people she knew in India and formed a pleasant circle of acquaintances, but with a

scandal broth brewing . . . There was only one way out. Robert
sighed.

"Indeed, I promise I will not make any difficulties," Esmeralda
said earnestly, hoping her general statement would be understood in
the emotional sense as well as referring to the journey south. She
imagined that Robert was plagued with women worshiping him.

"You won't, but others will," Robert said with a tinge of bitterness
and heaved another sigh. "There's nothing for it," he added, wearing
an expression of extreme dejection. "We'll have to get married."

Chapter 6

Esmeralda's mouth dropped open, and her eyes widened so far that they almost appeared ready to fall out of her head. In addition, shock drove the air out of her lungs while she was seeking words so that she uttered an indistinct and most inelegant gobbling noise. Robert, who had been staring past her concentrating on his private rationalizations, suddenly realized what he had done. He jumped to his feet, cursing himself for being ten kinds of a donkey. The last thing he had said to the girl was that it would be a long, hot ride, and then without the slightest warning or explanation he had proposed marriage. It would be no wonder if poor Miss Talbot had hysterics.

"No, don't," he said desperately. "I didn't mean to shock you. Oh, damn it all, you can't go riding all over the country with me and a bunch of Portuguese ox drivers. It isn't at all the thing. People would get to talking."

Now Esmeralda was in even worse straits. One cannot laugh while one is strangling for lack of air, but the form of Robert's explanation of his extraordinary proposal was inordinately comical. At the same time, the kindness of his intention and his obvious distress absolutely required a response that would put him at ease. Esmeralda struggled for breath while Robert stood halfway between her chair and his own, afraid to approach but equally afraid that the next thing that would come out of her mouth would be the piercing shrieks of a totally unhinged mind. He knew he needed female assistance, but the thought of what Esmeralda might say to any woman who offered her sympathy almost unhinged *his* mind.

"I'm all right," Esmeralda gasped at last. "I am sorry to have alarmed you. You took me so much by surprise."

Robert could have kissed her. He stared down into her large, dark-blue eyes, magnified now by unshed tears of stress, and again thought how remarkably beautiful they were. "I'll get some wine," he said anxiously. "Can't think how I could have been so stupid. Should have explained first. Dreadful shock for you. But I don't mean anything by it—I mean, I do, but I wouldn't expect . . . Oh, the devil with it. I'll get some wine."

Esmeralda was not in any need of a restorative, but she was glad to have a little time alone to reassemble her wits and get control over her feelings. Although she could now breathe evenly, she still did not know whether amusement or agony predominated. Captain Moreton, set on rescuing a maiden in peril, was clearly ready to go all the way, regardless of the cost to anyone. That was most laudable; only one could not help but laugh at the sad resignation with which he prepared to sacrifice himself; it was perfectly plain to Esmeralda that he scarcely saw her as an individual and did not care much for what he saw. No, Captain Moreton's sacrifice was not for the maiden, but for the propriety itself. Esmeralda started to giggle and choked on a sob.

He was such a dear person, so upright and honest, so obviously well brought up by a family that treated its women with the utmost consideration. But that was where the danger lay. If Captain Moreton had been as practiced a hand with women as his handsome face would lead one to suspect, Esmeralda thought she would soon have recovered from her infatuation. Such a person would doubtless try to flatter her and show her attentions, which she would know to be false. In that case, close association over an extended period would soon produce disgust.

That could never happen with Captain Moreton. He would most likely be careful and considerate of her because he had been trained to be careful and considerate of women. He would be kind because it was his nature to be kind. And Esmeralda knew that she would fall more and more deeply in love.

She should not do it. Esmeralda knew she would suffer horribly if she yielded to the temptation. Yet what else could she do? Without Robert, how was she to prove her identity? Perhaps she should return to India and obtain identification papers from Governor Duncan, but there was no way she could think of to pay for her passage, and she had no idea where to find a ship going to India. Would she have to travel to England first?

No, it was insane. Captain Moreton had offered the perfect

solution, simple and easy. Surely she was sufficiently adult and intelligent to keep her emotions under control when it was so very plain that he was utterly indifferent to her except as another duty. And she had intended to travel with him. A marriage of convenience could not possibly make any difference in how she would feel, since it was quite plain that Robert did not intend to act as her husband, but only lend her his name. But Esmeralda was lying to herself, and she knew it. It would make a difference. She would have to resist the idea of marriage.

Before her very urgent desire to snatch at even the most distant opportunity for an intimate relationship with Robert could take hold and manufacture arguments, he came back into the room, carrying a tray with bottles and glasses. Esmeralda could not help laughing, albeit a bit shakily. His anxious expression betrayed the reason for his acting as waiter. He did not want any witnesses if she had collapsed into hysterics again.

His eyes lighted at her laugh, and he said, "By George, you *are* a sport, Miss Talbot. I can't say how sorry I am. You see, I was sitting here and thinking about what you said—you know, about not having any family or friends in England—and that made me think that you wouldn't have anyone to—to stand up for you. Then I got to thinking about how long it would take to get the animals down to Leiria, and what might be said. . . . I swear I never thought . . ."

"Do set down the tray," Esmeralda suggested, driven to tease by her mingled misery and mirth. "But, really, you do not need to apologize or assure me that you had no dishonorable intentions. After all, you made me a proposal, not a proposition."

Robert set the tray down rather more abruptly than he had intended. Wearing a rather hunted expression, he turned toward Esmeralda. "But—"

She burst into laughter, interrupting him. "Oh, forgive me," she gasped. "I have a most improper sense of humor. I was only teasing you. I understand perfectly that you were most kindly offering a marriage of convenience to protect my reputation. I am very grateful, truly grateful, but I cannot think it to be necessary. Surely no word of so small an incident would get back to England."

Robert's expression had changed from anxiety to amusement at Esmeralda's confession and then back to anxiety again at her final words. "Unfortunately, that's just what I'm not at all sure of," he said. He hesitated, poured two glasses of the wine, and handed one to Esmeralda. Since it was obvious he was trying to find the right words to say something else, she sipped her wine and waited. "You see," he went on slowly, "I would have to bring you to headquarters, and Sir Arthur's staff is not only all very well connected but also very young. They wouldn't mean any harm; they would think they were making a joke at my expense. I could warn them," he went on hastily, "but I fear that would only impress the incident on their minds."

"That is quite true." Esmeralda was forced to agree. "What's more, it would make telling it even more irresistible," she admitted. "As soon as one knows something should not be said, it is always at the tip of one's tongue."

As the words came out, Esmeralda remembered that she was supposed to be arguing against the marriage, not for it. Even if the story of her unchaperoned days with him did get back to England, she did not think it would greatly impede her acceptance into society once the size of her fortune was known—a cynical view perhaps. Nonetheless, she was relatively sure that five days' lapse would be overlooked in the shadow of half a million pounds.

"Still," Esmeralda went on, determined to be sensible, "it seems to me to be too great an imposition upon you. I must take my chances. After all, I survived a shipwreck and escaped from old Pedro's schemes—"

"That's just why I decided there was nothing for it but getting married." Robert sighed and tossed off the glass of wine he had been holding. He refilled the glass and turned back toward Esmeralda. "No sense rescuing you from one bumble-broth and dropping you into a worse one. Not your fault the ship went down or that there aren't any ships going to England or that the damned Portuguese won't give me credit." Suddenly Robert smiled at her. "And you've been damned good about it, too. No vapors, no fuss."

Esmeralda laughed. "That would have been very poor thanks for your kindness, to saddle you with hysterics in addition to so awkward a burden."

Now Robert laughed also. "True enough, but most women don't seem to consider such things. Tend to get upset first, then they don't seem to be able to think at all. You're a very sensible girl."

"Thank you," Esmeralda said. "It is owing to having lived with Papa. He had very little sympathy with a display of the vapors.

However, I do not see that this marriage will really help. Will it not be even more exquisitely humorous to your fellow ADCs that you rescued a young woman and married her out of hand?"

"They *will* have a May-day frolic over the marriage," Robert agreed, grinning, "but I won't mind that, and they won't tease you. And when we have it annulled, they won't say a word to anyone about its ever having happened. They will think, you see, that something went wrong between us, and to have gossip about *that* would hurt me—and you also, of course. They would not wish to hurt us."

"Annulled!" Esmeralda repeated, and then added quickly, "Yes, of course. How stupid I am." She looked down at her hands, so tightly clasped that the knuckles showed white, afraid of what Robert might read in her face. "But will it not make a scandal to—to put an end to the marriage? Will that not negate the good effect you wish to produce?"

"No," Robert said eagerly, proud of his strategic planning and completely unaware of the blow he had delivered, "we can be married by the bishop, or by his priest or someone—I'm pretty sure I can talk him into that, since we're both heretics already. I mean, he wouldn't be taking a chance on having a Catholic soul corrupted, and maybe he would even think some good would rub off on us from a marriage in the 'true faith.' But the marriage wouldn't be valid in England, you see—at least, I'm pretty sure it wouldn't be. And since it wouldn't have been . . . er . . ."

"Consummated?" Esmeralda offered with seeming calm.

She was really numb with pain. When Robert had seemed so pleased with her and called her a sensible girl, she had for a few minutes almost permitted herself to hope that he would be willing to let the marriage stand.

"Yes," Robert said, with relief, smiling at her again. She really was a most unusual woman. "So there wouldn't be any trouble in obtaining an annulment very privately, and there wouldn't be any scandal. And I think I know someone who could help, too, I mean, help to keep things quiet."

"It is very good of you," Esmeralda said wearily.

"Not at all," Robert responded politely. "I like to see a thing neatly done—or, as the cavalry would say, get over heavy ground as lightly as I can—and this is really the best way. Moreover, if we should suffer any surprise by the French or any reverse in a military sense, you would have the protection of my name and rank."

"I had not thought of that," Esmeralda confessed. "I had almost forgotten the French."

Robert smiled indulgently. "I can see how you would, what with one shock after another, but it would never do for me to forget them. Now, sorry I shan't be able to give you more time to get used to all this, but it looks like the stock the bishop has collected for us will all be assembled by tomorrow. That means we must leave the day after. Can't have Sir Arthur bringing the troops ashore and having nothing to ride or to pull the wagons. So tomorrow will have to be the day."

"Very well." Esmeralda's voice was so colorless that even Robert, scarcely the most perceptive of men where women were concerned, realized something was wrong.

He looked at her closely and was shocked by the gray tinge beneath the sun-browning of her skin. "My dear Miss Talbot," he exclaimed, "do forgive me. You are exhausted. I will take myself off at once and let you rest. Would you wish to have a small supper sent up to your room, or—"

"I can scarcely come down in this dress," she began, then stopped speaking as a deep flush came up over Robert's face. "What is it, Captain Moreton?" she asked.

"About the gowns I asked you to order," he said, struggling with his embarrassment. "I'm afraid I should have explained the situation more completely, but I did not know myself, until after I left you, that I could neither change a reasonable sum in pounds for Portuguese money nor obtain credit."

"Oh, goodness," Esmeralda cried, getting up from her chair, "I never thought of it either. I will ring for a servant and send him at once with a note to the dressmaker. She was to bring tomorrow a riding dress and a morning dress, which she happened to have by her and which she said would need little alteration to fit my measurements. But she cannot have done much yet, so I hope it will cause no hardship to cancel the order."

"No, you must have those," Robert said. "I'm not so short as that. But I'm afraid any evening dresses—"

"I did not order any," Esmeralda assured him, forced to smile despite the lingering ache in her heart. "What would I do with evening dresses?"

Robert looked puzzled. "I don't know," he admitted, "at least, not until we settle into headquarters, but my mother and sisters never seem to go anywhere without trunks full of them." Then he burst out laughing but soon sobered and took Esmeralda's hand. "There aren't many girls who would be so sensible. You are one in a million, Miss Talbot, and if I *had* to come upon someone adrift, I'm glad it was you."

He raised her hand and kissed it and then left the room. Esmeralda did not permit herself to turn and watch him go out the door or to touch with her other hand the spot he had kissed. Her chest was heaving with sobs, but at the same time it was impossible not to laugh. Although Esmeralda was certainly not experienced in dalliance, it occurred to her that no man who was could possibly make so many stupid errors in dealing with a woman as Robert did.

Suddenly Esmeralda sat down hard. Could it be true? Could any man with a face and figure like Captain Moreton's not be a practiced hand with women? Odd pieces of evidence came together. Esmeralda knew Robert to be kind. If he did not wish to marry until after he had sold out of the army, a kind man who looked like Captain Moreton would avoid any except brief and casual social associations with young unmarried women of his own class.

As abruptly as she had sat down, Esmeralda jumped to her feet and began to pace the room, all sense of fatigue gone. If Captain Moreton's sole contact with gentlewomen was the kind one indulged in at balls and with his sisters—she paused and bit her lip, thinking back on their conversations, yes, the only women he had mentioned were his mother and sisters—then the unflattering remarks he made were not at all surprising. Such comments could not hurt a sister.

Esmeralda walked slowly toward the most comfortable chair, her lips curving into a wry smile. If she had not been such an idiot as to fall in love with the man least likely to be attracted to her, the remarks he made would not have hurt her, either. She might, if she were a fool obsessed with her own importance, have been offended at the clear and implied avowals that she was a nuisance and a burden, but she could not have been hurt by them. Sighing, Esmeralda leaned back and closed her eyes. She was very tired again.

It was dark in the room when a knocking on the door awakened her. She jerked upright, uttering a low cry as her neck and back, stiffened by sleeping in an awkward position, protested, and she looked wildly around, totally disoriented. A second soft tapping brought her to her feet. No one would tap on the door of the hut. The thought recalled the adventures of the day to her, and she called "Enter" in Portuguese.

Two servants came in, one carrying a candle, the other carrying a supper tray. There were apologies for not lighting the room earlier; Captain Moreton had told them not to disturb her until suppertime unless she rang for service. Esmeralda thanked them and agreed that supper should be set on a small side table. Then she started toward the door to the bedchamber, intending to wash her hands and face, but the servant who had carried the candle held out to her a small parcel, saying that the captain had asked him to give it to her. Esmeralda took it with a mechanical smile and hurried off to the inner room. She was quite certain that Robert had changed his mind about taking her with him and had sent her what money he could spare. She did not want the servants to see her distress.

When she tore open the parcel and a hairbrush, comb, and toothbrush tumbled out, she had to bite her lips hard to keep from either laughing or crying aloud. How ridiculous to think so odd-shaped a parcel could contain coin. And how clear a betrayal of her emotions that silly fear had been. No matter what pain she would suffer in the end, there was nothing she desired more than to marry Captain Moreton and travel south with him. But if they were to be married—an odd warmth suffused her—she realized that she would have to use his given name now. Robert . . . how nice it was to think of him as Robert. . . . Robert would have to call her Esmeralda, too.

She had been staring at the toilet articles without really seeing them while these thoughts ran through her mind, but when she focused on them, the realization of Robert's consideration rushed upon her. Very few men would have thought of her need. She had been so eager to leave the village, she had taken with her only the clothing she was wearing. Tears stung her eyes. He was the dearest, kindest man in the world. How unfortunate that he should be so handsome. If only he had been ugly, there would have been a chance for her to win his affection.

The hand Esmeralda had stretched out to touch Robert's gifts hung suspended as she considered her last thought. Was it utterly impossible that Robert could come to care for her? He seemed far more irritated by his own appearance than proud of it. Could it be possible that he was also annoyed or embarrassed by the pursuit of women attracted by his looks? If so, would not the presence of a wife be an advantage? Particularly a wife who would encourage his dedication to his career and never interfere with him?

But *never interfere* could mean something quite different from not making a fuss when one's husband went into battle. Esmeralda bit her lip again as fear washed over her, bringing a cold sweat out over her body. Still, she knew she could look outwardly calm and smile and speak cheerfully while she shook like a jelly inside. She had had plenty of practice at that when she had done things of which, had he discovered them, her father would have disapproved violently. And she was certain she would never show hurt, nor, indeed, feel it, when Robert dined with his mess rather than with her. But what if, protected by a plain wife for whom he did not care, he developed a taste for pretty women?

Esmeralda looked down at the brush and comb, which she had automatically laid on the mirrored dressing table. Robert was kind. He would not flaunt his affairs in her face. If she did not look for trouble, she told herself, she would not find it. But she would know. Esmeralda shuddered. Would she be able to bear it, loving him as she did? Would it be more agonizing to her to walk away from the marriage, as Robert now planned, or to try to induce him to continue it, knowing he did not love her?

Chapter 7

What devices Robert used to induce the bishop to direct his priest to marry them, Esmeralda never discovered. However, she needed to exercise considerable willpower to control a tendency to giggle all through the service, since the poor priest was so plainly astonished at what he was doing. Not that it took much that morning to make Esmeralda laugh. She had eaten her supper and gone to bed in a very uncertain frame of mind and spirits, quite unable to decide what she wanted. By the time she wakened in the morning, however, her depression had evaporated with her fatigue.

It was dreadfully foolish, Esmeralda decided, to worry about the future of her marriage as if planning in advance could help her direct that future. In this case, where she knew so little, really, of the person with whom she was involved and, in addition, had not the slightest notion of what would occur, it was impossible to lay plans. A far more sensible line of procedure would be simply to enjoy each moment as it came, without considering the future at all.

To encourage this brighter viewpoint, a note from Robert came up with Esmeralda's breakfast tray, "having the pleasure and honor" to inform her that the wedding was set for one o'clock that afternoon, and if Esmeralda had no objection, he would do himself the honor of joining her for a light luncheon at noon so he could escort her to the church. The formal tone tickled Esmeralda's fancy, but she realized she had no time to waste on amusement and sent an urgent message to the dressmaker with the waiter who had brought up the note.

By heroic efforts on both their parts, the morning dress was ready by eleven. It was not what Esmeralda would have chosen as a wedding dress under ordinary circumstances, but nothing else was available. The gown was made of a soft silk crepe in a dull orange

color, cut very low over the bosom, with tiny puffed sleeves, and with
the tight waist right under the breast. It was fortunate that Esmeralda's
breast was very firm and not overlarge. Looking down at herself,
Esmeralda resolved not to take any deep breaths, lest she become
totally naked above the waistline. In addition, the soft silk clung to
her body in a rather startling manner.

As soon as she saw the dress, Esmeralda had been aware that this
might be true and had sent the dressmaker's assistant to procure
pantalets and petticoats. Unfortunately, although several of each were
available in Esmeralda's size, they were all of silk and, although they
somewhat blurred the lines of her body, only encouraged the dress to
cling. The color, too, was scarcely suitable to a wedding, but when
Esmeralda looked in the mirror, her spirits lifted.

The gown *did* become her. She had a fine figure, which the dresses
her father insisted on her wearing had deliberately obscured, the color
lent warmth to her complexion, making her skin look rich and velvety,
and it also seemed to brighten her eyes. Only her hair was wrong. The
sun's bleaching had dulled its rich chestnut in irregular streaks, which
were made more apparent by the fact that it was drawn smoothly back
into a heavy knot at the nape. Esmeralda's small, round chin became
more prominent as a daring notion came to her.

She dismissed the dressmaker with strict injunctions to bring the
riding dress to her room by dinnertime at the latest, even if it was not
completed. They would work on it all night if need be. Then, as soon
as the woman was gone, she slipped out of her dress, undid her hair,
took a deep breath, and seized a pair of scissors she had asked to
borrow. Closing her eyes momentarily and offering up a prayer,
Esmeralda began to snip the hair surrounding her face. Although she
knew that some women cut their hair short and realized that it would
be much easier to care for that way, she did not dare attempt the back.
Besides, she was reluctant to sacrifice her heavy mane.

Fifteen minutes later, she gathered the cut strands from the floor and
dressing table, brushed short bits off her shoulders and breast, and put
on her new dress again. Then, taking a deep breath, she put up the
long hair in a high bun at the top of her head and attacked the short
ends around her face with dampened brush and comb. Finally she
permitted herself to inspect the result.

A long sigh eased out of Esmeralda. Her daring had not utterly
destroyed her. The trimming had not turned her into a beauty—

Esmeralda knew she would never be a beauty—but there was an improvement; she looked fashionable. A smile of pleasure further illuminated her features, but she was accustomed to her own expressions and did not realize the charm it added to her appearance. Still, she felt satisfied and happy so that when Robert entered less than half an hour later in full regimentals—which she realized he had donned in honor of the occasion—she greeted him with a glow of confidence.

His reaction was an additional delight, for he paused when he saw her and almost seemed about to excuse himself for intruding on a stranger. Then he grinned broadly. "That's a bang-up dress, Miss Talbot," he said. "I hardly recognized you. I'm glad it was done in time. I'm a little early, but I wanted to ask whether you would prefer to eat here or in the dining room?"

"In the dining room, by all means," Esmeralda replied. "I'm rather tired of this apartment. Orange isn't exactly the right color—"

"Why not?" Robert asked. "It certainly suits you."

"Thank you," Esmeralda said, her high spirits momentarily checked by the realization of just how unreal the wedding was to him. Obviously he did not associate her comment with the fact that maiden brides wore white. However, bubbles of mirth rose in her, and she said with abnormal gravity, "But do you not think you had better call me Esmeralda now? You will not be able to continue to call me Miss Talbot without arousing considerable curiosity among your fellow officers, and it is our first purpose, is it not, to avoid—"

Robert's hearty laughter interrupted her. "You're a bit of a tease, aren't you?" he asked with obvious enjoyment. "I was just about to suggest that we do away with surnames. In case you don't know, I'm Robert Francis Edward—the Honorable Robert Francis Edward, second son of the Earl of Moreton."

Esmeralda's big eyes opened wide. "No," she gasped, "I didn't know—that is, I remembered that your name was Robert, but I had no idea. . . . Oh, dear, whatever will your parents think of this escapade? Perhaps—"

"We aren't going to tell them," Robert said firmly, "but not because they'd have any objections. Thing is, my mother'd welcome you with open arms. Very set on seeing me married, no matter how often I tell her that it wouldn't do at all for a military man to take a wife. Damned unfair thing to do to a woman. Don't think my father would mind, either. After all, you're a gentlewoman. Nothing wrong with your family, even if . . ." He stopped abruptly.

"It's all right," she said a bit absently. "I don't mind that you think Papa was a queer nabs."

"Speaking of your father," Robert added, avoiding a direct reply to Esmeralda's rather unfilial statement, "I have obtained a certificate of his decease and burial. I think you will need that."

"Oh, thank you," Esmeralda replied, accepting the folded document Robert held out to her.

But her mind was not on what she was saying. Robert's statement about the unfairness of marriage for a man of his profession obscured every other idea, even the essential subject of proving her father's death so she could obtain her inheritance. At the moment it was more important to her that Robert's stated feelings came very close to her own thoughts on the subject and added considerable weight to her guess that his forthright remarks were owing to a relative ignorance in the handling of women rather than any intention of warning her off.

Even more interesting were his comments on his family's probable attitude to a sudden marriage under peculiar circumstances. He might be mistaken, but even if he were, the revelation of a dowry of over £500,000 would, Esmeralda was cynically certain, reconcile the Earl and Countess of Moreton to any slight irregularity in the marriage or the background of the bride.

The information could not resolve the problem of how she would feel about being married to a man who did not love her; however, the implication that the Moretons were not so high in the instep that they would add disdain to her problems or even attempt to dissolve the marriage increased Esmeralda's pleasure. She responded to another remark without being aware of what she had said, until Robert opened the door and stood aside for her to pass.

Having shepherded her down, seated her, and ascertained with the utmost courtesy what she wished to eat, Robert suddenly seemed at a loss. Esmeralda smiled as another piece of evidence was added to the growing record. Plainly Robert had no small talk suitable for a woman who was not a relative.

"Is all your stock in as you expected?" she asked.

His face lighted. "Yes. They even managed to turn up about a hundred and fifty horses, and there are over five hundred mules. On the other hand, there are very few oxen."

"I should think the mules would be better for military purposes," Esmeralda offered tentatively. "Oxen are dreadfully slow."

"That's true enough," Robert replied, beaming with approval and thinking that he had never come across so sensible a girl or one so easy to talk to. "But any draft animals at all are precious. As it is, I'm afraid half the guns will have to be left behind. It's those damned Spaniards. Almost everything they told us seems to have been a lie."

"Are you permitted to tell me about it?" Esmeralda asked, aware that she had made Robert comfortable and that he would remain comfortable and eager to talk as long as he could stick to his favorite subject.

Esmeralda had not the smallest objection. In fact, she was delighted that Robert was willing to discuss serious matters with a woman. Many men were not, Esmeralda knew, and she had been worried about being bored if Robert wanted to make the kind of conversation she had heard between young men and young women at the houses of friends. Being Henry's daughter had honed Esmeralda's mind, for what he said to her—although it was largely not addressed to her personally, being letters or instructions he required her to write to his bankers, agents, and customers—had given her a taste for exercising her brain. That, plus the fact that she had rarely been an object of more than the briefest civil attention, resulted in Esmeralda being no more accustomed to small chitchat than Robert.

"God knows, it's no military secret," Robert said. "The Spanish sent a mission to Britain in June to say that they had taken up arms against the French and to appeal for aid from us. I believe the government was given to understand that the Spanish army would push the French out, provided they were able to obtain arms and money and a leavening of experienced troops. The damned Spaniards said there would be no want of supplies or of horses and draft animals if the British could pay for them. Well, when Sir Arthur arrived, they wouldn't permit the troops to land, and though they were glad enough to take guns and money, they didn't like to be asked what they intended to do with them."

"That does not seem very open behavior," Esmeralda remarked to show her interest and encourage him to continue.

"Open!" Robert exclaimed. "I said they were damned liars. They told Sir Arthur that their General Blake had had a great victory, but it turns out that Blake had been beaten to flinders. Heaven only knows what's going on in the rest of the country."

"I hope you will find the Portuguese more honest," Esmeralda commented, frowning in thought.

Robert shrugged and mentioned the unwillingness of the Portuguese to advance him credit or even change money, and Esmeralda spoke soothingly of the fears they must have concerning the eventual outcome of the present effort to drive out the French.

This made such good sense that Robert complimented her on her perspicacity and went on to discuss methods for getting his cattle over the awful roads in the shortest time and for arranging that they not starve along the way. This led naturally to the question of the choice of a mount for Esmeralda, which permitted her to ask if she could come with Robert when he looked over the animals.

He agreed readily, even with pleasure, to this request and said, "We can do it right after the wedding, if that will suit you," and then looked stricken.

"If you dislike it so much—" Esmeralda began, her voice shaking.

"No, no, not at all," Robert assured her. "I just remembered that I forgot to get a ring. I remembered about the saddle, and I even remembered flowers—"

"Flowers?" Esmeralda repeated in amazement.

Robert flushed slightly. "I know it isn't real, but . . . well, it seemed wrong not to mark the occasion with some small observance. Why the devil I didn't think about the ring when I ordered the flowers, I don't know."

Esmeralda did not reply to that directly, only saying calmly that they could no doubt find a shop that sold trinkets on their way to the church, but she had to look down at her plate while she spoke to hide the mist of tears that rose in her eyes. She understood Robert's omission, even if he himself did not. Flowers were a kindness, a small gift any man might give to any woman on the slightest pretext; a wedding ring was a symbol of their union, no matter how temporary.

However, once Robert took the plunge, he was generous about it. He could not afford to buy Esmeralda a real ring since no jeweler would take pounds for gold and gems, but he would not allow her to choose the plainest and narrowest silver band, either. He searched through the stock of the shop until he discovered a lovely filigree ring set with tiny semiprecious stones.

"After all," he said, as he looked with satisfaction at the pretty ring on her finger, "one doesn't have an adventure like this every day. You'll want something to remember it by. I'm sorry the something can't be better, but this is at least attractive."

Again Esmeralda could find no more to say than a simple "Thank you." Her emotions were too tangled to make speech safe, for the joy of Robert's desire to please her was poisoned by the flat statement of his intention that the relationship be temporary. However, Esmeralda's immediate feeling that she really could not bear a life of this kind of unintentional brutality was considerably diminished by Robert's thoughtful gift of a posy of white camellias delivered to her at the door of the church and by his cheerful demeanor during the wedding ceremony.

Having adjusted to the situation, Robert was clearly no longer distressed by it. Esmeralda remembered that he had put on full dress uniform even before he had seen her in her new dress, and the way he blushed when he kissed her made her wonder if he might not be almost as innocent as she was. That blush restored all her determination to remain his wife if she could manage by any means to do so.

Nothing occurred during the remainder of the day to shake Esmeralda's resolution. Robert seemed pleased by her willingness, at his suggestion, to choose her own mount, then was impressed both by the animal she picked and her reasons for her choice. Esmeralda had pointed out a light chestnut mare, which she judged could carry her well but might be too small for a heavy trooper and was certainly unsuited for cartage. Robert agreed heartily and had the animal led out at once so he could examine her for soundness.

The mare seemed perfect on this score and in temper. She withstood Robert's probing most equably but did not seem to be broken-spirited for she stared with prick-eared interest around her and at anyone who spoke. Moreover, she responded to being stroked by Esmeralda by nuzzling at her and then took a tidbit from Esmeralda's hand with accustomed care.

"What will you call her?" Robert asked.

"I'll call her Boa Viagem," Esmeralda said, smiling. "Boa for short."

Robert grinned. He knew that much Portuguese, and it seemed characteristic of Esmeralda that she would choose a name like "Good Journey" rather than something silly like "Fairy."

The next step was the saddle, and by the time that was examined, placed on Boa Viagem, and both Robert and Esmeralda had agreed that it was unfortunate that her riding dress was not ready so that she could try the mare's paces, it was time for dinner.

In the most natural way possible, without specific invitation or any indication that it was not already an established pattern, they dined together. Then, since neither had any acquaintances in Oporto, Robert obtained a pack of cards, and they whiled away the evening in the most pleasant way, playing piquet. At first, Robert had deliberately underplayed, but he soon discovered there was no need for holding back, and they lost and won huge imaginary sums with a great deal of laughter.

Both were surprised when the mantel clock chimed nine, and it was with obvious regret that Robert rose and said that they had better retire for the night because they would have to be on the road as soon as the sun was up. His voice was just a trifle constrained as he spoke, but Esmeralda did not notice. It was not until that moment that she remembered her order to the dressmaker.

Her mind was immediately filled with the need to have her riding dress ready, so it was only when she and Robert were parting at the door of her chamber that she recalled her wedding and the briefest flicker of regret passed through her because Robert was not coming in as he would have done had the marriage been real. But by the time the dress was finished, Esmeralda was too tired to think of anything. She could barely stay awake long enough to ascertain that Robert had paid the dressmaker the preceding afternoon. She brushed her teeth and tumbled into bed.

Like a good soldier, Robert could sleep anywhere and at any time. However, this night when he got into bed he lay awake for a full fifteen minutes thinking over the events of the day. He felt considerable surprise at how much he had enjoyed himself. Miss Talbot . . . no, Esmeralda, was a delightful girl. No one could be more rational, and her pleasure, without cries of surprise or embarrassing flattery, at the most common polite attentions was most gratifying. She said thank you with genuine sincerity, and that was that, God bless her. She didn't go on and on about things or giggle or bat her eyes, and she knew horses and played a vicious game of piquet. . . .

Without realizing what he was doing, Robert sighed as he

wondered why he had originally thought Esmeralda so plain. She had looked very attractive in that new dress. Of course, her nose was too little and too round and her mouth was too wide, but it had been pleasant to kiss. Robert sighed again as a strong sexual urge caught at him. Wrong time, wrong place, he thought. Not the kind of hotel where such girls worked, and even if it were, he just couldn't, not with Esmeralda in the place.

He uttered a last sigh and tried to fix his mind on the duties of the next morning. Instead he found he was thinking about Esmeralda again, and it wasn't calming him down at all. Damn! Women, even the best of them, were always a nuisance. He *wasn't* married to her, and he had better remember it, especially since she clearly hadn't liked the idea and had only accepted it when she realized there was no alternative. Robert flopped over on his belly with an irritated grunt and determinedly began to calculate the probable cost of fodder and compare it with his available funds, which was so fruitless an exercise that he was soon asleep.

Chapter 8

Although it was still dark when a maid wakened Esmeralda, she suffered no fright or disorientation. Nor, although she had had far too little sleep, did she feel in the least reluctant to rise. She hopped out of bed at once, washed, and donned her new riding dress with a delicious sense of excited anticipation. It took her only a few moments to roll her toilet articles into her new undergarments, fold her morning dress around those so that it would not crease excessively, and then wrap the bundle in a blanket Robert had sent up with the maid.

The fact that Robert's greeting was barely civil and that he promptly buried his head in a newspaper did not trouble Esmeralda, either. She assumed that he was bitterly regretting what he had done, because he was imagining all sorts of horrors on the journey stemming from her presence. Owing to past experience, she was perfectly confident that there would be none. Thus, his grumpiness made her feel like giggling. That, however, would be most unwise, Esmeralda knew. One does not laugh at a gentleman at breakfast, particularly not a predawn breakfast, a time when the male sense of humor is at a low ebb.

In decorous silence, then, Esmeralda herself consumed a very substantial meal, interrupting her own stoking only to butter toast, refill Robert's teacup, and add slices of cold beef, ham, and eggs to his plate whenever the tide ran low. She also instructed the waiter to pack two hampers with additional cold meats, bread, and cheese, several bottles of wine, sufficient crockery, eating utensils, plus glasses for two, and a couple of flasks of water.

Realizing at last that his plate was exhibiting the characteristics of the miraculous loaves and fishes, Robert looked up. "Thank you," he said snappishly, "but there is no need to serve me anymore."

"I should hope not," Esmeralda replied too gravely. "I was beginning to wonder whether you had hollow legs."

"I meant in a general way," Robert retorted sharply.

Apparently breaking his fast had not restored Robert's good humor, but Esmeralda was still unable to resist teasing him. "But," she said most innocently, widening her eyes, "it would be most peculiar, indeed, if a wife did not do so." She saw his nostrils flare with temper and was aware he was about to say, "You are not my wife," so she went on hurriedly, "You did tell me, did you not, that we must behave as unexceptionally as possible to avoid talk?"

His guns effectively spiked, Robert rose from his seat in dignified silence. He was somewhat ashamed of behaving like a boor, but there was no explanation he could think of immediately to offer Esmeralda that would not be offensive. It was impossible, after all, to say he had found her company sexually stimulating and was annoyed at himself, not at her. Had they really been married, it would have been a compliment. As it was, to say such a thing would only alarm the poor girl needlessly since he meant her no harm and was scarcely *so* attracted as to be in any danger of ravishing her.

Still, it was annoying, particularly since he could not blame Esmeralda for doing anything deliberately to cause the effect. Even worse, the situation was not likely to improve. Robert thought she looked very handsome indeed in the tight-fitted, bright-blue jacket of her riding dress. A nice figure . . . Damn!

Esmeralda also rose with unimpaired calm, since she could not read Robert's mind and still believed him to be distressed about the coming journey. "I have ordered food for the trail," she said. "Would you prefer to have a pack mule brought to the hotel so the hampers can be loaded here, or would you like me to instruct them to send a servant to wherever the animals are being assembled?"

Jolted out of his bad humor by her practical forethought, Robert exclaimed, "Good God, I had forgot! Thank you, Miss . . . er . . . Esmeralda."

"Not at all," she replied, smiling at him. "I am sure you have far more important things to worry about than picnic lunches. Papa always left the food and drink for our journeys to me, and I will be very happy to take that burden from you. I only arranged for our own needs, however. If you wish me to order for the cattle drivers—"

"No. Why should you? They are being handsomely paid, far better than they would be by their own people. We are not responsible for their keep."

"I'm glad of that," Esmeralda admitted. "I did provide for our Indian servants, but to speak the truth, I have no idea what would be proper here in Portugal." Robert turned to go, and she laid a hand on his arm. "Will you send a mule? And what of your baggage?"

Robert barely controlled an urge to jerk his arm away. It was not that he found Esmeralda's touch unpleasant; he was merely surprised by the odd little quiver that ran up his arm. He wondered irritably what the devil was wrong with him and reminded himself yet again that the wedding ceremony was meaningless—certainly meaningless to Esmeralda. Her behavior could not be more natural or unaware.

"Yes," he said, "I will send one of the men with a pack animal. The hotel porter has my portmanteaus. Can you be ready in an hour's time?"

"I am ready now and will gladly come with you if that will save time," Esmeralda replied.

Robert had to smile. "You are entirely too agreeable and efficient." Then he pulled out his purse and extracted several coins from it. "Since you have more time than I, would you see to the vails for the servants? And you had better keep whatever remains, in case there is something you wish to purchase on the road. I will not be able to be with you much of the time, I'm afraid."

Esmeralda accepted the coins and assured him she would not only see that the tips were distributed properly but understood completely that his first duty was to the animals under his care. Obviously it would be necessary for him to range the line of march, making certain the beasts were not allowed to roam or that their drivers did not decide to accept the small prepayment as a sheer profit and go off to sell the horses and mules all over again.

Robert shook his head, smiling. "You are going to ruin me for dealing with ordinary women, Esmeralda—that *is* a pretty name, but quite a mouthful."

She laughed, her voice a little too high-pitched with the shock of hearing Robert put his finger so accurately on her plans; however, it was clear that he was not thinking of what he had said in the same terms she was, and she managed to keep her voice controlled and natural when she spoke. "Call me Merry, then. Most of my friends did so when I was a girl."

"When you were a girl?" Robert's brows rose. "You aren't exactly
an aged crone now, but Merry it is—and very appropriate, too, for
you certainly like your little jokes."

He went out without saying any more, and this time Esmeralda let
her eyes follow him, knowing he would not look back. Merry
. . . no one had called her that for many years, nor had the name
been appropriate since then. But it was just right now, for there was a
well of joy bubbling inside her. For now . . . For as long as she
could hold him . . . Esmeralda shook herself. She would not think
about that. She would enjoy every minute as long as she could, she
vowed to herself.

Esmeralda had no trouble at all fulfilling her vow. Despite the heat
and dust and the stench of the animals and sweat-drenched men, she
had never in her life been so happy—not perfectly happy; there was a
worm in the heart of her rose and she knew it, but it was sleeping now
and she did nothing to disturb it. Instead she blessed her father over
and over, often chuckling when she thought that she would learn to
love him at last not for the luxury she would someday enjoy at his
expense, but for the hardships he had inflicted on her. Whatever the
discomforts of this ride, they were nothing compared to those she had
endured in India—and the company was much better.

The journey had set out on the right foot. When she was informed
that her mare and the pack mule had arrived, Esmeralda went out at
once. For a moment she was very startled because it looked as if the
animals had come to the hotel on their own. Then she noticed a pair of
small, bare brown feet between the two sets of front hooves. Curious,
she went around to the front, where a diminutive Portuguese boy with
large, bright-black eyes regarded her soberly. He was completely
dwarfed by the two animals, but his air was one of confidence.
Esmeralda smiled. Shyly he smiled back.

"I have brought your horse and the mule, senhora," he said.

"I thank you," Esmeralda replied formally. She glanced at the boy
and repressed a smile. Clearly he could not lift her to the saddle.
"Would you be so kind as to take the mule to the kitchen entrance?"
she asked. "There is food to be loaded, two portmanteaus, and a
small parcel."

When he returned with the loaded animal, Esmeralda was already
mounted. She noted with approval that two large flasks of unglazed

and porous clay were slung on either side of the mule. The clay was already dark with moisture. This would evaporate under the hot sun, keeping the water within relatively cool. Seeing her mounted, the boy led the mule forward, and Esmeralda followed without comment until they turned south toward the bridge.

"Wait," Esmeralda said. "Where is Captain Moreton?"

"He will meet us at the bridge, senhora," the boy replied. "The cattle go by barge and ferry, but we will go ahead of them so as not to be choked by the dust."

"We!" Esmeralda exclaimed. "Surely you will go home to your parents."

The brightness of the boy's eyes dimmed. "I have no parents," he said softly, "and my sister, who I lived with, was . . . was taken away by the French. I was hiding Luisa here in the hills to keep her safe from them, and Theresa was not there when I came back. She never came home, although I waited many days. So when the bishop's men came to ask for mules, I brought Luisa. I go with you to fight the French."

"Have you spoken with Captain Moreton?" Esmeralda asked.

The boy's eyes dropped. "He chose Luisa," he said stubbornly. "Where Luisa goes, so do I." His voice trembled just a little on the last words.

Esmeralda bit her lip. The mule was probably the only thing in the world he owned besides his breeches, his shirt, and the brown cloth jacket flung over one shoulder. "Have you no aunts or uncles?" she asked gently. "You are a fine, strong boy. They would be sad if any harm should come to you. You will surely be needed for the flocks or the farm. It is not right that you—" The expression in his eyes, now turned up to her again, choked off Esmeralda's words.

"The French, they fed their horses and mules—no, our mules—on the standing grain. They killed our sheep. There is no time to grow new crops and no money to buy what cannot be harvested. If I eat, someone else will starve."

His mouth was set in lines of bitterness far too old for it, and the trembling of his voice was more apparent, but there was no pleading in it. Esmeralda knew he had stated the case exactly as it was. The boy's village must have been close to Oporto, and the French had stripped it bare. Old Pedro's village had suffered, too, but being farther from Oporto and supplied with fish from the sea, its condition was not nearly so desperate. She also knew she should tell him at once that it was impossible for him to accompany them.

"If there is no feed," the boy said more softly still, "they will sell Luisa. Or if no one will buy, they will slaughter her for meat. So I took her. I must go with Luisa."

Esmeralda's breath drew in. He had taken the mule without permission. Probably the animal was his, or had been his sister's, but the adults of the village would not care about that—not in a time of extremity. If he went back without the mule, he would be terribly punished. Esmeralda looked down at the bent head, and all the misery of her own youth after her mother's death welled up in her.

"Luisa is a very fine mule," she said, "and I am sure you know best how to care for her. I think I will keep her for my baggage and my husband's. You may call me Senhora Moreton." Esmeralda's voice trembled just a little over the last two words. It was the very first time she had said them, and she was a trifle concerned over Robert's reaction when he heard the boy speak of or to her that way. Then her lips firmed. Whatever Robert's initial reaction, it was best that he become accustomed. She brought her eyes back to the boy's face and asked, "What is your name?"

Great shining black stars filled with a passion of gratitude were turned up to gaze on Esmeralda. "I am Carlos Cerca," he said, "and I am twelve years old and very strong. I will care well for Luisa and for the baggage. I can find firewood and do many other things for you. Also, I have good eyes and ears. I watched and I listened. That is how I knew they were coming to rob us again and had time to take Luisa away."

The words tumbled out in a torrent of joy, and Esmeralda felt a dreadful pang of guilt. If Robert forbade the boy to go with them, it would be worse for him because she had given him hope. Down the long avenue, the bridge was in sight. To her relief, there seemed to be no one waiting there, although some traffic was already passing over the river.

"You go to the other side of the bridge and wait for me there," Esmeralda said. "I must talk to Captain Moreton before he sees you."

Chapter 9

Esmeralda's fear that Robert would forbid Carlos to accompany them was wasted. Robert was familiar with the results of war, and when he arrived, he made nothing of the matter at all beyond a single, sympathetic "Poor little beggar." And when she had finished the story with the request that Carlos be her servant, he nodded, smiling. "Yes, keep him with you. He'll be safer in the tail of the army than back in that village. At least he'll be fed—more or less—while he's with us, and being with the army will make him feel he's doing something. Lads like that often run off and join the native army and get killed."

"Join the native army!" Esmeralda echoed. "He said he was twelve, but I doubt it."

Robert shrugged. "Our drummer boys aren't much older, and there are babes in arms with the women. I think they're mad myself, but they fight to come with the men. You should have seen the rage when they were told only one out of five of the married women would be shipped with the troops. More than half say they're married but never bothered to go through the ceremony, so actually we only took one in about twenty. They chose by lot, and then we had to call out a unit to protect the ones who were going. Sir Arthur doesn't like it, I know, and neither do I, to speak the truth, but it's army practice. You can't stop them."

Esmeralda did not reply. She had not realized that families accompanied the troops to war. Naturally she was acquainted with a number of wives and daughters of the officers stationed in India, but she had always thought of that as "foreign service" rather than "fighting service." Her hopes seesawed back and forth between the fact that it was not unusual for women to accompany the troops and the fact that Robert and his commanding officer disapproved. Well,

she thought as they crossed the bridge and Carlos led Luisa back onto
the road, that was something else she could do nothing about at
present. Better put it out of her mind with all the other unpleasant-
nesses to be faced in the future.

At least there was nothing immediate to dim her pleasure. Carlos
was transported to seventh heaven by Robert's curt order to follow
Senhora Moreton closely at all times and to see that the baggage was
not mislaid or stolen. Esmeralda was nearly in seventh heaven herself
at the way Robert had called her Senhora Moreton, as if it were the
most natural thing in the world, without a frown or a hesitation. And
Robert himself seemed now to be in high good humor as the animals
were ferried across the river without a single disaster.

Long before the last of them arrived, Esmeralda and Carlos were on
their way out of Vila Nova, but not before the boy had given the first
proof of how valuable he would make himself. The sun had risen fully
just as they reached the outskirts of the town, and Carlos, turning to
say something, stopped suddenly and cried, "You have no hat,
Senhora Moreton."

"Oh, good gracious," Esmeralda agreed, "I have not. Do you
know where you can get one for me?"

He nodded and ran off after Esmeralda had given him a little
money, and she sat and waited, shaking her head at her own
distraction. How could she have forgotten so essential an item? One
would think her training in India would have hammered that into her
head. To ride in the August sun of Portugal without a hat was to invite
heatstroke.

Although the headgear Carlos brought drew whoops of laughter
from Esmeralda, it was really most practical, being a straw confection
with a tall, peaked crown and a very wide brim, worn by peasant
women when they worked in the fields. By noontime, she was
blessing Carlos's total lack of fashionable sense. The tall crown of the
hat kept her head as cool as the parasol-hat combination she had used
in India, and the brim shaded her eyes effectively also. Equally
important, she was delighted with the boy's honesty. She knew she
had given him far too much money, yet he had returned it all, saying
that he had been given the hat since it was for the English, who would
drive out the French.

During the first hour or two of the march, Robert would appear
periodically with his horse in a sweat and an anxious expression on his

face because he had forgotten about her. The first time, he was convulsed by the hat, too. He assured her that it would not break his exchequer if she obtained something more fashionable at the next town.

"I will do so, of course," Esmeralda replied, "if you feel that my present headgear will lower the tone of our most elegant expedition. Naturally, if you think I will embarrass the oxen, or that group of . . . ah . . . soldiers? that General Freire so kindly sent as escort . . ." She hesitated while Robert choked on laughter and then went on more seriously, "However, if I may have my preference, I should like to keep it. It is really most effective."

Robert chuckled. "Well, just don't come out to dinner with me in it. Sir Arthur is very nice in his dress. He'd have a fit."

"I think I shall embellish it with a band of ribbons and some flowers," Esmeralda remarked with spurious gravity, but she was thinking that it would serve her purpose best to avoid Sir Arthur entirely if he disapproved of army wives remaining with their husbands.

"Don't do that, or Luisa will eat it," Robert protested.

"Luisa is a very delicate mule," Esmeralda said indignantly. "She would never commit such an impropriety."

"Likely not," Robert agreed, laughing again. "No delicate lady would have anything to do with that hat." Then he looked anxious again. "You *are* all right?" he asked. "I'm sorry to neglect you, but I don't really trust the drivers so close to home."

"Carlos is taking excellent care of me," Esmeralda assured him, "and one cannot get lost because there is only the one road."

Robert agreed somewhat doubtfully, but when she remained equally calm and cheerful during his second and third checks, he seemed more relaxed and did not come again until he was ready to call a halt a little south of Grijo, where they found a stream at which they could water the animals.

Carlos soon chose a shady spot well away from the road where he unloaded the mule, spread a blanket upon which he set the hampers of food, and then took Luisa and Boa Viagem to the stream for water. Esmeralda laid out plates and glasses and took out a portion of bread and cheese, which she gave to Carlos when he returned, having tethered the horse and mule where there was a little dry grass on which they could graze. His eyes widened at the size of the portions, and he thanked her with the passion of one who understands hunger too well.

The kindness fortunately did not induce him to take advantage, which Esmeralda had feared might happen in a village boy without experience of society. Without instruction, he moved to the side of the road and sat down to eat at a decent distance from his benefactress. He was a clever boy in every way, Esmeralda thought, when about half an hour later, Carlos jumped to his feet to hail Robert. She had been watching the road herself, ready to call out because Robert had no way of knowing exactly where they were. He had only told them when to stop and had himself ridden back to instruct the drivers. But Carlos seemed determined to be the perfect servant, for he took Robert's horse and began to walk the animal slowly to and fro in the shade to cool it before he took it to drink. Robert raised his brows when he reached Esmeralda, and she shrugged.

"I don't know," she replied to the unspoken question. "I can't imagine where he learned, unless there is a gentleman's house in or near the village where he lived and one of his relatives served there— or perhaps he was a servant there himself and ran away. However, I'm not going to look too closely into the gift horse's mouth. I think we have found a treasure."

"I seem to have found one, too," Robert said, sinking down onto the blanket. "You have no idea how refreshing it is to have one's meals served in a civilized manner on a march." And then, after he emptied a tall glass of watered wine in a continuous series of long swallows, he exclaimed, "Oh, bless you, woman! I was as dry as the desert."

Esmeralda smiled as she filled glasses and plates, but she did not trust herself to speak. Everything was working so well, so exactly as she had hoped, that she almost feared to breathe lest the charm be broken. In particular, she did not wish to say anything that Robert would consider trivial, but she was also afraid to ask about how the drive was going, for Robert's appearance implied that there were problems. He was covered with dust from riding back and forth along the animal train, and he looked tired to death. So she ate slowly and silently, desperately searching for a remark that would allow him to talk freely if he wished to without actually implying that she expected him to tell her anything. And then she had cause to bless the indecision that had kept her from speaking at all.

Robert suddenly pushed away his plate, looked at her, and said, "'My gracious silence.' That's from *Coriolanus*. It's what he called his wife for not talking his head off and creating a scene when he said he was going back to Carthage. My whole family thinks I'm an idiot because I wanted to join the army, but a few things did stick in my head in school. I'm so tired I can barely chew. Bless you for not expecting me to talk."

"No, of course not," Esmeralda said softly. "Today must be dreadful, with everyone not knowing what is expected of him. If we are not too far behind schedule, perhaps you could sleep for an hour or so during the worst heat?" It was a question, not a suggestion, and she hoped he would not think it an attempt to interfere with his duty.

"If you wouldn't mind," he said gratefully, "I think I will. I'm sorry to be so rude. It isn't the company that's boring me, Merry, I swear it."

"Don't be foolish," she answered. "I will probably doze a little myself, although I am not very tired. It's a habit from India and customary here, too. Why don't you take off that coat and cool off."

He did not answer, just did as she suggested and was asleep almost as soon as his head went down. Esmeralda sat looking at his beautiful face, at the smoothly arched brows and long lashes, just enough darker than his golden hair to give character to his features, at the straight nose, the perfect arch of the lips. If she had been sure he was truly soundly asleep, she might have kissed them. She smiled, thinking of the way he had said his family believed he was an idiot. It must be a bookish family, then. Most parents in the upper nobility sent their sons to school because it was the thing that was done, not because they expected the boys to learn anything or cared if they did not.

Then Esmeralda turned away from him abruptly. Not only was Robert what she wanted, but his family sounded as if they would suit her as well. She was no bluestocking herself, but she liked to read and to think about things other than balls and clothing. Esmeralda sighed. She must not let herself believe her dreams would become reality; and yet, to be called "my gracious silence" . . . that was beautiful. And it had been his wife Coriolanus was addressing. She forced herself to remember that it was the silence, not the wife, for which Robert was grateful. But in time . . .

She pushed away the thought and busied herself with recorking the

wine and covering the food so it would be safe from insects. She did
not load anything back into the hampers yet in the hope that Robert
would be able to eat something more when he was rested. There
would be plenty of time for her to repack and reach the head of the
column, even if some groups set out before her. Then she leaned back
against a tree and dozed herself, waking periodically to check the
shadows cast on the ground.

When those were appreciable, she woke Robert. He sat up at once,
without protest, for he was accustomed to being called out for duty at
all hours of the day and night, but the soundness of his sleep was
apparent from the slightly dazed way he looked around. Seconds later
he was alert and aware and had pulled his watch from his pocket.

"Damn!" he exploded. "Why did you let me sleep so long?"

"I am very sorry," Esmeralda said.

"No, it's I who am sorry, Merry." Robert apologized at once. "I
remember now, I never told you when to wake me—or, in fact, to
wake me at all. But how the devil I'm to get those lazy damned fools
started and still get down to Oliveira to warn them we're on the
way . . ."

He stood irresolute for a moment, still a trifle bemused by sleep,
and Esmeralda said, "Is there any reason why I could not ride ahead
to Oliveira for you? I know it is not customary for a woman to do
business of this type, but perhaps because I am English it would be
acceptable. You could write a note, or several if necessary, on leaves
from your pocketbook—"

An expression of relief came into Robert's face. It wasn't at all
usual, of course, but it wasn't an army officer with whom she would
have to deal, only a town official, and Merry was an extremely self-
possessed young woman. She was right about being English, too. The
regador would almost certainly listen to her if she carried a note with
his rank and signature. Also, the Bishop of Oporto had promised to
send messages down to Oliveira, Águeda, and Coimbra, so the
information Merry brought wouldn't be unexpected or disbelieved.

As it was, the oxen would probably not arrive until nearly dark. If
he rode down to Oliveira and back before he got them started, he had
a horrible feeling half the animals would disappear into the dark. And
if he ordered the drivers to get started and did not keep an eye on
them, almost as many beasts would wander away and disappear in

daylight while the men argued about whose business it was to pursue them.

"You wouldn't be afraid?" Robert asked, relief giving away to an expression of anxiety. "I will, of course, send a man with you."

"Naturally, I shall do whatever you think is best," Esmeralda replied, "but you need not send a man unless you really believe there is some danger. I am not at all nervous, and I am sure the man will be of more use in keeping the animals moving than simply riding along with me. I will have Carlos."

"Well, I *don't* think there is any danger. If I did, I wouldn't let you go, with or without an escort, but I also don't think it would look right for you to arrive with official information without an official escort."

Esmeralda laughed. "Very well, but I'm not at all sure that one of those scarecrows you said General Freire sent will add much to my status."

"And neither will that hat," Robert remarked teasingly, as he sat down to write the notes.

He was joking, of course, knowing that Esmeralda would have better sense than to wear a peasant-woman's working hat when she made a call on the *regador,* but it showed his uneasiness. Nonetheless, everything worked out very well, and Esmeralda was able to send her escort back with the name of the inn in which they were to be quartered, as well as information on where the animals were to be held for the night. Moreover, by the time Robert arrived, a meal and rooms were ready so that he had no more to do than eat and tumble into bed—for which he was extremely grateful. Needless to say, that night he did not lie awake thinking about Esmeralda or any other woman.

This system of travel and lodging arrangements worked so well that they used it on each of the two succeeding days. However, as the animal drivers and soldiers moved into unfamiliar territory, farther from their homes, they were far less tempted to abandon the cortege. And, as they grew accustomed to their duties and also realized that Robert meant every word he said and would deduct the value of any animal lost or injured from their pay, but fully intended to add a reward if all arrived intact, they grew more assiduous and efficient. Robert was not pressed so hard and could spend some time each day riding and talking with Esmeralda.

As Robert's duties became less demanding, they played cards and talked in the evening—at least, Robert talked. Esmeralda said very little beyond what was necessary to encourage him. She learned a great deal about the European war, Bonaparte, the current political situation in England insofar as it pertained to the war, Robert's family, and Sir Arthur Wellesley. Since this was exactly what she wanted, Esmeralda had no fault to find with the entertainment, and Robert could not remember ever having enjoyed himself more.

Nor was his pleasure confined to the evenings when, having examined the stock and assignèd guards, he might with justice have put duty out of his mind. It was equally delightful to ride to the head of the column and find Esmeralda, cool and cheerful, under her funny hat. She had, as she had threatened, embellished it with flamboyant ribbons and large, ugly, paper roses, which she had begged from the innkeeper at their first stop. The hat and its decorations had begun Robert's second day, which he had wakened dreading, on a bright note of laughter.

He looked forward to their luncheons, too. Esmeralda always had some amusing or perceptive remarks to make about the march or the countryside, and the meal, whatever it was, was tastefully set out, which somehow lent a better savor to the most prosaic, and sometimes ill-cooked, food. More than once it passed through Robert's mind that this was the way to campaign.

Sir Arthur might be the most brilliant general England had—Robert judged him to be, although he felt Sir John Moore was almost his equal—but Sir Arthur was extraordinarily single-minded. On campaign he remembered the men had to eat and rest, since if they were not fed and rested, they would not be able to fight well; but he felt no such compunction about himself and his staff. They, he assumed, would do their duty fed or unfed, rested or unrested. Thus, the food and wine he offered his staff at mess was often very unpalatable, and he himself ate so fast that a man could choke trying to get enough down to stave off starvation before the plates were removed.

It would be very nice, Robert thought idly as Esmeralda was putting away the remains of the luncheon and he stretched out on the blanket in his shirt sleeves to doze through the worst of the heat, if there were a nice little supper waiting for him in his quarters near a cozy fire, with a companion who would be interested in what he had to say. If only there were some reason why Merry could not leave immediately . . . And then his eyes snapped open with shock. How could he be so selfish as to think for a moment of imposing more discomfort and inconvenience on her? Just because she was so good and never complained, or even looked dissatisfied, was no reason to think she did not suffer. He sat up so abruptly that Esmeralda was startled.

"We will meet Sir Arthur tomorrow at Figueira da Foz," he said. "I will try to arrange that you be accommodated on the first vessel that goes back to England with dispatches."

Taken by surprise, Esmeralda cried out, "Oh, no! Please do not send me away to England."

"Do not send you away?" Robert repeated. "But—"

Esmeralda swallowed hard and fought to control her impulse to fling herself into his arms weeping and pleading. "You cannot have thought," she said, her voice trembling, "that I am little better off now than when you found me in the village. I still have no friends, no relatives, no papers of identification, and nowhere to go. You may be the only person here or in England who can vouch for my bona fides. I am sorry that I have been such a trouble to you—"

"You haven't been any trouble at all," Robert interrupted. "In fact, you've *saved* me a great deal of trouble. I only thought that you would have had enough of this hardship and be glad to get back to civilization."

"But I have endured no hardship. Truly, Robert, I have enjoyed myself. I remember that you said Sir Arthur did not approve of women accompanying the army and I realize that in the future I may become a grave encumbrance to you, but still, I beg you not to send me away until my presence is truly inconvenient. I . . . I am afraid to go to England alone."

It was not true, of course. Going to England was not what Esmeralda feared. She knew that, with a letter from Robert and another from Sir Arthur to identify her, she would have no trouble being accepted by her father's bankers. It was the collapse of her dream that widened her eyes and filled them with tears, and drained the blood from her cheeks and lips. Robert leaned forward and took her hands in his own.

"Of course I shall not send you to England alone if you do not wish to go," he assured her.

It did not seem strange to Robert that Esmeralda feared making her way in English society more than she feared war. She must have heard tales enough of the horrible fate awaiting young ladies who could not obtain vouchers for Almack's or find a sponsor to present them at Court, and she knew nothing at all of war. He thought briefly of offering to send her to his own family, but immediately realized that the complications arising from that might be almost as appalling to her. Besides, he had few fears for the future. He was perfectly sure that Sir Arthur's campaign would be victorious. Thus, there would be no danger for Esmeralda if she stayed.

"I cannot ask for leave to take you home myself just now," he went on before she was able to control her voice sufficiently to thank him without bursting into tears.

"Oh, no!" she cried, so shocked at the appearance of this new danger to her plans that her control was restored. "I would not think of it," she added more calmly. "You must not allow the misfortune of finding me to interfere with your duty. I will manage very well. And if I stay out of Sir Arthur's way, perhaps you would not even have to tell him I was about."

"Well, no," Robert said. "I don't think I could go quite as far as that." He grinned at her. "I don't say I might not have tried if I thought I could get away with it, but he's sure to hear somehow. However, you needn't be afraid he'll order me to send you home. Sir Arthur is extremely chivalrous, and he tends to think of women as rather helpless creatures. When he hears your distressing story, he will be most sympathetic. Only, for God's sake, don't tell him you 'enjoyed' this little trip, careening around with muleteers and the dregs of the Portuguese army."

"No, no," Esmeralda assured him, her color restored and the mischief returning to her eyes. "I shall say no more than that setting me adrift alone in England would be the very greatest cruelty to my delicate sensibility. And I shall flutter my eyelashes." She batted them exaggeratedly.

"I don't think you've got the style of that exactly right," Robert said, chuckling, "and I'm afraid the delicate sensibility won't go over very well, either, unless you claim to have been in a faint the entire way down from Oporto."

"A shudder or two, then?" Esmeralda suggested. "And an expression of pained fortitude?"

Robert laughed, released her hands, which were now relaxed, and lay down again. He did feel one tiny prick of guilt because he had not said a single word to suggest that there were things he could do to pave her way in England, but it passed. She would be much happier, he told himself, if he took her home personally. Besides, then he himself could see to the settlement of her business with her father's bankers, make sure that the competence she expected was really adequate, and explain her situation to Perce and Sabrina, who would then sponsor her and arrange for her to meet the right people so that she would be properly established.

It would not be long before he was free to ask for leave, he thought. Probably they would go into winter quarters by November or at the latest by December. His eyes closed, and he was asleep almost immediately, too quickly for him to be disturbed by the wave of satisfaction that enveloped him when he thought that Merry would be around for months.

Chapter 10

They stayed at Coimbra that night in considerable luxury, for it was a large town. The next day, after getting the men started, Robert rode ahead to discover whether the troops were ashore yet and where Sir Arthur desired him to bring the stock. He was confident that the men would not desert or allow the animals to stray this close to the end of the journey. He was delighted to find the Riflemen already some miles inshore, and fortunately came across General Henry Fane, who greeted the news that baggage animals were on the way with considerable enthusiasm and tried to lay claim to most of them. Between the heat and the sand, he remarked dryly, he was likely to lose more men from exhaustion than from action. Unmoved, Robert said the stock was still a day's march eastward and asked for Sir Arthur who, he learned, was at Figueira da Foz.

Leaving the Riflemen to their unhappy struggles with the heat and the miserable ground, Robert rode to the temporary headquarters, where Sir Arthur received his report with a curt word of commendation. He then summoned his secretary and directed him to write an order absolutely forbidding any of his officers to preempt the animals and nodded dismissal at Robert. However, when Robert did not move, Sir Arthur lifted his head from the papers on the table to which he had returned his attention without noticeable irritation.

"Could I have a moment, sir?" Robert asked as the secretary left the room.

"You had trouble with the bishop?" Wellesley asked.

"Only in the sense that he wouldn't lend me money," Robert answered. "In fact, no one would give me credit or even change more than one or two pounds for Portuguese money."

"That's not—" Sir Arthur began, and then asked, "What the devil

did you need credit or more than a pound or two for? Good God,
Moreton, don't tell me you've taken to gambling?"

"No, sir, of course I haven't," Robert replied. "But I hadn't much
to do for a few days so I thought I'd ride around the country just to
take a look, show myself, and see if I could scare up a few more
beasts, and I found this girl—"

"Moreton!" Sir Arthur exclaimed in an exasperated voice. "Don't
you know better than—"

"No, sir, you don't understand," Robert interposed hastily. "I
know her. She's British. I'd met her in Bombay. She and her father
had been shipwrecked going home to England."

"You'd better sit down," Wellesley said. "I have a feeling this is
going to take longer than one minute."

Although it did, of course, take Robert longer than one minute to
tell the story, he managed not try his commanding officer's patience
since he had spent the hours it had taken him to ride to Figueira
composing his tale. He explained everything to Sir Arthur, including
the pretense of marriage and his reasons for it.

"Nothing else you could have done," Wellesley said in his abrupt
way, nodding approval. "It's unfortunate, but the country round about
here seems to be clear of the French, at least as far south as Leiria.
There shouldn't be any immediate danger. You had better bring
. . . er . . . Mrs. Moreton here. It will take several days longer to
disembark the troops, and she can rest. After that we may have to
move pretty fast, though." He paused, and his voice had changed,
carrying a roguish note when he added, "Pretty girl, eh?"

"Er . . . not a beauty, no, sir."

Robert was not prevaricating. He knew Sir Arthur to be a flirt, and
possibly more than a flirt, particularly with attractive married women.
There had been rumors that his relationship with Mrs. Freese in India
was not totally innocent; however, that was not the reason for his
ambivalent reply. Robert did not fear Sir Arthur would do Esmeralda
any harm since he knew her to be still an innocent girl. Actually he
was really puzzled for an answer to his commanding officer's
question. His recent impressions of Esmeralda were at war with his
earlier impression that she was not attractive.

"But she is a very sensible girl," Robert added, "not at all given to
vapors or complaining. . . ."

He had meant to assure Sir Arthur that Esmeralda would be as little trouble as it was possible for a woman in an armed camp to be, but Sir Arthur merely nodded again, waved dismissal, and looked back at the papers on the table.

Robert left the building with an inexplicable feeling of happiness. He knew part of it was relief. He had expected Sir Arthur to behave precisely as he had behaved, but there had always been the chance that some military order or some other stupidity of the Horse Guards would have exasperated him. In that case, he might have lost his temper over Robert's adventure to give a relatively harmless expression to his spleen. He would not have blamed Robert for his actions, but he could have provided funds enough to leave Esmeralda at Coimbra and have insisted that Robert do it.

If Robert associated his high spirits and sense of relief with anything, it was Sir Arthur's seeming satisfaction with the military situation. And when Lord Fitzroy pursued him out of the building, ostensibly to hand him the orders he had forgotten to take, but immediately said, "What sort of cock-and-bull story did you feed Sir Arthur? He called me in and told me to give you a hundred cruzados out of his private purse as a wedding present 'to outfit your bride' when you got back with the transport animals. What bride, damn it?" Robert found himself mischievously amused.

"Esmeralda Mary Louisa, née Talbot, now Moreton," Robert said, perfectly straightfaced, although his blue eyes sparkled. "And it isn't a cock-and-bull story. How kind of Sir Arthur."

"Kind!" Fitzroy Somerset sounded totally bewildered. "Mad, I call it. What the devil do *you* need money for, Moreton? I mean, you're plump enough in the pocket, even if you did get married. No, I don't believe it. Damn it all, *how* could you get married?"

"It isn't very hard," Robert said. "You just stand up in church and repeat—"

Lord Fitzroy made a sound remarkably like *grrr*, and his face took on an alarming hue, so Robert stopped.

"As to the money," he went on, "wait until you get away from camp and ask a Portuguese banker to change pounds. I virtually had to get down on my knees and plead. And credit is completely out of the question."

This explanation scarcely contented Lord Fitzroy. He still looked as if he were about to explode, and his voice was dangerously gentle when he asked, "But why does the bride need outfitting? Surely that's her parents' business."

"Oh, that. Well, she was shipwrecked." Robert laughed as Somerset raised a doubled fist. "No, no, I'm not joking. That's the truth, I swear it. Look, I promise to explain it all when I bring the beasts in. Meanwhile, give me those orders so I can get back. Merry's alone with that troop of half-wits Freire sent along as guards. I was just going to see if Mars or Jupiter had been brought ashore yet. If they haven't been, I'll have to borrow a mount from you or from one of the others. Hermes is about done up from racing up and down the line like a sheep dog."

Somerset's mouth opened to protest that last remark; he could not imagine Robert using his fine horse to herd cattle, but then an expression of strong self-control settled on his features, and all he said was "Yes, the horses are ashore. We have taken over that barn"—he pointed—"for a stable. I haven't had time to look the animals over, so you had better walk down yourself and see which of your mounts stood the voyage best." However, as Robert turned away, having tucked the order into his breast pocket, Lord Fitzroy seized his arm. "We will all be waiting to meet Mrs. Moreton when you arrive this evening," he said slowly and threateningly.

Not a muscle moved in Robert's face. "I am certain you will find her delightful," he said, and did not permit himself to begin laughing at his friend's expression until he was safe in the barn, although the restraint nearly choked him.

Under the circumstances, it was not at all surprising that Robert and Esmeralda were met about three miles from headquarters by a half dozen neatly attired young men on exquisite mounts. A few of the ADCs were on duty, and a number were still on the ships arranging the disembarkation from that end. All who were free, however, had ridden out of the camp as soon as the orderly they had set on watch had come galloping back to report that a huge cloud of dust was approaching. Of course, Robert had warned Esmeralda that this might happen.

"How the devil they imagine I planned to get away with it, I can't guess," Robert had said after he had assured himself that everything was under control with regard to the animals in his care and had come to ride beside Esmeralda. "After all, I served with Sir Arthur—by the by, a lot of the ADCs call him 'the Beau' because he is always so neat in his dress. As I was saying, I served with him in India, and I'm not likely to underestimate him. Still, Fitz, I mean Lord Fitzroy Somerset, clearly believes I picked up some Portuguese . . . er . . ."

"Light-skirt," Esmeralda supplied when Robert ran down, obviously realizing all of a sudden that he was saying something vastly improper.

"Sorry, I didn't mean to be offensive," he said, rather chagrined, "but you're devilish easy to talk to, Merry, and I end up forgetting myself."

"And so you should," Esmeralda assured him. "It will give us away completely if you do not feel free to say anything at all to me."

This, Esmeralda knew, was not necessarily true. She was not unaware that some husbands treated their wives as witless dolls—and sometimes with good reason. However, her primary purpose was to addict Robert to her company, and one of the ways to accomplish that was to make him as comfortable with her as he was with his male friends. Moreover, there was a double benefit, in that his conversation would be far more interesting for her if he felt free to talk about anything at all.

"Will it?" Robert asked, frowning in doubt. "Don't think m'father says anything *he* thinks to m'mother."

Esmeralda laughed. "I am quite sure you will not say anything to me that your father would not say to your mother. If you really believe that your mother is innocent of the existence of ladies of light and easy virtue at this time of her life and that your father would not mention them to her—in an impersonal way, of course—you are much mistaken. Probably your mother would not speak to *you* about such women—"

"You mean my mother thinks *I* am innocent?" Robert said incredulously. "I am seven and twenty years of age!"

Esmeralda laughed again. "I cannot imagine she thinks anything of the sort. Nothing you have ever said to me has given me reason to think your mother is a fool. But she would not wish to embarrass you. It is not the kind of thing a woman discusses with her sons, but that is no reason to think she is unaware."

"Well, I didn't think— Damn it, Merry, how did we get onto this stupid subject anyway?"

"You were saying that you did not know how your fellow ADCs thought you intended to pass off a Portuguese light-skirt on Sir Arthur as your wife," Esmeralda reminded him obligingly.

"Yes, well, that was not where I should have begun. The point is that they are very curious, and we should have a reasonable story to offer."

"It would be best, I believe, to stay as close to the truth as possible," Esmeralda said slowly. "I do not think we can completely conceal your chivalric motives." Robert made an uncomfortable noise, but Esmeralda continued without giving him a chance to interrupt. "Presumably your friends know of your past determination not to marry until you were ready to terminate your military career, and I am not the kind of girl over whom a man would suddenly lose his head—"

"Not in those clothes I found you in, anyway," Robert admitted, grinning.

A sense of satisfaction rose in Esmeralda. She was certain that only a few days ago Robert would simply have agreed with her statement or, if he had remembered to be tactful, have remained silent. He would not have attributed her lack of beauty to ill-fitting, unclean garments. Perhaps she had reason to hope that he was beginning to think of her as somewhat attractive.

"And Fitz already knows you were shipwrecked," Robert continued, unaware of what he had betrayed about himself and the pleasure he had given Esmeralda, "because Sir Arthur was kind enough to contribute a hundred cruzados toward a new wardrobe for you. But I could have . . . er . . . been enamored in Bombay."

Esmeralda giggled. "Not unless you were demented," she reminded him, but hope flared up again simply because he could say such a thing now. "And being aware that one is badly dressed makes one awkward, which only adds to the bad impression. However, there can be no harm in implying that we knew each other better than we really did and that you found me a pleasant kind of girl."

"It's true, too," Robert said. "I mean that you're a pleasant girl. Fitz and the others will see that for themselves at once."

"I hope so," Esmeralda answered most earnestly.

She did, indeed, hope to make a good impression on Robert's friends. It would be fatal to her plans if, after their first surprise was over, they continued to express wonder at what had made Robert so

foolish as to marry her. That would, of course, imply that he would
not have done so under normal circumstances and continually remind
him that he did not intend to remain married. On the other hand, if his
companions soon began to regard the marriage as reasonable—
perhaps enviable, although she could not really hope for that—it
would be another inducement for him to maintain the status quo.

"That will do it, I think." Robert nodded thoughtfully. "Sir Arthur
said there was nothing else I could have done, and if we were friends
in Bombay, all the others will agree."

Esmeralda was not so certain of that, but she raised no objections
and, indeed, hoped it was true. Now that the basic tale was settled,
she began to ask Robert questions about the men she would meet,
which he answered with as much interest as she had in listening,
realizing that he was clarifying to himself facets of his fellow officers'
characteristics that were useful to understand.

He had just said, "Burghersh is the best of fellows, but he will not
make a soldier," when a sound of shouting came from behind them.
An expression of irritation crossed Robert's face as he looked around.
He hated to have a conversation with Merry interrupted, but the noise
did not diminish. He turned his horse and, looking back just as he
started off, laughed and warned her, "And they are all top-of-the-
trees, so, for God's sake, take off that hat before we see them."

Esmeralda only waved gaily. She had never intended to allow the
elegant gentlemen of Sir Arthur's staff to see her hat before they knew
her well enough to appreciate the joke rather than to think she was
unaware of good style. But actually, it might not have mattered if
Esmeralda had worn it. It was apparent that the gentlemen who had
come to meet them were so surprised by her quite ordinary
appearance, her cultured voice, accent, and manners—all undeniably
British—that they probably would not have noticed. Quite clearly
Somerset had spread the word that Robert had married, with startling
suddenness, a completely destitute female about whom he had told
their commander some fantastic story. Considering Robert's own
breathtaking appearance and his previous resistance to feminine
charms, all had expected to see a ravishing beauty, perhaps no better
than she should be, who had sprung a trap that proved irresistible.

The shock, which left the young men incapable of doing anything
beyond acknowledging Robert's introductions, placed all the advantage in Esmeralda's hands. Thus, after the introductions, general

greetings and remarks had been exchanged, the party had sorted itself out somewhat, and Esmeralda found herself beside John Fane, Lord Burghersh. She seized her opportunity at once by asking eagerly how the landing was progressing.

"I know that it cannot be easy on this dreadful coast," she said, making her eyes large. "I will never forget my terror when I saw the cliffs and that huge surf."

"You were shipwrecked?"

Lord Burghersh's question did not imply disbelief. He had heard of the shipwreck from Lord Fitzroy, and he now recognized Esmeralda as a British gentlewoman. However, neither did his question express the shock and sympathy that would ordinarily be extended to one who had passed through so harrowing an experience. Although Lord Burghersh was quite young, as the scion of a politically active, noble family—he was, in fact, cousin to General Henry Fane—he had grown wary of manipulators.

"Yes," Esmeralda said. "It was horrible. The whole voyage was dreadful, storms alternating with awful calms, and then there was an unbelievable storm, and the *Ranee* went down north of Oporto. Papa and I were on our way home from India. He had been ill, and the climate became too much for him."

"India!" Burghersh exclaimed, "Moreton was in India for years. D'you mean to say you *knew* him?"

"Yes, of course," Esmeralda said with a faint smile. "I admit my situation here in Portugal was appalling, but even so, I do not think I could have brought myself to marry a person I did not know." Her lips twitched and she added mischievously, "Not even a person who looks like Robert. But he was in Bombay several times. We met at Governor Duncan's house at a ball and became moderately well acquainted."

"And your father . . ." His voice rose in a tentative question.

Esmeralda lowered her eyes and turned her head to look fixedly between Boa Viagem's ears. "He only survived the shipwreck by a few days," she said very softly. "He is buried in the village. As soon as it is possible for me to do so, I will have his grave properly marked. But money is such a problem, for no one would give Robert credit or—"

"Yes, we are having the same problem here," the young man said.

Then to change the subject, he added quickly, "And even if we had money, I am afraid that victualing will be a problem."

Turning her head toward him immediately and raising her eyes again, Esmeralda said even more softly, "Thank you. It is a difficult subject for me to speak about." Before he could reply she went on with deliberate briskness, "I agree that victualing may be a problem. It is very dry at this time of year so that I believe it to be impossible, in this area at least, for a second crop to be sown, even though the weather may remain warm long enough to ripen it. And my boy, Carlos, told me that the French had destroyed a good part of the crops in the vicinity of Oporto by using the standing grain for feed. I suppose we must assume that they would have done the same wherever they were camped en masse. What is more, I know from personal experience that the foraging spread at least fifteen or twenty miles out from the central concentration of troops. In that area, the people, who are normally very hospitable, have learned instead to be very clever in hiding anything they have."

Lord Burghersh made some noncommittal comment, but it could not conceal his surprise at Esmeralda's interest in and familiarity with the subject. He had expected her to say "too bad," or something similar, and then choose another topic for conversation.

She smiled and said tentatively, "I hope you do not think the subject unfeminine. Truly, my sympathy has been aroused for the people, and I find myself most eager to hear any detail that, even at some space of time, promises their relief."

Whatever Burghersh thought, he could not fail to respond with approval to a question phrased in those terms. And actually, he did not think the subject unfeminine. Many women exhibited a fine military fervor. All that had surprised him was Esmeralda's grasp of the practical aspects involved, and they spent the remainder of the ride in enthusiastic discussion. In fact, they were so happily engaged that Robert had to speak several times before he could get their attention. There was nothing at all in either Esmeralda's manner or Burghersh's that could have roused any suspicion, even in the most insanely jealous husband. Robert nonetheless felt a faint twinge of irritation, and he had to remind himself that he did not own Esmeralda. She had a perfect right to discuss anything she wished with anyone. But he found that reminder only exacerbated his feelings so that he spoke quite sharply.

This drew a quiet apology from Esmeralda, and no outward reaction from Burghersh at all, although inwardly he was somewhat surprised. He had already realized that Esmeralda was thoroughly in love with her husband. There was a slight change in her voice, a glow in her eyes, that utterly betrayed her every time his name came into the conversation.

Until Burghersh had heard the irritation in Robert's voice, however, he had been quite certain that the feeling could not be mutual. He and Robert had often talked about Robert's tour of duty in India, and Robert had given no indication whatsoever of any interest in that country or any regret in leaving it, aside from what he had learned and hoped still to learn in a military sense.

"I must see about quarters for you, Merry, and then for the men," Robert pointed out. "This is an army camp, not a town. And I must hand over the animals officially, although I'll probably have to make sure they all get into camp myself." He turned to look at Lord Burghersh. "Who's in charge of quartering and commissariat?"

"Not I," Burghersh exclaimed thankfully. "Ask Fitz. He's bound to know. No, never mind. You go back to your cattle herding, and I'll see about getting Mrs. Moreton settled and quarters assigned for your muleteers."

For one moment it almost seemed to Esmeralda that Robert would object and insist on seeing to her quartering himself, and her heart leapt. However, he said nothing to Lord Burghersh, merely turned back to look up at her, since she was still mounted, and asked, "Will that be all right, Merry?"

She put out her hands to him to be helped down from Boa Viagem and smiled. "You know that whatever suits you best will be perfectly satisfactory to me," she said.

"Well, to speak the truth," Robert remarked with raised brows, "I'd rather go with you and have a pleasant cup of tea, which is what I suspect this lazy lout is planning, but Sir Arthur likes his orders carried to completion. Don't let this crew finish up all the supplies. They will tell you the most pitiful tales of deprivation, but remember who comes first."

Chapter 11

It was not so easy to accommodate a gentlewoman in the overcrowded conditions of a small village filled to bursting, and Esmeralda was very glad Robert had been spared the trouble. At first, Lord Burghersh had suggested that she move into the building Sir Arthur was using as his headquarters, since it was the best and largest. Esmeralda was very reluctant to stay there, as she intended to avoid notice by Sir Arthur insofar as it was possible. If he did not recall that she was with the army, he was much less likely to consider the situation to be growing dangerous and order her sent to England.

She could not say this, of course, so she was greatly relieved when Lord Burghersh himself realized that the house was not really large enough to afford privacy, and the constant coming and going of officers at all hours would make it inconvenient for a lady. Eventually, a very small house on the grounds, in which several of the ADCs had been staying, was cleared for her. Gallantly, the young gentlemen made no complaint, but Esmeralda was worried.

"Will my accompanying the troops always make this much trouble?" she asked.

There was a brief silence that marked Lord Burghersh's shock, although his voice was expressionless when he said, "You intend to march on into Portugal with us? Would it not be safer and more comfortable for you to go back to England?"

"Safer, perhaps," Esmeralda was forced to admit, "but not more comfortable. You see, there is no question of 'back to England' for me. I was born in India and do not believe I know a single person living in England. I have never met Robert's family, and I have none of my own. Lord Burghersh, I assure you I am not a stranger to physical inconvenience, nor do I fear it, but to be thrust upon the Earl and Countess of Moreton without Robert's support quite sinks my spirits."

"But Mrs. Moreton," Burghersh protested, "there may be far more than inconvenience involved. There may soon be bullets and cannon-balls flying about."

"Surely not into the base camp or headquarters," Esmeralda said quietly, completely unmoved.

"I hope not," Burghersh replied, a trace of sharpness in his voice indicating the impatience he felt with the stubbornness and ignorance of women. "However, one can never be sure of the results of a battle. Camps and even towns at a considerable distance have been overrun."

Esmeralda raised eyes full of tears to him. "I am not ignorant of the risks," she whispered. "Please believe that there is a most compelling reason for my desire to remain with the army. And please do not tell Robert how unwise you think it to allow me to come. He is already too aware of the dangers to which I may be exposed and also of the fact that Sir Arthur does not approve, in general, of wives accompanying their husbands into a war zone. I have promised that—that if I am too great an inconvenience on the march, I will go without further protest, but I am very eager to remain as long as possible."

The tears that hung in Esmeralda's lashes and the intensity of her voice proclaimed the depth and violence of her emotion, and Burghersh was impressed by the control that permitted her to speak coherently and quietly. He could not imagine what had driven her to make the decision to stay, but he no longer thought it a trivial exercise of female impulsiveness.

"I assure you I will not interfere, Mrs. Moreton," he said, "but I must warn you that when your husband tells Sir Arthur of this, I doubt that Sir Arthur will permit it."

"But I am sure Robert has already told him," Esmeralda interrupted. "He said he must tell Sir Arthur *everything*, and Sir Arthur agreed that there was nothing else Robert could do. Why, he even was so kind as to instruct Lord Fitzroy to make us a present of one hundred cruzados."

Every word Esmeralda had said was literally true. However, the implications of the whole, when put together, were patently false. This did not trouble Esmeralda a whit. She took in the expression on Burghersh's face—he was looking down at her intently with his mouth slightly ajar—with considerable satisfaction. She was certain that he now believed what she wished: that Sir Arthur had given specific permission for her to go with the army for some secret purpose. Thus, Burghersh would not utter to Robert any criticism of her accompanying the troops.

Having seen her ruse work, Esmeralda promptly returned to the problem that had started this discussion. "But all this bother," she said. "Is there no way in which I or my servant can make arrangements for my lodging without troubling Robert or causing so much disruption?"

"Oh, certainly," Burghersh replied. "Now that you are on the rolls and the staff knows you will be with us, there will be provision made without any fuss. I will make sure that the quartering officer sends an orderly to show you to your lodging each day we move. And I must say, I am glad to hear that you are already furnished with a servant. Can I send someone to find him?"

"I doubt it will be necessary," Esmeralda said. "If I know Carlos, he and Luisa are right outside the door."

"Ah," Burghersh remarked with relief, "you have a woman with you also."

Esmeralda burst out laughing. "I suppose you could say so, but I fear Luisa would be a most unsatisfactory lady's maid, for she has four legs and very bad manners." Then, seeing that Lord Burghersh looked troubled, she said more soberly, "I imagine I shall be able to employ one of the soldiers' wives eventually, but I would like to leave that until I can discuss it with Robert. I am very hardy and shall manage very well with only Carlos for tonight."

Satisfied with that assurance, Lord Burghersh prepared to make his departure. Esmeralda, however, had not forgotten Robert's parting joke about not allowing his friends to eat up all the supplies. In fact, the previous evening in Coimbra, he had urged her to purchase substantial quantities of any delicacies she believed could survive the heat and transportation on Luisa's back without spoiling. Having also remembered what Robert said about the unfortunate state of Sir Arthur's table, Esmeralda was sure that he intended these supplies all along as a treat for his friends.

Thus, she forestalled Lord Burghersh's intended departure by saying, "Truthfully, I am rather concerned for Captain Williams and Captain Campbell and the others who were evicted to make room for me. Do you think they would be willing to come to a small supper at about nine o'clock so I can tell them how sorry I am? Nine o'clock should be time enough for Robert to wash and have a short rest."

Lord Burghersh had initially looked uneasy, but as soon as Esmeralda mentioned that Robert would be present, he smiled broadly. "I shall pass the word," Burghersh promised, nodding encouragingly.

Esmeralda hoped his expression meant that he would also pass along her explanation for remaining with them. If her expectations were correct, neither she nor Robert would be pestered with repeated statements of surprise or astonished questions. A seemingly indifferent acceptance of her presence by his companions would, she was sure, go a long way toward calming Robert's doubts.

Fortunately, Esmeralda's hope seemed to have been fulfilled. The supper that evening was a great success, and no one gave even the smallest indication of expecting that she would soon be leaving them. At first Robert was teased unmercifully about being the only man in the world who could be buried in manure and come out of the heap with a wedding bouquet. Soon, however, the talk turned to more serious matters. Captain Campbell remarked that he believed the disembarkation would be finished the next day.

"How many will we have ashore?" Robert asked.

"About eighty-seven hundred," Campbell replied, "but it's been a devilish landing. Half the supplies were overturned and soaked in seawater, and the horses got loose and went galloping up and down the beach. It took hours to catch them."

"Good God," Robert exclaimed. "Did we lose any guns?"

"No, but we lost about fifty men, two of them MPs. That will make a stink in England."

"And that isn't the worst of it," Lord Fitzroy said angrily. "Not that it has anything to do with the landing, but I don't suppose you've heard the Beau's been superseded."

"Oh, God damn it," Robert groaned. "That's just what I was afraid of right from the beginning when I heard we were going to Spain. Damn the Horse Guards! Damn them! For God's sake, Campbell, couldn't you manage to get whomever they sent out drowned instead of a lot of useful soldiers?" Then his face lightened for a moment. "Unless it is Sir John?" he asked hopefully.

"No such luck," Somerset replied bitterly. "Don't blame Campbell. Our new commanders haven't arrived yet. Sir Harry Burrard is coming out from England, and Sir Hew Dalrymple's coming up from Gibraltar."

Robert closed his eyes for a minute as if he were in pain. "Do any of you realize that the last action Burrard has seen was in America back in seventy-nine?"

"No," Captain Williams put in. "He was at Copenhagen."

"So was I," Robert snapped, "but he might just as well not have been. I was talking about action. And Dalrymple was with the Duke of York in Flanders. *That* was a brilliantly run campaign."

A universal groan attested to the fact that most of the ADCs had heard about the disaster in Flanders even though it had taken place thirteen years earlier. It was a classic on how not to run a military operation, the high-level officers and staff making merry with wine and women in the cities while the men froze and starved in inadequate camps in exposed positions until they were too weak and dispirited to fight. There was a discouraged silence.

"Please pardon my ignorance," Esmeralda said. "I have no knowledge at all of what is standard military practice. Does that mean we are to remain here until the new commanders arrive?"

Her question broke the gloom. Everyone looked more alert, and all heads turned to Lord Fitzroy Somerset. He might have read the orders or have information from Sir Arthur.

Somerset hesitated then shook his head. "There is no standard practice, Mrs. Moreton, but I do not believe in this case that we will remain here. It is not a good position."

A babble of talk broke out that was overridden by Robert's voice saying, "If there aren't specific orders, the Beau will move. I know him. If he can get in a few licks before those deadweights arrive, he will."

"But what the hell can we do with nine thousand men?" Lord Burghersh asked.

The more experienced officers explained at length what could be done with so small a force, but the question of whether Sir Arthur would have considered their optimistic plans any better than pipe dreams never arose. On August 5, before the disembarkation was completed, additional transports were sighted. These carried nearly five thousand more men under the command of General Sir Brent Spencer. Their arrival was most timely, for the landing operations merely continued in full swing, more efficiently now and with less loss of life and supplies.

The arrival of Spencer's division was also a blessing to Esmeralda personally. Although it was unavoidable that she be introduced to Sir Arthur, she had fortunately been presented at teatime just before General Spencer's arrival was announced. Having been briefed on General Wellesley's character by Robert, Esmeralda was at first surprised by his appearance. The admiration, bordering on awe, with which Robert spoke of him had made her imagine him a giant. On the contrary, Sir Arthur was shorter than her husband, of no more than medium height, and spare rather than heavy; however, the fit of his clothing showed him to have a wiry muscularity. Like the young men of his staff—who, Esmeralda now realized, had copied his style—his lightly graying brown hair was cut short.

He was, really, Esmeralda thought, a most ordinary-looking man, except for the high-bridged, aquiline nose that dominated his rather long, narrow-jawed face. And then her eyes met his, and all at once he *was* a giant. The color, like Robert's, was bright blue, but Robert's eyes, whether smiling or troubled, looked at you, not through you. Sir Arthur's had such intensity that one felt transfixed.

Fortunately, before Esmeralda could disgrace herself by stuttering or dropping a curtsy like a gauche schoolgirl, Sir Arthur's loud, whooping laugh broke the tension, and he came forward with a flattering comment about Robert's luck in picking up so handsome and charming a parcel of flotsam on the beach. Reminded by this gallant opening that Robert had told her Sir Arthur greatly enjoyed a gentle flirtation and seeing that, however piercing his look might be, there was genuine kindliness in it now, Esmeralda was able to respond naturally to this opening sally and the later conversation.

The half hour Sir Arthur had found in which to examine Robert's bride and assure himself that the young man had not fallen victim to some designing harpy passed most pleasantly. Although actually his doubts had been laid to rest the moment he saw Esmeralda, Sir Arthur was a very thorough man. He assured himself from reminiscences of India that she had, indeed, been a resident for many years, and her enthusiastic response to his offer to write to several Talbot and Connor families he knew in Ireland, among whom there was a strong possibility of discovering her relatives, was a good indication that her story was true.

Since these matters were Sir Arthur's first concern and the time he had to bestow on Esmeralda was limited, he never got around to any discussion of her departure. Ordinarily, this subject would have occurred to him at the time the ships were making ready to draw off, but on August 6 he was deep in consultation with General Spencer and on the seventh, the day the disembarkation was completed, he received a message from the Portuguese General Freire, requesting a meeting at a nearby town. Such a minor problem as Esmeralda faded out of Sir Arthur's mind.

Lord Burghersh, who had already shown considerable ability at diplomacy, accompanied Sir Arthur and returned in a state of emotional suppression that threatened a violent explosion. Urgently needing an outlet, he made his way at once to the little house that had already become a safe haven to most of the young gentlemen. To those flayed by one of Sir Arthur's icy outbursts, Robert offered philosophical consolation from his years of similar experience, while Esmeralda soothed the nerves with tea and sympathy. Here they were free to air their military opinions and complaints, get their buttons sewed back on, and damage to their uniforms mended.

Thus, when Burghersh burst in, neither Robert nor Esmeralda, who happened for once to be having tea alone, was much surprised. "I think everyone except us is insane," he snarled.

"And I'm not too sure about us," Robert rejoined placidly. "What's wrong, John?"

"Freire, that's what's wrong. Damn it, I thought the Portuguese were going to be different from the Spanish. You know we rode over to Montemor-o-Velho with five thousand muskets for that ragtag army of his. You'd think the man would be grateful, wouldn't you?"

"No," Robert replied, his lips twitching. "Native allies seldom are, and native generals, never. Sit down and Merry will give you a cup of tea."

"Well, good God, you're calm about it. I suppose you would have liked to hear him acting as if he were in command, telling Sir Arthur where and how to move his troops—"

"Where did Freire want Sir Arthur to go?" Robert asked with considerable interest.

"Inland," Burghersh said. "He wants us to follow the road to Santarém down to Lisbon."

"Why?"

"He says the road is better, the countryside is very rich there, and the army could live off the land."

"Well, there's nothing wrong with that," Robert remarked.

Burghersh took a deep breath and sank into a chair, leaning forward a moment later to take the mug of tea Esmeralda held out to him. "It's his manner, damn him," he said, and then, after a few sips, he sighed. "I don't know. I don't like him. I don't trust him."

"Don't let it worry you," Robert comforted. "I don't think Sir Arthur cares much for him, either. He'll listen and take any information into consideration, but he knows what's best for us and he'll do that."

"I know. We're still going to move along the coast where we'll be in touch with the fleet. But for a while Freire was threatening to simply take our muskets and go off on his own. Sir Arthur convinced him to meet us in Leiria instead. Freire says there's a good-sized magazine there, but he acted as if he were doing us a favor, as if—"

A knock at the door interrupted him. Robert shouted, "Come in," and an orderly put his head around the opening to say, "You're wanted by the general, Captain Moreton."

Robert got to his feet at once. "I think this means we'll move out tomorrow, Merry," he said.

"Very well," Esmeralda replied. "I will be ready."

Her voice drew Burghersh's attention, and he smiled at her and said, "I beg your pardon, Mrs. Moreton. I'm afraid I've been dreadfully rude, bursting in here and not even giving you a word of greeting, just grabbing cups of tea out of your hand as if you were a servant."

"Please don't apologize," she replied, smiling back. "I am very glad you feel so much at home in your brother officer's quarters. It gives me a great deal of satisfaction to be able to forward our purpose, even with so small a thing as cups of tea."

"Yes, do stay and finish your tea," Robert said rather stiffly.

"I'd better not," Burghersh answered, but not because he had noticed anything unusual in Robert's manner. "If you're wanted, I probably will be, too," he explained.

Esmeralda, however, had noticed. Nor was this the first time she had been made aware that Robert seemed to dislike it when she was alone with any of the other men. The first time she had noticed the reaction, she had anxiously reexamined her behavior, wondering if

Robert had perceived anything vulgarly inviting or flitatious in her manner toward his friends. She had been somewhat less generous with her smiles for a while, but it was really very difficult to resist the confiding friendliness his fellow ADCs offered.

This time, after Robert and Lord Burghersh had left, Esmeralda sat for a while allowing hope to rise more strongly than ever before. Was it possible that Robert was jealous? And, if so, what should she do? Was there any way in which she could invite him to make their marriage real without disgusting him or driving him away if her guess was wrong?

For all her bold use of words like "consummate" and "light-skirt," Esmeralda really knew very little about sex. Her mother had died before Esmeralda was told anything about the subject, and in recent years she had not been allowed to have friends intimate enough to discuss such matters. She had, of course, heard hints and innuendos, but these were dreadfully confusing. On the one hand, a young and lively matron, married very much to her own taste, would smile and wink with sparkling eyes and hint that her matrimonial duties were a most delightful pleasure. On the other, another would sigh lugubriously and cast up her eyes to heaven like a martyr. Both husbands had seemed pleasant enough to Esmeralda, but since she had never found either of them more physically appealing than the other, she was not a bit the wiser.

All she knew was that Robert had a very strong effect on her and that as their familiarity grew, the effect not only strengthened but changed. When they had first joined company, she had been satisfied just to look at Robert's handsome face, and to hear him speak was a pure delight. Now there was a growing sense of dissatisfaction mingled with her pleasure. It was not enough to look. Esmeralda wanted to touch—and to be touched.

It was a most frustrating desire, for there was little opportunity for "accidental" intimacy when they were alone. The tiny house had two rooms, one above and one below, and Robert did not share the upstairs bedchamber with Esmeralda. Although this must have been known to all, as Robert's cot stood against one wall, it caused no surprise or doubt. Few husbands and wives of Robert's class shared a bedchamber. In this particular case, the separation was even more natural because Robert might be called out at all hours. To rouse him if he had slept above-stairs would have been more difficult and even embarrassing; moreover, there was no reason for Esmeralda to have her night's rest broken by the demands of Robert's duty.

Nonetheless, living together as husband and wife did affect their relationship. Despite not sharing a bedroom, Esmeralda saw a great deal more of Robert's body than she would have under more formal circumstances. It would have been unnatural, considering the heat, for Robert not to take off his uniform jacket when he was supposedly at ease at home. Thus, Esmeralda was treated to a frequent display of her husband's manly form as his thin, sweat-wet cambric shirt clung to him, exposing every curve of muscle as clearly as if he had been naked. Nor did his tight breeches leave much more to the imagination.

Naturally, Esmeralda did not allow her eyes to linger on these most fascinating aspects of the male body. That, she knew, would be vulgar and unladylike. At least, she did not allow Robert or anyone else to catch her staring. But if she found her husband asleep when she came down from siesta, she would drink in the lines of his body, standing with hands tightly clasped so she would not reach out to caress him. Or at other times, when he was busy with writing some report, she would lift her eyes from her sewing and let her gaze slide from shoulder to thigh as if she were stroking him.

More puzzling to Esmeralda than her desire to touch Robert—she had long accepted the fact that she loved him, and it seemed logical to her that one should wish to touch a beloved object—was the effect merely looking at him had upon her. When her eyes rested on his strong shoulders and thighs, her skin would grow warm, and she could feel her breasts thrust against her bodice, the nipples hard and almost painfully sensitive. And her thighs would tremble and seem so weak that she had to press her knees hard together to make her legs behave.

It was very strange but also most fortunate, Esmeralda thought, that his handsome face did not cause nearly as strong a reaction. She giggled. That would have been a major disaster. It would have been impossible to look at him when answering a question or during normal conversation when his friends were present. And then the giggle died. Would it have been unfortunate? If she had given herself away, would Robert have responded? *Was* he jealous?

Esmeralda rose and went to look into Robert's shaving glass, propped on a shelf near the one window. She had to stand on tiptoe and could see no more than her face. She sighed. No, she was

allowing her own desire to twist her thinking. There was nothing in
the face that looked back at her that could tempt a man into love in
two weeks. It was far more likely that Robert, totally unaware that she
was in love with him, feared she would be attracted to one of his
fellow officers and embarrass him by misbehavior.

Insofar as Robert's conscious thoughts went, Esmeralda was quite
correct. The word "love" had never entered his mind. He was as
troubled by Esmeralda's presence as she was by his and was having as
much difficulty controlling where his eyes rested. But he accepted that
as quite natural, for Merry had a fine figure; he had acknowledged that
from the day he married her. It was quite normal, from Robert's point
of view, that a man's eyes should be attracted to a fine feminine figure
and that his body should be aroused by it. He did not associate
physical desire with love, and aside from sometimes feeling annoyed
when it delayed his falling asleep or when he woke with a powerful
urge, he could almost completely dismiss that aspect of his feelings
about Esmeralda.

There was, however, one small thing that puzzled him. Robert had
never been a three-times-a-night-and-every-night-of-the-week man,
even when he was idle. When he was deeply engaged in military
activity, as he now was, his sexual appetite was moderate. A girl once
or twice in a week, or even less frequently if he was really busy, was
enough to quench all desire and even all thought of women. Yet,
although he had found a willing girl in the camp the evening after they
had arrived, only hours later, when he had taken Merry's hand and
kissed it just before they parted for the night, he was suddenly no
better off than if he had not relieved himself.

A little logical thought as he was lying on his cot half an hour later
presented an explanation. The simple fact that there was an attractive
woman near him at all times when he was off duty was a constant
reminder and inducement. A little more logical thought presented a
solution. Get rid of the woman, and he would be rid of the sexual
problem. However, instead of relief, this solution produced a
profound depression of Robert's spirit, until he remembered that he
had promised Merry not to send her alone to England. He could not,
he told himself, go back on his word to her solely to provide himself
with a less tempting atmosphere. The immediate lifting of his
depression, he assumed, was the reward for his self-sacrifice; doing
right, he knew, always made one feel good.

It was less easy to explain to himself the uneasiness he felt at the attentions paid to Merry by his friends. Even if she had really been his wife, there would have been nothing to object to in them. In fact, when there was a group laughing and talking in the little house, Robert felt very proud of Merry's interest and intelligence and her ability to make everyone feel comfortable. However, when any single man settled beside her to talk seriously, or stayed behind when Robert himself had to leave, or arrived before he was himself in the house, Robert could feel a very strange sensation in his spine.

If he had been a dog, he thought ruefully as he and Burghersh walked quickly toward the headquarters, his hackles would be up. The simile was embarrassing because it made Robert think of a dog in the manger, snapping at an ox to keep it away from the straw the dog itself did not want. Or *did* he want it? he wondered. But that revelatory thought had no chance to take hold. At the moment it arrived, he entered the room Sir Arthur was using as an office and was enveloped in instructions pertaining to the march to be made the next day.

Chapter 12

Esmeralda was not totally discouraged by her guess that Robert might fear she would become interested or arouse interest in one of his fellow officers. Even so much as that was a large step forward. When he had rescued her, he would not have believed any man *could* be interested in her. The very fact that he was thinking about her at all was an achievement—at least, so long as he did not start to think in the wrong direction, that she was a nuisance who should be sent away.

That notion brought Esmeralda hurrying to the door to shout for Carlos. Robert had simply accepted her statement that she would be ready to move out with the army the next day, but there was still time, she feared, for him to change his mind. From long experience Esmeralda knew that the best way to escape unwelcome attention was not to be noticed. And the best way to do that was to be out of sight.

Esmeralda's call brought Carlos to the door at once, and again she blessed the twist of fate that had made Robert choose Luisa to carry their baggage. There were countless advantages to having the small Portuguese boy as her manservant. One of these was his youth and small size, which made it possible for him to go almost anywhere without challenge so Esmeralda did not need to bother Robert to obtain passes or identification for him.

"Go into the women's area, and ask Mrs. M'Guire to come to me," Esmeralda told him.

During the delay necessary for disembarking Spencer's troops, Esmeralda had had a chance to make inquiries and hire a womanservant. Of the many who had applied, she had chosen Molly M'Guire, a big, strong, fresh-faced Irishwoman who was not new to army service. In fact, M'Guire was Molly's second husband, her first having died in the West Indies of fever. Two of her three children had

died there, too, and Molly had left the one surviving little girl with her
mother in Ireland when she had been one of those chosen by lot to
accompany the men.

Esmeralda had asked her about leaving her child behind, because
she had been warned that more than a few of the women increased
their husbands' pitiful pay by whoring for the rest of the men or the
officers. Molly was good-looking enough to make that a possibility,
and she might have wished to be free of the child to be more available.
Of course, that did not fit very well with her application to be a
servant, but greed might make her think she could manage all three
occupations.

"I almost did not put me name in th' lot," she replied in her
appealing brogue, "but Oi tho'ght ibout it 'nd decided it were
M'Guire who'd need me most. Mam'll take good care o' Katy, 'nd if
they're sometimes a wee short 'nd flat i' th' belly, ah weel, it's loike
inough we'll be short, too. Oi've niver bin wit th' troops that we did
no outrun oor pay 'nd oor commissary carts."

It was a most reasonable answer, and Esmeralda was particularly
attracted to Molly's cheerful cynicism bred by useful experience, but
it was meeting M'Guire himself that decided the issue. When
Esmeralda had presented the problem to Robert, he had asked her to
have the husband up and see whether he was willing and capable of
being Robert's batman and groom.

"It's best to have a couple, if it can be arranged," he had said.
"And I never heard of an Irishman who couldn't handle horses, so
that will be all right. Find out with what regiment he's serving if he
seems suitable."

Not only was M'Guire willing and capable, but Esmeralda liked
him at once and liked even more the obvious good feeling that existed
between Molly and her husband. It was clear that M'Guire was years
younger than his wife, much less experienced, and not at all the type
to look elsewhere if Molly played around. Esmeralda therefore settled
matters as soon as she was certain that M'Guire was country Irish, not
London slum Irish, and thus that his claim to be "well inuff wi' th'
horses" was probably true. He would be responsible for Hermes,
Jupiter, Mars, and Apollo.

Nor had there been any trouble about M'Guire's temporary
detachment from his regiment. Caitlin Crawfurd did not wish to
disoblige a member of Sir Arthur's staff and, making the stipulation

that M'Guire should be with his company in time for any action, excused him from all duties except roll call. And since Robert was far more interested in having his horses and weapons well cared for than in the perfection of the shine on his boots, M'Guire was an adequate servant.

When Molly arrived, Esmeralda gave her the news, which did not seem to be much of a surprise to her. They made quick work of the packing and, far more important, plans for finding each other during the march, if it became necessary, and in camp or quarters. Molly suggested that if they passed through any town, Esmeralda should try to buy food, specially cured meat, cheese, and rice—plus anything else that would not spoil—adding that she knew ways of cooking such ingredients together so that they were truly good eating.

Esmeralda nodded agreement, as much because of what Robert had said about Sir Arthur's carelessness in feeding his ADCs as because she feared the supplies would be inadequate. And since Esmeralda now had money—one hundred beautiful silver cruzados—she intended to shop for more than food as soon as possible. There was no need for a dressmaker for the simple gowns she would need; if she could find attractive fabrics, she could sew them herself with Molly's help. Those hundred cruzados would go a long way, Esmeralda thought. She would send Carlos to buy the food—a poor little orphan boy, driving a mule for the English, should be able to obtain excellent bargains. And, accustomed as she was to Indian merchants, Esmeralda herself could drive a mean bargain.

All the while she and Molly were talking and working, Esmeralda prayed that Robert would be kept too busy to come back before time for bed. He would dine with the mess, she was sure, but usually he was free by nine o'clock. If he came back at that time, she could not avoid him. To be absent when he expected to see her would fix his attention on her just as surely as getting in his way when she should not be about.

Esmeralda got her wish, and even a little more, for Robert sent an orderly to tell her that he would not be in until late. This gesture, touching in its consideration for her, also troubled Esmeralda. She did not want Robert to feel any guilt if his duties kept him away. Guilt is a most unpleasant burden, a nagging irritation, and could quickly wipe out any pleasure he derived from her company. The concern followed her into her dreams so that, although she slept well enough, she woke as soon as the first sounds of activity from the camp drifted through the open window, with the same worry in mind.

Thus, she hurried her dressing and ran down to make Robert's tea and cut bread and cheese for his breakfast, working as silently as she could until he woke. A convention had been established between them: Once Robert began to stir, Esmeralda kept her back turned to him until he pulled on his breeches and boots and went out to wash and visit the jakes. When he returned, she allowed him to get well started on his breakfast before she spoke to him, unless he addressed her first. Since Robert did not seem to be in any haste to leave, Esmeralda followed the established practice for a while, but when he held out his cup to be refilled, she assured him that it was not necessary for him to inform her of his coming and going if it was not convenient.

"I didn't want you to worry," he said, staring at her rather intently.

"I know, and I am very grateful," Esmeralda replied, feeling a trifle puzzled by his steady gaze, "but you must not think of me as gnawing my fingernails to the nub or filling a bucket with tears if you are unable to return to our quarters at your usual time. Of course, if you can send word, I would be glad to know when you are delayed, but if it is inconvenient, do not give it a thought."

Robert lowered his eyes to the piece of cheese he was about to spear. It was considerate of Merry to assure him that he need not fear she would worry about him, but somehow he wished she had not said it. Not that he wanted her to be fearful, of course, but . . .

"Is there something wrong with the cheese?" Esmeralda asked. "I can cut some fresh for you."

"What?" Robert started and looked up. "The cheese? No, there's nothing wrong with it." He looked down at it again somberly, suddenly finding it very uninviting. "Except that it is cheese." Then he looked up quickly again, and his voice had a slight edge when he spoke. "No, don't apologize. I know there's nothing else to be had. Are you ready to leave? If so, you would do best at the very head of the baggage train. You won't be smothered in dust there, and I'll know where to find you."

Esmeralda could not understand what had annoyed him and did not dare ask. At least he had given her instructions about the first stage of the march. Since she knew that their objective was the inland town of

Leiria, there could be no question of her being ordered aboard ship until they reached another shore point.

Thus all she said was "Yes, I am ready. Do you know whether there will be any towns along the route? Molly suggested that I buy food, and—"

"Don't you dare wander away from the troops," Robert interrupted. "So far the people seem well affected, but we don't know whether Freire has stirred up any trouble." He stood up abruptly.

"I will not leave the baggage train," Esmeralda assured him immediately. "I only thought if we passed *through* a town, I could buy what I needed before the wagons got through. Then I could easily catch up to the front of the train because Boa Viagem is so much faster. . . ." She stopped because her voice had begun to shake, and she was afraid Robert would think she was acting like a spoiled child deprived of a chance to shop.

"I suppose you can do that, but have M'Guire with you as a guard," Robert said rather ungraciously. He hesitated and then added harshly, "I *do* worry about you, you see."

Esmeralda had been so alarmed by his seemingly unprovoked ill temper that his parting words with their sarcastic emphasis took some time to sink in. When they had, she jumped to her feet and ran to the door, but Robert was out of sight. She stood biting her lips, knowing it was impossible to pursue him to explain. That would only add embarrassment to his irritation. But how dreadful that he had misunderstood her; how ungrateful he must think her to be if he believed she could imply that she did not care what happened to him.

One fortunate result of Esmeralda's misery was that it insulated her from the difficulties of that first day's march. Robert had spoken as if she were to leave at once, and in almost trembling haste she washed up and packed the crockery they had used. Nonetheless, it was several hours before the troops were out of the camp and even longer before the long train of baggage mules and ox carts began to follow them. By then, the sun was high and brutally hot.

Accustomed as she was to India's temperatures, Esmeralda was only minimally aware of the heat. Carlos and Luisa were just behind her, and the water flasks were full. She could drink whenever she wanted. Nor did she notice how heavily Boa Viagem was plodding, pulling her hooves one at a time from a road so dry and sandy that she

sweated from the effort despite the slow pace. As long as the mare did
not stumble, Esmeralda's own unhappy thoughts held her attention.

She saw, without really taking in, the bodies of stragglers propped
against their packs or lying limply along the road. They had fallen by
the wayside, exhausted by the weight of their unwieldy packs. The
intense heat, combined with the labor of marching under so heavy and
awkward a burden, seduced the unwise to make frequent use of their
canteens, which were soon emptied—and there was no water to be
found after they had left Figueira da Foz and the Mondego River. The
new men dropped by dozens. A few died; most were picked up and
thrown onto the baggage carts, where the blazing sun only increased
their torment.

Although Esmeralda was not overtly aware of what she saw, the
sights and sounds did penetrate some part of her mind, and all along
the way the patrolling subalterns acknowledged her presence, sometimes with expressions of surprise and sometimes with shy nods. A
few came up and spoke to her; those addressed her by name and
remarked genially on her aplomb, saying one would think she was
"an old campaigner." At the time the comments puzzled her; later she
understood it was because she had made no attempt to interfere or to
aid the fallen men. She had, of course, seen far worse things on the
west coast of India, which was partly why the sights had not
penetrated her self-absorption. Nevertheless, she might have stopped
and tried to help had she not been cautioned against it.

Fortunately Sir Arthur had examined the terrain himself and knew
the troops were raw. Thus, the first march he planned was no more
than twelve miles to the village of Lavos. The army was ordered to
camp in the open nearby, and the senior officers and staff sought
quarters in the village. By the time Esmeralda arrived, there was an
orderly waiting to tell her that she and Captain Moreton were to have
rooms in a farmhouse conveniently close to the building Sir Arthur
had chosen.

There was no sign of Robert nor, indeed, of any of the other ADCs,
so Esmeralda went directly to their quarters and ordered M'Guire to
take Robert's horses to the barn and then help Carlos unload Luisa.
Carlos was chattering away in a mixture of Portuguese and English
about how good a mule Luisa was. Esmeralda hardly listened. Her
mind was ranging the countryside, wondering where Robert was and
whether he was so angry that he was deliberately staying away. When

M'Guire returned, she forced herslef to consider more practical matters. Having carried up the clothes bags and other essentials, he asked whether she wanted the cots brought in, since there was already a bed in the room.

Esmeralda went up, searching for a reason that would sound natural to have at least one cot carried in and, at the same time, hoping there would be an absolutely inescapable reason not to do so. Then she could share the bed with Robert. She could make herself small, pressed against the wall so that he might not at first notice she was there. And then . . . And then, she admitted, staring blankly at the bed, he would be furious with her and so disgusted that he would probably give up the pretense and quarter himself with the other ADCs until the first opportunity to be rid of her.

At that moment her eyes focused on the bed, and she shuddered. "Bring up *both* cots," she ordered, "but don't set them up yet. Just put them as far away as you can manage from that nest of six-legged pests. And take the mattress out. Leave it in the corridor or carry it downstairs, but get it out of here."

The shock of disgust did her good, however. She had managed to keep herself reasonably clean in old Pedro's village by insisting that she sleep on clean straw and by bathing frequently—a habit all residents of India established for the sake of the cooling effect. The rooms she had stayed in on the road from Oporto had been the best available, and she had insisted on clean sheets in each place. The little house in Figueira da Foz had been cleaned out for the young men who lodged in it before she arrived. Now, Esmeralda realized, she would be faced with the problem of making her quarters habitable.

Forgetting her personal problems for the moment, Esmeralda went out to discover whether the few shops in the village carried such things as soap and brushes. Once in the stores, she remembered the other things she had intended to buy. Cloth of a sufficiently delicate quality was not available, but there was rice and other dry grain in plenty, dried fruit of various kinds, and other provisions. Clearly the French had not foraged excessively in this area—or the inhabitants of Lavos were more clever at hiding things than most. Certainly they were hiding nothing now. Word that the English would pay had apparently preceded them.

However, this information had also raised the expectations of the merchants. Esmeralda's need to get the best price on everything

stretched the time she spent in the shops, and in the end she ran into
Robert in the street as she was edging her way around a group of men
pushing and jostling to get into a wineshop. His arms were full of
bottles, as hers were full of bundles, and he stopped short and glared
at her.

"You are incorrigible!" he exclaimed. "Did I or did I not tell you
to keep M'Guire with you as a guard?"

"Oh, dear, I forgot," Esmeralda admitted guiltily. "But if you had
seen the bed in the room and the fleas on the walls—"

"Don't tell me about it." Robert groaned. "You should have seen
the look on the Beau's face when we were escorted into 'the finest
house' in the village."

"You should have seen the look on mine!" Esmeralda countered.
"Anyway, the only thing I could think of was soap and scrubbing
brushes. I'm sorry I forgot to take M'Guire along, but the whole town
is so small, he would have heard me if I called him from anywhere.
And there wasn't any danger. The people *are* well disposed."

"They should be," Robert replied dryly. "They will make a year's
profit on this visit of ours." But he smiled at her with easy good
humor as he nodded at the packages she was carrying.

"Not out of me, they didn't," Esmeralda responded with pretended
indignation, although she could have wept with relief at seeing the
smile. He must have realized, she thought, that he had misunderstood
her. "I'm no downy chick for plucking," she added, laughing. "I
learned to bargain in Indian bazaars." Then she nodded in turn at the
collection of wine bottles he was carrying. "You will be late tonight, I
gather?"

"Not unless I'm the lucky boy who will have to ride back to
Figueira with the dispatch Sir Arthur is writing. The general officers
are invited to dinner and, I imagine, to a planning and scolding
session. I'm not sure the Beau will want to have the 'messenger boys'
present."

"Scolding?" Esmeralda repeated. "But—"

Just then an altercation broke out among the men around the
wineshop, and Robert glanced back over his shoulder. "I'll tell you
later," he said. "Get into quarters now, Merry, and stay there. The
natives won't make trouble, but these drunken devils may. I'll come
when I can."

She hurried away obediently, not afraid at the moment but realizing

Robert was right. Sober, not a man in the army would have dreamed of touching her; in fact, most would hardly dare smile at her or speak to her. Her clothing and speech marked her as "officer class." However, blind with drink, any one of them might play too rough before he realized who she was. It would be a disaster for Esmeralda to be involved in that kind of trouble. Even if she escaped unhurt, she would be sent away at once.

Molly was already in the room, cleaning. She was startled, almost horrified, when Esmeralda proposed sharing the task. "Ye're no used t' sich work," she exclaimed.

"Well, I certainly was not used to it in the past," Esmeralda admitted. "When I lived in India there were plenty of servants. But I am not so fine anymore. In the village where I was shipwrecked, I scrubbed my own clothes, and I helped in the house. There is too much for you to do alone, Molly, and I would rather help scrub than put up with the fleas. I'll have to find something to wear, though."

She settled on a shirt of Robert's that was already soiled and needed washing. Since there was nothing else and it was very warm, she just put it on over her pantalets. Molly choked with laughter, and Esmeralda giggled at the sight she knew she must make; however, under the laughter she was strangely stirred by wearing Robert's garment. She soon forgot, though, and became sufficiently absorbed in what she was doing that she lost count of time. Nor did she pay any attention to the sound of footsteps on the stairs. M'Guire had been emptying slops and bringing up fresh water, but he had been warned not to enter the rooms. Molly had just left to put out the last of the dirty buckets.

Thus, Esmeralda straightened up without concern from giving a last wipe to the wall and looked with satisfaction at her work. She did not turn as the door opened but said, "It's odd, but despite the work there is a real pleasure in seeing a room properly put to rights."

Since the only reply she received was a shocked intake of breath, Esmeralda whirled about to confront Robert, who still had his hand on the door and looked paralyzed with surprise. Esmeralda could feel the blood rising in her face; both of them stood staring, unable to speak or move. Robert swallowed convulsively as Molly's voice came through the open door calling down to M'Guire that when he had emptied the bucket he should set up the cots.

Somehow the combination of Molly's voice and Robert's aston-

ished face recalled to Esmeralda how ridiculous she must look.
Although she was mortified, she had very little personal vanity, and
the whole thing struck her as extremely funny. Her hands flew up to
her mouth, but they could not repress the giggles that shook her. "I am
so sorry," she gasped. "Molly wouldn't think to warn you, and I am
afraid I forgot the time."

The unnatural color faded from Robert's face, and he grinned.
"Shall I go out again?" he asked, but his eyes flicked appreciatively
over her legs, bared from the knee down by her unusual attire, before
they were tactfully averted.

"No, I will go next door and make myself decent," she replied,
still smiling, not at all ill pleased with the flash of admiration she had
seen. "Shall I tell Molly to bring in your bags so you can change to
regimentals? You will wish to change for dinner if the general officers
are invited, I expect."

Robert burst out laughing at a sudden vision of himself in full
formal dress escorting Esmeralda in her present costume, then
choked. "I beg your pardon," he said, striving desperately for
gravity. "I will change if you like, but I am not dining with Sir Arthur
tonight. If you will give me the honor of your company, I will dine
with you this evening. The staff is excused, as there is not room
enough at the table for us and the general officers."

"I know *just* what you are thinking," Esmeralda remarked, trying
to look severe and failing lamentably because she thought it was
funny, too. "However, it will not do. We cannot count on being alone
with our little joke. If Lord Burghersh or one of the others should
come in—"

The mischievous sparkle in Robert's eyes was quenched at once,
and he stood away from the door. "Go and get dressed immediately,"
he said.

Esmeralda fled, embarrassed all over again as soon as the light
teasing between them ended. She would have liked a few minutes to
think over the implications of Robert's manner from the beginning to
the end of the incident, but she did not dare leave him alone with *his*
thoughts. They might, of course, be greatly to her advantage, but they
might also lean the other way, emphasizing the embarrassment and
discomfort of sharing quarters with a woman with whom he was not
genuinely intimate.

Thus, Esmeralda tore off Robert's shirt while she told Molly to go out and see if she could get an adequate dinner cooked for them somewhere, pulled on her one gown, and rushed back—only to find Robert stripped down to his breeches. This time it was Esmeralda's gasp of surprise that drew attention, but when their eyes met, both burst out laughing.

"Oh, I am so sorry," Esmeralda cried. "I thought I had told you not to change. I have sent Molly out to bring in dinner. We will both be more comfortable here, I think, than trying to struggle through the crowds in the town. Shall I go?"

"Not if you don't mind seeing me put on a shirt," Robert replied.

Esmeralda smiled and moved toward a chair near the window. "I hope you do not think me shockingly bold," she said, "but, you know, after living in India all my life, I cannot really feel much dismayed by a bare upper body. Really, there is little of the male form with which I am not acquainted. The men working in Papa's go-downs wore hardly anything at all."

"You should not have been in the go-downs," Robert remarked. "I do not wish to speak ill of your father, particularly since he is dead, and even more because I have profited by his peculiarities in that you are very . . ." He hesitated and then, as if he had not left the sentence unfinished, went on, "But it was most improper. You will need to be more careful in England."

He turned away to rummage in his bag. Esmeralda forgot to reply while her eyes rested on his broad shoulders, then slid down his hard-muscled back to his narrow waist. She had done it before, but only when he was asleep or deeply absorbed in some task. This time he seemed to feel her gaze on him, and he turned back toward her, but in the split second it took Robert to look at her, Esmeralda was staring most innocently out the window.

"I don't think I am likely to be in the same situation in England," she said blandly, and then, when he did not answer, she grew nervous and retreated from the personal conversation to what she knew would interest him and put him at ease. "What did you mean when you said Sir Arthur was going to scold his general officers?" she asked.

For the first time in his life, Robert had to exert considerable effort to focus his mind on a military subject. "The march," he said vaguely, thinking that he must be more careful in the future; he kept seeing Merry in those provocative pantalets, damp with sweat, and clinging to her buttocks and thighs. With considerable haste, Robert pulled his shirt on and reached for his coat.

"You'll be too warm if you wear your coat," Esmeralda commented innocently, her voice tinged with surprise, for Robert seldom wore more than a shirt during the heat of the day in their own quarters.

Robert wondered irritably whether he should inform her of certain facts of life, but when his eyes met hers and saw the puzzled concern in them, the words froze in his throat.

"What was wrong with the march?" Esmeralda asked.

"Good God, didn't you notice that about a third of the men fell out along the way?" he retorted.

"I did see a number of men along the road," Esmeralda admitted, "but I am very ignorant of what is usual under these circumstances."

"Well, the troops are very raw," Robert conceded, "but Sir Arthur felt that the officers were not sufficiently attentive, and he wishes them to know that he was not satisfied with the performance of the men. It did not really matter today and probably will not until we reach Leiria. After that, however, we may meet the French any time, and we cannot have a third of our forces lying along the roadside, complaining of the heat."

"Have you received definite information about where the French are?" she asked.

"No, but that almost certainly means that they are not close," Robert replied soothingly. "There is nothing to fear."

"I am not—" Esmeralda began, but her denial was interrupted by the sound of several pairs of boots on the stairs, which heralded a polite scratch on the door.

"Come in," Robert called, and grinned as he remembered that Merry had warned him they were not likely to be left alone for long.

"I just thought I would let you know that it would be better to keep Mrs. Moreton off the street," Lord Burghersh said immediately after greetings had been exchanged. Then he stared around the room and twisted up his face. "You are a lucky dog, Moreton," he sighed. "You're likely to be the only one who sleeps tonight. The rest of us will be too busy scratching."

The remark was fervently echoed by the others and led naturally enough to jokes about Robert having all sorts of unfair advantages. He responded to the teasing in his usual way, but he was aware of a very odd mixture of feelings: He felt guilty because he now realized why

Esmeralda had been wearing that odd costume—she had been cleaning the room. Yet the knowledge that she had done it and made nothing of it, adapting so easily and uncomplainingly to each new situation, gave him a sense of satisfaction. It also aroused in him an uneasy indecisiveness regarding his once firm conviction that following the drum was no life for a woman. It certainly seemed to agree with Merry.

Chapter 13

The march from Lavos to Lugar the next day was, for Esmeralda, much the same as that from Figueira to Lavos. For the men there were differences. A far stricter watch was kept by the officers all along the route, and fewer fell out of ranks. Problems in the quarters were much the same but were easier to deal with because of past experience—and Robert was much more cautious about entering rooms without announcing himself so there were no further embarrassing incidents, a little to Esmeralda's regret. On August 10 they came to Leiria.

This was a town of modest size rather than a village. Sir Arthur took over a decent inn, and all of the officers had clean and comfortable lodgings. The state of the men was not as good. When they had camped near villages, the people, either because they were truly glad to see the English or as a preventive measure, had been most hospitable. They had carried fruit out to the camps, oranges, melons, grapes, and figs, and even brought calves to be slaughtered to add to the salt meat and biscuit the men were issued. The townsfolk of Leiria were not so generous.

There was a magazine of supplies in the town, collected by the Portuguese authorities for the sustenance of the troops. However, it was seized by General Freire, who then refused to share it with the English. He also refused to cooperate further with Sir Arthur, insisting that the English supply any Portuguese troops who followed the coast road. Sir Arthur refused to do this, partly because he did not think it reasonable but also because he did not think most of the Portuguese troops reliable enough to be of much assistance. Eventually a compromise was reached. About 260 of the Portuguese cavalry and 1,600 infantry were to accompany the English under the command of

Colonel Trant. The remainder of Freire's army was to remain near
Leiria to protect Sir Arthur's rear.

Robert was so busy and so furious that he had no time to ponder any
personal concerns. He was aware only subliminally of the comfort
Esmeralda brought him by providing for his physical needs and by
listening sympathetically to the tirades it was not safe to express
elsewhere. As one of the senior ADCs, it was Robert's duty to soothe
the younger men so that they would not show their true feelings even
by cold looks or haughty manners and complicate or, perhaps, ruin Sir
Arthur's negotiations. Had Robert not had Esmeralda to confide in, he
might have burst.

Over the days of the march, owing partly to conversations with
Robert, partly to her casual snippets of talk with the young officers,
and partly to the tales and anecdotes she heard from Molly and her
husband, Esmeralda had begun to identify with the army. Thus, her
response to Robert became deeper and more sincere; the army became
"her" army, and she encouraged Robert to tell her everything he
could because of genuine interest rather than because she wished to
please him.

As a result, Esmeralda's indignation about the treatment they were
receiving from Freire was sincere, but she was herself so happy that
she could always see a small advantage here and there to ameliorate
the problems Robert described. Her days were very full. Good fabrics
were to be had to make gowns; Robert's friends and many of the
young officers from the regiments were very much at home in her
apartment; Carlos was there to be taught both English and the fine
points of being an excellent servant.

Only two shadows clouded Esmeralda's serene sky: One had
existed from the beginning; how was she to make her marriage real?
The other was new. As the army became more real to her, its purpose
also became more real. The English were in Portugal to make war on
the French. Men died in war. Too often now, when Esmeralda talked
and laughed with the young men who sought comfort and entertainment in her quarters, a chill of fear would pass over her. And
Robert . . . He, too, was flesh and blood. He, too, was vulnerable.

Late in the evening of August 12, the second of Esmeralda's clouds
gathered substance and blotted out the brightness in her life. She
knew that something important was about to happen because none of her
usual guests showed up for tea and Robert was unusually late in

returning after dinner, but she was at first fooled by Robert's sparkling eyes and brilliant smile—especially since it was quite apparent that the gaiety was not owing to drink.

"Something has gone right at last, I see," she said. "Can you tell me?"

"We are moving out tomorrow," Robert replied, tossing his hat into the nearest chair. "And we will be rid of General Freire."

"I am delighted we will be shot of Freire." Esmeralda laughed and shook her head. "But I cannot quite match your enthusiasm for leaving Leiria if we are to be again quartered in villages." Nonetheless, she was smiling as brightly as he. If Robert was happy, a few fleas were nothing to Esmeralda.

"Oh, you won't be going—at least, not tomorrow," Robert told her. "Sir Arthur is leaving most of the baggage train here until we have some definite news of the French."

It was lightly said as Robert walked toward the table where several bottles of wine and glasses stood ready, but Esmeralda caught a peculiar sidelong glance from him as he went by the chair in which she was sitting. She rose to her feet as he passed and barely prevented herself from catching at him. It was the look that held her back; she took warning from it and choked down the impulse to throw her arms around him and plead to be taken along. By now Esmeralda knew enough about military matters to understand that if Sir Arthur had decided to leave his baggage train behind, it was not just news of the French he expected to find, but their army.

Fighting the terror that threatened to choke her, Esmeralda said, "You will not leave me for long, will you? I—I will be very eager for news."

Robert turned toward her, smiling. He had almost expected her to say "Thank God," or just "Oh, very well." Instead, her statement that she was eager for news gave him an intense pleasure that he did not understand, but he just accepted the warmth and gladness as part of the general feeling of joy Esmeralda produced in him. The clear thought in his mind was that Merry was the most perfect girl. She never made a fuss.

"Perhaps I could come back tomorrow night," Robert said. "We won't have moved too far for me to ride in if I can get leave from Sir Arthur."

"Oh, please do, Robert," Esmeralda cried. She was about to say she would be worried sick if he did not come, but she bit that back, remembering that she had resolved not to ask for any attention that, if necessarily neglected, would place a burden of guilt on him. Instead, she added, "And if there is no sign of the French, I could move forward with you in the morning, could I not?"

"I suppose that would be safe enough," Robert replied slowly, again feeling inordinately pleased, but then his conscience smote him. "But why should you? You will be more comfortable here."

"I was only joking about the bad accommodation in the villages, truly I was," Esmeralda assured him, struggling to prevent a note of pleading from entering her voice. "If I move up, you see, I will still be in reach the following day. . . ." She hesitated, unsure of how far it would be safe to go, and then said uncertainly, "Unless it would be too much trouble for you to ride back each night like that."

"No trouble at all." Without analyzing the idea, he knew he would go as far as necessary to join Esmeralda.

They discussed the route the army would take and the fact that he and Esmeralda would have to be on the road just at dawn to be certain that Robert would arrive at Sir Arthur's headquarters—wherever it might be—by the time his commanding officer might want him. A number of practical complications arose from Robert's spending his nights apart from the other ADCs, but he soon found a reason for his eagerness to involve himself in so much trouble.

"It will be much easier for me, too, if I ride down with you in the morning," Esmeralda had just assured him, laughingly. "That way I will have the whole day to get the fleas out of the place instead of only a few hours, and you will not return to find me most improperly clad."

Robert laughed, too, but a disconcerting vision of Esmeralda in pantalets rose again in his mind. He blanked out the vision most firmly. *Of course*, he told himself, *it is perfectly reasonable to look forward to decent lodgings. An hour's ride is well worth a full night's sleep and an escape from scratching all the next day.*

In any event, Robert did not take Esmeralda with him the next day; there was no place for her to stay. Sir Arthur himself had found nothing better than a miserable mud hut, and when Robert left, the staff had been settling down to sleep—if it could be called sleep— under a nearby tree.

"They called me all the names they could think of when I got permission to come back," he said, laughing. "Sir Arthur wasn't pleased, but he conceded that it was necessary to reassure you that all was well, so long as I was on duty by six."

"I won't mind staying wherever Sir Arthur was," Esmeralda offered. "We have the cots, and I can load Luisa with food. Molly would follow me, too, I'm sure."

Robert shook his head firmly, insisting that the place was not fit for her. She did not argue, only lowered her eyes to her hands, which were tightly clasped in her lap. Somehow Robert could not say the words he had planned, which were that in a few days, as soon as they found a satisfactory place to camp, the whole baggage train would follow since it would be necessary to bring supplies. Instead, he laughed and told her that he was growing addicted to the fleshpots of Leiria himself and would come for her the next night if it were possible.

As he said it, he wondered if he were mad. It would mean riding twenty miles in the dark after a full day of scouting the road ahead and riding up and down the line of march with messages and reprimands from Wellesley to his line officers. But Merry's beautiful eyes had risen to his, glowing with gratitude, when she said she knew she was being ridiculous and that he must not put himself to so much trouble to satisfy her whim. So Robert laughed again and said not to worry about that.

They reached Alcobaça on August 14 and learned that a brigade of the French army under Thomières had been there until the preceding day and that General Delaborde was somewhere to the south in the area of Óbidos with a weak division. Clearly the French were drawing together and would make contact within a day or two.

Robert was aware of an unaccustomed dichotomy in his emotions when he heard these reports. Normally, the information that action was near thrilled him. After a battle, when he saw the dead and, more particularly, the wounded, he felt regrets; but beforehand he thought only of the excitement, of the thunder of the guns and the exhilaration of riding with messages and seeing the results of the troop movements. This time he also felt a sharp pang of disappointment. Perhaps it would be unwise to bring Merry so close to the action.

Almost immediately Robert banished the disappointing doubts. Merry would not be near the action at all. Thomières was no longer in the area; Óbidos was over seventeen miles south of Alcobaça. Surely she would be in no more danger staying in Alcobaça than in Leiria. If they retreated—and Robert did not really believe that any retreat would be necessary; the troops were in good condition, morale was high, and Sir Arthur had not yet lost a battle—Merry would be well in advance of retrograde movement. Thus, it would be perfectly safe to bring her to Alcobaça.

When Robert again asked permission to return to Leiria, Sir Arthur looked at him most peculiarly; however, since there were several other officers in the room, he did not comment cynically about Robert's being surprisingly attentive for a husband engaged in a marriage of convenience, which he might have done had they been alone. Nor did he make any objection to the request because Robert had been waiting that morning with the other ADCs when Sir Arthur had finished shaving and been ready to give orders. In fact, Sir Arthur was beginning to believe that what had started as an act of duty had turned into a love affair. A romantic himself, although he kept his soft heart very well hidden, Sir Arthur felt considerable empathy with his handsome young ADC. If he wished to spend a last night with his love, why not?

Had Sir Arthur known that Robert intended to bring his wife south, he might have remonstrated, but no mention was made of that. It was not a conscious omission on Robert's part. He had reasoned it all out, and it seemed logical enough to him. To his mind it was silly to annoy Sir Arthur with unessential, personal details. Nor, for the same reason, did Robert mention the next morning when he appeared for duty that Esmeralda had taken over the quarters that the ADCs had just vacated.

To Robert's mind, Merry had listened to the news of the proximity of the French army with absolute indifference, and she had agreed with complete conviction with Robert's analysis of the situation. In fact, Esmeralda believed Robert was right, but she knew she would have agreed with equal fervor even if he had told her the sky was bright red and that the officers would attack riding flying pigs instead of horses. Not that she was still ignorant of the ways of war; she realized that a total rout completely out of control might endanger her, even as far as seventeen miles away. However, even if she had thought certain destruction very likely and had been terrified, Esmeralda would have pretended indifference.

Having heard that action was imminent, she was determined to be near Robert. If he should be hurt, she intended to nurse him. It was her conviction, from stories she had heard, that as many wounded died from neglect and the inadequate medical facilities as died from the effects of the wounds themselves. And actually, Esmeralda was not at all afraid. Her military opinions having been molded by Robert and his friends, she was even more confident than Robert that the British would be victorious in any action Sir Arthur decided to undertake. It was not herself, safe in Alcobaça, for whom she feared.

Fortunately, Robert had taken her frozen rigidity of absolute horror to be indifference. And when he began to tell her of the distance between the armies and that it was likely that the French would retreat for several days longer while they grouped their forces and brought up reinforcements, Esmeralda's immediate anxiety had melted enough for her to reply to his conversation rationally. Even so, Robert had his doubts as to the wisdom of Esmeralda moving farther south, but the two evenings he had spent alone with her had sharply reinforced his pleasure in her company. As on that first evening in Oporto, they had talked about army affairs, played cards, and laughed a great deal.

By now Robert was growing quite expert in finding excuses to keep Esmeralda close, and she aided and abetted him with the agility of mind developed by years of outwitting her father. Between them, they found reasons enough for her to continue south with Robert to Caldas on the morning of August 15. There had not been even a smell of the French, Robert told himself; there could be no danger in moving her south once more.

His conscience should have stabbed him, because early the next morning four companies of the Sixtieth and of the Ninety-fifth Rifles came upon French pickets established at the windmill of Brilos, just about a mile outside of Caldas. Upon order the English troops drove the French out without the smallest difficulty, but their officers, being more gallant than sensible and lifted to enthusiasm by finally coming upon the enemy, unwisely followed the fleeing French troops, firing as they ran.

When the mill was clear, Sir Arthur dismounted to climb to the top of it to survey the countryside. He examined the terrain minutely while the sound of the firing diminished into the distance. After fifteen or twenty minutes, he dropped his glass from his eye and cocked his head to listen to the intermittent sound of the guns still fading. Then he *tchk'd* and lifted his glass to his eye. After a few minutes more, he turned his head toward his staff.

"Campbell, Spencer's division should be well forward to our left. Tell him to send a brigade on to Óbidos with all the speed they can make. Moreton, ride after those idiotic Rifles and tell them to stop at once. They can hold their ground if it is reasonable to do so, but they are to retire to Spencer's protection without further contact if threatened by a superior force."

Campbell was already gone down the stairs, and Robert followed him, leapt into the saddle, and kicked Mars into a full gallop. The skirmishers were well in front, however, and it was apparent by the time he came close that it was too late. The sharp cracks of the rifled weapons still came intermittently, but there was a heavy roll of the duller explosions produced by unrifled muskets. Robert could see a thick fog of gun smoke spread over the rising ground, behind which, he presumed, lay the village of Óbidos.

Cursing fluently, he drove Mars even faster. It was clear that the advance skirmishers had run into the rear guard of Delaborde's division, for whom they were no match. Quickly Robert ran over Sir Arthur's orders in his mind. Sir Arthur expected his orders to be obeyed as they were given, but sometimes there was leeway in how to obey. Robert did not believe it was still possible to retreat without bringing the rear guard after the English troops. If he had been certain just where Spencer was, that might be a clever move because Spencer's division could then surprise and overwhelm the French; however, he did not know how far away Spencer was.

At this point in his ruminations a ball whizzed by so close that Robert flinched automatically. It was nearly spent and could have done little harm even if it had hit him; nonetheless, he began to look for cover. Aside from low bushes, there was none. All Robert could do was ride off the road itself to where bushes and irregular ground might confuse the eye. For all of that, he had scarcely slackened his pace. Mars was sagacious about where he put his feet. A shot plucked at Robert's sleeve, and he cursed again. Then, off to the right, he saw a Rifleman sitting behind a bush trying to stanch the bleeding from one shoulder.

"Have you come back far, Rifleman?" Robert shouted.

"Haven't fallen back at all, sir," the man replied. "I was one of the first hit."

Seeing as he came closer that the bush was taller than he had first thought, Robert pulled up and dismounted. He ripped off his sash and tied it quickly around the trooper's shoulder, hoping the pressure would decrease the flow of blood. It was not a gratuitous act of mercy; Robert wanted to use the man.

"Hold my horse in this shelter," he ordered. "If you go faint, tie him to you or the bush. I don't wish to walk back to Sir Arthur."

The Rifleman nodded, and Robert began to run forward. Bullets flew by with more frequency, but they were, he thought, the result of bad aim rather than any attempt to shoot him. Most of the fire was still concentrated ahead of him. Another two minutes brought him to a corpse, then another, then a man doubled forward, breathing hard.

"Where are your officers?" Robert called.

"Lieutenant Bunbury's dead, sir," he gasped, and waved vaguely farther to the right.

A dead officer was of no use to Robert, so he veered off to the left, hoping positions had not been so inextricably mixed that another officer would be toward the center of the action at a distance. Robert's movements were now necessarily erratic as he ducked and darted, using whatever cover he could find.

"Damn your bloody ass!" a voice bellowed at him suddenly. "Get down and use your gun."

Robert sighed with relief as he bent double and crawled in the direction from which that enraged and authoritative voice had come. "Staff!" he shouted, not wanting his blue coat to be taken for a Frenchman's uniform.

"I suppose if I don't get shot here," the young officer said bitterly as Robert flopped beside him, "the Beau will have us all shot when we get back."

Robert laughed. "You deserve it, but no, I don't think it will be as bad as that. He's likely to peel off your ears, though." As he spoke he had pulled out his Ellis and cocked it. "What he said," Robert went on as he peered intently through the fog created by the repeated powder explosions for a target within pistol range, "was to tell those idiots to stop at once. You are to hold the ground if you can but retreat to Spencer's protection without further contact before a superior force."

The officer groaned. Robert started to laugh again, but an errant breeze pulled the smoke apart, and ahead of him just barely within

pistol range a blue-coated figure rose and leveled a musket. Robert
fired. The figure cried out and fell backward. The fog closed in again.

"How the devil can we retreat?" the officer snarled. "They'll be
down on us like hounds on a fox."

"You might not need to," Robert offered, working the cocking
mechanism on his pistol. "A brigade of Spencer's is coming to the
rescue. It depends on how far forward his division is, how fast he can
move them, and how long you can hold out here."

"The French will run over us if they charge."

Robert shrugged. He knew it. He knew, too, that technically a staff
officer should be able to offer advice within the bounds of the orders
he carried. The theory was that, owing to experience in the field and a
wider view of the battle situation, a staff officer could provide
information a field officer would not have. Robert was in a better
position to offer help than most of the ADCs since he had nearly ten
years of military service and had seen considerable action. However,
he had never served in the field, and in this case the possibilities were
so limited that advice was useless. Obviously the lieutenant with
whom he was speaking could not make any major decision, either.

"Where is your captain?" Robert asked.

"Ahead, if he's still alive. Bunbury's had it."

"Yes, I know," Robert said, rising to a crouch and starting off in
the direction pointed.

Because the troops were pinned down, Robert thought he could find
the captain of the company in the same position, but he had moved.
Robert hunted for another fifteen or twenty minutes before he found
Captain Leach, with whom he was acquainted, worrying all the time
he searched about what he could say aside from the orders he had been
given. Fortunately, just as he squatted down to speak, the sound of
Spencer's drums came, very faint and distant, but nonetheless
unmistakable.

The crisis was not over; in fact, the indication that a supporting
force was close might induce the French officers to order an
immediate attack to do as much damage as they could before they
retreated. However, with help coming, the solution was obvious.
Robert delivered his orders, identified the oncoming rescuers, and
when Captain Leach snapped orders to the buglers for the men to fall
in to close defensive formation—which was what Robert himself
would have suggested—he relaxed. Sometimes a field officer resented

suggestions from staff that were not direct orders from a commanding officer.

Robert did not, however, leave at once. It was his duty not only to pass along orders but to report accurately concerning the situation, and there was little he could say about it until he knew whether the beleaguered troops would be rushed and, if so, whether they could hold out. Essentially, however, the action had ended. The men successfully formed three deep around the summit of a little hill, and although there was enough firing to keep them pinned down, the rush they expected never came. When the light began to fail, Robert made his way back to his horse, assured the Rifleman, who was still conscious, that help was on its way, mounted up, and galloped back to make his report to Sir Arthur.

Robert was too wise after years of service with Sir Arthur to advance any personal opinion unless asked for it or to offer any excuses for the action of men and officers as he might have done had he been serving with Sir John Moore. He reported exactly what he had seen and done—no more, no less.

"Casualties?" Sir Arthur asked.

"Lieutenant Bunbury dead, sir. That was reported by one of the men and one of the officers. I saw about a dozen wounded, three dead, aside from Bunbury."

Sir Arthur made a small sound of irritation, but his expression held none of the rigidity that appeared when he was reining in his temper. "Ah, well," he said, his voice sounding indulgent, "it was very foolish, but it shows an excellent spirit. They behaved very well, after all, if not with great prudence."

The army advanced into Óbidos with due caution, but the French were gone. Small detachments of cavalry were sent out with strict orders not to engage, but they found nothing as far as three miles south of the town. Pickets were set up within the perimeter that the cavalry had covered, and Sir Arthur settled into quarters. His genial behavior that evening showed he was well satisfied with the march of events, and Robert was so exhilarated by his first taste of action since the affair at Copenhagen that he forgot Esmeralda's existence entirely.

Even when the ADCs left the mess, the talk was all of the coming action. It was not until Robert began to strip off his clothing to go to sleep that he remembered Esmeralda would be expecting him and he had not even sent a message. He paused in his undressing to consider whether he should ride back to Caldas, but he was a little the worse for wine—Burghersh had laid his hands on a very tolerable vintage.

After a moment Robert continued with his disrobing. After all, Merry had told him that he was not to worry himself if it was inconvenient to send a message. If she did not care, why should he? It did not take much more effort for Robert to decide that he was not fit to present himself to a lady, and he tumbled into bed.

Chapter 14

The next day it was discovered that the French had retreated only a few miles farther than Sir Arthur's scouting parties had gone, to a village at the meeting of the roads leading to Tôrres Vedras, Montachique, and Alcoentre, called Roliça. Sir Arthur decided to ride out to examine the land himself, as was his habit, and his staff would naturally accompany him. Fortunately, Robert had expected this and had made arrangements to warn Esmeralda that he might be absent for several days.

Since more action was imminent, Robert could not detach M'Guire from his unit, but he managed to locate one of the men of the Sixtieth who had been hit in the upper arm and could not fire a gun but whose wound was slight enough to permit him to walk the three and a half miles to Caldas. Robert scribbled a note to Esmeralda to be delivered by this man. Having relieved his conscience, he went buoyantly about his duties.

The position at Roliça taken up by the French commander Delaborde was a good one. The sandy plain that stretched south of Óbidos became enclosed on either flank by bold hills in the region of Roliça, and behind the villlage lay a connecting cross ridge, broken by a sort of gorge through which the road passed southward. To the right of the defile of the road just below the heights of the ridge was another village called Columbeira. On the other side, but some distance behind, was Zambugeira. However, Delaborde had placed his men on an isolated rise of ground some distance ahead of the cross ridge. On the eastern slope of the isolated rise was the village of Roliça.

The names of the villages beyond Roliça and the lay of the land were determined by a combination of observation and information obtained from the local people. Robert was detailed to the duty of questioning the inhabitants of Óbidos, since he had become reasonably fluent in Portuguese. Often when he missed a word and had to ask for repetition or explanation, he found himself wishing for Esmeralda. Once or twice he found himself wondering whether it would be possible for him to get back to Caldas—and he was rather shocked at having such an idea when it was plain Sir Arthur was waiting only for the whole army to be assembled and given a night's rest before they attacked in earnest.

Nonetheless, once the idea got into Robert's head it kept recurring, and with each recurrence it seemed more reasonable. It was less than four miles to Caldas. He would not stay the night, he told himself; he would only ride over for an hour or two to tell Merry what was going on. She was always so eager for news.

Now and again common sense reared its ugly head to point out that visiting with Merry, even for an hour or two, was an invitation to sexual discomfort—if not actually to a sleepless night, then to very restless dreams. That, Robert told himself as he finished the written report of the information he had gathered, was not Merry's fault. Merry never flirted with him or made suggestive remarks. Robert paused with the report in hand. How odd that was. All the young women he knew flirted and made suggestive remarks to him if he gave them half a chance. Yet he had spent hours alone with Merry and she had acted just like his sisters—except, of course, a hundred times more sensibly. Why? It had been pleasant at first because he was able to be relaxed with her. Why was it no longer pleasant?

The questions were not to be answered immediately. Somerset came out of the room Sir Arthur was using as an office and said, "Oh, there you are. Sir Arthur's ready for you."

But at that moment Sir Arthur himself came out and said, "Come along, Moreton. We're going to compare all the information we've picked up, and there are likely to be questions that can't be answered by a report."

Robert followed Sir Arthur into a larger chamber, in which most of the general officers were already sitting and talking. Lord Fitzroy Somerset and Lord Burghersh had preceded him and Sir Arthur. Burghersh was refilling glasses as they emptied, and Somerset remained seated inconspicuously at a small table with writing implements and paper for taking notes. Sir Arthur greeted his officers genially. Nothing could have pleased him more than a chance for action. With the immediate threat of supersession hanging over him, he was very eager to make some mark.

"Well, Taylor," he said to the commander of the Twentieth Light Dragoons, which had been scouting the area, "what have your men to tell us?"

He listened to that report and to other fragmentary information, to the details Robert had extracted from the local Portuguese, and at last turned to Somerset and asked, "What have we, then?"

"General Delaborde seems to have four to five thousand men and about five or six guns," Lord Fitzroy summarized. "All reports agree that he has taken up a position on the hill behind Roliça. The Portuguese believe that General Loison was recently as close as Alcoentre and is marching to support Delaborde with as many as ten thousand troops and twenty guns."

"How reliable is the last rumor?" General Henry Fane asked.

Sir Arthur looked to Robert, who replied, "I should say the numbers are exaggerated. I got wild variations in estimates of troops. Those who are afraid we will run immediately give ridiculously low numbers. I have been told over and over that Delaborde has no more than fifteen hundred or two thousand men. Then there are those locals who fear that if we fight and *then* run, the French will punish them. They give much higher numbers—six or eight thousand for Delaborde and ten or fifteen guns—to discourage us from fighting. I've heard as many as twenty thousand for Loison and that he is hiding just over the hills at Zambugeira until we launch an attack."

"What I like," Caitlin Crawfurd said sardonically, "is the universal opinion that we will be beaten. The only doubt seems to be whether we will run away before the fight or after it."

Fane laughed. "There seems to be considerable surprise among the locals that we dared challenge the pickets at Brilos."

"The less said about that the better," Sir Arthur remarked, but not with any great severity. "I like to see dash in the men, but a little prudence would have accomplished the same result without any loss at all."

"I have spoken to my brigade," Fane said, with just a shade of stiffness in his voice.

"What *I* want to know," Rowland Hill put in smoothly, "is what Delaborde thinks he is doing on that silly hill in the middle of nowhere. If the information we have about his guns is correct, he can't hope to hold us off with artillery. As the ground lies, he's just asking to be encircled and swallowed. I wonder, could Delaborde have more guns than we believe? Could he know more of Loison's position than we do?''

"Anything is possible," Sir Arthur admitted without a shade of worry, "but it is my belief that Delaborde is afflicted with the same conviction as the Portuguese. Frankly, I am convinced he thinks we are afraid of the 'invincible' French. I imagine he hopes that we will either retreat or sit here trying to find the courage to attack until Junot's main force comes up from Lisbon.''

There was a low, throaty sound in the room. Robert was surprised by it for a split second and then, as he realized he was contributing to it himself by growling like an animal, he almost laughed. Gentility, he thought, was spread very thin when a man's courage was brought into question; and Sir Arthur, he realized with another near spurt of laughter, had deliberately poked his finger into a sore spot. How many of his officers *did* think Bonaparte's troops were invincible? How many might have counseled caution before Sir Arthur had made that statement? Robert repressed a temptation to smile. Not one would do so now.

Quite naturally, Sir Arthur now moved into the planning stage of this conference. Just as Robert had surmised, there was not a single protest or suggestion that more reconnaissance might be necessary. Indeed, the only objections voiced at all, and those were humorous, were by the officers relegated to reserve positions. Once the general designations were made, Sir Arthur suggested that they have dinner before they got down to particulars.

The night of August 15 was the worst of Esmeralda's life since that of her mother's death. She had not worried much at first; occasionally Robert had come in very late, even when they had been at Figueira. However, by midnight she had given up hope and gone to bed. Over and over she told herself that there were endless reasons for his absence, but none she could think of gave her any comfort. Even the most harmless, that Sir Arthur had required some service that sent Robert too far to return to Caldas, implied some serious situation had arisen. And there was the recurring fear that the quiet evenings had become boring and that Robert simply preferred being with his cronies.

She now cursed herself for telling Robert there was no need to keep her informed of his whereabouts if it was inconvenient to do so. At the time it had seemed wise to her, but now she feared it was an excuse he had seized eagerly. But painful as it was, that idea was preferable to the fear that the army had met the French and Robert had been hurt. She had told herself that Sir Arthur would not have neglected to inform her—but would he? He might be too busy if the British had suffered a serious reverse—or even if they had had an important victory—to think about one woman. Nor was Esmeralda sure that Sir Arthur knew she was in Caldas. What if he had sent a message to Leiria?

At that point, Esmeralda remembered she was less than four miles from the army. Had there been a battle, she would have heard the artillery. Still, when Robert's messenger arrived, she barely managed to tell Molly to offer the man, who identified himself as Tom Pace, something to eat and drink. She read Robert's note, standing quite still in the middle of the bedroom fighting her terror. All women fear for their menfolk who are exposed to the dangers of war, but Esmeralda's situation was far more painful than that of most others. She had no family, no close friends. Robert was all she had in the world.

It was possible for Esmeralda to face the fact that she might not be able to make Robert love her or be able to hold on to the marriage, because she knew that even if the legal relationship were severed she would not lose Robert completely. She was certain they were good enough friends by now that he would never abandon her. She did not wish to make do with half a loaf, with a friend instead of a lover, but to think that she might never see him again, never talk to him again, never laugh with him again, nearly unseated her reason.

Esmeralda had been emotionally isolated for years after her mother's death. She had grown accustomed to that cold state. Then, at the governor's ball in India, Robert had brought a tiny but glowing warmth into her life. She had no thought that the feeling could ever be more than a lovely memory, but she had cherished it. Their meeting in Portugal, their marriage, had enlarged that little core of warmth. Not only had Esmeralda's love for Robert developed from a dream into a consuming passion, but their relationship had opened to her a wealth

of real human contacts; however, Esmeralda believed that every one
of those contacts depended upon Robert.

She would have had hysterics if the need to obtain more
information from the messenger had not been so acute. Having lost all
sense of time while she was locked into her terror of losing the one
human being in all the world who had meaning for her, Esmeralda ran
into the kitchen in a flurry of fear that the soldier had eaten his fill,
rested sufficiently, and already departed. But in reality, less than a
quarter of an hour had passed.

As she paused just outside the open door to assume a calm she did
not feel, she heard the soldier tell Molly that M'Guire's unit had not
been engaged in the action. Esmeralda heard Molly's sigh of relief.

"It was a nothing of a business," the man said, "and not a one of
us would have been hurt, only it was such fun to chase the Frenchies,
we got a bit carried away."

Just then Molly saw Esmeralda and stood up. Tom Pace also stood,
and Esmeralda bent her lips into a smile. She was a good actress from
long experience; the smile looked natural. "Please sit down, both of
you," she said. "I hope I will not make you feel awkward if I join
you. Molly, would you be kind enough to get me a cup of tea, too? I
have so many questions, and I didn't want to wait until you finished
your meal, Pace. Also, I don't know when you must report back."

Pace had resumed his seat, a little stiffly, but he answered readily
enough. "I have time, ma'am. I'm on sicklist."

"Are you hurt?" Esmeralda asked. "Is there something Molly can
do for you?"

"No, ma'am, thank'ee. I was hit in that little set-to we had, but it's
nothing. The ball was near spent—only it caught me in a place so's I
can't hold a gun. Be right as rain in a week."

The thoughtful interest Esmeralda had shown had relaxed him, and
he sat more easily and answered Esmeralda's questions with considerable verve. Of course, a common trooper knew very little, but
the ranks were rife with rumor and this he relayed with gusto. In this
case, it so happened, the rumors were not far off from the truth.

The French, Pace said, were holding a position somewhere not far
south of Óbidos. If they were not doing so, he pointed out, Sir Arthur
would not have stopped the march. He would have sent more
screening parties ahead while the main force advanced cautiously, as
they had been doing. He also said they would attack the French the

next day. His evidence for this was more tenuous: It rested on the facts that inspections were being carried out on the men's fighting gear and battle drill was being practiced.

Having drunk her tea and obtained every scrap of rumor Tom Pace had heard, much of it so wild that Esmeralda, frightened as she was, had sense enough to dismiss it, she went upstairs to her own room. At first she felt only relief. A day's respite had been granted her. For one more day Robert would be safe.

However, the day's reprieve soon became more painful than pleasant. Her mind ran from one misery to another. If Robert did not come—and it was not likely that he could because Sir Arthur's staff must be constantly employed before a battle—there was a chance she would never see him again. Esmeralda's throat closed so tight that she could not breathe. Black swirled before her eyes, and her mind blanked in a near faint so that she gasped air unconsciously. As she swam toward consciousness some defensive mechanism inside her shut away that ultimate terror. She fixed on a safer problem.

If Robert found time to visit, how was she to control herself? Even if she said nothing, he would see the fear in her eyes. Would she be able to speak without bursting into tears? Suddenly she remembered Molly's sigh of relief when Pace said M'Guire's company had not been involved. Molly had been an army wife for years. How did she bear it?

Esmeralda ran down the stairs and peeped cautiously into the kitchen. Pace was gone, she saw with relief, and Molly was bending over the sink, probably washing the dishes. For one moment Esmeralda's pride struggled with her misery. Was it wrong to show her fear to a servant? In the next instant she knew she did not care what was right or wrong.

"Molly," she said, "aren't you afraid?"

The woman turned from the sink and, seeing Esmeralda's face, put down the cup and hurried forward wiping her hands on her skirt. "Och, me luv," she said, "tis ye'er first toime. Sure Oi'm afeared, but ye'ev t' remember he's no th' onny one. Ye'er thinkin' that ivry gun on t'other soide's pointed at him onny, but 't'isn't true. Theer's thousinds uv 'em. Think. Me first man, he wuz i' action many a toime, but it wuz th' fever got him."

Esmeralda sat down heavily on a chair, and Molly sat down

opposite her, this time without invitation. She understood that for this little while they were two women together, not mistress and maid.

"But I have no one else, no one else in the world," Esmeralda quavered. "You have your mother and your daughter. I have no one."

"Ye'er a young bride 'nd in luv," Molly soothed. "It seems so, surely, but . . ."

"No, it *is* true," Esmeralda insisted, and told Molly about her father and her life in India.

"Poor luv," the older woman said, "I cin see thit he's moor precious thin most, 'nd o'coorse ye feel thit he stands oot t'all as he stands oot t' ye, but 'tis no true. Ind he's staff, too. Y'know, if th' battle goes loike Sir Arthur planned, staff wun't even be neer. Thiy'll sit on a hill wit th' gineral 'nd watch. That's why th' dukes 'n th' earls are willin' t' send theer young'uns oot as staff."

There was no bitterness in Molly's voice and only kindness and concern in her face, but Esmeralda again became aware of the gulf between them. What Molly said about the possibility that Robert would never be involved in the fighting at all was true. Moreover, even if he should be hurt, his chances of survival were many times greater than that of the ordinary soldier: Robert would be missed and searched for; he would be treated before any common trooper; he would be transported behind the lines separately with more care. And all the rest was true, too. She had been feeling as if every single enemy gun would be trained upon Robert just because he was so precious to her.

"I'm being very foolish, I'm afraid," Esmeralda said with a watery smile.

"Well, y'are," Molly agreed, smiling also. "No fer fearin'. We all fear. There's no help fer thit. But 'tisn goin' t' help *him* fer ye t' be faintin' 'nd whoinin' wit red eyes 'nd a pale face whin he comes back roarin' wit good spirits—fer that's how he'll come—and a stink on him loike ye wouldn't believe. So ye'll want changes fer him from breeks out. Now, 'tisn't lady's woork t' wash smalls, but ye'll be th' better for somethin' t' do, so what say we do all frish 'nd clean?"

"Yes," Esmeralda agreed, "I'd like that."

It was not that she lacked employment. She had several gowns cut that needed stitching up and tasteful embellishment with bows of ribbon and knots of floss, but she could not bear to work toward an adornment Robert might never see. It was very steadying to the spirit, on the other hand, to clean his clothing because she expected him "home with a stink on him." That was real, a fixed idea to cling to: Robert striding in with his eyes sparkling, "in roaring good spirits," to tell her all about what had happened, and her listening eagerly until the main points were out and then telling him to change his clothing while she set out their supper and their wine.

But even that was not enough; washing clothing could not keep her occupied until Robert's return. She felt she had to know moment by moment what was happening. For today, she really did know. Tom Pace had described the activities of the camp, and even to a certain extent of the officers, vividly enough to make a satisfactory picture in Esmeralda's mind. Everyone was preparing. She washed clothes; the men cleaned and checked their weapons, went over their drill; the officers planned and conferred. But what of the next day? All the preparations would be finished. Robert's clothes would be clean and dry; there would be nothing for her to do but wait—and she could not simply wait without knowing.

Esmeralda gave the kettle a hasty stir and went out. Just before she entered the stable, she stopped to consider what she was about to do. If Robert ever learned of it, he would be furious and might send her away. But why should he hear of it? Very likely it would not even be possible and, in any case, she would have plenty of time to change her mind.

"Carlos," she called.

There was a delay, and Esmeralda repeated her call more sharply, hoping that the boy had not run off. He had been sulking ever since they had been left behind. At Leiria he had begged Robert to be allowed to go along with the army rather than following with Esmeralda, crying passionately that he had come to fight the French. Robert had given him as stern a lecture as his limited Portuguese and Carlos's limited English had allowed, pointing out that he was useful to Esmeralda but that he would be a useless burden with the army. He was untrained and too small to hold a gun, even if anyone was lunatic enough to teach him how to load and fire one.

To their horror, Carlos had said that he was not too small to follow the soldiers and use a knife. That had called forth an even sterner lecture on the rules the English obeyed concerning prisoners and wounded enemies. Everyone had heard horror stories—all the more horrible for being true—of the torture and murder of sick and wounded French stragglers by the Portuguese peasants. Admittedly, the French army's custom of living off the land had worked great hardship on the peasants. Moreover, some French commanders had ferociously repressed any resistance in towns they were able to control. The mass executions, sacrilege, and brutality Loison had permitted, and some said encouraged, at the sack of Évora were a byword all over Portugal. But the behavior of one army to another did not permit such excesses, and Robert made it clear that if Carlos wished to remain with the British, he would have to abide by their rules.

Carlos answered Esmeralda's second summons, however, and the dreadful vision that had begun to take hold of her dissipated. She smiled with relief and because she knew that what she was about to ask the boy to do would make him happy and keep him harmlessly occupied.

"I would like you to go around the town," Esmeralda said, "and ask whether there is a retired ship's officer or the widow of a ship's officer living here. What I desire is to borrow a glass."

"A glass? Have we no glasses to drink from?" Carlos asked, astonished. "And why must we borrow from—"

"No, no," Esmeralda interrupted. "Not a glass from which to drink, but the kind one puts to one's eye to see things a long distance away. If that is called something different here, use the right word."

The boy's eyes brightened at once. "You wish to watch the battle?" he asked, his voice shaking with excitement.

"Yes," Esmeralda admitted, her own voice shaking a little, "but do not tell anyone that. Say . . . say I am a mad Englishwoman and I wish to . . . to watch the birds."

Carlos burst into giggles, but then he frowned. "But you will not be able to see anything from here. Even with what you call a glass, it is too far. Besides, we are too low. There are trees and buildings in the way."

"First find me a glass," Esmeralda replied, "and then we will consider a place from which to use it."

By noon, shortly after Esmeralda had finished her laundering, Carlos returned almost dancing with glee, to say that he had heard of just such a man as Esmeralda needed. She was hot and tired, and, as Molly had predicted, physical labor had reduced her tension and dulled her fear. She might have abandoned her wild project except for the positive change in Carlos. It could do no harm, she told herself, to try to borrow the telescope. Very likely whoever owned it would be unwilling to lend it to a perfect stranger.

Thus, Esmeralda went upstairs and changed into a beguilingly simple confection of sprigged muslin trimmed with dark-blue ribbons, which she and Molly had finished the day before. She put on a charming straw bonnet, purchased in Leiria—*the* hat was safely stowed away, a precious relic now—and set out with Carlos. He led her to a large, handsome house near the center of the town. When she saw the place, Esmeralda was taken aback. She had envisioned dealing with someone like a tradesman.

However, far from being turned away at the door, as she expected, she was welcomed in with grave courtesy by an elderly, one-legged servant as soon as she identified herself as the wife of an English officer. Carlos was dismissed to the kitchen quarters; Esmeralda was told that she would be taken to the master of the house, Dom Aleixo de Solis, and led to a large room furnished in a handsome, heavy style but embellished with carvings, ivories, and brasses, which could only have come from India. Before she thought, she had exclaimed in recognition and with a quaver of homesickness in her voice.

"Ah, you know India, Senhora Moreton."

Esmeralda turned to see a very thin, old gentleman with a fringe of white hair surrounding a bald head seated in a large, cushioned chair near a window. Instinctively she curtsied, and the old man smiled.

"Forgive me for not rising, senhora, it is not possible for me."

"Oh, please." Esmeralda made a gesture of appeal. "It is I who should ask pardon, Dom Aleixo, for intruding upon you without a proper introduction, or—"

Dom Aleixo smiled again. "These are strange and unruly times, Senhora Moreton, but to tell you the truth, I am delighted to be intruded upon. My life is very quiet, perhaps too quiet. My servants pick up rumors in the market, but when I heard an Englishwoman was at my door, I thought I might hear some real news."

Esmeralda knew that the Portuguese people as a whole were violently opposed to the French, but that did not hold true for all of the Portuguese nobility. Some of them had thrown in their lot with the invaders. This might be such a man. She smiled sweetly after the briefest hesitation and said, "I will tell you what I know, but I am afraid it will be little more factual than the market rumors. You see, I have not seen my husband since he brought me here."

"But the English do intend to stand against the French, do they not?" Dom Aleixo asked.

"Yes," Esmeralda replied, without hesitation this time, since she did not see how such information could be of any harm. "I know the general, Sir Arthur Wellesley, intends to drive Junot out of Portugal. He is also convinced that Portugal can be defended against the French once they are driven out, no matter how strong a force they send."

"And the men of the army and the officers, do they believe this, too?"

"The officers, certainly. I have very little contact with the men, but the trooper who brought me a note from my husband this morning said it was 'great fun to chase the Frenchies,' so they must have done so."

The old man nodded, then sighed. "It would have been better if we had driven them out ourselves as we did the Spanish in 1640, but . . . ah, well, times change, men change. Now, Senhora Moreton, what can I do for you?"

Esmeralda had been so busy running over in her mind what she could and could not say to Dom Aleixo about military matters that his question caught her quite unprepared, and she stared at him blankly for just a moment before she gasped, "Oh! Oh, I heard that you had retired from a life at sea, and I wondered whether you would have a—a seeing glass. We call it a telescope in English, but I do not know the correct word in Portuguese."

"Indeed, I have. I have more than one. But what use have you for a spyglass?"

Dom Aleixo's lips twitched as he asked the question. He was an old man, who had lived a long and varied life and had learned much about humanity. He had understood that slight hesitation before Esmeralda said she would tell him anything she knew. In fact, Dom Aleixo *was* opposed to the invaders of his country, but he had no way to prove that to Esmeralda and did not think it worthwhile trying. Protests would only make her more suspicious.

However, there was no reason, Dom Aleixo thought, why he should not have a little innocent amusement. From the look on the lady's face when she said "my husband," Dom Aleixo had understood that Senhora Moreton was very much in love—well, it had to be so for any gentlewoman to follow the drum. When he added to that the youth of the lady, which indicated that she had not been long married, and her total lack of expression when she mentioned the telescope, he had a pretty fair idea of her purpose. He was curious, however, to hear what excuse she would give.

A slight color rose in Esmeralda's cheeks when she heard Dom Aleixo's question. She was not new to a flatly stated lie and had, over the years, told more than one to her father, but she discovered that it was not so easy to be untruthful to a stranger who had been kind. The fact that Dom Aleixo had asked so few questions about the British army after he had said he was hungry for news indicated that he had sensed her reluctance to give him information. He could easily have taken offense, but he had, instead, considerately abandoned the topic.

Nonetheless, she did not dare tell the truth. If she did, she was certain he would refuse to lend her the telescope. Perhaps that would be best, but she had the crazy feeling that if she were watching the coming battle, nothing could happen to Robert. And, as soon as she had heard there *was* a glass available, that feeling had grown even stronger.

"Birds," Esmeralda said desperately, her blush growing deeper. "I do not know whether you are aware that the English are—are very fond of birds. We—we like to watch them, to see where they nest, and how they feed their young, and—and such things."

"You will not find many nests at this time of the year," the old man pointed out very gravely, his dark eyes shining with amusement as he wondered what she would now say.

"No—no, of course not," Esmeralda admitted, scrabbling about in her mind for scraps of information she had picked up from bird-watchers in India, "but they—they fly about. Their—their patterns of flight are important, and—and they feed. Some eat seeds, and others . . . er . . . eat other things."

Naturally in a time of emergency one's mind failed, Esmeralda thought despairingly. All she could think of were the most inappropriate bits of information, like the tales she had heard of birds that picked fleas or some such insect off cattle, and those she herself had watched picking over feces. Those were not items one could relate to an elderly and elegant Portuguese gentleman.

That "er . . . eat other things" was too much for Dom Aleixo. His gravity departed, and he began to chuckle. "My dear—oh, I beg your pardon, Senhora Moreton, but you are young enough to be my granddaughter—I am most ungenerous and unkind to tease you. I will not only lend you a glass but show you how to use it, for it is not so simple as just looking through it. And we will say no more about your purpose, but, my child, I must tell you that a seaman's glass is not at all appropriate for watching birds."

By now Esmeralda's cheeks were flaming red. "I am so sorry," she murmured. "I did not wish to lie, but I was certain that you would refuse to lend me the glass if I told you my real purpose."

He shook his head. "I knew your intention from the beginning, child, as soon as you asked for the glass." He reached out and pulled the bell cord conveniently near his chair. "I will ask you no questions," he went on while they waited for the servant to answer the bell, "but I have lived all my life—at those times when I was not at sea, of course—in this part of my country. It seems to me that the only easily defensible area near Caldas are the heights of Columbeira. This, I imagine, is where the battle is most likely to take place. To see them, and not come too close, one could watch from the tower of the Church of San Mahmed. It is not very high, but the land is flat there, except for the hill on which Roliça stands. Also, there is Amiais, a tiny hamlet about one-half league to the west. There is no church, but the village lies on rising ground."

As the door opened, he paused and turned his head to order his manservant to bring him the four-draw Dollond glass. The one-legged man looked a little surprised, but he bowed and went out without speaking. Dom Aleixo smiled.

"It is a powerful instrument," he said. "You will have to rest it on something if you wish to watch any particular place, for the smallest shaking of your hand will move your view a good distance."

Then, while they waited for Sebastiano to bring the telescope so that Dom Aleixo could show Esmeralda how to use it, he explained more fully how to reach the village and tiny hamlet he had named.

"You are very kind," Esmeralda said at last. She had been listening in stunned amazement, hardly able to believe her ears, but finally coming to the conclusion that Dom Aleixo's desire to help her was a quixotic impulse of a bored old man.

When Dom Aleixo was satisfied that Esmeralda was reasonably proficient in using the telescope, he asked most politely if she would like some refreshment. She had eaten no luncheon because of her fright, but that was only a minor part in her eager acceptance of his offer. Talking to Dom Aleixo would keep her mind occupied and prevent her from thinking about the events of the next day. In the end, she dined with the old man, enjoying their comparison of their memories of Goa and Bombay. It was soothing to see how much pleasure he took in her company.

When the light started to fail, Esmeralda said she must go, and Dom Aleixo agreed at once, apologizing for having kept her so long. She smiled and shook her head. "I wished to stay. I hope I have not imposed on you and tired you with my chatter. You have saved me many hours of useless worry. I do not know what time I will return your glass, but I assure you I will take the greatest care of it while it is in my possession. I do not mean to offend you, but would you like me to leave some token with you to guarantee I will return it? I have only this locket with my mother's picture, but—"

Dom Aleixo laughed, interrupting her. "I am sure that is far more precious to you than the glass, however valuable, is to me. No, child. If I had not been sure from the beginning that you would return it, I never would have lent it. The time does not matter," he added wryly after a short pause. "I will be here."

Chapter 15

The army broke camp and marched for Roliça in the early morning of August 17. Still earlier, Esmeralda, mounted on Boa Viagem, and Carlos, riding Luisa, had left Caldas. They reached the outskirts of Óbidos in time to watch the last units of the reserve march out of camp. Esmeralda hung back, fearing that some officer who knew her might recognize her riding dress even at a distance. When the troops were well clear of the town, Carlos and Esmeralda rode cautiously forward again.

They reached San Mahmed with only one fright, a belated ammunition wagon that came rolling down the road behind them so that they had to ride off into the scraggly bush and hope they would not be noticed. At the church, which was the most prominent building in the village, Esmeralda dismounted. She went in quietly, carrying Dom Aleixo's glass while Carlos took Luisa and Boa Viagem to the wineshop, where there was a shed to shelter the asses and mules of the patrons.

Coming out of the narrow walkway provided for servicing the church bell, Esmeralda gasped and shrank back behind the arch. She felt for a moment as if she were close enough to the army to be seen herself, because she could see the soldiers so clearly. Then she realized that was an illusion. She could see the massed lines of troops because of their bright-red coats and the number of men standing close together in the sunlight. She, a lone figure in the shadow of the bell tower, would be invisible.

Esmeralda could see nothing of the French, and she had a single flash of hope that they had run away. But it was too much to expect that driving away a few pickets would cause panic to sweep through the entire French army. Then Esmeralda realized that the troops were

moving. At first, because of the distance and the fact that the units all
moved together, she had thought they were standing still. Hastily she
pulled the glass from its leather case, extended it as she had been
shown, rested it on the ledge of the arch, and applied her eye to the
eyepiece. Figures leapt into individuality as the powerful telescope
caught them, but they passed out of view almost immediately as they
moved forward. What had seemed barely a crawling pace to the naked
eye was greatly speeded by the magnification of the lens.

In a way, it was most disappointing, for the telescope narrowed the
scene of action to a few individuals. Esmeralda looked out at the mass
of men again, unaided by the glass. She could see three distinct
groups, which formed a crescent with the right and left well forward
of the center. Nothing seemed to be happening at all, just a very slow
progress toward the rising ground. As she swept her eyes from one
end of the field to the other, she realized that at the rear of the center
there was a mounted group. She had not noticed them at first despite
the horses because they all wore dark coats and hats, which were not
as eye-catching as the red-clad troops.

A moment's thought told Esmeralda that the group must be General
Wellesley and his staff, and her heart leapt. She might be able to see
Robert. She spent about fifteen minutes maneuvering the instrument
into the correct position until she was at last able to pick out the group
she sought. At first, she was again disappointed because even the
powerful telescope did not provide a clear enough image to make out
faces. But she had barely absorbed that disappointment before it
became irrelevant as, with a shock of joy, she recognized Robert.
There was something in the way he carried his body and sat his horse
that identified him quite clearly.

By now, Esmeralda had gained considerable expertise in using the
telescope, and she was able to keep Robert in view with little
difficulty despite the steady forward movement of his horse. Her
mood had been unsettled ever since she had left Dom Aleixo, periodic
panics fading into mere anxiety. She had slept very little, as her desire
to follow the army did battle with her knowledge of how furious
Robert would be if he discovered what she had done.

It was the thought of continuing in unknowing terror that drove her
from her bed before dawn to follow through with the preparations she
had made. And now, seeing Robert within the quiet group at the rear
of the army, Esmeralda felt a great relief. It was a proof of what Molly

had said. Robert was not in the front lines; the staff was not expected
to fight.

At that moment, Carlos came running up the stairs. He cried out in
excitement, and Esmeralda lifted her head, rather startled, asking,
"What is it?"

"There!" the boy cried, pointing. "There! See, the battle has
begun."

Esmeralda's heart leapt into her throat as her eyes followed the line
of Carlos's arm, but what she saw was not at all frightening. Far to the
left just where the ground began to rise, there were intermittent, tiny
puffs of smoke. It took another moment before Carlos's remark
connected with the minute man-made clouds in Esmeralda's mind and
she realized that what she was seeing were guns being fired. She
hastily reapplied her eye to the telescope, but she did not move it to
cover the area in which the firing was taking place. It was the mounted
group of staff officers she sought.

When she found them, relief flooded her again. Clearly Wellesley
and his staff were aware of the action; their heads were turned in that
direction and a number of them, including Sir Arthur himself, had
spyglasses to their eyes. However, they were still moving slowly at
the rear of the central group. No evidence of any excitement was
apparent among them, and Esmeralda did not think any member of the
staff had left. Robert was certainly there; she picked him out
immediately.

After assuring herself that Robert was in no danger, Esmeralda tried
to find the area where the shooting was taking place with the
telescope. By the time she was able to locate it, there was little to see.
She knew what was happening only because Carlos was jumping up
and down, crying out that the French were running away. Esmeralda
abandoned the glass and looked out. She saw at once that the puffs of
smoke on the higher ground were fewer and were moving backward
while those that had come originally from the plain were more
frequent and advancing onto the rising ground.

This condition was maintained for a while longer and then ceased.
After repeatedly confirming that Robert was still with Sir Arthur,
Esmeralda began to grow bored. From her point of view, the battle
had not been very interesting. What was more, after a while the whole
force began to move again and it was apparent that they would soon
be hidden from her view by the bulk of Roliça hill. Esmeralda bit her

lip and began to collapse her glass. She could move west to Amiais, but she had no idea whether she could find a vantage point there or whether any further action, if there were to be any, would be visible to her even with the aid of the telescope.

Esmeralda was not the only person dissatisfied. Sir Arthur, who had hoped that Delaborde would be sufficiently contemptuous of the British force that he would stand his ground, was even more disappointed than she. The French general, however, was not a fool. As soon as he was assured that the attack was determined and that his position was in danger of being enveloped by the right and left wings of Sir Arthur's army, he gave the order to abandon the isolated hill and retreat as quickly as possible to the heights behind Columbeira.

Had Sir Arthur's army been less raw or had he twice the force, he might have tried to prevent such a move by occupying those heights himself in a night march. As things were, he did not dare permit his army to be divided or permit the French to come between him and a safe line of retreat to the coast. The action at Brilos had showed good spirit, but the light companies were the best in any regiment, seasoned men trained to act independently. How the regular troops would behave under fire was still questionable, and Sir Arthur had determined to take no chances in this first real action.

Therefore, when the French retreated, Sir Arthur had little choice. On the one hand, half the morning had been wasted; on the other, nothing had been lost. He sent Captain Williams off to tell General Ferguson to continue along the crest of the hills in a wide flanking movement to the left; Campbell went off to order Colonel Trant to continue his movement along the base of the hills and bring his Portuguese regiments in on the right flank. The center moved in pursuit, Hill's division heading quickly westward around the isolated high ground, followed by Nightingale's, which had held the center. General Fane's went round the other side of the hill along the main road.

Sir Arthur's intention had been to hold back the frontal storming of the heights until Ferguson and Trant were positioned to attack simultaneously on the left and right flanks. However, it was soon apparent that the fate of the too-intrepid light companies at Brilos had not made sufficient impression on all his field officers. Everything went smoothly enough at first: Two batteries of guns were established near a windmill on the northern slope of Roliça hill and began to bombard the new French position while the divisions redeployed.

Unfortunately, Colonel Lake of the Twenty-ninth had misunderstood his orders, thought he saw an opening he could fill with little loss, or simply suffered a rush of mistaken heroism. Long before there was any hope of Trant or Ferguson being anywhere close enough to begin flank attacks, Lake led his regiment up a deep gully just beyond the village of Columbeira. When he heard the crackle of firing begin, Sir Arthur's lips tightened. He combed the area ahead with his spyglass, but the depth of the ravines and the growth of brush and trees along them obscured the view.

"Go and see what that is, Moreton," he said quietly after a few minutes. "If you think the situation can be salvaged, you may request assistance from General Hill."

Robert rode off, skirting the eastern edge of Columbeira, and entered the gorge. Now that he was in the ravine, he was better able to see what had happened. The high ground protruded to some extent around the dry streambeds that had cut the gorges, and as the cut slanted left, it exposed the attacking troops to fire on three sides. Nonetheless, they had forced their way a considerable distance up.

Just as he realized it would be unwise to push his horse much farther up, Robert heard voices above him. Most were indistinguishable shouts, but among those were a few voices crying "Friend." Apparently Lake and his men had gained the heights, and the troops facing them were not determined to hold out. That, however, was no guarantee that other enemy troops in the vicinity would feel the same. Lake's one regiment, which must have taken considerable losses, could not hold the ground alone. They would need General Hill's assistance. Robert turned back and made the best speed he could, calling out for information about General Hill's position as he rode.

He found the general on the extreme right, where, having already noted the movement of the Twenty-ninth, he had just directed the light companies of his brigade and the first battalion of the Fifth Regiment to start up the most westerly of the ravines. He listened to Robert's report and Sir Arthur's order and nodded calmly.

"You may tell Sir Arthur," he said to Robert, "that I will take the Ninth up myself. You may also say that I have begun an assault on the far right, as it is impossible, in my opinion, to wait for the flanking parties without losing the Twenty-ninth entirely."

As he spoke, General Hill urged his horse into motion. Robert
wasted no time himself, knowing that the sooner the entire army was
in motion, the better it would be for all. By the time he reached Sir
Arthur, however, all units except the reserve were already in motion.

"Do you know just where the Twenty-ninth is?" Sir Arthur asked
after he had acknowledged Robert's report. His voice was raised, for
the general and his staff had closed in as the troops moved forward
and the intermittent boom of the artillery was now only a background
to a rising roar made up of shouts, screams, and the constant
explosions of muskets.

"Yes, sir," Robert shouted in reply.

"Very well, then, follow General Hill up and tell him I am moving
one of Crawfurd's battalions to cover Columbeira. If the Twenty-ninth
is not able to re-form and Lake needs Hill's support, he may send
down for them."

Not able to re-form? Obviously Sir Arthur had seen some action on
the heights that had fulfilled Robert's fears of the regiment's inability
to hold the position. Robert had seen that the Twenty-ninth had taken
losses, but they were not so severe in his judgment as to make it
impossible to re-form.

Robert made directly for the place he had seen Hill enter when he
rode back earlier with his message to Sir Arthur. The gorge wall that
had then looked impassable was now open at an angle, a cannonball
having taken down a small tree and the passage of a number of men
having leveled the brush and beaten down the earth somewhat.
Beyond was a small wood in which some wounded men, who had
retreated there for what shelter they could find, were lying.

After pulling up his horse to let the animal breathe, Robert looked
around for a man capable of answering his questions. Before he could
ask, however, a tremendous noise broke out above and to the left.
Robert opened the saddle holsters of his guns, but he did not draw
them, being uncertain about exactly what the violent eruption of
gunfire portended. His movement in the direction of the noise was
almost immediately blocked by a group of men stumbling down the
precipitous hill in retreat.

"Hold up!" Robert bellowed. "Stop."

To his intense delight, they did stop as soon as they reached the
shelter of the wood, but he could see others coming down. "Move

back," he ordered. "Make room for your fellows. Now, face about. Reload." He drew his saber.

" 'M' out o'bullets, sir," one man shouted.

"Anyone short of ammunition, help himself to the bullet bags and powder horns of the wounded," Robert ordered.

More and more men were pouring down the hill into the shelter of the wood, but as soon as they saw their fellows standing quietly or busy scavenging ammunition or reloading their pieces, they too steadied. After about fifteen minutes the flow downhill stopped. Although there had been a pretty free play of bullets into the wood at first, that tapered off without doing any damage.

Robert looked around and judged that he had about a hundred soldiers and that they were not beaten men. Indeed, from the remarks he heard, he was sure that they were ready, in fact, determined, to assault the French again; however, there did not seem to be any officer with them. Robert would have loved to lead the attack himself, but he dared not. His duty was to continue his search for General Hill, particularly because the reserves might be necessary. On the other hand, he did not like to leave the men without any officer in charge.

"Has anyone—" he began when a horse burst through the brush on the far side of the wood.

"Who's in charge here?" the officer roared.

Robert recognized Captain Leach of the Ninety-fifth, which surprised him since the men in the wood were mixed companies of the Twenty-ninth and the Ninth. Normally an officer confined his attentions to his own men, but Leach might have been sent by a superior officer to try to stem what looked like a rout.

"The men halted on my command, Captain Leach," Robert called.

By then Leach was already headed in his direction, having spotted the single mounted man. They met about midway, in front of the troops, some of whom were leaning on their guns and others sitting on the ground catching their breaths. As they approached one another, Leach recognized Robert.

"Why the devil don't you get yourself a line regiment, Moreton?" he asked, laughing. "Every time I look around, there you are in the midst of the action, waving a pistol or a sword."

"M' father won't hear of—" Robert's voice was drowned as a cannonball hit a tree with a tremendous crash and rolled among the men slowly enough, owing to its original impact, for them to step

aside. "—it," he continued, curbing his horse, which had taken
violent exception to the sudden increase and change in the noise.
"And m' mother has the vapors every time she sees me in
regimentals."

"And you went and married?" Leach remarked with mild astonishment.

"Merry's not like that at all!" Robert exclaimed.

Another cannonball crashed through the trees. This one did not
strike any object large enough to impede its progress and rushed in
among the men. The sound had given warning, however; some
dodged, some threw themselves flat on the ground. One man was
bruised as the ball barely touched his shoulder going by, but no one
was seriously hurt.

"One's a mistake," Leach said, "but two means they've found
us." He turned his head toward the men. "On your feet, there," he
bellowed. "Form into your companies, smart."

"Do you know where General Hill is?" Robert asked, holding
Hermes on a tight rein.

"On the left wing," Leach replied.

"I'm off, then." Robert gave a casual salute and loosened his reins.
Hermes bounded forward, but Robert had to curb him almost
immediately, the ground being unsafe for too rapid movement. His
eyes were busy between watching the ground and seeking General
Hill, but his mind had somehow stuck on his statement that "Merry's
not like that at all." It was true. Merry never made a fuss. She never
had, right from the beginning when she was really in a terrible
situation without money or identification. She hadn't even mentioned
her troubles until she had to explain why she was so eager to travel
with him.

Had he been wrong, Robert thought suddenly, to assume she didn't
care what happened to him just because she said it wasn't necessary to
tell her every time he was delayed? That was part of the same thing—
not wanting to make a fuss. And then, with a terrible feeling of guilt,
Robert remembered he had not sent her a note that morning. She
would know a battle was about to take place. Tom Pace would have
told her that if she had asked, and Robert, knowing how much interest
Merry took in anything to do with the army, was sure she would have
asked.

Tonight he would have to ride back to Caldas, no matter what. Just as he made that decision, a burst of shouting came from over a rise of ground to Robert's front. A horse came trotting forward, followed by a wave of men. A second company followed, led by an officer on foot with bare saber in hand. Robert angled Hermes in that direction, but had to hold back until the troops passed. Then, before he could cross the ground, he saw a group of horsemen led by General Hill charging forward on the far flank.

He turned to follow and heard the first roll of musket fire, an answering roar, and a reply to that. As he drove Hermes up the last steep rise, bullets were flying pretty freely about, but most of them were directed too low to do him any harm. The fourth volley sounded ragged, and Robert muttered an obscenity, fearing that the charge had been broken. He drove his heels into Hermes's sides, urging him to greater speed, but topping the rise seconds later, he was relieved to see the redcoats still moving forward. The weaker gunfire must have come from the French, and then another rolling volley came from the British line. Robert cursed again because the gunsmoke obscured his view and he lost sight of Hill and his staff once more.

Driving forward in the general direction, Robert was startled to see a figure rise out of the smoke almost alongside him. Instinctively, he slashed with his saber, which he had not even remembered was still naked in his hand. As he struck, he cried out himself, fearing that he had injured one of the Ninety-fifth, whose dark-green uniforms could easily be mistaken for those of some French regiments. His conscience was immediately salved, however, for a ball whistled by his head as his blade came down, and the shrieked word the man uttered was not English.

A minute later another gun went off so close that Hermes screamed, shied, and stumbled. Robert thought he had been hit, but he recovered and leapt forward. He must have stepped on the wounded man who had fired the gun, Robert realized, hastily thrusting his saber into its scabbard and drawing and cocking a pistol. He was just in time, as another soldier ran at him with a bayonet. He fired, and the man twisted away as he fell.

For a while longer he was too busy to look for anyone, but a new wave of red-coated troops soon flooded into the area, and Robert was able to abandon self-defense. Fifteen minutes later he found General Hill and delivered his message, although it was fairly obvious that the British were now well lodged on the crest and assistance from the reserve would not be necessary unless a massive French counterattack was launched. Since this was most unlikely, considering Delaborde's limitations in numbers, the general confirmed Robert's unspoken opinion, added his thanks, and scribbled a brief note for Sir Arthur about the current situation.

But Wellesley was little easier to find than Hill, and by the time Robert caught up with Sir Arthur, the French were beginning to retreat in earnest. There was no panic. Robert could feel nothing but admiration for the French, who fell back in regular formation, two battalions holding off the somewhat disordered British troops while the other two retreated.

Robert felt immense pride in their own men also. Although they were not as disciplined, owing to lack of experience in the field, their spirit could not be faulted. Their organization was not nearly as good, largely because their officers were too enthusiastic and excited to control them properly, but they went forward hotly, driving off several charges by the polished *chasseurs à cheval* and pursuing the French with such determination that in the narrow pass behind Zambugeira they managed to capture three of Delaborde's five guns and take a number of prisoners.

The steady retreat took on some aspects of a rout then, but it was growing late and Sir Arthur was not willing to allow his raw troops to pursue farther than Cazal da Sprega. In the more open ground there was too great a chance of the French re-forming and the British getting completely out of hand. By the time all units were informed of this decision, every staff officer had ridden several horses into trembling exhaustion, and Sir Arthur's young gentlemen were themselves not in much better physical condition than their horses. Emotionally, however, they were exultant.

No matter that the force opposing them had been smaller than their own; the troops actually involved in the battle had been nearly a match in numbers. And possibly Delaborde would have tried to hold the ground with more determination had the British not outnumbered him, but they *had* dislodged him from the heights of Columbeira—a very strong position—with no more men than he had. *The British had beat Boney's "invincible" troops.*

Chapter 16

The army was ordered to camp on a ridge of high ground above the road leading to Lourinha while Sir Arthur set up temporary headquarters in Cazal da Sprega. As soon as they could, all senior officers rode in to consult and receive orders. They found Sir Arthur in good humor despite Colonel Lake's ill-considered advance. Sir Arthur said more than once that he had never seen more gallant fighting than that of the Twenty-ninth and the Ninth, and he complimented all the senior officers on the behavior of the troops.

Under the circumstances, the wine bottles passed with unusual freedom during dinner, and even after the ADCs who were off duty were dismissed, they had no inclination to curtail their celebration. Someone had unearthed a new supply of wine, and they settled down in a house adjoining Sir Arthur's temporary headquarters to describe to each other their individual battle adventures.

The family of the house they had taken over had at first been terrified; however, when the young men brought out money and Robert explained to them in their own language that they would be much safer with British officers quartered in their home, their welcome became quite enthusiastic. The eldest daughter of the house, who was helping her mother serve the young men, was particularly free with her smiles, the warmest of which along with the most frequent offers of food and more wine were bestowed on Robert. Naturally, it was not long before his fellow officers noticed this favoritism.

"I think," Colin Campbell said, "I am going to start a petition to get you sent home, Moreton—or, at least, to get you quartered in the next town. It was a pleasure at Alcobaça and Caldas when you rode back to Leiria. The girls paid attention to *us* for once."

"It's damned unfair," Burghersh complained. "You've already got a wife."

"Wife," Robert said. "Good God, Merry will be worried! I've got to ride back to Caldas and tell her we won. She'll be so glad."

"Can't ride back alone." Campbell shook his head. "There are bound to be French stragglers. Shoot you for your horse."

Robert glanced out the window. "Not dark. No more than ten miles altogether."

"Horses are all half-dead," Burghersh pointed out. "You won't get much speed out of any of them. It will be dark before you pass Roliça."

"Got to go back anyway," Robert insisted. He was just drunk enough to make him stubborn. "God knows what we'll be doing tomorrow."

"Sweet woman, Mrs. Moreton." Captain Williams's voice was slightly slurred. "Wouldn't want her to worry. Some of us can ride back with him. That would be safe enough. No sense staying here anyway. Once a girl's caught sight of Moreton's pretty face, the rest of us might just as well not be alive. We'll do better in Caldas. There was a girl in a wineshop there—"

"No, that was in Óbidos," Campbell said. "But you're right. Let's ride back, push Moreton in with his wife, and be rid of him. Save him from himself. New married man, don't want to see him in the petticoat line—at least, not so soon."

Young and active as they all were, their exhaustion had mostly been cleared after dinner and the few hours' rest they had taken. Moreover, enough excitement remained from the action they had seen and the perils they had personally experienced to make them restless. Thus, the idea of escorting Robert back to Caldas was seized upon with enthusiasm.

Burghersh had sent his servant to get the least exhausted horses saddled. Not wishing to waste time or permit their high spirits to be dampened by exercise, each young man took along a bottle. Whether Campbell had exaggerated the dangers or the group was just large enough to discourage attack, they saw no one except a few belated carts carrying wounded into Roliça, French and British mixed together with a fine indifference.

The village was hopelessly crowded, and with the stench of blood and death and moans of the wounded, not inviting as a spot to pause.

Besides, as Burghersh had predicted, it was getting dark. They pressed on toward Óbidos at the best speed the jaded horses could make. On the way, however, the argument between Williams and Campbell broke out anew about whether the wineshop where the girl had flirted with them was in Óbidos or Caldas.

Each held firmly to his own opinion, claiming he knew exactly where the wineshop was and what it looked like. Then, since the bottles were empty and it was quite dark by the time they reached Óbidos, Burghersh suggested a logical way to end the argument: They would find the wineshop Campbell said he remembered in Óbidos, buy some more wine, and wait there for the moon to rise. If the girl Campbell remembered was there, he could stay in Óbidos while the remainder went on to Caldas to leave Robert with his wife and perhaps discover the wineshop Williams remembered. Thus, everyone would be happy.

This program was immediately accepted. Campbell did lead them unerringly to the wineshop—no great feat since it was on the main street and there were only two. Moreover, the serving girl certainly did greet them with most delighted smiles. But Williams still insisted that it was not the right wineshop, though he was not averse, any more than the others, to sitting down and having a few sustaining glasses until the moonlight illuminated the road.

Williams was still determined to find the wineshop *he* remembered, and several others also clung to the jolly notion of Mrs. Moreton's happy surprise when they returned her husband to her intact. They were not quite steady when they mounted, but they assisted each other with the greatest good humor, and Campbell rushed out just before they got their horses into motion to be sure that each had a bottle to take along. He was still absolutely certain that Williams's memory was at fault and did not want his friends to suffer if there was no welcoming wineshop in Caldas.

Drunk as he was, and by then they were all very drunk, Williams found his wineshop when they reached Caldas. To call the process by which they got off their horses dismounting would be a gross exaggeration; however, all reached the ground without injury, and that was a considerable accomplishment. When all were standing—more or less—and dusted off, they surged forward toward the door. Here, Captain Williams and Robert collided. Each staggered back and turned toward the other with grave politeness to bow—a somewhat perilous activity that required deep concentration—and to beg pardon, and each began to gesture the other forward, but Captain Williams aborted his gracious gesture and stared at Robert with a puzzled frown.

"You're not shupposed to be here," he said thickly.

"I'm not?" Robert asked uncertainly. "Where'm I shupposed to be?"

But the answer had escaped Williams's mind. They turned to their companions and explained the problem to them. After some deep thought all agreed that Robert had been supposed to leave them at some point, but they had no idea where. Finally Burghersh asked where they currently were. If they knew that, he pointed out gravely, it might be easier to decide where Robert was supposed to be. Then one of the others had the brilliant idea of inquiring in the wineshop. This suggestion obtained instant approval, but it seemed only polite to order some wine before asking questions.

The arrival of the bottle temporarily diverted them from the less immediate problem of determining their location. Having sampled the wine and found it very good, they decided they wished to order more.

"The trouble ish," Burghersh said, each word very carefully enunciated, "I don't believe m' father'sh vin-vintner carriesh thish."

"Silly thing anyway," Robert remarked, with even more care, having noted that Burghersh's speech was not all that it should be and resolved that, being older, he would control his tongue better. "Why sh-send an order to England? Wine's right here. Order it here."

"Where'sh here?" Burghersh asked. "Need the direcsh-direction t' shend an order."

"Right." Robert nodded approval of this perceptive point. Vaguely he heard Burghersh calling to someone and asking where they were. It seemed silly. After all, they *were* here. Why ask about it?

A moment later he felt his shoulder being shaken. "It'sh weird," Burghersh said apologetically. "Don't shpeak English here—only Portuguese. You shpeak it, don't you? Ash them where to shend an order for wine."

That was entirely too complex a question for Robert to compose in his present condition; however, he did remember that none of the others spoke Portuguese and one must, of course, do one's best to oblige a friend. The compromise he reached was simply to ask where they were. Indulgently, the wineshop owner replied that they were in Caldas.

"Caldash!" Robert exclaimed, the name having struck a chord in his muddled memory. "Merry'sh in Caldash."

"There," Captain Williams remarked with enormous satisfaction. "I shaid you weren't sh-supposed to be here. You were shupposed to tell Mishush Moreton about the battle. Doeshn't matter, though. The girl'sh not here, either. You can shtay."

"No. Can't," Robert said, reminded of his purpose and determined to carry it out. "Merry'll be worried. Ish very late."

"Right," Williams agreed. "Sh-sweet woman. Mushn't worry. Take you home now. Come back and fish-finish the wine."

This, however, was easier said than done since no one, including Robert, could remember how to get to Esmeralda's lodgings. The situation was resolved by Burghersh, who suggested with rare perspicacity—considering his condition—that, owing to the fact that he lived in the town, the wineshop owner might know. Restraining his mirth at the mangling of his language when Robert asked for directions, and realizing that Robert was probably incapable of understanding them, much less following them, the man suggested that he provide a guide.

Esmeralda had descended from the church tower in San Mahmed in considerable doubt as to what her next move should be. From what Dom Aleixo had told her, she would be able to make out mass movements from Amiais, but no individual figures. Was it worthwhile to take the chance that Robert would hear of this crazy excursion to watch maneuvers she would not even understand? But that was not completely true, Esmeralda admitted. She had understood that the French had withdrawn.

Perhaps the battle was over? As she and Carlos walked toward the wineshop to reclaim Luisa and Boa Viagem, Esmeralda voiced this hope. Carlos's laugh was answer enough when her own common sense agreed completely that it could not be so. More likely, she thought, it was only more pickets that had been driven off. The real action would take place farther away in the ring of hills she could see in the distance.

As Esmeralda mounted with the help of a bench Carlos dragged from the wineshop, she was still in some doubt as to what to do.

Then, as Carlos scrambled to Luisa's back, he pointed to a narrow lane at the side of the shop.

"This goes to Amiais, Senhora Moreton," he said, his eyes gleaming with expectation.

It can do no harm just to look, Esmeralda told herself. She was much calmer than she had been all the previous day, which was the advantage of doing *something,* even if that something was rather pointless. Besides, there could be no risk at all because both the French and English armies were moving away and would be farther from her when she was at Amiais than they had been when she had been in San Mahmed. She nodded, and they set off for Amiais.

Although the people of the tiny village were very excited because the Portuguese units of the British force had passed right by the town earlier in the day, Esmeralda found no sign of either army anywhere in the vicinity of Amiais. But when she mentioned that she had a spyglass and might be able to see what was happening if she were high enough, a woman with a house on the edge of town a little way up the hillside eagerly offered her a place from which to look. However, all she could report was that a march was underway. She was then offered refreshment: bread and cheese, melons, figs, grapes, with milk or wine. While they were eating, a distant, dull thudding began. At first no one paid much attention, for the sound was certainly not threatening. After a few minutes, however, the regularity of the thuds impressed themselves on Esmeralda, and she jumped to her feet with a gasp. That was the sound of cannon.

She rushed up to the loft and leveled her glass through the tiny window. Sure enough, there was smoke rising in the air, but a shoulder of the Roliça hill hid the actual position of the guns. Desperately Esmeralda adjusted the glass, but she had no idea where to aim it, and it took her more than half an hour before she made out the patches of red that were probably whole brigades. Still, she watched eagerly, but more and more of the red coats disappeared into the brush and trees on the rising slopes of the farther hills, and no matter how carefully she swept the area within her view she could not catch the smallest glimpse of Sir Arthur or his dark-coated staff.

Her frustration increased. It was ridiculous to go on staring at virtually nothing. Either she should go back to Caldas or find a closer vantage point. As she moved impatiently, the glass swung left, showing her the slope of Roliça hill. She stared at it blankly at first, then with more attention. Perhaps she would be able to see better from Roliça. Even as the thought formed, Esmeralda knew it was unwise. She was not worried about the French. She could see they were retreating, and Robert had said the British would win, so it must be so. What worried Esmeralda was that there might be some British units in and around the town and someone might recognize her.

Frustration was a stronger emotion in Esmeralda than caution, and although she had been strongly reassured by seeing Robert safely in the rear throughout the early action, she had a desire to catch at least one more glimpse of him. If she could see him once more, still in the quiet group that surrounded Sir Arthur, she would be convinced he was in no danger and go back to Caldas. That compromise eased her conscience, and to further assure herself that she was acting reasonably, she carefully examined the area between Amiais and Roliça hill with her glass. She could see nothing aside from a country cart or two and a few tiny moving specks in the tilled fields, which was reassuring. Surely the people of San Mahmed would not be out tending their fields if there was danger.

Her departure was regarded with alarm, the woman of the house asking fearfully if the British were running away.

"Of course not," Esmeralda replied rather indignantly. "They are advancing," she averred with conviction, although she had not really seen anything to support her statement. "They are now too far away to see properly. I am going to ride across to Roliça."

As she said it she felt uncertain again, but Carlos's whoop of joy and the village woman's smiling nod—both of which, of course, were based on her own previous statement—reassured her. Nor was there anything besides the mounting heat to shake her confidence as they rode back toward San Mahmed. There were farm carts on the road, and people waved in a friendly way from the melon patches. Here, with the bulk of Roliça hill between them and the action, even the sound of the artillery could not be detected, and it really seemed as if any conflict was very far away.

When they were south of the village, Esmeralda asked a passing woman about the road to Roliça. She pointed it out to them and described the route with a smile that held neither doubt nor fear. Esmeralda rode on, satisfied, thinking that if she could not see from the town itself, she might find a way to the top of the hill. Intrigued by the idea, she examined what she could see of the slopes.

They did not look excessively rugged, and when she and Carlos reached the place where the hill bulged northeast toward the path, Esmeralda knew that the village was just around the bend. There was the shining trickle of a stream, which often meant a gentle slope, so she suggested that Carlos take Luisa, who was more surefooted than Boa Viagem, across to the hillside and see whether it might be safe to climb, while she continued slowly by the path. She thought she would be able to parallel Carlos's course, but there was a little wood into which he disappeared. Still, he could not get lost. Esmeralda continued around a bend in the path, her attention more engaged with the hill than the road.

"Halte!"

The harsh command startled Esmeralda so much that she cried out and jerked hard on Boa Viagem's reins. Equally startled by the sudden shouts and rough pull on her mouth, the mare rose on her hind legs and then backed away. Simultaneously, a French soldier leapt up from the side of the road where he had taken cover, displaying a musket. Esmeralda screamed again, but it was less the sight of the gun that frightened her than the fact that half the man's face was covered with a brown crust of drying blood.

"Halte-là! Descende de cheval!" the man shrieked, lifting the gun as if to aim.

Although she knew no French, the soldier's meaning was unmistakable. What was more, the blood, the uniform, and the gun all indicated that the soldier had been left behind; he wanted her horse so that he could return to his own army. The revelation came in a flash and was followed by another, equally swift, that he would not dare fire while Boa Viagem was moving up and down, because there was a far greater chance of his hitting the horse than hitting the rider. Moreover, Esmeralda was far more afraid of losing her horse and having Robert find out what she had been doing—a real and immediate terror—than she was of death, which was a concept that somehow had little reality with regard to herself.

Immediately Esmeralda screamed again, much louder than her first startled cries, kicked Boa Viagem as hard as she could, and at the same time pulled back on the reins. Completely confused by the kicks that meant *go forward* and the jerking at her mouth that meant *go back*, and frightened by the loud shouts and wild gestures of the man ahead and the piercing shrieks of Esmeralda on her back, the mare reared wildly, began to plunge forward, was violently checked, backed and reared again.

The soldier shouted some more incomprehensible gibberish and began to run forward. Esmeralda promptly uttered a whole series of ear-splitting yells and beat her reins back and forth across the mare's shoulders, kicking wildly at her ribs. Since the restraining pressure on her mouth was gone, Boa Viagem began to charge ahead, but her direct path was blocked by the threatening form of the gesticulating soldier. Too mad now to turn aside, the mare reared once more, flourishing her hooves in an instinctive defensive gesture. The Frenchman staggered backward, tripped, and fell, discharging his musket harmlessly in the air.

Esmeralda promptly stopped shrieking. She realized that as long as he could not grab her or the horse, the soldier was no threat until he could load his gun again. By then she hoped she would be well out of range—except that Boa Viagem was so frightened that Esmeralda was not able to turn her and dash away. She could have let the mare bolt ahead toward Roliça, but she did not dare do that because she was afraid there would be other stragglers, perhaps many more, even a band of them who might surround her.

Suddenly there was the sound of oncoming hooves. Inspired by terror, Esmeralda wrenched the mare's head around by sheer force and began to kick, beat, and scream again. Boa Viagem struggled then yielded, leaping over the Frenchman, who was desperately trying to roll away from her dancing hooves, and galloping back down the path toward San Mahmed. In the next moment, Esmeralda heard a harsh shriek of terror, which cut off abruptly only to be succeeded by a shrill yell of triumph.

"Oh, my God," Esmeralda cried. "Carlos! That was Carlos!"

Desperately she struggled to check her flight. She had to go back and see how badly Carlos was hurt. Surely the soldier would not have killed a little boy. Finally, sobbing with grief and remorse, she was able to stop the mare and turn her, but before she could start back she heard Luisa coming. Esmeralda sat paralyzed for an instant, but then Luisa burst around the turn of the road. Esmeralda gasped and raised her reins to bring Boa Viagem around, but she did not complete the movement.

Chapter 17

Once the offer of the wineshop owner to send a guide with Robert and his friends was comprehended, it was accepted with gratitude. After regaining their feet—with difficulty and assistance—they set off. Fortunately the distance was not great, and the night air was cool enough to restore a modicum of sobriety so that no one fell by the wayside and all of them remembered their purpose was to get Robert back to his wife. They were not very noisy, but Molly, restless with worry, heard them discussing how to get into the house without waking the whole neighborhood and leapt from her bed.

She got the door open just as Robert raised his hand to knock. His reflexes being somewhat disordered, he made the motions of knocking anyway, barely missing hitting Molly in the face. This unbalanced him so that he staggered right past Molly into the house. Poor Molly was so startled by this seemingly threatening gesture from Captain Moreton, who had always been as pleasant a gentleman as anyone could wish to serve, that she jumped aside with a startled gasp. She also recognized the smell of wine on him as he went by; her breath drew in again, and she hunched her shoulders defensively.

Molly had had personal experience with a generally good-tempered man who turned nasty on drink. She cast a single glance after Robert, but she had no intention of going near him or drawing his attention for any reason. In fact, she swung around to the door, thinking she would be better off spending the night in the stable with Carlos. This movement brought her face to face with Lord Burghersh, who had just come carefully up the two stairs that led to the entryway.

Both of them recoiled a trifle. Burghersh would have fallen down the stairs, except that Captain Williams was close enough behind to steady him. However, Lord Burghersh was scarcely aware of his friend's support. Having been startled by Molly, all of his attention was fixed on her. For the moment he did not recognize her. He blinked owlishly, realizing there was something very wrong. Servants who came to the door did not, in his experience, dress in the kind of shapeless object in which Molly was wrapped.

"Me lord," Molly whimpered, "no!" She had smelled him also and seen the dark forms ranged behind him. Horrible tales of the cruel and violent excesses of gentlemen had been whispered around her home village.

The English words had made a definite impact on Lord Burghersh. He was still drunk enough that his balance was uncertain, but the exercise and cool air had brought him to a moderate rationality. He peered more closely and saw that the servant who had opened the door was Mrs. Moreton's maid—not improperly dressed, but wrapped in a blanket.

"Good God," he said, "is it so late that you were in bed?"

The voice was thick, but far from being threatening there was a note of apology in it, and his lordship stood quietly, except for swaying a little, not reaching to grab her or trying to push his way in. Molly took hold of her courage.

"'Tis viry late," she said, trying to speak firmly but unable to hide the quaver of her voice.

"Didn't mean to frighten you, Molly," he said, smiling broadly. "We won! There's nothing to be afraid of. Didn't realize it was so late. We—we've been celebrating."

"Oh, Oi'm thit glad, me lord!"

Molly was glad, but she still didn't want to let them in the house, and she didn't want to stay in it herself, either. As soon as her worst terror subsided, she heard Robert's feet going uncertainly up the stairs. Now she expected momentarily to hear sounds she did not want to hear, but she could not think of a way to get rid of Robert's friends or to escape from them. Thus, the quaver of her voice and the tense rigidity of her body were not much reduced.

Alerted now, Lord Burghersh noticed, and he whacked his forehead with his palm. "Fool that I am, you'll be worried about your man. I'm sorry, but—"

"Wait a bit," Williams said, coming from behind. "That's M'Guire, isn't it? Moreton's batman?"

"Yes, sir," Molly agreed, stepping forward eagerly, fear forgotten in her desire to hear news of her husband.

"He's all right," Williams said. "I saw him coming into Cash-Cazal da Sprega. He'sh all right."

"Thank God fer thit," Molly sighed, barely above a whisper.

The soft sound of her voice was not enough to cover the slam of a door on the upper floor of the house. Molly jumped. Both Lord Burghersh and Captain Williams looked up. "Oh, sir, me lord—" Molly began, her voice shaking again.

"Never mind," Burghersh said. "Won't intrude. Know it'sh too late for a vish-visit."

They turned and, in concentrating on getting down the stairs without falling, did not notice that Molly had closed the door behind her and sidled away, jumping lightly down from the side of the small platform whose steps they were negotiating. Discovering that the man from the wineshop who had led them to Esmeralda's lodging was still with them—he had waited because he was not at all sure they knew which house they wanted—they demanded to be taken back to their unfinished wine.

Inside the house, Robert had made his way up the stairs. Here he paused for a moment, realizing that it was very dark, all the candles having been extinguished. He thought about that muzzily until it occurred to him that it was later than he and his friends had thought, too late for them to visit Merry. He started to turn to tell them that, then remembered that Molly had opened the door. She would tell them that Merry was in bed.

As he thought it, Robert smiled slightly, aware of a sense of satisfaction. He would rather have Merry to himself. The smile did not last long as he realized, with a sharp pang of disappointment, that if Merry was in bed, he couldn't see her, either. He wanted to tell Merry that they had beaten the French, and answer her excited questions, and tell her of his own part in the battle. He stood in the corridor a moment longer, feeling sullen but knowing he must go to his own room. Then he blinked. He had not spent a night in Caldas with Merry. He had no idea which room was his. He glanced toward the lower floor, where Molly seemed to be telling the others it was too late to come in, and thought of going down to ask where he was to sleep, but the very idea of navigating down the stairs made his stomach turn.

This, on top of the angry feeling of ill usage he was already experiencing, was too much. Damn it all, he thought, what if Merry *was* in bed? She was his wife. He could poke his head in and ask which room he was to use without doing her any irrevocable damage. She would be covered, and even if she were not, he had seen her in next to nothing already. A flush of warmth ran across his groin and thighs, and unwilling to allow himself to think about it, he opened the nearest door. There were windows and enough light to show that it was not a bedroom. Robert slammed the door ill-temperedly.

Esmeralda had had a very exhausting day. Her shock had almost equaled her relief when she had seen Carlos, well bedaubed with blood, on Luisa's back. Even after she discovered that the blood was not the boy's, she had felt little better. Carlos's exultant description of how he had leapt off Luisa onto the Frenchman and cut his throat certainly did Esmeralda no good. She had felt no animosity toward the soldier who tried to steal her horse until the fear seized her that he had hurt Carlos. Even then she had blamed herself for the stupidity of getting into the situation more than the man, who was only trying to escape.

Still, it was impossible really to blame Carlos either. The boy could not have known that her shrieks were not the result of terror but a deliberate action designed to keep Boa Viagem in frightened motion. Possibly he had seen the Frenchman point the gun at her. Certainly he had heard the report when the musket fired. Carlos might not have realized that the gun went off by accident. He had been trying to protect her.

She had said it would have been enough to have taken the gun away, but she had to acknowledge the force of Carlos's argument that if he had tried to do that, the soldier would have had opportunity to seize him or Luisa. And to have ridden past swiftly, leaving the Frenchman with the gun, might well have meant the death of some innocent Portuguese farmer who happened past with a mule or cart. She knew the French had often been ruthless in seizing what they wanted from the peasants. Nonetheless, she could not help wishing she had not been the instrument of the soldier's death.

What weighed on her spirits far more was the knowledge that she would have to confess the whole adventure to Robert. She had at first thought she could warn Carlos and Molly to say nothing; however, the boy would not part with the musket and bayonet he had taken as prizes of war, and, on further consideration, Esmeralda realized that sooner or later one of the three would let slip too much. Then, if Robert questioned Carlos, disaster would ensue. It would be better if she told Robert herself, in her own way.

She had spent some time composing her explanation before she went to return the spyglass to Dom Aleixo. Returning the glass turned out to be far less simple than she had hoped because the old man had insisted she keep the instrument, but had extracted payment by asking questions he intended to have answered. Esmeralda had found providing answers very trying, since the old man was perceptive and *had* got the truth from her. Then he had Carlos summoned from the kitchen, had tipped him lavishly and praised him for his heroism, upsetting Esmeralda still more. By the time she returned to her lodgings, she was nearly weeping with exhaustion and had barely been able to swallow part of her dinner before she collapsed into bed.

Tired as she was, Esmeralda had slept through the entire exchange on the doorstep. It was the slam of the door next to her own that wakened her, and the dull crack was so much like that of the gun she had heard earlier in the day that she leapt out of bed. Her first wild glance around the room showed nothing. Esmeralda told herself she must have been dreaming, but she was frightened, and she turned up the wick of the lamp that Molly had left burning low beside the bed and lifted it high to examine the room.

Simultaneously, the door opened. Esmeralda drew breath to emit a shriek for help and instead gasped, "Robert!"

If she was surprised, Robert was transfixed. The lamp cast just enough light for Esmeralda to recognize him, but she herself was completely illuminated. In the limited time she had had for sewing, nightwear was the last and least of her concerns, and she had contented herself with the use of a thin shift for sleeping. In this, with the light glaring down from the upheld lamp, she might as well have been naked, for the dark nipples of her breasts and the dark pubic hair showed clearly through the translucent fabric.

The vision was brief. Having seen who it was, Esmeralda immediately set the lamp down on the table and rushed forward. This gave Robert little relief, for now the light was directly behind her and her body was outlined in unbearably provocative relief—the curve of the breast bending inward to the narrow waist, the swelling hips, the

division between the legs showing light and then dark as she ran
toward him.

Even sober Robert might not have had either the strength of mind or
the will to withdraw. Drunk, he stood still, gaping. In any case he had
little chance to act. Esmeralda threw her arms around his neck and
buried her head in his breast. Unfortunately, Robert was in no
condition to withstand this loving impact. He staggered back, flinging
out an arm to seek support; all he caught was the edge of the door,
which swung shut behind him, leaving him precariously off balance.

Esmeralda managed to save them both, but she was badly
frightened again, thinking that Robert was weak owing to an injury.
She should have known better from his breath, but it did not occur to
her that he was only very drunk. He often smelled of wine—all men
seemed to do so after dinner—and she had seen him "a little on the
go," as the saying was; still, she had never seen him so drunk that he
was unable to balance or articulate clearly or even think logically. Her
reaction was to swing him around and support him toward the bed,
where the light of the lamp fell most strongly and she would be able to
see him clearly.

When he was thrown off balance, Robert unthinkingly clutched
with the arm he had not flung out at the only solid support available,
which was Esmeralda. While this saved him from falling physically, it
unbalanced him further emotionally. He could not really feel the
warmth of Esmeralda's nearly naked body or the softness of her
breasts through his clothing, but his imagination readily supplied all
the missing sensations. So violent a surge of desire gripped him that
he uttered a soft inarticulate cry, yet his reactions were slowed and
disorganized and he could not hold Esmeralda when she swung
sideways.

Robert tried to protest, but before he could get his tongue and lips
under control, he realized Esmeralda was not trying to free herself
from his grip but was leading him toward the bed. This caused another
upsurge of desire but also awakened his conscience. He knew the
desire was wrong. This was not a girl for whom he would leave a few
coins. Merry was a good woman . . . his wife. His wife . . . The
words echoed in Robert's mind, riding dizzily atop the waves of
sexuality.

Esmeralda had loosened her hold around Robert's neck as soon as
he made that first sound and had asked anxiously whether she had hurt

him, but she was herself so breathless with surprise and with the fear generated by his staggering that her voice was virtually inaudible. Almost immediately, however, she became aware of his grip and of her near nakedness. She meant to ask again whether he was injured, but she was suffused with a violent sensation to which she could not put a name, and her voice became completely suspended.

Because she had already fixed her mind on the move, Esmeralda was able to get Robert to the bed where the better light showed the tears and dark stains on his clothing. Robert had, of course, intended to ride back to Caldas before he had been caught up in the minor action at Brilos, and he had not taken along fresh clothes. Thus, he was still wearing the garments in which he had taken part in the fighting. The rips on sleeve and shoulder from the near misses gaped.

Anxiety swamped all other emotions in Esmeralda and made her voice high and frightened as she asked, "Where are you hurt, Robert?"

He had allowed her to push him gently to a seated position on the edge of the bed, relaxing his tight grip, but the hand that had clutched her to him still rested on her hip. The fear in her voice came through to him, distracting him momentarily from the feel of her flesh under his fingers.

"Hurt?" he repeated. "Who'sh hurt?"

Esmeralda was nearly intoxicated herself by the concentration of wine on Robert's breath and reeled back half a step, but the odor and the blurred speech were a welcome revelation. Still, to be sure, she asked again. "You. Are *you* hurt?"

But the intensity was gone from her voice, and Robert's attention fixed again on the lovely body exposed to him. Now Esmeralda was illuminated from the side, but that view was equally entrancing. He was dimly aware of the question, however, and replied after a short delay, rather at random, "I don't think sh-so."

Since the light from the lamp was full on his face, Esmeralda was in no doubt about where Robert's attention was fixed. She could also see that he was somewhat flushed rather than pale, as he would be from weakness or loss of blood. Moreover, before he answered her, his eyes had moved slowly from her throat to her breast to her hips to her bare legs and up again. Esmeralda flushed, but she felt no impulse to hide herself. Her body responded to the touch of his glance with an odd, inner trembling that was intensely pleasurable and with an increased

sensitivity that made her suddenly aware of the tiny movements of her
shift against her skin as her breathing quickened.

At the same time, her mind seemed equally stimulated. She
realized that if she wished, her marriage would be consummated that
night and that once he made love to her, Robert would honor the
commitment; there would be no annulment. With the thought came a
prick of conscience. It was not really fair to take advantage of his
drunkenness. And that knowledge was followed by a pang of fear.
Would he hate her for trapping him? Was the desire he so plainly
exhibited only bred of wine?

When Esmeralda had stepped back a trifle, Robert's hand had
slipped from her hip. The loss of contact was painful to him, and as he
spoke he looked up into her face, his eyes both puzzled and pleading.
She asked if he was hurt, and he was deeply confused, knowing he
was hurt although not by war. She was his wife. Then why was she not
his wife? Why was it wrong to touch her as he wished to touch her?
Why did she withdraw from him? He raised his hand again,
uncertainly, not grasping for her body but seeking reassurance—
although for what he did not know.

The look and the gesture ended the war in Esmeralda's heart. She
did not understand either one completely, thinking that the pleading in
his eyes and the reaching out were born solely of sexual need. Far
from angering her, this only stimulated her own passion. She had to
know what it was to be a woman, and she had to know it with
Robert—whatever the cost. There might never be another opportunity. It had to be now. And his words had given her the perfect opening.

Esmeralda stepped close again and bent forward. Robert's out-
stretched hand fell upon her breast. She drew a short, deep breath and
murmured, "Let me take off your coat. That way I can see if you are
hurt."

To Robert at that time, the movement seemed an answer to his
unasked questions. It assured him that it was not wrong to desire
Merry. He heard the words, but they did not trouble him then. He was
too taken up with the offering under his hand, and he fondled it gently,
cupping it and extending his thumb to stroke the nipple. He could feel
Merry's breath catch, and he looked up at her again and smiled slowly.
He no longer felt drunk, only slightly light-headed and very, very
happy.

Despite the distracting sensation that made it hard to breathe and made her knees feel like jelly, Esmeralda had managed to unbutton Robert's coat. She could not draw it off, however, without pushing his hand away from her breast, and she could not bear to do that, both because the sensation was so exquisite and because she was afraid any movement of denial would break the spell. She had lingered motionless, eyes locked with Robert's until he smiled. Then she put her hand on the edge of the coat to pull it off, but he released her breast and took her hand and kissed it.

"Boots first," he said, his voice clearer than it had been. He felt very odd, at one and the same time throbbing with eagerness and yet not at all in a hurry. In fact, he wanted every moment to last forever.

Esmeralda knelt at once and seized one boot. It came off more easily than she expected, and she fell back, sitting down hard. Robert reached forward and caught her, drawing her back toward him with one hand, lifting her face with the other so he could kiss her lips.

"I'll manage the other," he said, but Esmeralda shook her head and pulled it off. "I never had such a beautiful boot boy," he commented, laughing and kissing her again.

It took a long time to get the rest of his clothes off. Wherever she moved, his lips followed. When she pulled off his coat and shirt, he kissed her arms and breasts; when she bent to undo the buttons of his breeches and slide them off, he kissed the back of her neck and her shoulders, played with her hair, pulling it so that he could reach her lips and ears with his mouth. Under the circumstances, Esmeralda was not very efficient. Her fingers trembled so much that she had difficulty pushing buttons through buttonholes, and her breathing became so erratic when she began to pull off Robert's smalls that she felt dizzy and had to stop what she was doing altogether.

Robert seemed to understand. He held her against him, stroking her back to quiet her. However, as soon as she seemed steady, he upset the apple cart again by running his fingers between her legs. Esmeralda began to shake.

"Please," she whispered, "please." But she did not know for what she was pleading, only that the sensations Robert was generating in her body seemed about to tear her apart.

He gripped her hard, then reached down with one hand and pulled off her shift. She uttered a short, wordless cry, not of protest but of eagerness.

"All right, love," Robert murmured. "It's all right."

He stood up suddenly, lifting her in his arms and turning to lay her on the bed. Then he bent over her and began to caress her with lips and tongue, licking her breasts and her belly, kissing her nether lips, sliding his tongue along and between them.

"God help me! God help me!" Esmeralda whimpered.

Her hands scratched blindly at the bedclothes, pressed Robert's head tighter against her, then pulled it away. The teasing was driving her mad, but she was totally ignorant of what was necessary to satisfy her.

"Help," she gasped, "help."

Because he was drunker than he realized, Robert's body had not responded with its usual speed to sexual stimuli. Had he been ready, he might not have extended his foreplay so long; however, the prolonged caressing of Esmeralda's body had a cumulative effect. When readiness came upon Robert, it came in a red, blinding rush that would not be long denied. He heard Esmeralda whimper, "God help me," and then gasp, as if she were dying, "Help." By then it was too late for consideration or thinking about what Esmeralda meant. He heard the words, but they mingled with his own feelings and had no associations for him outside of passion.

He mounted her swiftly then, passing a hand between her thighs to position himself. The head of his shaft slipped easily between the lips he had so thoroughly lubricated. Robert groaned softly with pleasure, removed his hand, and thrust gently, expecting to slide home. However, nothing much happened. He thrust harder. Esmeralda gasped. Robert slid in an inch or two and met a barrier. This was outside his experience. He opened his eyes, which he had closed in the expectation of total bliss when he first entered, and gazed with gentle reproach at Esmeralda.

The lamp still burned high, and at first glance Robert realized that whatever was obstructing his path, it was no deliberate act of Esmeralda's. She looked both surprised and frightened. And then he realized what was wrong. Of course, Merry was a virgin. Robert hesitated for just a moment, torn between his urgent need and a qualm of doubt. But passion and the destruction of inhibitions caused by the alcohol in his blood urged him on, and below those physical pressures was another desire, deep and hidden, to make Merry his own forever.

He bent his head and kissed her lips and her throat, murmuring between the caresses, "This once, just this once, I must hurt you, love." Then he slid a hand down her side, brought it back up, moving his fingertips in gentle circles along her hips and ribs and on up to her breast, rubbing the nipple gently. Esmeralda's breath shuddered in, and he took that for acceptance; but he had closed his eyes again so he could not see her face. She would fight him, he told himself, if she were unwilling, or cry out, but he hardly gave her time to respond, drawing and thrusting again with the greatest force he could bring to bear. She did cry out then, a muted whimper, for Robert's mouth was on hers, but it was too late for second thoughts. Robert was lodged, and Esmeralda was no longer a virgin.

His purpose achieved, Robert lay still, kissing and caressing and murmuring love words. The tight grip on his shaft was heavenly, and there seemed to be an infinitesimal quivering inside Esmeralda that sent chills of pleasure up and down his spine. For the moment he was content not to move, and he concentrated on trying to arouse Esmeralda again.

His efforts were rewarded. After a minute or two, she moved against him in a way that was unmistakable, and he took the chance of drawing out a little way and pushing in again. The sensation was too exquisite to resist, and he continued moving, slowly at first but then faster and harder as all consciousness beyond that of his own intense pleasure was blotted out.

Esmeralda felt his growing rapture, and it increased the excitement generated by his hands and lips. There was a swelling thrill in her own body, a deeper, stronger echo of the pleasure Robert's mouth had wakened in her earlier. It was too mixed with pain to come to fruition; although as Robert finally cried out and convulsed in his climax, Esmeralda gasped with an empathic reaction that was very near fulfillment.

"Wife," Robert murmured as he subsided swiftly into a sleep demanded by the exertions of the day, the wine he had absorbed, and this last effort. "Lovely wife."

His voice was blurred again, and Esmeralda's eyes filled with tears. He had called her beautiful when she took off his boots and now, lovely. Was it only the wine and the sexual need that had elevated her plainness to beauty? Was it at all possible that Robert's growing affection for her had illuminated her ordinary face in his eyes? And affection added to desire—was that not love?

Robert's weight atop her was making it difficult for Esmeralda to breathe, but instead of pushing him off, she embraced him—the first time she had dared to do so aside from throwing her arms around him in excitement when he first came in. He made a soft sound, and Esmeralda tensed, not knowing whether it was satisfaction or a protest, but he did not move away, and she lay, holding him, the tears that had formed trickling gently down her temples.

She would not let him hate her, she vowed; she would not let it come to that. If he showed anger, seemed to feel trapped, she would let him go. And then, the thought of her great wealth came into her mind. That would help. No man would object to a wife with more than half a million pounds as a dowry. Surely the money in addition to the real liking she knew Robert felt for her would reconcile him to the bargain he had so unintentionally made. But if he accepted her only for the money, could she bear that? Not *only* for the money, she thought. Robert's family was wealthy, and he seemed to have plenty of money of his own. If he loathed her, the money would not matter, and she knew he did not loathe her.

Then another specter that had haunted her from the beginning rose again. Would Robert consider himself heart-free even if he accepted the legal bond? Would he give that free heart to another woman? But there were no other women with the army, except camp followers and soldiers' wives, and they were not likely to be a danger. It was a stupid thing to worry about just now. The first question remained: Was it only wine that had brought Robert to consummate their marriage, or had he had some desire—no matter how small—to do so anyway?

The question was unanswerable at this time, Esmeralda knew, but the morning might give the answer. New tears formed in her eyes, and she bit her lip. She did not want the answer; she wanted to cling to hope as long as she could; she needed more time to demonstrate how perfect a wife she could be to a military man.

Robert made a slight movement, and his softened shaft slipped completely from between Esmeralda's legs. He stirred again, started to slide sideways off her body. She uttered a very faint sob, helplessly devastated by the feeling that he was retreating from her totally and forever. Robert stretched his neck and kissed her cheek, mumbling almost indistinguishably except for two words that Esmeralda made out—sleep, which could have been expected, and love.

That last word spread like a balm over Esmeralda. She did not allow herself to think of the many, many reasons Robert could have had for using the word, all of which had nothing to do with her at all. She only repeated it over and over to herself until the mingled remains of her fatigue, anxiety, and reaction from excitement pushed her into a sleep that was deep and, as far as she ever remembered, dreamless.

Chapter 18

Although Molly's personal anxiety was greatly relieved by the information that her husband was safe, her sleep was not easy. It was not physical discomfort that kept her tossing and turning; she had slept soundly in far worse conditions than the soft hay of the stable loft. It was her conscience that invaded her dreams, waking her with nightmares of guilt and fear. Each time she woke, she told herself that there was nothing she could have done to protect her mistress. In fact, it was most likely that Mrs. Moreton would have been furious if she had tried to intervene. Most women, at least in the beginning, preferred to take their beating instead of having the fact of their husbands' brutality exposed.

Still, Molly felt vaguely guilty. Mrs. Moreton loved the captain so much. It was a shame to have her dream broken. The guilt and the regret continued to permeate her restless sleep, and it was with relief that she saw the lightening of the sky, which presaged dawn. Molly knew that Robert had returned to duty each morning, and she had been a soldier's wife long enough to know the seriousness of absence from one's post. Anyway, whatever had happened was now long over. The captain had been very drunk. He must have slept soon after he went into his wife's room, and he would have a most unpleasant awakening. That thought gave Molly a little satisfaction.

She hurried to the house, dressed, and tapped softly at Esmeralda's door. After a moment, she tapped again and called. She was just about to open the door and go in, although she did not wish to enter without giving her mistress a chance to cover her bruises, when she heard the latch click.

" 'Tis near dawn, ma'am," she said into the opening.

Esmeralda stuck her head out. She looked sleepy and startled. "What's the matter?" she asked.

" 'Tis near dawn," Molly repeated. "Will th' captain no be goin' bick t' his post?"

"Oh, heavens!" Esmeralda exclaimed. "I'll have to wake him."

But she did not look frightened, as Molly had expected. Instead, she blushed so deeply that Molly could see it even in the very dim light of the hallway. At first Molly was surprised, but then she barely stopped herself from laughing. It seemed that Captain Moreton had not mistreated his wife; quite the opposite, he apparently had provided better than usual entertainment and then had fallen asleep in Mrs. Moreton's bed.

It seemed strange to Molly that that should embarrass her mistress, but she knew the gentry were odd that way. They slept in separate rooms and acted as if babies were generated by magic. Amused and relieved, Molly ran down to start up the fire and heat water.

Molly's rapid departure left Esmeralda in a dreadful quandary. What was she to say to Robert? More horrifying yet, what would he say to her? Perhaps it would be best to call Molly and tell her to wake him, hide herself away, and pretend nothing had happened. He might have been drunk enough not to remember.

This cowardly idea was so attractive that Esmeralda turned back toward the door and was actually reaching to open it when she remembered why she had only stuck her head out in the first place: She was stark naked. She hurried to pick up her shift from the floor, but the act reminded her of the way Robert had looked at her, and inadvertently she cast her eyes down at her own body—and gasped. Her thighs were all streaked with the brown stains of dried blood.

For a moment she stood paralyzed, but not because she was afraid she had suffered an injury—she remembered immediately the sharp, tearing pain when Robert had penetrated her and the color of the stains was proof enough that the bleeding had stopped hours ago. Her escape route was closed. Robert, too, must be covered with bloodstains. It was impossible for him not to wonder where they had come from and then to remember.

Instinctively Esmeralda began to pull on her clothing, delaying the inevitable for just a few minutes more. Her mind scurried about seeking another escape route, but none presented itself and she did not dare spend any extra time thinking about it, for she could see the sky was growing lighter. It would only make things worse if Robert were late and Sir Arthur reprimanded him. Drawing a deep breath to steady herself, she leaned over the bed and shook his shoulder gently.

"Robert. Robert. It's dawn. You must get up."

His first response was a heartrending groan. Esmeralda bit her lip and fought back tears, thinking the sound to be an expression of regret. Nonetheless, she persisted, shaking him again, a little less gently, and repeating, somewhat louder, that he had to get back to camp. As she said it she realized that she had no idea what had happened in the battle. Had Robert been drinking to drown the sorrow of a defeat?

"My head," he moaned. "Don't. Oh, God, my head."

Esmeralda bit her lip again, but this time to stifle a giggle. How foolish she was. She had forgotten the morning punishment for drinking too much the night before. Her father had very rarely drunk to excess, but occasionally he had done so; Robert's plaint recalled the results of that overindulgence to her mind. And then a brilliant thought occurred to her: Perhaps Molly knew of a remedy. At least, she could say she was going to ask for one. Then she could allow Robert to remember what had happened on his own. She would not have to see his first, unguarded reaction.

"You must get up," she repeated. "Sir Arthur will expect to see you at six o'clock. I am going down to find out whether Molly knows of something that will help your head."

She fled the room as Robert rolled over toward the edge of the bed, groaning pitifully and reaching blindly for the chamber pot. As she closed the door, she wondered whether she was being unkind. If he was going to be sick, should she have stayed to hold his head? She would not have minded doing so but thought that it might embarrass Robert. Somehow being sick seemed a rather unromantic first contact with one's bride, even on a delayed wedding morning.

Esmeralda's spirits had risen mercurially. She was delighted with the excuse she had found to leave the room, which had permitted her to act just exactly as a good, loving wife should act and still would allow Robert to remember in her absence that he had consummated their marriage. Even if he were appalled at what he had done, he would be far too kind to show it once he had mastered his first shock of realization. And if he showed no open rejection of the situation, that would provide time—time for her to show what a good wife she

could be in every sense, since it would be ridiculous now that she was
no longer a virgin for them to continue to live apart, and time for him
to grow accustomed to the idea that she was a permanent acquisition
rather than a temporary one.

Presented with a most moving description of the sufferer's anguish,
Molly laughed. "Ah, weel," she said indulgently, "he's no doin' it
often, 'nd he's no mean with it—is he?"

The last two words were a trifle pointed, but Esmeralda only looked
puzzled. "Mean?" she repeated.

"Theer's men as git to foightin' or hittin' theer woives whin they
drink," Molly remarked.

"M'Guire?" Esmeralda asked, shocked.

Molly laughed again, for it was plain that her mistress could not
even associate such an idea with her husband. "No, niver M'Guire,"
she assured Esmeralda, "nor me first man, but me da wuzn't above it,
though no often. He's dead, God rest him, 'nd God forgive him, too.
Now, whut the captain'll be needin' is a hair o' th' dog wit a wee boite
to it. Jist let me gi' a thought to whut's heer."

"Yes, and you had better show me," Esmeralda said. "It's just luck
that you are here this morning instead of in camp with M'Guire. If it
should happen again, I want to know what to do right away."

Upstairs, Robert had indeed been sick, although it was mostly dry
heaves that shook him. After the first spasms were over, he opened his
eyes cautiously. The dimness of the predawn light seeping into the
room was helpful. A stronger light would have intensified the lances
of pain that stabbed through his head and made him sick again. The
half dark permitted him to look straight ahead without any new
disaster overtaking him, although he was sure that if he moved his
head or his eyes, he would expire at once.

What he saw was so startling, however, that he temporarily ceased
to feel his physical symptoms. There were his boots, neatly side by
side, but in the middle of the floor. On the other hand, his coat, shirt,
and breeches were strewn about in untidy heaps here and there. His
smalls were nowhere to be seen at all. Robert stared around the room.
He knew he had been very, very drunk, but he had been very, very
drunk many times before. Occasionally he had slept in his clothing,
but never had he thrown it hither and thither. Nearly ten years of
military service had ingrained in him certain habits. One of them was
to fold his clothing neatly when he took it off, particularly when he

had been drinking heavily. That way he could find his things and get them on no matter how sick or blind with pain he was, and he would look tidy outside no matter what the wreckage inside.

Surprise still holding back pain and nausea, Robert bent his head to look closer to the bedside for his smalls, and in sweeping from the foot toward the head of the bed, his gaze passed over his own naked thighs. He gasped with shock at the brown stains on his skin and the clotted blood that matted the golden curls of his pubic hair.

"Oh, my God," he whispered. "Merry."

But there was no regret in his voice, and a definite feeling of triumph swept over him. Perhaps he should not have done it, but she was his now, for good. As the thought came and he remembered more clearly the events of the previous night, his shaft stirred and began to rise. Robert laughed shakily. He wished he were not on duty so he could get Merry back into bed. The notion lingered pleasantly for a moment or two, Robert even toying with the idea of sending Carlos to headquarters with a note to say . . .

He grinned at the thought of requesting a day's leave to continue making love to his wife. He could imagine Sir Arthur's face as he read the note. It was never a serious intention; Robert would not really consider sending a young boy unfamiliar with the area alone through a countryside where a battle had been fought. Then the grin froze on his face as it occurred to him for the first time that Merry might not be willing.

There was evidence that he had not been very gentle with her. He got up, wincing at the renewed pain in his head, and walked unsteadily to the stand that held a basin and pitcher of water for washing. What the devil was he to say to Merry? he wondered, as he poured water into the basin and washed away the dried blood. When he stooped to pour the soiled water into the slop pail, he almost fell, shuddering as he fought a renewed desire to retch.

Better leave the bowl. He shoved it onto the stand and staggered back to the bed. His smalls must be under the bed, he thought, shuddering again at the notion of bending down to retrieve them. However, before he could put this hazardous enterprise into motion, there was a brief tap and the door opened. Robert barely had time to sit down and pull part of the tumbled blanket across his lap when Merry was in the room.

"Here is a horrible concoction that Molly says will put you to rights," she said.

Her voice was light, but she was blushing furiously. Robert stared at her, almost ready to weep with gratitude. There was no woman in the world like Merry, he thought. No matter what, she never made a fuss. Whatever happened, she picked up the pieces and went ahead as brave and steady as the best trooper. He saw her glance at his naked body and shift her eyes, and he blushed, too.

"I couldn't find my . . . my . . ."

Ridiculously, Robert could not say the word, even though he knew Merry had packed and unpacked his undergarments. Besides, it was a crazy thing to say. He had meant the statement as an apology for his nakedness, but the words came out almost as an accusation, as if he were blaming her for misplacing his garments. She came closer without speaking, but hesitated at about arm's length and held out the mug she was carrying. Robert took it from her. His gorge rose at the idea of trying to swallow anything, and his hand shook so that some of the contents slopped over. Merry took another step forward and put both her hands over his and the mug to steady them.

"Never mind about the clothes," she said softly. "I'll bring you clean ones. Those will have to be washed and mended before you wear them again anyway. Oh, Robert, Molly told me you beat the French. It's wonderful!"

He had been looking at the liquid in the mug, trying to nerve himself to take a pull at it, while at the back of his mind he wondered if it would frighten Merry if he kissed her hands. He looked up as she spoke, just catching her eyes as they lifted from his body. She was red as fire again in an instant and turned away quickly. Robert swallowed and tried to speak, but nothing came out on his first attempt.

"I'm sorry I hurt you, Merry," he said desperately, just as her hand fell on the door latch.

She stiffened, almost as if to withstand a physical blow, and the remainder of what Robert intended to say—assurances that he would be more gentle in the future, apologies for his drunkenness—died in his throat because she so quickly turned back toward him and smiled, although the expression was rather strained.

"We haven't time enough to talk now," Esmeralda said rapidly. "Molly told me Lord Burghersh and some others were with you. You'll have to find out whether they went back last night. If they didn't, you might have to wake them. You'll be late on duty, and Sir Arthur won't like that." She was not sure whether the stricken expression on his face was owing to his physical discomfort, to regret, or to her seeming rejection of his apology—and she was afraid to find out—but she could not bear it. "Don't worry so, Robert," she added softly, and then went out before he could speak.

The gentle assurance almost brought tears to Robert's eyes again, and he felt silly for being so emotional. Merry was just being herself. What the devil had ever possessed him to mention the possibility of an annulment back in Oporto? Why hadn't he realized then how lovely she was and how perfect? And then his conscience lashed him: Did he have the right to ask Merry to follow the drum? But she seemed to love it. Or was that only another instance of her not making a fuss?

Robert's head whirled, and he knew he was too dizzy and too sick to think straight. And he had forgotten all about his convivial companions again. If they had been as drunk as he was, they would never have made it back to Cazal da Sprega. Besides, he seemed to remember someone saying they intended to return to the wineshop and finish the wine they had ordered. Oh, God, they would be in prime and plummy order this morning!

He looked with loathing at the liquid in the mug, but decided that despite the smell it could not make him feel worse, even if it were poison. Better if it was. If it killed him, at least his troubles would be over. Taking a deep breath, he gulped at it.

Raw fire exploded in his mouth and throat as it went down, and the breath he had taken whooshed out of him in an anguished moan. He tensed, expecting a volcanic eruption from his stomach, but he really felt no urge to bring up the hot lava he had swallowed. There were certainly fireworks—Robert let out another huge breath almost expecting to see flames spew from his mouth—but the fireworks seemed to be beneficent. Sighing like a martyr, he closed his eyes and downed the rest of the fiery liquid.

Meanwhile, with shaking hands Esmeralda gathered up fresh clothing for Robert, but she had difficulty fixing her mind to the task and ended up with four stockings, two pairs of smalls, two coats, and no shirt or breeches. She had to put everything down and begin again. It was ridiculous, she thought, that Robert's bare body should have so violent an effect on her. She had seen him nearly naked before. It was true that the sight had always affected her, but the experience of

making love had heightened her reaction to him almost unbearably.
She had had a nearly irresistible impulse to touch him, to run her lips
and tongue over him as he had run his over her. And he had caught her
looking at him twice! He would think her more abandoned than any
light-skirt.

And what had that apology meant? Was he sorry *only* about hurting
her? If that were so, Esmeralda thought, she would have achieved a
state close to heaven. She knew, however, that she had cut him off
before he finished what he intended to say. Perhaps that had been
wrong; perhaps he would have said what she wanted to hear—but
perhaps he would have said just the opposite. She had not dared take
the chance.

Poor Robert, he had looked so ghastly. It was obvious he could not
think straight about anything. Later in the day he would feel better. He
would have a chance to consider the ramifications of what he had done
and also have a chance to adjust to the situation. After that, she would
no longer be able to avoid talking to him about the future. That
thought was so sobering that Esmeralda gathered up a full comple-
ment of clothing without any more romantic tremors.

When she reentered the room Robert was still sitting on the bed, but
she saw the mug was empty and that his complexion had lost its
earlier green tinge. True, his eyes were tearing and he was breathing
out as if he had eaten something too hot for comfort, but all in all he
looked better. He held her gaze steadily only once. As soon as she
blushed, hating herself for her inability to keep her color steady, he
dropped his eyes.

"I will come back as soon as I can," he said. "I don't think there
will be any more action for a day or two, and I will ask to be excused
from mess tonight."

"It will be pleasant to have dinner together," Esmeralda ventured.

"Merry—" he began, flashing a glance at her and then biting his
lip. "No," he went on, "you are quite right. We don't have time to
talk. Will you send Molly for Carlos, please? I left my horse at the
wineshop last night, and I haven't the faintest idea of how to get back
there."

"I can send him to fetch the horse so you can rest a few minutes
longer," she suggested.

Robert hesitated, then said no. He didn't dare shake his head yet,
although he did feel less as if it would fly off if he did. "The walk will

do me good, I think. I just hope someone had sense enough to unsaddle Apollo and give him something to eat and drink." He glanced up again fleetingly, flushed, and reached for the pile of clothing Esmeralda was still holding.

Silently she gave it to him and fled, just barely biting back an offer to help him dress. Had the offer come to her mind out of kindness, she could have said the words. Unfortunately, Esmeralda knew her motives were not in the least of such purity as kindness. Her desire to help Robert dress had been born solely out of a most immodest lust, and she probably would have been more hindrance than help in getting his clothing on.

It was dreadful. Esmeralda was well aware that she should be ashamed of such raw sensuality, but she was not. She had not run away to put temptation behind her but to prevent Robert from finding out what a coarse wretch she was. The fear drove her not only down the stairs but out of the house. Instead of sending Molly to wake Carlos, she went herself to the stable and shook the boy, telling him to go up to the bedchamber to help Captain Moreton dress if he needed help.

Then sternly admonishing herself, Esmeralda went to the kitchen to tell Molly it was possible Robert would be back for dinner. They were talking about what to buy that could be cooked and then kept for a day or two without spoiling if he could not get leave after all, when his booted feet came down the stairs. Esmeralda dropped the spoon with which she had been fiddling and bent down to pick it up so that Molly could not see her face and so her flush would seem to have a natural cause. It was dreadful to blush every time she saw Robert or even expected to see him. Esmeralda wished miserably that she could stop.

However, Robert did not come in. Although he felt a flicker of disappointment and worry when Esmeralda did not appear even briefly to say good-bye, he buried the emotions quickly under a determined effort to remember enough about the wineshop to permit Carlos to find it. Robert knew his physical condition was affecting both his emotions and his ability to reason, and he was resolved not to think about Merry until he felt human again.

To his surprise, as soon as Carlos led him to the main street of the town, he recognized the wineshop. He had the devil of a time routing out his companions and bitterly regretted that he had not asked Molly to make a gallon of her volcanic restorative. It was not that he felt well—his head still pounded and occasionally his stomach made threatening noises—but he was at least ambulatory and did not have to lean off his horse every few minutes to vomit. Worse yet, the party that had remained in Óbidos was not in much better condition.

Naturally, they were all late reporting to duty. Sir Arthur glared and spoke very coldly, but Robert, who was the only one in any state to notice, detected a definite twinkle in his eyes. Although he no longer indulged in such behavior, Robert was well aware that Sir Arthur had been there before them. There were tales of bacchanals during the early years of Wellesley's Indian service that made his ADCs' celebration sound like a nursery tea.

Sir Arthur might not have been quite as understanding if he had not had some good news just before his young gentlemen arrived. He had learned that General Acland's brigade was offshore and General Anstruther's was close behind, which meant four thousand men would be added to his force. This was of considerable importance, since he had reason to believe that the original estimates of the men available to Junot were too low. Better yet, both brigades could be put ashore at Porto Novo at the mouth of the little river Maceira only about ten miles south of where they were. To protect the landing, the army would take up a position on the heights east of the mouth of the river with headquarters in the largest village in the area, Vimeiro. With more than eighteen thousand troops, five thousand of which had proved themselves in action and all of whom were in high spirits, Sir Arthur felt his situation to be good.

Some of the army was already in motion toward Vimeiro, but there was work enough for the ADCs in transmitting Sir Arthur's commands to the remainder, making arrangements for the worst wounded who could not be moved and for those who could be shipped home in the emptied transports, plus seeing that the inexperienced commissary agents would have food and other necessities available, setting up quarters for staff and line officers who would need to be close to Sir Arthur—endless details. As the least disabled, Robert was busiest; but he found that he had lost his ability to concentrate his mind on military business to the exclusion of everything else.

The first thing he did as soon as he understood the situation was to ask Sir Arthur's permission to absent himself from the mess dinner that evening. The second was to find M'Guire, arrange the loan of a troop horse for him, and send him back to Caldas to see that Merry and the others followed the army to Vimeiro. The third was to make sure Fitzroy Somerset knew that Merry was on her way so that there would be quarters waiting for her. Then and only then did he set about the errand upon which Sir Arthur had sent him. True, there was no great urgency about the errand, but never before in his military life had Robert set a personal consideration before even the smallest duty.

Now Robert understood very clearly why—aside from the hardships they must undergo—Sir Arthur was so antagonistic to the idea of wives accompanying their husbands into the field. And he also understood why some officers would ignore their commanders' displeasure. Despite pricks from his conscience, which he soothed by reminding himself that he had several times urged Merry to go to England and it was she who had begged to remain in Portugal, he had not the slightest intention of parting with his wife unless danger threatened.

Chapter 19

M'Guire arrived at Esmeralda's lodging midmorning. Although Robert had described the place as best he could, it had taken M'Guire some time to find it, since he spoke no Portuguese. By then Esmeralda had finished the shopping and Molly had finished cleaning Robert's clothes. Both Molly and Esmeralda asked eager questions concerning why they were going and where, but aside from the name of the place, M'Guire knew nothing. The captain, he said, had been in a tearing hurry and sharper tempered than usual. He had said no more than that they must catch up with the army and get to a village called Vimeiro.

Esmeralda's heart sank right down into her slippers, which she ran to change to riding boots, but really she was too busy to spend much time worrying. She had to pay for the lodging, write and send off a note to Dom Aleixo with thanks and farewells, help Molly pack, make sure M'Guire and Carlos did not load Luisa in such a way that fragile or perishable objects were under heavy ones, and see to it that nothing was left behind.

It was not until they had passed Óbidos that she remembered the attack of the previous day. As it came into her mind, she also remembered that she had not yet confessed her spying to Robert, and she hesitated about confiding in M'Guire. Second thoughts convinced her that she must tell Robert for safety's sake. Then she discovered that, despite Carlos's limited English, he had already managed to communicate both to Molly and M'Guire the most exciting and important event that had taken place—at least, as far as he was concerned—since Robert had agreed he could accompany the British. M'Guire smiled shyly at Esmeralda and assured her that there was nothing to fear now. Troops had been out to sweep the area and to spread the word of the English victory. Any Frenchmen left behind had been happy to come out of hiding and go along with the English because they knew they would certainly be tortured and killed if they were found by the Portuguese.

Whether or not M'Guire was right, no one interfered with their small party. They arrived quite safely in Vimeiro about five o'clock. They had traveled unusually quickly because Molly and M'Guire had taken turns riding the troop horse, with Carlos intermittently in front of them on the saddle bow. Thus, no one had to walk the whole twenty or so miles, and one rest period to allow the mule and horses to drink and Esmeralda to stretch her legs was sufficient.

Although the whole area was a swarming mass of men and animals by the time Esmeralda and her party arrived, there was less actual confusion than there had been at Figueira. The largest house in the place had already been commandeered for Sir Arthur; orderlies and ADCs came and went. Lord Fitzroy's efficiency and attention to detail were already becoming a byword—and because he had been on duty the preceding night, he was not half-dead like those who had accompanied Robert.

M'Guire got the direction of Captain Moreton's quarters, which were back to back with Sir Arthur's, and in half an hour Molly and Esmeralda were hard at work. Molly started dinner while Esmeralda went up to look over their quarters, see whether they needed to be cleaned, and unpack necessary items. To her relief, the large room seemed to be in perfect order, and with great joy she saw there was a double bed. Holding her breath, she pulled back the covers to inspect the sheets. They were not fresh, but that did not matter. If there were no fresh sheets in the house, Esmeralda now had her own. What was important was that they were not all spotted with blood, which meant that the bed was probably not infested with fleas or bedbugs.

To her greater joy, she discovered that the one room was all they had been allotted. Because Sir Arthur felt it was possible that the French would attempt to interfere with the landing and in any case that there might be renewed action at any time, he wanted his commanding line officers close by for planning. Their rank entitled them to spacious quarters, and room had to be available for their staffs also; thus, Sir Arthur's ADCs were crammed in as tightly as possible.

Esmeralda could not have been better pleased. Her one doubt was what to do about Robert's cot. Not to set it up, she was afraid, would be too blatant an invitation; on the other hand, setting it up might be taken as a signal that she was unwilling to share her bed with him. Then she thought that it would sound reasonable if she said she considered it more important that M'Guire get Boa Viagem and Luisa fed, watered, and rubbed down than to be setting up a cot, which could be done later. And Molly had not really seen her husband for several days. Surely it would be a kindness to dismiss her to attend to him as soon as she had dinner at a stage where Esmeralda could watch over it.

She sent M'Guire off with the animals at once and told him that he need not come back unless she sent a message with Carlos. Nor did it take long to get rid of Molly. Then she realized that, if she wanted privacy, they would have to eat in the bedchamber. What would Robert think of that? Would he accept the excuse that it was too hot in the kitchen? Would he notice at once that the extra cot was not set up? Should she change from her riding dress? Esmeralda hesitated, suddenly regretting that she had sent Molly away. If only she had not, she could have arranged to be half-undressed when Robert came up.

The thought was so pleasant and had so insidiously slipped into her mind that Esmeralda was well on her way to devising another method of achieving the same purpose before she realized how shocking it was. And just as she became aware of how appallingly immoral her true nature was, Robert appeared in the doorway. It was as if her guilty conscience had taken flesh to reprimand her. Esmeralda gasped and stepped back.

"For God's sake, Merry," Robert said, "don't be afraid of me."

"Oh, no," she said breathlessly, "I'm not. Really, I'm not. I was only startled. I was thinking about something."

Those words were unwise because, of course, they brought *what* she had been thinking about clearly to mind and she blushed hotly. Robert was distressed. For the first time a horrible notion leapt into his head. Had he *forced* Merry? He remembered now that she had cried for help several times. Had she been screaming? It had sounded soft to him, ecstatic, but he had been so drunk! He stood staring at her, appalled.

Frightened by his expression, Merry took a step forward. "What is it?" she cried. "Robert, what's wrong?"

"D-did I . . . Merry . . . did I *force* you?"

Of all the questions he could have asked, that was the most unwelcome, the most embarrassing, but Esmeralda knew she must answer. Yet if she said no, she was a whore; and if she said yes, Robert would never come near her again. Clearly stated in her mind, Esmeralda knew at once which was the more dreadful to her and cast her reputation to the wind without a second thought.

"No," she said firmly, and then, trying to salvage something, she added, "you are my husband, Robert. You have been so kind, have done so much for me. How could I refuse?"

"That's . . ." He tried to smile. "Well, I certainly am your husband now. Annulment's out. . . . Right?" The last words were uncertain.

For a bare instant Esmeralda hesitated again. Then she said, "Yes, I agree."

She had tricked and manipulated her father for years without a single qualm of conscience, but to do it to Robert, who was himself so transparently honest, was horrible. With a few words, she could free him from a burden that he did not seem to welcome. But Esmeralda knew that those few words would be final. Robert would never think of making love to her again if he believed annulment was still possible, and that would cause so great a strain in their relationship as to make any continuance of it impossible. *Not yet*, she thought as she spoke. *I can always offer him his freedom. I must try to make a complete marriage work first.*

Although Robert was far from the most perceptive of men where women were concerned, his sensitivity with regard to Esmeralda had been greatly heightened because of his desire for her and his guilt about having possibly mistreated her. The slight hesitation before she answered, which he would not have noticed under other circumstances, was markedly apparent to him in this case. He felt an odd sinking in his midsection, thinking that, even if he had not forced her physically, she had had little choice, then or now. He would make it up to her, he vowed to himself. He *would* make her happy.

His troubled expression wrung Esmeralda's heart. She put out her hand to him, saying, "Robert . . ."

He took the hand and drew on it, very gently, very tentatively, as if he were afraid she would resist coming closer—or as if he hoped she would resist. Esmeralda pushed that second thought out of her mind and yielded to the hint of a pull, smiling up at him.

"I'm sorry I hurt you," Robert said, his voice as soft and as uncertain as his grip.

"Is that what's worrying you?" she asked hopefully. "Because if it is, I wish you would forget about it. You must have noticed that I survived."

Her cheeks were pink again, but Robert saw with intense relief that her eyes were amused. "Well," he began with renewed confidence, "it's been on my mind, you see, because I . . . er . . ." The confidence trickled away as Robert sought for what he considered proper words for what he wished to say.

"Yes?" Esmeralda asked encouragingly.

"I . . . ah . . . I hope I have not . . . er . . . given you a . . . a distaste . . . a permanent distaste. . . ."

"Oh, dear," Esmeralda said, and then feeling Robert stiffen slightly, and his grip on her hand, which had tightened, loosen again, she said quickly, "No. Oh, Robert, I don't know how to answer you, not because I don't know what I wish to say but because I don't know the way to say it. My mama died before I was old enough to have the proper mode of response explained to me."

"The proper mode of response," Robert repeated in a much more natural voice. "What the devil does that mean?"

"I am not very sure," Esmeralda replied doubtfully. "Are there not correct ways, I mean ladylike ways, of responding? I obtained a book of manners to learn the correct modes for entertaining when I was in India, and it had pages and pages of proper responses, even one for marriage, but not for . . . oh, dear. I . . . I would not wish to seem coarse or . . . or to shock you."

Robert burst out laughing. If Merry didn't wish to shock him, she could not intend to refuse him. He had no experience at all with "ladies," but, from what he had heard from other men and the plays he had seen, he knew that refusal was always proper and modest; only acceptance could be shocking.

"Well, *I* can't tell you the proper mode." He chuckled. "My mama never explained it to me, either." He hesitated, and then went on, much more seriously, "And to tell the truth I don't care what mode you use so long as . . . so long as you say yes. . . . I mean, so long as you say you are willing to be my wife."

He seemed so earnest and sincere that Esmeralda's heart leapt with joy. "Yes, indeed, I am willing," she replied eagerly. Then she giggled. "And it is most fortunate that we have come to this agreement just now, because we have only been assigned a single bedchamber. It would have been very awkward. . . . I did not know how to explain to M'Guire so . . . so . . ."

Robert pulled her closer. "It may not be exactly correct, but I like your mode very much," he murmured, and kissed her.

For a very little while Esmeralda remained passive, but she found the embrace so much to her taste that she soon attempted to wrap her arms around Robert. She had forgotten that she was holding a basting spoon, which rapped him smartly on the ear as she brought her arms up. He lifted his head in surprise.

"Oh, I'm so sorry," she exclaimed, her eyes wide with fright because Robert might have thought the blow deliberate.

"Now that," he said, chuckling, "I can say outright, was not the proper mode."

Esmeralda's expression changed from fright to laughter. "I am not so sure," she remarked merrily. "It seems appropriate, now that I think about it. If a gentleman assaults a maid in the kitchen, a rap with a spoon—"

Robert interrupted her by seizing her and kissing her again. This time she dropped the spoon, and it fell to the stone floor with a loud clatter. He released her, uttered an exaggerated sigh, and took a step backward.

"I take your point. Not in the kitchen." Then he looked around with surprise. "What are you doing here anyway? Where's Molly?"

"I sent her away." Esmeralda's color rose at this confession, and she continued quickly, "I . . . we had to talk privately, and the only place to be private would have been the bedchamber if Molly was in the kitchen."

"You *are* afraid of me," Robert said with a worried frown.

"Yes, but not of what you think," Esmeralda put in hastily. "Robert, we have been joking about the proper mode, and in a way it is funny, of course. Perhaps people should be able to express freely what they feel, but—but a free expression in some cases might give— give a wrong impression. I *am* afraid, but of seeming too bold, or—"

"Too bold?" Robert took her up on that at once. "Never mind what other people might think. I am as ignorant as you are of proper maidenly behavior. I want to know—I *have* to know—did you hate what I did or did you enjoy it?"

But Esmeralda could not bring herself to answer his question directly. Instead she stepped closer, put her arms around his neck, and lifted her face to be kissed, murmuring, "I also thought that Molly would like to be with M'Guire."

Robert understood what she meant and accepted her gesture with pleasure, even though she had not answered in words. The embrace lasted some considerable time, as he explored not only her mouth but her ears and neck with his lips. He received enough encouragement that no doubts of Esmeralda's pleasure were raised in his mind, for she kissed whatever part of him was available when he was not occupying her lips with his own. He was just insinuating his hand under her chin so that he could unbutton the front of her riding dress when voices sounded outside. They jumped apart, both flushed with embarrassment.

"Damn it," Robert growled softly, reaching out for Esmeralda again, "why shouldn't I kiss my wife?"

"Oh, you should," Esmeralda murmured, nonetheless evading him as she heard booted feet in the corridor and then mounting the stairs, "but not while dinner burns." She giggled softly. "I am sure that would cause comment. You never did so before."

"The more fool I," Robert said, but he laughed.

"We could eat upstairs," Esmeralda suggested. "There is a table. It is small—"

"We will manage very well," Robert agreed quickly. "If we remain here, we will have half the camp tramping in and out." He paused and sniffed appreciatively. He had eaten nothing all day, of course, and now that his stomach was settled, the savory odor had wakened a sharp appetite. "And you will invite them all to dinner because you are much too charitable. Don't. I intend to eat it all myself."

Esmeralda stooped to pick up the fallen spoon, and Robert ran a hand over her buttocks. She jerked upright with a gasp.

"Yes, indeed," Robert went on, "I am very hungry."

"Well, if you do that again, you won't get any dinner," Esmeralda said severely. "I will end up putting sugar over the chicken and salt in the tea."

"It was an irresistible temptation." Robert looked innocent as an angel, but his eyes glittered. "And anyway, I don't take sugar in my tea."

"You don't take it on chicken, either," Esmeralda retorted, and brandished her spoon at him. "Sit down. I am afraid to turn my back on you, and I must baste the chicken or, hungry as you are, you will not be able to eat it. Neither will I, and I am just as hungry as you are."

The words were innocent enough; the blush that accompanied the last few made them into a suggestive promise. Naturally, instead of sitting down, Robert took a step forward, but Esmeralda slid sideways toward the sink.

"If you feel so energetic," she said quickly, tipping what remained in the water bucket into a washing pan, "you can pump up some water for me."

Robert laughed. "That was not the activity I had in mind," he protested.

"I know," she admitted, laughing too, "but it will do you good."

A door slammed on the floor above, and the floorboards of the upper corridor creaked. The footsteps came down the stairs.

"Cold water is said to have a beneficial effect," Robert remarked, sighing.

He laughed again at Esmeralda's puzzled expression, grasped the handle of the water bucket, and went out the back door. Although Robert claimed ignorance, he was not being completely truthful. He did, in fact, know the convention that required "good" women to find lovemaking a trial rather than a pleasure. He had heard it used as an excuse by husbands who frequented houses of pleasure, and it had struck him as a most peculiar and unpleasant idea. Now he was certain that it was also wrong.

Everything Merry said and did marked her innocence. As he moved the pump handle, Robert began to laugh again at the idea of finding the proper mode of response to lovemaking in a book of etiquette. Perhaps it was cruel, because it was apparent that Merry had loved her mother, but with a husband like Henry Talbot it was probably Robert's good fortune that Mrs. Talbot had died before she could pass along to her daughter her notions about the correct behavior of a wife to a husband. As it was, Robert believed he could teach Merry to act in any way that pleased him best. He began to pump with more vigor as he contemplated that delicious prospect and was so absorbed that the bucket overflowed and flooded his boots before he realized what he was doing.

When the cold water seeped through the seams and wet his feet, Robert jumped back with an oath, but then stood still, frowning. Cold water did have a beneficial effect, he decided somewhat grimly. It was all very well to revel in Merry's innocence, but it could easily get her into trouble. He had been a fool to fondle her as he had in a relatively public place. That sort of thing wasn't done, and he must not give her the impression that he wanted her to violate convention. She was so mischievous that his bad example might make her push a joke too far.

Until now Merry's natural modesty had protected her from behavior that would be censurable by the toffee-noses home in England. But he now realized that he must be careful not to lead her astray. Merry was very conformable to her company. She had been totally ignorant of military matters when they met; now she was as interested and probably more knowledgeable than any army-mad subaltern. And she was right, too, about his never having behaved affectionately before; nonetheless, any change in his manner toward her *would* raise comment, which was best avoided. Bedroom manners had best be kept in the bedroom.

Besides, Robert thought suddenly, he couldn't jump Merry for a quick tumble before dinner as if she were fully accustomed, as many troopers' wives were, to snatching at any brief opportunity for lovemaking or as if she were a camp follower. He would have to be very careful this time. She said she was not frightened, and she had kissed him willingly; however, if he hurt her again, she might become less willing. That was a worrisome notion, but it was soon overlaid by a contemplation of the many pleasant ways of making Merry not only willing but eager. A minute later Robert jerked his mind back to reality. If he went on thinking along those lines, he told himself, he would have to find a way to work off his energy that was more effective than pumping water. Maybe he ought to sit in the bucket.

The idea made Robert laugh and considering how he would explain his wet breeches in addition to his wet feet was amusing enough to permit him to pick up the water bucket and enter the kitchen in a less indecent condition than that of a few minutes earlier. As he lifted the bucket to the counter, however, the bottom just caught on the edge. Had the bucket not been overfull to begin with, this would not have done any harm, but Robert had not been thinking of water or buckets and had not poured away the top two inches of liquid as he should have. A gush of cold water spilled out over him. Merry uttered a little cry of warning, but it was too late. Robert jerked, tilting the bucket even farther, and half the contents cascaded down his thighs.

Esmeralda clapped both hands to her mouth in an agonized mingling of an urgent desire to laugh and real fear that Robert would be very angry. After all, she had sent him for the water. However, to her surprise, he burst into roars of laughter himself, nearly spilling what remained in the bucket. Esmeralda seized it before this could happen and pushed it back to a safe spot on the counter.

"I am so very sorry," she cried. "I should have known you were not accustomed to fetching water."

But Robert only gurgled something about the beneficial effects of cold water and, still laughing, staggered up the stairs to find their room and change his clothing. He did not come down again, which made Esmeralda rather nervous. She had visions of entering the room and finding Robert naked in the bed. This was exciting and repellent at the same time. She would have to put the dinner aside and take off her clothes with him watching. She was still dusty and sweaty, too, from the long ride and the heat of the kitchen. She had been too busy to wash and had not expected Robert so early.

However, Esmeralda's fears were unfounded. She found Robert wearing a shirt, pantaloons, and slippers. He was sitting quietly at the table, staring out the window, so deep in thought that he did not hear the click of the latch, and Esmeralda caught a glimpse of an expression of deep concern on his face. Instinctively she said, "Robert—" and he jumped to his feet and came toward her.

"Good God, Merry, why did you carry that heavy tray up the stairs?" he exclaimed, taking it from her.

"Shall I be cruel and say I lacked faith after the water incident?" she replied lightly.

Robert smiled as he set the tray safely on the table, but his look of concern returned as Esmeralda detoured around his boots, which he had set to dry in a patch of sunlight in the middle of the floor. "Merry," he said, "I have been thinking of what to write to my parents and of how . . . how peculiar all this will sound in a letter. I do not like to lie to them—"

"No, don't," Esmeralda interrupted. "They would never forgive me if they discovered I was the cause of such unfilial and dishonest behavior." She sat down in the chair opposite Robert's and stared at him. "I don't know what to say, Robert. I would not for the world be a cause of discord between you and your parents. I did not love Papa, but I would have done anything for my mother. I do understand how dear parents can be."

"It's nothing to do with *you*, Merry. My parents won't have any objections to you. Can't see why they should. You're a lady, and you've got something as a dowry—not that they'd be likely to worry too much about that anyway."

Esmeralda opened her mouth to tell him that she had a good deal more than *something* as a dowry, but the words would not come. For one thing, keeping the amount of her fortune secret had become second nature; for another, she wanted very much to have Robert accept her for herself rather than because she was exceedingly rich.

Absorbed in his problem, Robert did not notice and went on. "No, it's nothing to do with you, it's just that I never wrote them about it when we were married. I guess I thought it would worry them, and I didn't want to give m' mother any ideas. And I've never mentioned you in any letter I wrote—well, there were only two—since then. It's not only that they might be hurt if I write now and say we've been married since the twenty-eighth. I guess I can explain that, but how the devil am I going to explain why I'm telling them *now*? I mean, I could explain it to Fa if I could talk to him, but in a letter? And if m' father's not home, m' mother would open any letter from me."

"Oh, no!" Esmeralda cried, "Please do not. . . . What will they think of me!"

"Think of you! Fa'll want to take a horsewhip to *me* for getting so drunk I'd treat a decent girl like a whore."

"Perhaps," Esmeralda whispered, "but more likely they would think I . . . I did not behave as I should." It was the truth, of course. Robert had been very drunk, but if she had not encouraged him, she believed he would not have persisted.

Robert frowned. "I hadn't thought of that," he admitted. "Damn it. Once they set eyes on you, they'll know it was my fault, but I'm not very good at writing letters anyway, and this is so complicated. . . ." He looked at her appealingly.

"Oh, Robert, no!" she exclaimed. "I may be much better at writing letters and explaining, but your parents would know at once that you had only copied out what someone else had written, and think of the impression *that* would give."

"Oh, Lord," he sighed, "they'd start to imagine that I'd fallen prey to a particularly clever harpy. They should know better, of course, but m' father thinks I'm an idiot anyway, and m' mother's convinced I'm still ten years old."

Esmeralda was not really as worried as she sounded. She was cynically certain that whatever Robert's parents thought originally, they would be happy to welcome her as a daughter as soon as they discovered the extent of the deposits at her bank. However, it seemed to her that the longer his affectionate parents had to think and worry about what Robert had done, the worse their opinion of her would become. If she and Robert returned to England together and Lord and Lady Moreton saw that Robert was happy, that she was socially acceptable, and simultaneously heard about her fortune, they might still be shocked but not, she hoped, antagonistic. She could take the blame upon herself, too, saying she had been so frightened, she had begged Robert not to tell them. Fear was not nearly so reprehensible as seduction.

"Do you think the extent of time will be significant?" Esmeralda asked.

"What do you mean?"

"Well, do you think your parents would be more deeply hurt or worried if you wrote a week or a month from now instead of immediately?"

"Probably not," Robert said, his expression lightening. He was not at all reluctant to put off an unpleasant duty, but then his face clouded again. "But I don't see that it can help, either."

"It may not," Esmeralda agreed, smiling, "but I think this is not the best time to consider so important a subject. You are hungry and tired, and, I suspect, still a little disordered from your potations. If it cannot do serious harm, I would suggest that you put the question of the announcement aside for a day or two, at least. Perhaps something will occur to us." She pushed the chickens invitingly nearer to him and extended a carving knife. "If you will carve, I will serve out the rice and greens and sauce. I'm sorry it's so very simple a meal, but we didn't arrive until five o'clock, and Molly didn't think there would be time to cook anything besides chicken. If you hadn't come when you did, I would have sent Carlos to discover whether there was a cookshop, but I didn't even have time for that."

As she spoke Robert had swiftly carved both small birds and distributed pieces on the plates Esmeralda readied. He took a bite and smiled. "Simple but tasty. I swear Sir Arthur must hire a cobbler and tell him to cook old shoes." He chewed for a while in silence, then reached for a second helping.

As she added the garnishings to his plate she asked, "Robert, where are we and why? Can you tell me? I mean, I know the name of the town, but M'Guire couldn't tell us anything else."

His eyes lit, and he began to describe the battle of Roliça. Esmeralda shook her head. "First tell me why your coat is all torn and your breeches all stained."

Robert looked surprised. "That had nothing to do with the fight at Roliça," he said, quite truthfully but giving Esmeralda a totally false impression. "That was at Brilos when I had to leave my horse and go climbing around on a stupid hill to tell those idiots in the Sixtieth and the Ninety-fifth that help was on its way."

"Then you weren't in the fighting?" she asked.

"Not really," Robert said regretfully. "Fa won't hear of my taking a line command. I'm going to have to talk to him about it again. I really think I need some field experience before I command a regiment of my own. But what I did isn't in the least important."

As far as Robert was concerned, he had told the truth. He did not consider riding through shot and shell or even the hand-to-hand combat in which he had engaged as taking part in the fighting. To his mind, to take part in the fighting meant leading men into action and being responsible for what they did. But, of course, Esmeralda did not know this. She was therefore left with the notion that he had probably torn and stained his coat and breeches scrambling through brush and over rough ground.

Comforted and content, she turned her full attention to Robert's detailed explanation of the overall significance of the battle of Roliça: The actual advantage gained militarily was far less important than the significance in terms of morale. "If we could have pursued them, cut them off from Loison's force and from Lisbon, and wiped them out, it would have hurt Junot. As it is, I'm afraid we haven't done the main French force much harm, but we've done ourselves a lot of good."

"Did Sir Arthur think it too dangerous to follow?" Esmeralda asked eagerly. "Would we have been caught between the two armies?"

"Sir Arthur never says too much about what he thinks," Robert admitted. "It's one of the things I don't like about serving with him, but I can usually figure it out afterward or if I ask after the action, he'll explain. And he's so good a general that it's worth waiting for. But anyway, coming to Vimeiro hasn't much to do at all with French movements. Sir Arthur received word that Acland and Anstruther are off the coast with four thousand men. We have to protect the landing site. And it's important to have the extra men because those idiots in Whitehall—or maybe the old fools at the Horse Guards—got the wrong information about what Junot has to put up against us."

"Is the difference serious?" Esmeralda frowned with concern but her voice was steady and her expression was not in the least fearful.

Robert smiled at her. "It might have been if these two brigades had not arrived. Once they are ashore, I believe we will be strong enough to throw off any attack by Junot."

"Did not the Spanish troops desert as expected?" Esmeralda asked.

"Yes and no." Robert grinned. "There are still about six thousand Spanish troops in Lisbon, but they're doing more for us than for Junot. In fact, he only managed to prevent them from deserting by arresting them in small batches, and now he's got a whole battalion tied up guarding them."

"From what you have said about the abilities of the Spanish army, keeping the troops prisoner may cost the French more men than allowing them to return to Spain and fight," Esmeralda remarked.

Robert laughed aloud. "You are becoming a better general than Junot," he teased. "But there is another funny part to this. There is a Russian fleet in Lisbon harbor with about six thousand seamen under Admiral Siniavin. They haven't done a thing since they arrived but eat. When the Portuguese started to rebel, Siniavin refused to help the French. He said that the tsar had never declared war on the Portuguese nor recognized the French annexation of Portugal. He wouldn't even let his men guard the Spanish prisoners."

"But why?" Esmeralda was puzzled. It seemed very odd behavior for an ally.

"Because there is a strong party in Russia violently opposed to the peace Alexander made with the French, and Siniavin is in sympathy with this party. It also seems that Siniavin is Royal Navy trained and served with our fleet for a few years. He has no intention of helping the French against us if he can avoid it. Naturally, he can't disobey orders, but he can draw the line pretty tight and do *only* what his instructions specifically command. And that, I gather, is nothing. He's been at sea since before Russia declared war on England, and I don't think he's got any orders."

"How convenient," Esmeralda remarked.

"Yes, isn't it?" Robert responded, grinning.

"Then what does Junot have?" Esmeralda asked, returning to the point of the discussion that affected them most directly.

"A lot more than the fourteen or fifteen thousand men Sir Arthur was led to expect—at least twenty thousand, we think."

Esmeralda thought for a moment and then said, "So all in all, the numbers are about even, aren't they? The French may have a little edge, but—"

"But they don't have Sir Arthur," Robert replied with grim enthusiasm. "He's really the best general I've ever seen in action. And he's used to being the underdog and winning anyway. That's important. And because of Roliça, for the first time our men and officers *believe* they can beat the French."

Esmeralda looked so astonished that Robert laughed again. He realized that she had accepted as gospel his conviction that under Sir Arthur's direction, a British victory was inevitable. It was a very pleasant feeling that she trusted him so completely.

"I guess you never paid much attention to what Boney was doing in Europe, did you, Merry?" Robert asked.

"No . . ."

"Well, Boney beat everyone to flinders," Robert told her.

"I knew that—I mean, I knew he rolled up the Austrians, Russians, and Prussians."

Robert nodded. "Yes, well, you see that's been part of the trouble. Everyone is so afraid of Boney's French troops that they're half-beaten before they start. I'm pretty sure, although no one said it outright, that our own men and officers felt the same way. But we've had phenomenally good luck. That little action at Brilos—I'll swear it was half bravado and half hysteria that made those four companies chase the French pickets too far. But they held out like heroes after they'd run into the whole rear guard, and then we *beat* them at Roliça."

"You said you would," Esmeralda put in, smiling.

But Robert did not return the smile, and he shook his head. "I swear God's on our side, Merry. Everything went wrong at Roliça. Colonel Lake got a rush of heroism to the head—or maybe he didn't

understand the orders. We'll never know because he's dead now, but
he started the attack long before he should have—before the artillery
had a chance to soften up the troops and before there was any hope of
support on the flanks from Ferguson or Trant."

"But Robert, if everything went wrong—" Esmeralda hesitated,
unsure of how she wanted to finish the sentence.

"We beat them anyway," Robert pointed out with blazing eyes.
"We drove the French out of a very strong position by sheer courage
and fighting skill." He drew a deep breath then and smiled wryly. "At
least, that's how the men and officers see it. And it's put them on top
of the world. They may even believe they're better soldiers—that's
not true, but it doesn't matter—"

"Isn't that dangerous?" Esmeralda remembered the tears and stains
on Robert's clothing and was suddenly frightened. "Overconfidence
can lead to rash actions. You said Lake had behaved rashly and upset
Sir Arthur's plan."

"You don't have to worry about overconfidence. Sir Arthur will let
all the officers have the rough side of his tongue for not obeying
orders. They'll be more careful—"

"Moreton!"

A roar from the stairwell cut off whatever more Robert had been
about to say. Esmeralda saw his lips tighten and his nostrils flare with
temper, and a thrill went through her. It was the first time Robert had
ever shown the smallest sign that he preferred her company to his
duty. Nonetheless, as Robert went and flung open the door, a definite
feeling of relief was mingled with her joy. She could have kept him
talking for a while longer, but eventually he would have resumed the
amorous activities he had begun earlier.

Not that Esmeralda objected to that. Despite the pain she had
suffered, she was eager to renew the experience, partly out of
curiosity, partly out of a recollection of the pleasure and excitement
that mingled with the pain, and partly because she understood it was a
way to bind Robert to her. Her problem was that she felt she could not
be very appetizing at the moment. She wanted to wash and comb her
hair and put on a pretty new dress so that she would not fall too far
below the standards to which Robert was accustomed.

Thus, although she lowered her eyes, she was not really disappointed when Robert came back from the door still tight-lipped with

displeasure to say, "I'm wanted. I hope it won't be for long, but I don't know."

"It's all right," she said, putting out her hand to him. "I have to clear up anyway. Whenever you come, I'll be waiting."

Chapter 20

As soon as Robert's footsteps died away down the stairs, Esmeralda tumbled all the plates together onto the tray and carried them to the kitchen. She did not bother to wash them. Molly would do that in the morning. Getting herself sweet and clean was more important than anything else, particularly as it would not be easy to do. First, water had to be heated. Esmeralda emptied what Robert had left in the bucket into the kettle and set it on the stove. Then she lugged the bucket out to the pump and filled it, brought it back to the kitchen, topped up the kettle, and emptied the remainder of the water into several other pots—as many as could be set on the stove.

While those heated, she searched the house, the pantry, and finally the outhouses, but she could not find a bath. In the end she found a pan, possibly used for baking, that would be wide enough for her to kneel in. It was far too flat to bathe in, but it would catch the excess water while she sponged herself clean.

Esmeralda first took the large pan upstairs, then filled the bucket with cold water and carried that up. At that point she realized that she needed a second bucket for the hot water. She recalled seeing one while she was looking for the bath, but she was getting flustered because everything was taking so long and she could not remember where she had seen it. She ran about looking in all the least likely places only to discover the bucket in the most logical spot—under the sink. When she saw that it was dirty, she almost wept with anxiety and scrubbed it clean with frantic haste.

She had a vision of herself elegantly dressed, with her hair neatly combed, sitting quietly by the lamp sewing. She felt that was how Robert would expect to see his wife. He would not like to see her carrying buckets of water. He had been surprised when he saw her working in the kitchen, and it would be most unromantic for Robert to see her sweating, or struggling to get clean.

By the time she had the old bucket suitably scrubbed, the water in the smaller pots was boiling and that in the kettle too hot to touch. With trembling haste, she emptied all the hot water into the bucket and started for the stairs. Voices outside made her freeze for a moment, but they passed and Esmeralda hurried up the stairs, gasping for breath and shifting the bucket from one hand to the other, as she felt her arm might be wrenched from its socket by the weight.

Having assembled her paraphernalia and found the soap and sponge, Esmeralda finally removed her clothing and began to add cold water to the hot until the temperature was reasonable. Then she knelt down in the baking pan, dipped her sponge, soaped it, and began to wash. The removal of dust and old sweat soothed her immediately. Her breathing slowed and so did her movements. When her face and neck were clean, it occurred to her that until she was ready to wash her legs, she could sit in the pan with her knees raised. That would be more comfortable.

Esmeralda got up, emptied the water that had accumulated in the pan into the slop bucket, and sat down. It worked quite well, the sides being low enough not to cut into her thighs, but when she tried to rise to empty the water again, she found it very awkward. By now, however, she was feeling much better and she giggled happily as she tried to find a way to lever herself upright without tipping the pan. At which point the door flew open, and Robert said, "Merry—"

Shock deprived Esmeralda of voice and movement for the one second it took Robert to look around and see her. His eyes opened wide, his lips parted—and then he stepped in and shut the door behind him. Blushes dyed her face and throat scarlet and even reddened the upper portion of her chest. In contrast, her breasts were very white. She and Robert stared at each other for another moment in a silence that was less shocked than appreciative on Robert's part, and more calculating than embarrassed on Esmeralda's. Slowly she moved her hands, which had been braced against the floor, up toward her breasts as if to shield them.

Robert grinned. "It's too late now," he said cheerfully. "I've seen all there is to see—and very nice it is. Merry, you need a keeper. You didn't lock the door. *Anyone* could have walked in on you."

As he spoke, he reached out and turned the key, but his eyes were on his wife. Her color had started to fade and then intensified when he teased her, but after another short silence, she lifted her head defiantly, dropped one hand, and held the other out to him.

"I can't get up without spilling the water," she said with only the smallest tremor in her voice. "Will you help me?"

"With the greatest pleasure in the world," Robert replied, coming forward, but he did not take her hand; he bent and lifted her.

"Oh, you idiot!" Esmeralda exclaimed. "Now you've got your one clean coat all wet with soapy water."

"It is not in the proper mode to call your husband an idiot," Robert said gravely, and kissed her.

"It is not in the proper mode to intrude on a lady naked in her bath," Esmeralda retorted as soon as her lips were free. "You should have apologized and stepped out." She had, however, spoiled whatever effect the reprimand might have had before she delivered it by putting her arms around Robert's neck and responding enthusiastically to his kiss.

"But then the door would still be unlocked, leaving you at the mercy of less well accredited trespassers," he pointed out.

He bent his head to kiss Esmeralda again, but she recollected what she had just complained about and said, "Put me down, Robert, do, and let me sponge off your coat."

"Just as you are?"

He began to laugh so hard that he almost dropped her, and she slid to her feet.

"You said yourself that it was too late for modesty." She started to bend down to retrieve and rinse the sponge, but saw Robert move, and came upright. "Don't you dare pat my . . . my . . . me there," she warned.

"Perish the thought," Robert replied, widening his eyes into a look of angelic innocence. "Would I be so crude? Am I not a gentleman? Don't you like it?"

"Do I have to answer those questions?" Esmeralda giggled, sidling around the bath to a place where she could safely clean the sponge.

Having accomplished that, she advanced on Robert, holding the sponge out almost as if it were a white flag signaling a truce. He eyed her speculatively, a smile pulling at the corners of his lips, but he allowed her to clean off the front of his coat and sleeves without interference.

"Have you finished your bath?" he asked blandly when Esmeralda was satisfied that the coat would dry cleanly.

She hesitated, then said with a note of defiance, "No, I haven't. Why don't you take off your coat so it can dry?"

"Why don't I take off everything?" he suggested. "You cannot have washed your back yet. If I wash your back, will you wash mine?"

A flash of doubt crossed Esmeralda's face, and she half turned away, color rising in her cheeks again.

"Merry," he said softly, "I know you are a good, innocent woman. Don't be afraid to be playful. But if you will be made uncomfortable by my nakedness, I will not force you—"

"Oh, no," she murmured. "I am only afraid of passing the line of what is pleasing. I am so very ignorant."

"There is no line," Robert said firmly. "Anything that gives us both pleasure in private is right and proper—so long as it is kept private."

Esmeralda lifted her eyes to his, smiling wryly. "My good sense tells me that such a warning implies we are already beyond the line."

Robert's grip on her tightened, and he drew her closer. "Who knows?" he remarked. "But I doubt we are the only couple who has ever shared a bath."

"If we share this one, it will be by miraculous intervention." Esmeralda laughed, looking at the pan in which she had barely fit, and then said hastily, "No, Robert. If you pull me against you, I will have to sponge your coat again."

"You are right," he admitted, promptly letting her go. "And that will only waste time. Besides, it will be much more fun to kiss you when we are both soapy."

"I am sure this is wrong," Esmeralda said in a small voice, watching him tug off his coat. He laughed aloud, raking her with his eyes. "You are growing more and more outrageous," she complained, but bubbles of joy were exploding inside her. "Robert, really, when you think of this tomorrow, will you not also think I should have checked you and put on some clothes?"

"Before you finish your bath?" He had his shirt off and kicked off his pumps as he unbuttoned his pantaloons. "No, you ninny. When I think of this tomorrow, I will be trying to discover something still more outrageous to make you blush. You are very pretty when you blush, Merry. It makes your eyes shine."

He began to push off pantaloons and smalls at the same time and had his wish, for Esmeralda blushed hotly again. Not knowing what else to do, she knelt and emptied the dirty water from the pan. When she looked up, he was standing very close, and her eyes widened in astonishment. Before she could move, he knelt beside her and took her in his arms.

"Do I frighten you, Merry?" he asked gently.

"I don't know," she whispered. "It—it seems impossible, but I know—"

"I was drunk last night," he said. "I'll be more careful. Don't think about that now. Let me wash your back."

But it was more than her back he attended to, and it was not only the sponge he ran over her body. And he took her place in the pan and urged her to wash him, allowing her to grow accustomed to handling him. She grew bolder slowly, finding his sighs and wordless exclamations as exciting as the caresses he lavished on her even while she bathed him.

Like most other young men of his class, Robert had read a fair amount of erotic literature. In fact, it was the only reading, aside from military history and theory, that he did voluntarily. His physical experience, however, was limited mostly to camp followers, upon whom he wasted no time. Both parties, in fact, were concerned more with the speed and completion of the act than with elegance or technique.

During periods in England, Robert had tried one or another high-class courtesan, but those experiences, although much pleasanter, had been blurred by the intake of far too much wine. The fact that he had been so drunk also obscured the details of his previous night's lovemaking. Actually, this time with Merry was Robert's first experience with a gentlewoman when he was stone-cold sober. He had never enjoyed anything so much in his life and was quite determined to discover whether the rapturous litanies in the books he had read could be reproduced by putting into practice the techniques described.

Esmeralda was only too ready to assist him in this laudable purpose. She had come to the conclusion that she had already offered enough protests to prove her maidenly modesty. She thus put away all doubts, determined as she had been from the first to enjoy every

moment of what had been an impossible dream and, nonetheless, had
come true.

The light was failing by the time they got around to drying each
other off. The water had long since cooled to room temperature, but
neither of them noticed. Robert carried Esmeralda to the bed then and
lay down beside her. Both were nearly ready, owing to the lingering
caresses they had mingled with the more practical activities of
washing and drying each other, and there was a special delight in the
sweet, clean smell and taste of each other's fresh body.

Innocent and curious, Esmeralda copied every movement of
arousal Robert practiced on her. He was so perfectly beautiful to her
that there was no part of him she was unwilling to caress with fingers,
lips, and tongue. His disjointed remarks were somewhat puzzling to
her at first, for he would sigh, "Oh, my God, how wonderful," and
then, almost instantly, "No, don't." And when, obediently, Esmeralda paused, he would whisper, "Please, please, again." She understood later, however, when he groaned, "Stop, Merry, stop. I'll go too
fast, and I'll hurt you."

But by that time, Esmeralda did not think anything could hurt her.
And, in fact, when Robert finally mounted and entered, the pain of
stretching only seemed to excite her more. She thrust and writhed
against him, impelled by age-old instinct, for she no longer really had
any conscious thought; her body independently sought a satisfaction
she did not know existed. It came in explosive spasms of pleasure that
wrung moans and near shrieks from her.

Her frantic movements had surprised Robert. By and large, the
army whores lay still, unwilling to waste unnecessary energy. The
courtesans had, of course, simulated pleasure—or may really have
felt it, since Robert was a dish that did not come often to a paid
companion's table—but they had complete control. Merry's total
abandonment was new to him and, coupled with the long foreplay,
brought him in moments to an unthinking state of instinctive drive
toward climax in which the convulsive spasms of her body completed
his act as well as hers.

Robert, more accustomed to the results of sexual activity, recovered
first, although this particular experience exceeded any in his memory.
Faint tremors still ran from his groin through his abdomen and down
his thighs, but he became aware of Merry gasping for breath under

him and he tried to lever himself up to relieve the pressure on her, only
to discover that his arms were shaking and weak as reeds.

"Good Lord," he said softly, and then, with a shock, he associated
the sounds that had rung in his ears during his climax with his wife.
"Merry," he whispered urgently, "Merry, are you all right?"

"It's hard to breathe," she said faintly.

A second, more determined attempt to raise himself succeeded, and
Robert tilted sideways. "God in heaven," he mumbled, "I was right
out of my head. I didn't even realize you were screaming. What—"

"I wasn't screaming," she interrupted. "At least . . . I guess I
was, but . . . but not because . . ." She hesitated again, and then
said quickly, "You didn't hurt me, Robert. I liked it."

He did not respond at once, lying quietly and thinking over the
experience. The first thing that came into his head was that a man was
a fool to bother with whores when a wife could provide more
pleasure. Then he laughed softly. *His* wife did because he had the
good sense to tell her not to be afraid to be playful. The thought
brought a rich sense of satisfaction, and he sighed and stretched.

"You aren't displeased?"

That ridiculous question made him open his eyes, which had been
closing. "Displeased?" he repeated in a bemused voice.

"I thought perhaps my—my exclamations had disturbed you."

Robert began to laugh. "I don't think a full cannonade could have
disturbed me." He slid an arm under her neck and drew her close.

"I am very glad to hear it," Esmeralda said, resting her head
comfortably on his shoulder, "because I don't think I could have
refrained. I mean, I had no idea I was going to make all that noise.
Perhaps you should have warned me."

"*I* should have warned you. How the devil was I to know you
would screech like a banshee?" He was amused, but after a moment
he remembered Merry's habit of smoothing everything over and he
asked rather anxiously, "Why did you cry out like that, Merry? I
thought I had hurt you again, but you said not. Was that only for my
sake?"

"Oh, no. No. It was . . . I don't think I *can* explain. I never
knew a person could feel so . . . so much. But . . . but it was
perfectly splendid!"

Anxiety was dissipated into a pleasant sense of pride. Robert
yawned, tensed, and then relaxed his legs, which were coming back

to normal but still felt limp and heavy. His whole body was deliciously languorous, and the air coming in the open window was just cool enough to make Esmeralda's warmth against him an added pleasure. His eyes closed again. He felt the movement of the jaw and the deep intake of breath that indicated Merry was also yawning.

"But I think," she continued in a very drowsy voice, "that you had better put your hand over my mouth next time. After all, we would not want everyone to think you were murdering me."

Robert chuckled softly. Those two words "next time" fell very pleasantly on his ears. "I will," he promised, his voice showing he was smiling, "that is, if I'm in any state to remember at the moment." But he did not really care whether the whole world heard her. He was not in the least ashamed of making his wife sing out in pleasure. And, as he dropped off to sleep with the sound of Esmeralda's deep breathing near his ear, there was probably not a happier man in the entire world.

The morning brought no diminution of cheerfulness. Robert found washing, dressing, and shaving much pleasanter now that he did not have to hurry for fear of embarrassing Merry. In the past, he had sometimes sensed her attention and wondered if he was offending her. There could be no doubt now. They went down to have breakfast together in the kitchen, laughing when Esmeralda again asked Robert to bring water and warned him against spilling it.

"No fear," he had replied. "I'm not distracted now by wondering whether you are putting me off."

"Oh, no," she said lightly. "I shall be a model wife."

She meant it more sincerely than Robert could know, but the words reminded her that she still had not confessed her adventure at Roliça and that Robert would be sure to hear of it from M'Guire. It was the very worst time to tell him, too, she thought, with transport ships right offshore. If her adventure convinced him that she would be safer in England, she could be packed off onto a transport ship within hours. She could not bear the thought of losing the precious joy that Robert's body could bring her for months or even years.

When he returned, she glanced at him sidelong, nervously, as she put the food on the table. At first, Robert was fully occupied with his meal, but he had grown sensitive to Esmeralda's moods. Something pricked at him; still, he had almost finished eating before he suddenly pinpointed what was bothering him and put down his cup.

"What's wrong with you?" he asked.

"I have a spyglass," Esmeralda burst out desperately.

Robert blinked. The remark was so far out of any context with which he could relate that it almost seemed his wife had lost her mind. "What?"

His unbelieving question brought forth a tumbled story in which Dom Aleixo and the spyglass seemed to have exerted some mysterious influence that induced a French soldier to climb up the tower of San Mahmed church to steal Boa Viagem because Esmeralda had not been able to see the battle from the house on the hillside in Amiais. Robert sat listening with eyes wide open and a dropped jaw.

"But there really wasn't any danger because Carlos was there, on Luisa, you know, and he killed him because he didn't understand that I was really riding away. And I will never, never do it again, I promise. Indeed, I promise most faithfully, even though Dom Aleixo wouldn't take the spyglass back."

"But I saw Carlos when I left my horse in the stable yesterday afternoon." Robert sounded confused, and his eyes were slightly glazed.

"Oh, Carlos will never do it again, either. It was only because I had screamed, you see, not because I was in any danger, but only to frighten Boa Viagem."

Robert closed his eyes for a moment. He had heard his mother and sisters offer similarly incomprehensible explanations to his irate father. Robert knew that he was being led up the primrose path. The question was whether it was worthwhile to spend the time and effort to untangle the real facts. He opened his eyes.

"Just tell me how you got Boa Viagem down from the church tower by screaming," he asked blandly.

Now it was Esmeralda's turn to look stunned. "How I got what?"

"Never mind," Robert said. "I only wanted you to know that I may not have understood what you said, but I am not such a fool as to be led around by the nose." It had occurred to him that the mention of Carlos gave him an easier source for discovering the truth. He pushed back his chair.

"I promise I will never be so foolish again," Esmeralda vowed desperately. "Don't send me to England, Robert."

A slow smile curved his lips. "No," he said, "I won't do that. Not unless we get into serious trouble here."

Chapter 21

There was, however, no news of any threat from the French, nor was it Carlos who explained Esmeralda's adventure to Robert. Carlos had remembered Robert's remarks with regard to the cutting of French soldiers' throats, and he was keeping out of his master's way. Robert got what details he could from M'Guire, which was just as well because the big Irishman was not inclined to give much credence to what he thought were a young and excitable foreigner's exaggerations. As told by M'Guire, Mrs. Moreton had been startled by a wounded French straggler, had screamed, frightening her horse, which had carried her out of the Frenchman's power. But Carlos had heard her screaming and had rushed to the rescue, acting to save his mistress before thinking.

Of course, Robert was not pleased by Esmeralda's carelessness in riding around in a war zone, but she had already expressed contrition and promised not to act so foolishly again. Nor could he say much to Carlos, since he was caught between needing to praise the boy for risking his own neck to protect his mistress and blaming him for going too far. It was best, Robert thought, to allow the incident to slip away unremarked.

He had enough to keep him busy through the day, too. It was no easier to disembark Anstruther's men than it had been to get the troops ashore at Figueira. The surf on the beaches was tremendous, and the slope of the land into the sea made the water too shallow to allow the ships in close. Despite the best efforts of the landing parties, several boats were overturned, and supplies and lives were lost. Having investigated the slow and arduous process of the landing, Sir Arthur sent a party to the tiny village at the mouth of the river, saying, "Moreton, anything called Porto should have ships—or, at least, boats—and a way to get the boats ashore. See if you can get the people down there to show you.''

Robert's Portuguese was much improved, but there were still gaps in his vocabulary. Up until now, he had been concerned with draft animals, supplies, and questions about numbers of men and guns of the enemy. Ports, ships, and the maneuvering of such vessels were out of his range. He struggled for a little while, meeting unexpected opposition for so innocent a request. He suspected from the villagers' apprehensive expressions that there was some basic misunderstanding. Then he remembered that Merry had said something about the villagers with whom she had lived being fishermen and that she might have the right vocabulary as well as being more fluent in the language.

Robert considered briefly whether it was correct to bring a woman into a military matter and decided quickly that it would be far better to involve Merry, who knew how to hold her tongue, than to spend all day arguing with people, only to discover they did not understand what it was he wanted. And, indeed, when Merry arrived, Robert found that he had somehow implied that he wanted to take the boats of the local residents to sea. Once Robert's real intention was clarified, he had no further difficulty. There was a passage at the mouth of the little river, but whether it was suitable for Sir Arthur's purpose remained to be seen.

Having served her purpose, Esmeralda, with characteristic good sense, promptly said polite farewells and was escorted home. She and Robert had exchanged no more words than those necessary and only one glance that was not directly associated with the business in hand. Nonetheless, Esmeralda returned to her lodgings in the best of spirits. Her adventure in Roliça was a dead issue, and her usefulness had again been proven.

More secure than she had ever been, Esmeralda decided that the moment had come to announce her father's death, her marriage, and her temporary residence in Portugal to her bankers. She went out into the village and purchased paper, pen, and ink. And in the same shop, which seemed to carry everything, she was delighted to find a thin muslin in a delicate shade of pink that she felt would be most satisfactory for a nightgown—an item of attire about which she had not previously worried but which now seemed very necessary.

Instead of writing the letter to her bankers, Esmeralda spent the entire day cutting out and sewing up her new nightgown, but she got very little use out of it because she barely put it on before it was off again. She did not find this any source for complaint. She was, in fact, much flattered by Robert's lazy remark, after they had made love, that she was a source of naughty inspiration because he didn't usually . . . His sentence was oddly truncated, as if he had been about to say something more and had decided it would be unwise, but Esmeralda was able to finish it herself quite easily.

The next day she did write her letter, but she had no opportunity to give it to Robert. The convoy carrying Acland's brigade had arrived; however, it was late afternoon before the ships were brought inshore, and the disembarkation went on until it was too dark to see. Most of the men did get ashore and were left to sleep on the beach, but when Robert came up to their room it was very late, and he was in a white-lipped rage.

Esmeralda had been sitting by the table, mending one of Robert's shirts by the light of the lamp. She jumped to her feet when her husband slammed the door shut and, seeing his face, cried, "Oh, heaven, what is wrong?"

"Sir Arthur's been superseded. That—that dotard Burrard is here, in the *Brazen*."

"How dreadful!" Esmeralda exclaimed. "Has he already upset Sir Arthur's plans?"

"No." Robert's lips curled in a nasty sneer, but then he sighed. "I'd almost have preferred it if he had. Sir Arthur went out to greet him, and—you won't believe this—Burrard wouldn't even come ashore to look over the land and the disposition of the troops."

"But, Robert, perhaps that is a good sign. Perhaps it means that he trusts Sir Arthur and will not interfere."

"Don't you believe it." Robert's voice shook slightly with rage. "All it means is that he's too damned lazy. He's like all those blasted Guardsmen, the Duke of York's pets. Burrard calls Sir Arthur a sepoy general and looks down his nose at him, but Burrard's never commanded more than a brigade—no, a division it was, at Copenhagen, and he didn't do a thing. Sir Arthur was the only one who was in action."

Esmeralda bit her lip. "Did he give any indication of what he plans to do?"

"Plans to do?" Robert's voice scaled upward. "Burrard hasn't got a plan in his head. That old dotard didn't even want to listen to Sir

Arthur's report. There's plenty of time, he says. Sure there's plenty of time. Time to let the French bring in reinforcements from all over Portugal. If it's up to Burrard, we'll sit here until Boney gets back from wherever the devil he is—Austria, I think—and brings the whole damned Grande Armée down on us."

"No," Esmeralda said, "I meant Sir Arthur. Will he stay and serve under Burrard?"

Robert sighed and shook his head. "I don't know. This has hit him hard. He knew, of course. Somerset told us in Figueira that Sir Arthur had been informed he would be superseded. But I know he's been hoping that we would have the French out of Portugal before Sir Harry got his orders."

His voice was now more tired and discouraged than furious. Esmeralda put down the shirt she had unconsciously been clutching. "Come, sit down," she said. "I'll get you a glass of wine. Would you like something to eat?"

He came across the room and dropped heavily into the chair Esmeralda had pulled out invitingly. "No, nothing to eat." He smiled wryly. "Sir Arthur's damned old boots are still sitting pretty heavily in my stomach, but I'll take that wine. Sometimes he's a devil to serve under. I've never eaten such awful food, and the wine's nearly as bad. We were just talking the other day about how we could convince him to let Burghersh buy his wine." The smile died. "It's so cursed unfair."

"But Sir Arthur did have a victory against Delaborde. Perhaps if Sir Harry doesn't act, Lord Castlereagh can use that to make the Horse Guards put Sir Arthur back in command," Esmeralda suggested hopefully.

Robert sipped the wine. "The trouble is that it would probably be too late. Junot's not going to let us sit here enjoying the lovely countryside. I know Sir Arthur planned to move tomorrow and attack, maybe to clean out Peniche so we'd have a decent landing site or maybe move right on Lisbon while Junot isn't ready for us. But if Burrard waits for the additional division coming with Sir John Moore—which was the only thing he said that had the slightest military significance—the chances are that the French can collect a big enough army to overwhelm us."

He had been staring into nothing as he spoke, and Esmeralda could not think of anything to say that would comfort him. Gently she put a hand on his shoulder, almost expecting him to shrug it off angrily. Instead he tossed off the wine and then looked up at her. "My gracious silence. Come, let's go to bed and seek our comfort there."

It seemed to Esmeralda that she had barely closed her eyes when there was a pounding on the door. Before she had even struggled to a sitting position, pulling up the blanket hastily to cover her bare breasts, Robert was at the door and had it open a little way. The voice from the other side of the door was too low for Esmeralda to make out the words spoken, but Robert exclaimed, "Good God, what luck! Yes, I'll be there in five minutes."

He did not bother to turn up the lamp, since the dim light was enough for him to see his clothing—neatly and properly laid out this time. As he dressed, he said to Esmeralda, "Junot's on his way. I told you God was on our side. Nothing could be better. Burrard can't tell us not to fight if we're attacked, and Sir Arthur will have the troops all set so Sir Harry can't make a mess of that. If Sir Arthur had a grain of sense, he wouldn't even send a message. Like as not, that old dotard will come ashore at the last minute and take the credit for winning the battle."

Esmeralda started to get out of the bed, and Robert shook his head at her. "Don't get up," he said. "I have no time for breakfast now—don't want it, anyway. Go back to sleep. Nothing will happen for hours and hours." He shrugged into his coat, grabbed his hat, and strode toward the door, where he stopped suddenly and came back to kiss Esmeralda quickly. "I'll try to stop in around six to have a cup of tea with you if I can. If not, don't let it worry you."

Although she wanted desperately to beg Robert to be careful, Esmeralda knew that if she opened her mouth she would burst into tears. That would never do. She knew how much he disliked wailing women. If he thought she was going to make a scene before every battle, he might change his mind about not sending her to England. He had reached the door again and opened it, but he paused and turned around sharply.

"You may use your damned spyglass," he said severely. "In fact, the church tower would not be a bad place to be while the battle is going on—unless they start to shell the village, in which case you come down out of there at once, understand? But if I discover that you have left the village and gone wandering around the country-side . . ."

Still speechless, Esmeralda shook her head emphatically. Robert
eyed her for another moment and then went out. She sat perfectly still,
fighting fear, afraid to cry lest Robert had forgotten something and
returned. But the fear this time was not a panic that threatened to
choke her. She remained innocently convinced that Robert would not
be personally involved in the fighting. Still, as far as Esmeralda was
concerned, it was dangerous enough that he should be out in the open;
there might be stray bullets flying about or stragglers like the one who
had threatened her.

She could not sleep, of course, but after a time she lay down
obediently to wait for the sun to rise. Then it would be time to make
tea and sit in the kitchen to wait again until Robert came—if he came.
Esmeralda both eagerly desired and dreaded his coming. He might not
have thought it odd that she did not speak during the short time it took
him to dress. She hoped she had seemed half-asleep. But it would be
different later. She would have to speak, to seem cheerful.

This task turned out to be easier than Esmeralda had expected. She
went down to the kitchen at half after five, just in case Robert should
come early, and was greeted with cries of delight from several of the
other ADCs staying in the house. They did like her, of course, but
Esmeralda knew that their joy at her presence was owing to the fact
that she would slice bread and cheese, brew tea, provide cold meat if
there was any, and in general save them from the onerous task of
feeding themselves. Despite this casual commandeering of her
services, Esmeralda was as delighted to see them as they were to see
her. While his friends were there, doubtless Robert would address his
remarks to them and she could hide her terrors behind the teapot.

Actually, it was hard to continue to be frightened in the face of the
tearing high spirits of the young men. They laughed and joked, and
Robert was equally animated when he arrived. No one seemed to
doubt that they would be victorious, and all seemed almost tearfully
grateful to Junot for attacking them, calling him the best of good
fellows to arrive when he was most wanted. Each time a new person
came in, everyone jumped up asking eagerly, "Are the French in
sight?"

The last arrival was Lord Fitzroy, and as soon as he appeared in the
doorway, cups were set down with a clatter, food dropped, and hats
and whips were grabbed up. "Sit. Sit," he said, grinning broadly as a
groan went up. "Just came by for a handout. Be a while yet before

Johnny Crapaud gets here. They're down by the bridge near Villa Facaia having a nice sit down and some breakfast."

"Well, I wish they'd get a move on," Colin Campbell said fretfully. "It's getting late."

"What do you mean, late?" Burghersh asked. "It's true the Beau ordered the troops into position an hour before sunrise, but they aren't standing to attention or anything. Our men are probably having something to eat, too. You don't think the waiting will put them in a pucker, do you?"

"It's nothing to do with the men," Campbell replied. "They're all right. But Burrard's likely to wake up sooner or later and decide to come ashore."

There was an appalled silence. In the excitement of delivering orders and seeing the battle lines drawn up, everyone had forgotten Burrard.

"He can't stop the action now," Williams pointed out. "Even if he wanted to retreat, there isn't anywhere to retreat to."

"That's true enough," Robert agreed. "But there's always the chance that he'll take it into his head to run the battle himself. And it would be a shame if Sir Arthur lost the credit."

"He wouldn't do that, would he?" Burghersh asked, looking at the more experienced of the ADCs.

Robert shrugged, but Williams shook his head slowly. "I don't think so," he said. "Sir Harry is really a pleasant and good-natured person."

Nonetheless, the reminder of Burrard's right to interfere put a damper on the breakfast party, and a few minutes later there was a general movement toward departure. Robert lingered just a half step behind as if he intended to say something to Esmeralda in private, but his name was called and he did no more than wave at her gaily as he went out. Esmeralda found that she was having difficulty in believing in the reality of this battle. Was it possible that soon men would be maimed and die, and that what worried Robert and his friends was whether or not Sir Harry Burrard would undeservedly take credit for Sir Arthur's work?

The anxious ADCs were relieved to find no sign or message from Burrard. Nor had any come when Sir Arthur had word that a dust cloud had been sighted coming along the Tôrres Vedras road. It was nearly nine o'clock by then, and everyone breathed a sigh of relief,

having begun to fear that possibly Junot had heard of the landing of
four thousand additional troops and had decided not to attack. After a
quick personal inspection of the broad front of men, indistinctly
visible among the woods and rolling uplands, Sir Arthur rode out to
check on his troop dispositions.

Vimeiro village lay in a small valley created by the river Maceira,
surrounded by a range of hills, particularly steep and formidable
toward the south, and it was from the south that Sir Arthur expected to
be attacked. He had stationed the brigades of Hill, Bowes, Caitlin
Crawfurd, Nightingale, and Acland, with eight of his few guns, on
the ridges of the southern range.

Just in front of the village was an isolated hill, partly covered by
vineyards and thickets, which would provide excellent cover for
defenders. Fane and Anstruther held that as the first line, with six
guns. Ferguson and Trant were behind Vimeiro on the lower heights
to the north, ready to serve as a reserve to Fane and Anstruther. The
tiny cavalry—240 English and 260 Portuguese—waited on the banks
of the river.

Having assured himself that all was in order, Sir Arthur returned to
the hill in front of Vimeiro and watched the approach of the great
French column. He expected to see the head of it swerve left and
move along the valley of the Maceira, but it did not do so, continuing
on north completely past the heavily defended right wing on the
southern ridge. He watched quite calmly, waiting to make certain that
this was not a feint. Two of Junot's brigades began to deploy just in
front of Fane and Anstruther, but away to the north the cavalry
advance guard was still riding, and it was obvious that infantry was
following them.

"I see that General Junot has decided to leave the southern heights
alone," Sir Arthur said. "Well, well, I had been led to believe he had
more dash, but it appears he intends to throw most of his weight at us
here."

He swept his glass around the area to be quite sure his right wing
was safe, then drew out his notepaper and unstoppered the inkhorn.
When he had written his messages, he took another look around. The
sound of rifle fire was drifting up toward them, as the small pickets
Fane had stationed a mile forward of his position were driven back
toward the main lines. The French were forming a line of battle with
its southern end opposite Wellesley's center.

"Captain Williams, will you please take this to General Ferguson? Tell him to make all haste to the heights behind Ventosa, avoiding notice if he can. It would be nice to provide the French with a little surprise. Also, please tell General Ferguson that Generals Nightingale and Bowes will follow to support him as quickly as they can, and Colonel Crawfurd will be near Mariquiteira to protect his left."

Sir Arthur then passed out notes and messages to the other officers involved in the shifting of the battle line. Robert was sent to General Acland, who was to act as reserve to General Ferguson and the others. "Also," Sir Arthur said, smiling, "pass my apologies to General Hill. He will likely have a very dull time of it, but I cannot leave the right flank completely unprotected, and, after all, he and his men had the liveliest sport during the engagement at Roliça."

By the time Robert returned, the action had started in earnest. The usual thick line of French *tirailleurs*, or sharpshooters, were advancing up the hill with about four battalion columns close in their rear. But the *tirailleurs* were not sniping easily at massed British troops. The riflemen of the Sixtieth and Ninety-fifth were taking a toll as they retreated. Behind, on the slope of the hill but hidden by a convenient dip of the ground, the Fifty-second and Ninety-seventh waited in line, well covered by the full-leafed vines of the vineyards. As the Riflemen melted in among their comrades, the six guns on the crest roared in a fierce volley.

Robert saw Sir Arthur stiffen to attention, and he did so, too. Those guns were loaded with an experimental type of cannon shot invented by Major Shrapnel. Instead of being solid, this was a shell packed with smaller, individual shot. The theory was that having been fired, the shell would burst and spray the individual shot over a wide area. For once, theory actually worked in practice: Major Shrapnel's shell worked like a charm—or, rather, like a blast out of hell.

The advancing troops, already shaken by the murderous cannon volley, were then charged by the British line, the Ninety-seventh meeting them head on and the Fifty-second taking them in the flank. Sure and determined, the British held their fire until they were little more than ten paces from the French, who were somewhat disordered, and then released a smashing discharge that almost literally blew away the front ranks of the opposing regiments. Those still able to move recoiled amid the screams and moans of their comrades.

Another volley from the second line penetrated deeper into the column, which broke apart and retreated pell-mell down the hill.

This time when the drums beat out the orders, the British halted their pursuit and formed up again, only cheering when the word was passed that they had not only beat off the first attack but had captured seven of Junot's guns. Sir Arthur smiled, and there was warmth in his piercing blue eyes.

"They will make good soldiers," he said to General Fane, who had just given the order to send the Fiftieth and the reserve Riflemen down upon another regiment.

There was a breathing space while the remnants of the shaken French regiments were rallied outside of musket range and two battalions of grenadiers from the reserve were sent ahead of them up the hill for a second assault. The British guns came into play at once and fired regularly. Changing tactics, the French launched a narrow attack, intended to break through the British line and spread out behind them, but the attempt was a disastrous failure, for the compact formation was blown to pieces by Shrapnel's shells and the converging fire of the Fifty-second and Ninety-seventh.

With determined courage, the French reserves managed to struggle halfway up the hill, but they could not withstand the intense fire, and they retreated. The British pursued, but with caution, keeping in contact so that they could present an adequate front to any new counterattack, and the battle rolled down into the little pinewood at the base of the hill. It was apparent, even through the screen of the trees and brush, that the French could not rally.

At this point, it seemed that Junot decided not to send the remainder of his reserve into this conflict and attempt to push the British back. He had apparently despaired of taking the hill by frontal assault. He threw in his last reserves in an attempt to turn the flank of Fane's brigade and penetrate to the village of Vimeiro.

When the direction of the third attack became clear, Robert's hands tightened on the reins of his horse so that Jupiter backed and fidgeted. Although he had been in personal danger many times during his army career, Robert had never been frightened. He knew, in an intellectual way, that he could be wounded or killed, but the possibility was never real to him.

Now, for the first time in his life, Robert was terrified. There were no units directly in the path of the French thrust, and he broke into a cold sweat, imagining the infuriated troops charging into Vimeiro, breaking open houses, looting, seizing Merry. . . . He opened his mouth to say he must go to protect his wife, but it seemed as if his throat was frozen shut, his lips and tongue paralyzed. Before he could make a sound, an ADC was already galloping headlong toward General Anstruther's position and Sir Arthur himself had moved away, riding quickly toward an area from which he could observe the action.

Robert threaded his horse through the other officers surrounding the general. "Sir Arthur—" he began.

"Take this to General Acland," Wellesley said, handing him a note, as if he had not heard—and perhaps he had not, for there was still considerable noise. "He is to attack the left flank of the French. Anstruther will be taking them on the right."

Although Robert's heart was still pounding so hard he could feel the vibrations in his throat, he had enough common sense to know that the best way to protect Merry was to prevent the French from getting into Vimeiro at all. The fact that Sir Arthur had immediately planned the most efficient troop movements to accomplish that purpose and was already giving orders to start the counterattack further helped to steady Robert.

The trouble was that he could not believe there was enough time. He was afraid that by the time he got to Acland and the general set his men into action, some of the grenadiers would have been able to pass around behind the men holding off Anstruther's counterattack and reach the village. He would save half a mile by riding across in front of Vimeiro. Of course, he would be riding right across the front of the oncoming French troops also, and if he were shot down, Sir Arthur's orders would not arrive at all.

Robert was an experienced soldier. Under normal conditions, he would have known that the likelihood of what he was envisioning was nil and that the time saved by cutting half a mile's travel on a fast horse could have no effect. But fear does very odd things to the mind. At the moment, every second seemed like a very long time, a period in which French troops could cover great distances and perpetrate unspeakable crimes. When Robert's mount reached the easy slope of the base of the hill, he did not turn left toward the river to go around behind the sheltering buildings of Vimeiro but charged straight forward.

When he reached the Tôrres Vedras road he saw the main body of
French troops in the distance, coming into the small valley along one
tributary of the Maceira. They were too far away to be any danger to
him, but Robert knew there must be skirmishers preceding the
columns. The first shot rang out simultaneously with his though   he
crossed the road, and then another.

Robert used his whip to inspire the last ounce of speed of which
Jupiter was capable and then drew his pistol. He did not really expect
to be able to use it. He hoped the skirmishers would be too far away
for accuracy with a pistol, and he had no intention of wasting shot and
powder in a vain effort to discourage their advance. Experienced
soldiers would pay no more mind to pistol shots from a galloping
horse than to flies. There was a small chance, however, that a few men
would be close enough to pop up and try to stop him. The pistol would
be useful for that.

Several more single shots rang out. One was close. The bullet
buzzed by Robert's head like a bad-tempered bee, and he bent low,
close to his horse's body, to present a smaller target. Just then several
guns exploded together, very near. Jupiter screamed, gave a huge
convulsive leap ahead, and crumpled forward. Robert yelled, too, but
with fury and chagrin rather than from pain. Nonetheless, his feet
were free of the stirrups as the animal fell—it was not the first time he
had had a mount shot under him—and he rolled away as the horse
dropped.

There was a moment, as his legs tangled in the scabbard of his
saber, when he almost despaired, for one arm was under him and the
other hand carefully holding the pistol away so that if it went off, he
would not shoot himself. He rolled again, closer to the kicking,
screaming horse, working his legs to push the scabbard out of the way
and praying that Jupiter would not get him in the head or break any
bones. His luck in war held, and he found himself free and unhurt in
the next instant.

His first shot was into the head of the horse. Even if the skirmishers
were atop him, he could not allow Jupiter to suffer. But actually he
was reasonably sure that the French were at least fifty yards away.
Now the still body was also a defense, and he knelt up a little, looking
out warily as he worked the reload mechanism on the Ellis repeater.

He was only just in time, for he had been wrong about the distance
between him and the French soldiers. Three men were rising out of

the brush hardly more than twenty paces away. Robert did not know whether they had seen the pistol in his hand and waited for him to fire, thinking he would not have time to reload and thus would be little threat to them, or whether they had only delayed to reload their own guns. He grinned, not caring which mistake they had made. Either was equally fatal.

Aiming carefully, Robert fired and grinned again as one of the oncoming Frenchmen went down and the others uttered surprised cries. Robert ducked behind the horse's body once more to reload, this time with greater care. The Ellis repeater had a tendency to jam. But a single-shot pistol would have left him helpless now, and the Ellis was more than accurate enough for his present purpose—if only the French had not taken fright and hidden themselves in the brush again.

In ten seconds the gun was safely loaded. Cautiously Robert raised himself high enough to see and breathed a sigh of relief. The two remaining men had come on boldly, either simply determined to stop him from delivering the orders they must know he was carrying or perhaps thinking that he had had two guns and had now expended both their charges. Another man went down, the force of the bullet at the close range carrying him backward. The other man fired as his comrade was hit, and Robert was twisted to the left as a blow struck his upper arm. He exclaimed, more in anger than in pain, and dropped down, snarling as he heard a triumphant cry from the remaining French soldier.

All that bothered Robert was the temporary numbing of his arm, which was interfering with his ability to reload. He knew pain would come soon and that the Frenchman was either fixing his bayonet or reloading his piece, but Robert's mind was on his own immediate problem. The shadow loomed over him just as the lever finally went home. Robert flung himself backward, flat on the ground, raised the pistol, and fired as the bayonet came down. The power of the striking bullet saved him, deflecting the soldier's aim so that the weapon plunged into the body of the horse instead of into Robert, which permitted Robert to jump to his feet, knock off the man's shako, and strike him brutally on the head with the pistol.

It was hardly necessary, but Robert had not realized the soldier was falling sideways rather than trying to pull his bayonet out of Jupiter. It was, in fact, the gun fixed into the animal by the bayonet that had kept the man upright for the few seconds it took Robert to strike the blow.

He went down with his victim but shook loose of the weight and came
to his feet again to dash toward the banks of the stream. Several shots
followed him. Fortunately, however, none of the Frenchmen farther
back had hurried his advance, and no one was close enough to fire at
point-blank range or to interfere personally. Robert could only assume
they had been sure he was finished when his horse went down and
three of their own men had advanced on him.

Once in the brush he was relatively safe from their bullets, and he
ran through it and into the stream as fast as he could, ignoring the pain
in his arm and the way the brambles tore his face and clothing. He was
bitterly aware of his stupidity. Instead of saving time, he had lost
double what it would have taken to ride the long way around. He was
so concentrated on his self-blame that he was scarcely aware of the
scratches or the increased pang in his arm when he tripped on the
pebbles and stones of the streambed and fell in the water—he only
gasped curses under his breath and struggled on.

The French had lost track of him in the brush so that he was
halfway through the stream before they began to shoot at him again.
His irregular movements as he slipped and slid on the unstable footing
of the streambed made him too difficult a target, and he stumbled up
the far bank and into the brush and small trees there without being hit
again. After that he was essentially out of danger. It was possible that
he would be pursued, but he did not think they could catch him. He
was out of sight of the skirmishers, and they could not know what
direction he would take.

Actually, the skirmishers had abandoned their interest in him once
he disappeared afoot on the opposite bank. Their business was with
any British force coming down the valley to oppose them. They did
not know of Acland's brigade a short distance to the north. But Robert
had no idea they had given up, and he struggled on northward,
keeping within the shelter he had found until he felt he must be just
below Acland's position. Then he came out of cover and began to
climb the rising ground—but there was no sign of the troops he had
expected to see.

Chapter 22

Esmeralda and Molly finished washing the dishes and setting the bedchamber to rights, and then there was nothing else to do. Although Robert had given her permission to watch the battle, Esmeralda really had no inclination to do so. Her previous experience had been very disappointing. Nonetheless, she did go to the church and climb to the tower since she could not bring herself to sit quietly sewing. This attempt to discover what was going on was futile because Vimeiro was behind and below the rising ground on which the troops were stationed. She could see nothing at all but the hillsides upon which only a few sheep and goats moved.

Exasperated, she returned to her lodging. There was nothing to do but sew, and Esmeralda decided to embark on an ambitious and difficult enterprise—a second riding dress. She had got as far as laying out the new cloth on the table when the first crash of gunfire came. Involuntarily she gasped and dropped her box of pins all over the floor. Molly, who had been holding one edge of the cloth, jumped also and turned her head in the direction of the sound as if she could stare through the walls.

"Whose guns . . ." Esmeralda faltered.

"Oors. 'Tis got t' be oors. It sounded s' close. Th' others'd be fainter, dooller."

Had Molly's voice been more certain, Esmeralda might have been more reassured. Without speaking again, both moved at once toward the door and out into the garden behind the house. They stood still, straining to hear, but the sounds had become confused—only a few sharp rifle cracks stood out from a general roar of musket fire, dulled and distorted by distance and the hill between them. After what seemed a very long time, the sounds seemed to die away.

Esmeralda turned eagerly to Molly. "Is it over?"

"No, ma'am. Only th' first charge. If we beat 'em bad enough, 'ey moight retreat, boot our men'll have t' follow."

This time there was not the uncertainty that Esmeralda had heard before, and, indeed, she herself was reasonably sure that the British army had had the best of it, because if the French had advanced, the noise would have approached them and it had not. They waited, but not for long. Realizing that their petrified vigil in the garden was useless, they returned to the task they had abandoned.

Esmeralda had finished picking up and setting her pins as markers for cutting the front of the skirt when the second phase of the battle began. She and Molly looked at each other and then toward the door, but there was no sense in going out into the garden again. They could hear the thunder of the big guns quite clearly enough from where they were. Esmeralda picked up the scissors, which she poised over the cloth. After a moment, she put them down again.

"I'll only spoil it, Molly," she said. "My hand is shaking too much."

The older woman smiled and held out her own hands, which were also trembling. "'Tis a shame," she said, "thit th' hoose is decent. Oi'd be glad o' some scrubbin', thit Oi would."

Esmeralda sighed. "I, too. I feel like running around and screaming—and much good that would do."

Molly looked surprised. "Doos it take ye thit way, too, ma'am? 'Tisn't thit Oi'm scared—'cept fer M'Guire a bit—Oi swear it. 'Tis jist thit Oi need t' *do* somethin'."

About to nod agreement, Esmeralda paused. There was a new sound, closer than the battle noises, and this one was approaching steadily. It took her a little while to identify it as the screech of cart wheels because other noises mingled with and obscured the regularity she had come to associate with the sound. Esmeralda started for the front door, but Molly caught her arm.

"'Tis no for ye, ma'am. Thit'll be th' wounded comin' in. Oh, 'tis too near we are. Had th' captain toime, he would've sint ye away, Oi'm sure."

"The wounded," Esmeralda repeated.

Now that the sounds were identified, she was able to pick out the groans and occasional screams that mingled with the screech of the cart wheels. She stood undecided for a time, unable to go back to a task that seemed so puerile in contrast to what was taking place, but afraid to thrust herself in where she might not be wanted. She did not think she would be sickened or made faint by the blood or mutilations. There had been accidents and injuries in her father's go-downs and even in the houses, and she had not been overset, only truly sorry and quite willing to help the doctor. There must be something she could do that would be more important than cutting out the skirt of a riding dress.

"Find out where they are taking the wounded," she said to Molly. "I am accustomed to nursing. My father was ill for a long time. I know how to give a drink or feed a person who cannot help himself. I could write letters for those who wish to say a last word to their loved ones."

Molly looked very doubtful, but the truth was that she was herself eager for an excuse to go to the hospital area, not so much to help— although she was willing to do what she could—but to see whether there were men of her husband's regiment there and whether any of them had seen or heard of him. She found the buildings that had been selected easily enough, and almost at once was hailed by a friend of M'Guire's with a gory but not fatal hole in his thigh, who told her that her husband had come through the first attack without a scratch.

Much cheered by this news, she went back for Esmeralda, who had sensibly wrapped a sheet, apron-style, around her delicate morning dress and collected paper, a stoppered inkhorn, and several pens, as well as a cup, bowl, and spoon into a small sack that she fastened around her waist. Thus armed, she followed Molly, trembling a little because she grew less and less sure of herself as she approached the hospital area. At first it was harder than she thought. Wounds made by bullets were far messier than those made by a misdirected knife or ax, and Esmeralda did feel sick; but there was a young man, hardly more than a boy, weeping, and she knelt down by him and murmured soothingly, and soon she was too busy to feel queasy at all.

When Robert came out into the open about halfway up the flank of the hill, he stared around, feeling that he had been caught in a nightmare. He had been very sure of Acland's position, having taken Sir Arthur's first order to move to him and carried back General Acland's reply. And even if Acland had been some distance off, a brigade of men cannot be confined to a small area. In any case,

Acland would have pickets out, and Robert now realized that he should have stumbled on one of those as soon as he came out of the brush. Nor could Acland have been attacked, beaten, and driven away; not only would the noise have been apparent during the action, but there would be dead and wounded lying about. But there was no one—no one at all.

Unbelieving, Robert labored higher up the hill, trying to convince himself that Acland's troops might be on the reverse side, hidden behind the crown of the rise. He did not believe it, but he was dazed and in pain, and it seemed to be his last hope. However, as he reached the summit, he heard the thud of artillery to the north and a low confused noise, which he knew must be a combination of musket fire and the screams of men. Robert sank down, panting. He was too late. Acland had been instructed to act as reserve to Ferguson and those supporting him on the left flank. He must have been needed and gone off, possibly even before Robert started.

It was little help to know that his own foolishness had not caused the disaster. The fortunes of war . . . Robert shuddered. Death or rape might be the fortunes of war for Merry. He started to rise, again nearly frantic with the desire to go to Vimeiro to protect her, but his knees gave way and even as he struggled to get up once more, he remembered his duty. He must get back to Sir Arthur at once and report Acland's movement. He gritted his teeth. Both duty and good sense dictated exactly the same action: return to Sir Arthur, who could order troops to fill in and play the part Acland was supposed to have played, possibly Fane's reserve could—no, they were already in action.

Robert fought back tears and levered himself to his feet. It would do no good to anyone for him to sit and weep. Sir Arthur would manage something; he always did. He started down the hill, staggering slightly, aware now not only of pain but of the fact that blood was running down his arm. That did not trouble him except for the fear that too much bleeding would weaken him, and speed was again essential. Yet if he ran, he would lose more blood. Crazily he thought of a line from Shakespeare: "A horse! A horse! My kingdom for a horse!"

The moment the idea came into his head, the instinct to protect Merry personally, which had been suppressed but not extinguished, made him think of Vimeiro. He could get a horse there, or if not, there was Luisa. And Vimeiro was not out of his way. The strength of hope flooded him, and he began to run, but a crash of musket fire made him drop to the ground and look around wildly. There was no one near him nor any sound of bullets humming or thudding into the ground. Robert sat up and listened to a second volley and then to the roar of cannon. A broad smile took the place of anxiety and fear in his expression, and he began to unwind his sash. There could be no mistaking those sounds nor the direction from which they came. General Acland had apparently seen the threat of the French thrust along the valley and had acted on his own to prevent an attack on Vimeiro.

With relief, Robert removed his coat and shirt and leisurely examined the damage to his upper arm. His shirt sleeve was soaked with blood, and there was an ugly gash in the flesh of his arm, but the injury obviously was not serious. His coat sleeve, however, was a total ruin, beyond repair, the whole back of it shredded apart where the bullet had blasted a path out.

Robert clicked his tongue wryly. His one good coat, aside from his regimentals, spoiled. Merry would have a fit. Well, perhaps she could patch it. He wound his sash as tightly as he could around his arm, slung shirt and coat over his good shoulder, and started for Vimeiro, where he knew he would find a surgeon to sew him up. As he walked, he laughed softly. His arm ached, but didn't hurt nearly as much as it had before he knew how slight the damage was, and he no longer felt particularly weak, either.

Having forded the little tributary of the Maceira, Robert paused and listened. He was now too far north to see the battle, which was around a bend and screened by trees and brush, but it did not seem to be moving either way. The French, he thought, were stout fellows to withstand the heavy fire pouring in on them from both flanks. They were good soldiers with great pride, but they would not break through now—not unless Junot had another brigade or two to push into the valley and attempt a three-pronged assault. Robert shook his head. Not after those two bloody attacks on Vimeiro hill and sending all those regiments north.

He wondered how the battle on the left flank was going and began to walk again more quickly, despite the discomfort of his wet boots. If he wanted news, he had better get back to Sir Arthur. Nonetheless, Robert made no attempt to cut the distance by angling south. In his present condition he had no intention of coming closer to the action

than necessary. His pistol was wet, and while afoot his saber was a
poor weapon to oppose either a gun or bayonet.

Robert came into Vimeiro by the back lanes, but it was a small
village and he had no difficulty finding the hospital buildings.
Stepping into the nearest, he stopped dead in the doorway and
watched as Esmeralda, with infinite gentleness and patience, dribbled
water into the mouth of a man whose jaw had been half shot away.
She was covered with blood, but her voice was steady as she
murmured comfortingly.

Swallowing back a bellow of outrage, which he knew would make
Esmeralda jump and hurt the wounded man, Robert waited until she
rose to her feet and then said sharply, "Merry, what the devil are you
doing here? I can't turn my back on you for a minute—"

She whirled to face him, her features illuminated by joy, which
changed to terror as she took in his appearance. Her tanned skin
turned pasty gray, her lips parted as if to scream, and her eyes began
to roll upward in their sockets.

"Merry!" Robert exclaimed, startled. He jumped forward, dropping his coat and shirt, grabbed at her, and held her against him with
his good arm. "It's all right, my dear. I didn't mean to sound so
angry."

She clung to him dizzily, reassured by the strength of his grip.
Then, reminding herself that a soldier's wife must not show such
faintheartedness, she pulled herself together and straightened up.
Still, she could not prevent herself from asking breathlessly, "What
happened to you? How badly are you hurt?"

Robert smiled and let her go. "Hardly at all. It's nothing but a
crease, and all my own fault, too." Then the smile disappeared, and
his clear blue eyes clouded. "Jupiter's dead. I stupidly rode right into
the enemy's forward scouting parties instead of going around behind
the village. I should have known that Acland was too canny to let the
French cut him off from the rest of our army—but I was so—"

He stopped abruptly, realizing that he could not tell Esmeralda it
was fear the French would break into Vimeiro and harm her that had
sent him, against his better judgment and his military experience,
across the face of the oncoming enemy battalions. He did not wish her
to feel guilty or frightened by the nearness of the fighting. His
decision was correct, but he had made it for the wrong reasons.
Esmeralda would, indeed, have been terrified, but only by the risk he

had run, for she was far less concerned with her own safety than with his.

"Oh, poor Jupiter," she cried, knowing that Robert felt much worse about the horse than his single statement betrayed.

Before she could say more, however, an orderly came up behind Robert, sidestepped him without looking, although he glanced at the blue coat Robert had dropped on the floor, and said, "Mrs. Moreton, there's a man who'd like you to write to his wife for him."

"But—" Esmeralda began to protest.

Still without a glance at Robert, the orderly continued, "I don't think the man has much time, and I wouldn't bother with a Frenchie—not if he's walking. He can wait."

Robert had to laugh at Esmeralda's affronted expression. He had now recovered from the shock of finding her employed in an activity that he could not imagine his mother or sisters undertaking and which he knew must frighten and disgust her. On second thought, he felt proud rather than horrified that she should be willing to subdue her own feelings in order to help the men who were fighting.

"This is not a Frenchman but my husband, Captain Moreton," Esmeralda had exclaimed.

The orderly turned sharply, looking rather frightened, but Robert laughed again. It was obvious to him, if not to Esmeralda, how the mistake had come about. The rags of his blue coat and stained white breeches could easily be mistaken for the ruins of a French uniform.

"That's all right," he said to the orderly, who was stammering apologies. "Just go and ask one of the surgeons if he'll stitch me up at once. I have to get back to duty."

The fright those words caused Esmeralda paralyzed her momentarily and prevented her from crying out in protest as the orderly hurried away. She felt dizzy again and stiffened to resist the sensation. Robert would not annul their marriage, but he could still insist that she be sent to England if he felt her to be an encumbrance. She swallowed hard and moistened her dry lips.

"You seem to have lost a lot of blood, Robert," she said, her voice flat and cold with the effort she was making to keep it from quavering into tearfulness. "Is it wise to go back to Sir Arthur?"

"Oh, most of the blood isn't mine," Robert said easily, but he was aware of the rigidity of Esmeralda's stance and the coldness of her tone. It was an odd contrast, both to the words of concern she had spoken and to the soft sympathy her voice had held when she had been talking to the wounded soldier. Robert wondered whether she was angry or simply indifferent, and then dismissed both notions as ridiculous. There was nothing for her to be angry about, and she could not be indifferent to his welfare; he was her passport to the social connections she needed in England.

That idea, clearly and suddenly stated in his mind, was so unpleasant—although it had been implicit in their relationship from the beginning—that Robert hastily urged Esmeralda to find the dying man who wanted a letter written at once.

"But I would rather wait until—" Esmeralda began.

"There's no need to wait," Robert said. "There isn't much wrong with me, and the orderly will be back. . . . See, there he is now. Go along, Merry, a dying man's last wish is more important than a scratch on the arm."

It was not, of course, more important to Esmeralda, not if the scratch was on Robert, but she was still too insecure about their relationship to oppose him in anything. She did not realize that Robert would have welcomed her insistence on remaining with him—or any other sign of affection. It had not entered Esmeralda's head that Robert could have fallen in love with her; that had not even been a part of her impossible dream. The most she had hoped for was that he would grow accustomed to her company and find it pleasant. And of course, Esmeralda knew that men could enjoy sexual intercourse with women for whom they had not the slightest regard.

In fact, Esmeralda associated Robert's urging her to go to the dying soldier with his own stated intention of returning to his duty. She believed Robert felt that, having taken on the task of assisting the wounded, she must perform it. Thus, she turned away in the direction from which the orderly had originally come without saying anything more. In a sense, it was a relief to go, because her struggle with tears was growing momentarily more difficult. Esmeralda had already become somewhat hardened to the dreadful sights around her, but the wounded men were not Robert. She was not at all sure she would have been able to maintain her composure had she actually seen her husband's torn flesh.

Once Robert could not see her face, Esmeralda allowed the tears she had been withholding to flood her eyes. The rigidity went out of her body, and sobs of fear rose in her throat. Blindly she hurried forward, afraid that by some mischance Robert would hear or notice that she was crying. Unfortunately, although his eyes followed her, all he perceived was the relaxation of her tension and a seeming eagerness to get away, which puzzled him very much and hurt him, too.

Like Esmeralda, Robert did not associate mere sexual pleasure with love and thus did not reason that, because she obviously enjoyed their physical relationship, Merry loved him. Actually, he had not yet even associated his own eagerness to be with her or his anxiety about her safety with the fact that he loved her. If he had been asked at that moment by someone he trusted implicitly whether he loved his wife, Robert would probably have answered no. He still thought of his marriage as an act of compassionate duty, although he would have admitted freely that it had turned out far better than he could have expected, and he felt no regret.

The orderly's voice drew Robert's attention from Esmeralda's hasty retreat. "What?" Robert said dully.

"Mr. Neale will attend to you right away if you will come with me, sir," the man repeated.

"Oh, yes," Robert replied, finally taking in what had been said to him, and feeling a sense of relief.

What a fool he was, he thought. Here he was blaming Merry for the unpleasant sinking feeling he was experiencing and thinking she was behaving in an unnatural way, when probably he was just trying to avoid contemplating his visit to the surgeon. This conclusion was so satisfactory that Robert's spirits rose at once. Strangely, he did not notice the contradiction, and by the time Adam Neale had finished sewing him up, Robert had convinced himself that there had not been anything at all unusual in Merry's manner. Nothing could be more reasonable than that she should hurry to write a letter for a dying man, particularly when he had twice told her to go.

Although the surgeon insisted Robert rest for a little while after he had sewn the wound, no time was lost as Mr. Neale permitted his patient to send one of the lightly wounded men to find him a horse. And he smiled when he advised Robert to keep his arm in the sling he had fixed for him, raising his brows at the ruins of coat and shirt the orderly had brought in from the outer room. It appeared the sling would cover almost as much of him as what was left of his clothes.

Of course Robert could have asked for Esmeralda so that she could bring him fresh clothing, but for some reason he refused to define or even think about, he did not mention that his wife was in the building. Instead he simply abandoned the shirt, thinking it too far gone to bother about, and inserted his good arm into the coat, which he had the orderly button at the waist.

By the time he returned, Sir Harry Burrard, who had finally come ashore at Porto Novo late in the morning, had arrived at Sir Arthur's command post and was inquiring of Lord Burghersh where General Wellesley was. Burghersh was unable to answer his question, since he himself had only just ridden up. Under the circumstances, Robert's appearance was fortunate, as it diverted Sir Harry's attention. That gentleman was at first considerably shocked by Robert's dishabille and then seriously concerned that Captain the Honorable Robert Moreton, son of the Earl of Moreton, should have so little regard for his health and safety as to return to the battlefield after having been wounded.

Sir Harry was too much of a gentleman to give orders to another officer's ADC, but he was gently suggesting that Robert report himself unfit and retire, when Sir Arthur rode up. General Wellesley did not at first notice Sir Harry because his eye had been caught by Robert's golden hair and bedraggled condition, and he cried out sharply, "Where the devil have you been, Moreton?"

Burrard's eyes widened slightly at this seemingly unfeeling remark and Sir Arthur's expression of cold disapproval, but Robert grinned. He knew Sir Arthur well enough to recognize the question as a mark of great anxiety. "Doing something stupid, sir," Robert replied, "but General Acland had already gone into action, so it didn't matter. And General Burrard has arrived, sir."

As he spoke, Robert backed his horse so that Sir Arthur's view would be unobscured. Although he was as sorry as all the other ADCs about the fact that General Wellesley had been superseded, he was grateful that Burrard had arrived at this precise moment. He knew that he had been saved a scathing, but deserved, reprimand by Burrard's presence. In the next instant, however, he was punished for the brief, selfish emotion. Instead of turning immediately to his superior, Wellesley took the time to look searchingly at Robert and then to ask, "Are you fit?"

"Yes, sir," Robert replied. "It was only a crease, and Mr. Neale has sewed me up." Now he felt horribly guilty and wished that Burrard were back in England, even if it cost him a hundred of Sir Arthur's painful scolds.

"Good day to you, Sir Harry," Wellesley said courteously, if with no marked enthusiasm. "The situation—"

"No need for any details, Wellesley," Sir Harry said. "You seem to have everything well in hand, and you must finish what you have so ably started."

"Thank you."

A note of warmth appeared in Sir Arthur's voice, a recognition of Burrard's generosity. It was not every general who would allow a subordinate officer to reap the reward of a victory. Usually the superior officer grabbed the credit, even if he arrived after the fighting was over. Although Sir Arthur was not often forthcoming with military information, he understood generosity and responded to it.

"But," he continued, "I should like to tell you, as exactly as I know it myself, just what is happening."

"Very well."

Robert exchanged glances with Sir Arthur's other ADCs. The lack of enthusiasm in Burrard's reply was noticeable. Although each young man had a different interpretation of the cause, all were equally appalled. As Sir Arthur's voice had cooled noticeably again, it was obvious that the general also felt Burrard's lack of interest was not a good sign.

Having summed up the disastrous results of Junot's attempts to dislodge the British from Vimeiro hill, Sir Arthur concluded, "The attack along the valley has also been checked with heavy losses for the French. I have just ordered that the Forty-third be brought in from the east, and that action should begin at any moment. If you would like to ride down with me, sir, we will be able to see the results more clearly."

Sir Arthur told Colin Campbell to remain where he was and direct any messengers down to the small knob of high land above the station of the Twentieth Light Dragoons, whereupon he began to ride downhill toward the battle scene. Indeed, he had come up principally to make certain no extremely urgent messages had come from the left flank. Robert had guessed that and guessed also that the quick turns of Sir Arthur's head and the frequent use of his glass implied some uneasiness with regard to the silence from that area.

Robert's mind was divided between those thoughts and a new wash

of anger and disgust. It was clear that Burrard was surprised by Sir
Arthur's intention of surveying the battle at close range. Not that Sir
Harry was the least afraid; he was merely astonished at Wellesley's
notion that a commanding general should go and see for himself.
However, Robert was soon distracted by the action itself. The French
were still resisting stubbornly, and by this time both sides were in near
chaos because the outlying houses and walls had broken the formation
of the regiments. The charge of the Forty-third only added to the
confusion. Volleys were exchanged at almost point-blank range, and
there was fierce hand-to-hand fighting with very free use of the
bayonet.

It was soon apparent that the courageous French grenadiers could
not turn the tide. Sullenly the drums rolled the order to retreat. It
would have been virtually impossible for the disordered masses to pull
out and protect themselves, and Junot sent out a regiment of dragoons
to cover the retreat.

Sir Arthur, of course, did not want an orderly French withdrawal.
He decided at once to use his handful of cavalry, the 240 light
dragoons, supported by 260 Portuguese in two squadrons, which were
drawn up below the rise. Lifting his already well-known cocked hat,
Wellesley waved it and cried, "Now, Twentieth, now is the time!"

Colonel Taylor, who had been watching anxiously for some signal
from Wellesley, wheeled his regiment from behind the sheltering hill
and charged at the retreating French. At first the Portuguese rode even
with the British, but when the French paused and began to fire, the
Portuguese broke and fled back to the safety of the re-forming lines of
Anstruther's brigade, who greeted them with hoots and catcalls.

Sir Harry uttered a shocked exclamation, and smothered groans
came from the ADCs of both generals. Sir Arthur alone watched with
unmoved expression. Taylor's men rode on, crashed through the lines
of French dragoons, and plunged in among the fleeing infantry,
sabering right and left and taking prisoner those who threw down their
arms. Now Sir Harry was smiling, and if he had not been, so to speak,
a guest of Sir Arthur's, he would no doubt have waved and cheered
them on. However, as the Twentieth continued onward right through
the terrified infantry, Wellesley's mouth tightened in furious disapproval.

A short while later the result Sir Arthur had foreseen came about.
The overenthusiastic troopers were checked by a stone wall on the hill

and simultaneously charged by two fresh regiments of French horse, which had been kept in reserve. Sir Arthur disliked and distrusted cavalry regiments, having said more than once that they were never properly disciplined and got carried away, thereby turning a victory into a defeat.

Robert had to admit that the charge had been carried far beyond reason. The end result, which he learned about the next day, was, however, not quite disastrous, for by some miracle the overexcited troopers were not annihilated.

Actually at the moment the action was taking place, Sir Arthur had essentially lost interest in it. He had mentally given up the Twentieth for lost. Moreover, a muted roar had come down from the slopes north of the Maceira, which could only have been produced by a full regimental volley. That meant the troops Junot had sent north to flank the British had finally come into contact with the forces Wellesley had set up to oppose them. Sir Arthur politely lifted his hat to Sir Harry, who was still contemplating the headlong rush of the Twentieth, and spurred his horse away in the direction of the new fighting, with his staff streaming along behind him.

They splashed through the tributary of the Maceira. The small valley was noisy now and littered with dead and wounded among whom unhurt and lightly wounded moved, some looting the dead bodies and others giving what assistance they could to those hurt worse than themselves. There was, at least, a fine impartiality about both activities, the French wounded receiving as much assistance as the British and the British dead being looted about equally with the French.

Despite the noise and confusion in the area, Robert's eye was drawn inexorably to Jupiter's body, and he gave it a long, regretful look as they passed. Sir Arthur rode north along the ridge where British troops were pursuing the remnants of some French columns. The troops were moving in good order, pausing periodically to fire another volley into the fleeting French. Then, near three abandoned French guns, the Seventy-first and Eighty-second halted to rest and re-form their ranks. General Nightingale, who was moving forward with the Twenty-ninth, which had been in the second line, saw Sir Arthur and rode back to him.

"There are more French somewhere," he said. "They came to the

edge of that ravine just below my position and then went on farther
north until we lost sight of them completely."

"Do you have any idea how large the force is?" Sir Arthur asked.

Before Nightingale could reply, the question answered itself. From
the summit of the heights above the plateau on which the Thirty-sixth
and Fortieth regiments were driving the French northwest, four
battalions of infantry and two squadrons of dragoons poured down.
The British regiments reeled back in disorder, abandoning the
captured guns. With an oath of dismay, General Nightingale charged,
calling orders toward the Twenty-ninth, which had paused uncertainly.
Tactfully Sir Arthur halted. He was not in the least discomposed by
the setback. Bowes's division was at hand and had not yet fired a shot;
Caitlin Crawfurd and the Portuguese—for whatever good they would
be—were about a mile away, near enough to lend a hand if necessary.

It was not necessary. In a very short time the new French attack was
broken. The three guns were again in British hands, together with
three more that the new French battalions had carried with them. Sir
Arthur did not stay to see the end of the action. He instructed Lord
Burghersh to give his compliments to Generals Ferguson and
Nightingale upon their handling of the situation and the behavior of
their men, and rode hastily back in the direction from which he had
come.

The battle of Vimeiro was won, and Robert realized Sir Arthur
believed that the French army of Portugal could be utterly destroyed if
action were taken quickly, before Junot could reorganize or call in
reserves. Unfortunately, Robert knew that Sir Arthur did not have the
authority to initiate that action. Burrard had given his permission for
Wellesley to complete the battle he had started, but that could not be
stretched to include the pursuit of Junot's broken force.

But Sir Arthur hoped that in the first heat of real victory over the
"undefeatable" French army, Sir Harry's supine nature might be
roused to action—or, at least, to permitting Sir Arthur to take action.
Sir Arthur rode up to Burrard, waving his hat and crying, "Sir Harry,
now is your time to advance. The enemy is completely beaten, and we
shall be in Lisbon in three days."

Chapter 23

Esmeralda had written the letter to the dying soldier's wife, with tears streaming down her face. It was mostly of her own composition, for the man could barely summon strength to whisper the name and address. He was pathetically grateful for what he believed to be her sympathy, and poor Esmeralda was racked with guilt although, in truth, her fear for Robert gave her a poignant understanding of the sorrow of an unknown woman. She even made a note of the name and address, thinking she might be able some day to assist the widow if she were worthy and needed help. She felt futile and angry, knowing there was no way, even with the wealth that would be at her command, that she could help the womenfolk of all those who died, but the small gesture toward this one person soothed her a little.

Soon after the letter was finished, the man lapsed into unconsciousness. Esmeralda looked about vaguely, wondering if it would be very wrong and cowardly to abandon her self-imposed duty. Before she could decide, however, she heard her name and saw a familiar face, one of the young officers of the line who had often stopped to speak to her on the march. She hurried over, anxiety making her almost forget the danger to which Robert had returned.

Fortunately, in this case the anxiety was largely unnecessary. The young man had had a ball in the shoulder, but it had been extracted without difficulty, and his chances for recovery were excellent. In fact, he intended to return to his company in a day or two. His purpose in summoning Esmeralda had not been out of a need for assistance but to soothe her, since he had seen how distressed she was while she wrote.

Half an hour of pleasant talk restored Esmeralda considerably, particularly since she could not resist mentioning that her husband had

also been wounded but had insisted on returning to Sir Arthur. She had
been assured that he would not be sent out again and that, more likely
still, Sir Arthur would send him home. Thus cheered, Esmeralda went
back to the less pleasant aspects of the task she had undertaken. It was
disheartening, for there was so little she, or even the doctors, could
do. Nonetheless, she persisted, as she assumed Robert would wish her
to do, but not for long. She had barely attended to the wants of two
men whose limbs had been amputated when Carlos's voice, high and
frightened, interrupted her.

Esmeralda rose so abruptly and was so terrified by the fear Carlos
was displaying that she had to catch at the wall for support. Nor could
she call out to the boy, but her movement had caught his eye, and he
hurried over, crying, "Come home, senhora, come home."

"Oh, my God," Esmeralda whispered, "is it your master?"

"He has gone mad," Carlos breathed, his big, black eyes wide with
fright. "He shouted at me and tried to hit me, and his face was all
red."

Esmeralda's breath caught as she was torn between relief and a new
fear. At least he was not dead, but . . . Fever, she thought. It was
bad, but not the worst. He was young and strong, and cinchona was
quite effective against fever. She tore off the bloodied sheet that had
partially protected her gown and ran toward the house in which they
had quarters. She could hear Robert's voice, hoarse and angry, all the
way down in the street. Just outside the door she hesitated. If he was
really out of his head, she would not be strong enough to control him,
and Carlos, frightened out of his wits, poor child, could be no help.

Esmeralda had turned to send Carlos back to the hospital area to get
Molly, when another voice she recognized—just as furious as
Robert's—struck her ear, and then a third. She promptly dismissed the
notion of fever; it was rage she heard in all three voices. Could the
battle have been lost? That notion was cast aside with her original idea
about delirium. Had the battle been lost, the French would have been
flooding into Vimeiro.

Still Esmeralda hesitated. Although she was no longer worried
about needing to control Robert while he was out of his head, she had
never seen her husband really angry and had no idea how he might
react toward her. In general, Robert had a sunny disposition. He had
occasionally displayed irritation, but it had not lasted long. If he had
really tried to strike Carlos, would he relieve his feelings by beating

her? Not, she decided, in the presence of his friends, and she quickly
entered the house and ran up the stairs.

". . . have to do it all over again, and God knows whether it will
be possible now that Junot will be better prepared."

Esmeralda made out the words, but they were uttered in so fury-
choked a voice that she was not sure who was speaking until she was
far enough up the stairs to see that it was Captain Williams. "What
has happened?" she asked, but either no one heard her or all the men
were too taken up with their subject to heed her interruption.

"We won't be *able* to do it again with that incompetent, lazy
numbskull in charge," Robert roared. "He'll have us out in a flat
plain all lined up like a parade to be shot to pieces."

"Maybe he could have an accident," Colin Campbell snarled.

Esmeralda shuddered. It was not unheard of for really bad officers
to have "accidents" on the field, and there was a vicious, uncon-
trolled note in Campbell's voice that showed he was not joking.

"I'd help you if I thought he'd ever get close enough to any action
to make it possible," Williams said bitterly.

"What has Sir Arthur done?" Esmeralda cried.

This time her voice was quite loud. The three men seemed to be
working themselves up to commit an atrocity, and although frightened, she knew that an interruption and the presence of a witness
might induce second thoughts. For a moment she was afraid that all
she had accomplished was to draw the rage onto herself, for all three
turned and glared at her. Instinctively her hands came up, and she
backed away. Meantime, Campbell's eyes had fallen on her blood-
stained gown, for the sheet she had used as an apron had not protected
her fully, and he jumped forward with a hand out to support her. To
Esmeralda the gesture seemed so threatening that she shrank back still
farther, stifling a cry of fear and wavering on her feet.

"Good God, Mrs. Moreton's hurt," Campbell exclaimed.

"How could that happen?" Williams asked simultaneously.

"Merry, what's the matter?" Robert cried, getting an arm around
her.

The realization that she had completely misunderstood Colin
Campbell's movement and at the same time accomplished her purpose
restored Esmeralda immediately; however, she did not reject Robert's
support nor disclaim faintness at once. Quick-witted as she was, she

recognized that it would be best to keep the men's attention on her for a minute or two until their tempers cooled.

"I am all right," she murmured. "The blood is not mine. I was in the hospital area—"

"God damn it, Merry," Robert said, "you haven't the sense of a three-day-old kitten. It's one thing to help out but quite another to get so exhausted you are ready to faint. Come and lie down."

But Esmeralda had no intention of leaving the three men alone. She knew that in minutes the discussion they were having would resume and there was a good possibility that they would work themselves into a rage all over again. She had no expectation of keeping them off the subject but hoped that her presence would have an ameliorating effect.

"No," she protested. "I'm better now, and I am dying for a cup of tea. Come downstairs with me and tell me what Sir Arthur has done to make you all so angry."

Actually Esmeralda now realized that it could not be Sir Arthur about whom they had been speaking. He did, quite often, infuriate his ADCs, but even in a blind rage Esmeralda could not imagine one of his staff calling him lazy, incompetent, or a numbskull. She had introduced his name as another calming red herring.

Whether it was her presence or the soothing effect of fresh, strong, hot tea, relative rationality was maintained while Esmeralda learned how Sir Harry Burrard had managed to snatch defeat right out of the tight claws of victory. The tale was rather disjointed, since several more of the staff joined them, and the tellers periodically flew into rages and shouted at her and each other; however, no one reintroduced the subject of Sir Harry having an "accident," so Esmeralda was satisfied.

Actually, it was fortunate that she was not called upon to voice any opinion because emotionally she was far more in sympathy with Sir Harry than with the furious young men who castigated him for refusing, despite Sir Arthur's lucid reasoning and clear, practical plans, to pursue Junot's broken army. Intellectually Esmeralda knew Sir Harry was wrong. Robert said the French could have been destroyed in Portugal and the war in that country ended if Junot had been pursued; whereas letting him retreat unmolested would permit him to rearm, reorganize, and call up reinforcements. Moreover, with the inept Sir Harry at the helm, the British might be defeated in the next battle. Thus, in the long run, Sir Harry's orders to wait until Sir

John Moore arrived with another ten thousand men were stupid and dangerous to the British cause.

Nonetheless, Esmeralda's heart would not listen to her head. Her heart only knew that Robert was sitting safe and almost sound beside her instead of riding off to God knew where on the heels of fleeing men who would fight desperately to save their lives. In addition, there was some hope that Sir Arthur would take offense and return to England, in which case his staff would no doubt go with him and Robert would be safe.

As this thought crossed her mind, Esmeralda sighed deeply. She knew she was deluding herself. Although he admired Sir Arthur greatly, it was the army and, to a certain extent, war itself that Robert loved. He might, indeed, go back to England with Sir Arthur, but he would stay only long enough to find a way to get back into the action—and then another thought, so horrifying that Esmeralda shuddered at it, came into her mind. If they went to England, Robert would almost certainly leave her there when he returned to the front.

At this point Lord Burghersh came in. He was late because he had been ordered to remain on the northern slopes until the end of the action there. Although calm now, he at first had been as furious and disgusted as the others. He had seen the Thirty-sixth and Fortieth regiments of Ferguson's command pin one of the French brigades into an angle of the hills from which there was no easy escape. Burghersh had ridden back to Sir Arthur with Ferguson's ADC, who carried his general's request to advance, and had seen Sir Harry absolutely forbid any further action. The ADC had been stunned speechless, and Sir Arthur had made one more attempt to convince Sir Harry that the French could not stand another attack. He pointed out that one good push would send them in a rout into the rugged spurs of the Sierra da Baragueda where starvation, hardship, and the Portuguese peasants would likely finish off those who had not yielded as prisoners.

"Oh, I think the men have done enough for one day," Sir Harry had replied.

"But Hill's division and those of Bowes and Crawfurd have not even been in action. They are quite fresh," Sir Arthur countered, his voice even although it trembled just a little with anger.

But Sir Harry had stuck stubbornly to his decision that there would be no further advance that day, whereupon Sir Arthur had turned his horse and said bitterly to those of his staff who were present that they all might as well go and shoot red-legged partridges.

This report had led to a renewed discussion of the disaster that would undoubtedly follow Sir Harry's assumption of command, at which point Esmeralda—who had hardly listened, consumed as she was by her terror at the idea of being left in England—sighed and shuddered at her own thoughts.

"We are distressing Mrs. Moreton," Lord Burghersh said.

"Oh, no," she protested, "I am not frightened, only sorry that so many men have been killed and wounded to no purpose."

However, the worst prognostications of Sir Arthur's angry staff were not fulfilled, though this was not immediately apparent as matters seemed to worsen the next day when Burrard was in turn superseded by Sir Hew Dalrymple. Sir Arthur had immediately approached Sir Hew with a plan to advance to Mafra, which would cut Junot off from Lisbon and the heights of Tôrres Vedras, but Sir Hew was even less accommodating than Sir Harry; not only would he not listen to any plan for prosecuting the war, he was less polite about it.

To add to the complications, the army was sullen and recalcitrant. They wanted, and would take orders only from, their "old general," who had led them to victory. How far this spirit of rebellion against having their glory snatched from them would have gone was never tested, fortunately. In the afternoon of August 22, General Kellerman, who had led the French grenadiers that had fought so stubbornly on the outskirts of Vimeiro, arrived bearing a flag of truce. He had come to negotiate a total French withdrawal from Portugal.

Again Esmeralda presided over a tea table around which furious arguments raged. The younger and less experienced ADCs maintained that Sir Arthur should enter a formal protest and refuse to have anything to do with the negotiations. Robert and Colin Campbell, although not happy with the outcome because they knew General Wellesley's original plans would have done Bonaparte much more harm, argued that a convention of withdrawal was now the lesser of the evils they faced.

"For, you know," Robert said to Esmeralda in the quiet of their bedchamber after the futile meeting was over, "we have already lost our chance to cut Junot off from a safe retreat to Lisbon, and it is likely that with these bunglers in charge, any action would be delayed so long that reinforcements could be brought in from France. In any case, if we do not agree to a withdrawal, the war would be greatly protracted, which would mean heavy casualties, probably the bombardment and destruction of Lisbon and a number of other Portuguese cities, and possibly the complete ruin of Portugal.''

"It is too heavy a price to pay," Esmeralda agreed. "It is very fortunate that Sir Arthur has recognized the facts, since the armistice must surely go against the grain for him."

"He hasn't said much. He never does, but he's a very longsighted man." Robert's eyes brightened, and his lips started to curve a little. "There'll be plenty of fighting before we finally whip Boney."

There was a slight pause while Esmeralda swallowed the fear these words engendered in her and reminded herself of the conclusions she had reached: Robert was going to find a war to fight in somewhere all of his life, and if she showed the fear she felt, he would simply leave her behind. And that brought to mind a more immediate problem. Now with armistice in the wind, would they return to England?

"Has Sir Arthur given any indication of what he intends to do once the negotiations are over?" Esmeralda asked.

"Not to any of us," Robert replied, smiling wryly. "All of us have been after him, but he's tight as a clam—as he should be." Then the wry twist left his lips, and he wound a finger into one of Esmeralda's curls. "One thing's sure. We'll be leaving here and moving into Lisbon very soon. You'll like that. There'll be lots of parties. Sir Arthur loves balls. Now you'll have to get some evening dresses and I'll have to see about getting you some trinkets to wear with them."

Esmeralda touched the hand playing with her curls. "And will you enjoy it, too?"

"Enormously," Robert said, "if you will save some dances for me."

Robert's prediction was correct, but he and Esmeralda remained in Portugal only because of Sir Arthur's very real patriotism, which outweighed the chagrin, fury, and disgust he felt at the way the convention with the French was negotiated and the way Dalrymple allowed Junot to interpret the provisions in it. By the end of August, it was clear that Sir Arthur wanted no more to do with the present management of the campaign in Portugal and that he intended to return to England as soon as he received permission to do so.

Nevertheless, he was troubled about abandoning the army and the people of Portugal to almost certain disaster in the hands of Dalrymple and Burrard.

Robert first became aware that Sir Arthur had been giving serious thought to how the situation might be amended when he was summoned to the room Sir Arthur was using as an office early on September 17, the day before they were to leave for England. He waved Robert to a seat and asked him if he remembered correctly that Robert's initial appointment in the army had been to Sir John Moore's staff.

"Yes, sir, it was."

"And you parted with him on . . . ah . . . good terms?"

"Most excellent terms, Sir Arthur," Robert replied, somewhat puzzled. "I only left him because the Peace of Amiens had been signed and Sir John was going on inactive service, which I did not wish to do." Then he grinned. "I was concerned, also, that my family would endeavor to persuade me to leave the army altogether since 'the war was over.' It seemed to me expedient to put some distance between them and myself, and I had heard of your brilliant campaigns in India. Well, India was a good distance."

Wellesley loosed his whooping laugh. "I hope your family is now resigned to your military ambitions?"

"Pretty well, sir. You remember, I suppose, that Fa insisted that I go inactive while my brother Perce was with the Russian army and Fred was at sea, but that was only reasonable. There's Moreton to consider. But he didn't kick up a fuss when I said I wanted to join your staff again after Perce came home."

"Very good," Sir Arthur approved. "Now, are you eager to get home, or would you consider changing your plans on very short notice, transferring to Sir John's staff and remaining in Portugal?"

Robert blinked. Personal staff was a personal matter, although most generals were saddled with an assortment of army-mad and ne'er-do-well younger sons of influential people. Actually Robert had thought of applying to Sir John again, but not until he was sure that Sir Arthur was accepting inactive status and returning to his post as chief secretary for Ireland rather than obtaining another military command elsewhere. There was, after all, the question of a decent loyalty and not giving the appearance of abandoning a "sinking ship," for there were already signs that England was furious about the so-called

Convention of Cintra, which had been signed on August 31. Many
members of Parliament and most of the public were demanding that
those who had signed so pernicious a document be called to account.

Sir Arthur misunderstood Robert's hesitation, which was owing
exclusively to surprise, and frowned. "I suppose it is inconvenient.
You must be all packed to leave."

"Oh, no, it isn't the inconvenience, sir. I just—"

"Good Lord!" Wellesley exclaimed. "You must want to take your
wife home. I had forgotten for the moment about Mrs. Moreton's
situation. *Hmmm.*"

"No, it's nothing to do with Merry," Robert assured him. "I was
just surprised. I didn't know that you and Sir John were in
communication."

"We aren't," Sir Arthur said, "but I have just written to him, and I
would like you—since you know him—to deliver the letter and urge
him to meet with me, as I have requested, sometime today at his
convenience. I understand that he has had a disagreement with Lord
Castlereagh." Sir Arthur's lips twisted wryly. "He was dissatisfied
with the expedition to Sweden on which he was sent and also did not
like being placed as third in command to Sir Hew and Sir Harry."

Robert choked.

Sir Arthur eyed him frostily but continued without comment, "The
good of the nation and the successful prosecution of the war against
Bonaparte are far more important than Sir John's personal feelings—
or mine. Or, for that matter, Mrs. Moreton's convenience. If you
would like, I will escort her to England myself and see that her affairs
are placed in proper and competent hands."

It was a very generous offer. Sir Arthur must know he would be put
to a great deal of trouble. Nor was there any reason for it beyond
genuine kindness. He could simply have ordered Robert to ask for the
transfer and ignored any personal problems his orders caused. Robert
flushed.

"That's very good of you, sir, but I—I don't know what Merry will
want to do," he said. "It's—there's no longer any question of
annulment."

Sir Arthur raised his brows. "Well, then, it is simpler. I need only
place Mrs. Moreton under the protection of your family."

Poor Robert flushed even darker, but he only repeated that he must

discuss the matter with his wife and then said desperately, "I also
think it would be best to settle matters with Sir John first."

"Very well, Moreton, it is your affair, of course, but keep in mind
that I am willing to help in any way I can."

Robert thanked him again and, having obtained the direction of Sir
John's quarters, took his leave. But his mind would not stay fixed on
what to say to Sir John. The truth was that Robert did not want to put
Sir Arthur's proposition to Merry. He felt that she would jump at the
chance. With Sir Arthur's support, she could establish herself, and she
was all packed and ready to go. He would miss her damnably.

Surprisingly, Robert's loins tightened, as if he had been too long
without a woman—but that wasn't the case at all. He had made love to
Merry only a few hours before; they made love almost every night,
and sometimes even twice. It was crazy. Before he had met her, a few
times a month was enough when he was on campaign, but he seemed
to want Merry all the time. Just crazy. She wasn't even beautiful. She
was plain. . . . Or was she?

As Robert mounted his horse and rode off, he was trying to
visualize Merry's face, but there seemed to be many images
superimposed. That was odd, but odder still was the fact that he
responded just as strongly when he remembered her as plain as
dishwater as when he imagined a dramatically beautiful face, pale and
large eyed, surrounded by masses of gleaming dark hair, a face he
knew could not be real. It didn't seem to matter how she looked. He
just wanted her.

Well, he didn't have to tell her about Sir Arthur's offer. He realized
that Sir Arthur must have some notion he intended to present to Sir
John that would place the command of the Portuguese campaign in Sir
John's hands, but Robert told himself that the Horse Guards would not
be easy to circumvent. If those wooden soldiers had their way and
Dalrymple remained in charge, there probably wouldn't be any more
action. Then there wouldn't be any danger or hardship for Merry to
endure. Would it be so wrong in that case to explain the situation and
not tell her that Sir Arthur had offered to escort her to England?

Robert had found no answer that would satisfy him when he
dismounted, but he was greeted with considerable enthusiasm by such
old friends as Major John Colborne, now Sir John's military secretary,
and Colonel Thomas Graham of Balgowan, who teased him about
arriving so early in hopes of getting a good breakfast to make up for

the bad dinner at Sir Arthur's table the previous evening. Robert laughed and shook his head, happy to push the problem of Merry out of his mind. It was not the first time he had seen his old friends, of course. He had paid a courtesy call soon after Sir John arrived in the Lisbon area, but when he said he was on business, he was escorted without delay, although with looks of considerable curiosity, into Sir John's chamber.

Moore smiled at him, but with a question in his eyes, and asked in what way he could be of service. Robert handed over the letter and repeated Sir Arthur's hope that he and Sir John could meet. Moore stared at Robert for a long moment without answering, then broke the seal and began to read Sir Arthur's letter. The rather austere expression that had given his handsome features the look of a fine carving relaxed as he read, and when he looked up, his warm and enchanting smile assured Robert of the success of the first part of his mission.

"I would be honored to meet Sir Arthur, anywhere and at any time," he said. "He writes most excellent good sense, and he is a brilliant officer."

"That he is, Sir John," Robert agreed, "and thoughtful of the men and kindhearted, too. Don't be put off by his manner," he added. "He has an air of great reserve, but he is a good and steady friend."

Robert would never have volunteered that kind of personal comment in speaking to Sir Arthur, who always wished to see and judge for himself. But Sir John's disposition was very different. He was of open and friendly temper—though he could be cold and distant enough to those he did not like—and he valued a free proffering of well-meant information from those he trusted.

He nodded, smiling, and said, "So I have heard, and I have also heard he has a reputation for keeping his own counsel, but his letter seems very open and honest."

"I would not say that he is, in general, open," Robert said carefully, "but what he says is always honest, and in this case I am sure he believes openness to be necessary. What he said to me was that the good of the nation and the successful prosecution of the war against Bonaparte were far more important than your personal feelings or his."

Moore looked rather startled, but after a brief pause nodded. "I agree most heartily."

"What is more," Robert continued, "he desires me to ask for a

transfer to your staff. I know a good deal about the difficulties of
working with the Portuguese, I know the Bishop of Oporto personally,
and I can speak the language moderately well."

Since the Bishop of Oporto was now a member of the ruling junta
of Portugal, Robert's acquaintance with him might be of considerable
value.

"Really," Sir John remarked thoughtfully. "How kind of Sir
Arthur. Well, I will be delighted to have you back, so you may
consider that settled. Now there is only the question of where and
when to meet. I assume Sir Arthur would not like me to come to him,
nor would he wish to come here and perhaps give the impression
of . . . er . . . collusion."

Robert smiled broadly. He had not wanted to suggest such a thing
himself but it had been in his mind. There could be little doubt that
Dalrymple had his knife out for Sir Arthur and very likely for Moore,
too, since Moore was a passionate advocate of new methods, both for
the training and disciplining of soldiers and of battle tactics.

"There is a palace, a fascinating little gem of a palace actually, just
outside of Lisbon at Queluz," Sir John went on. "Do you know it?"

"No. But the local people will know, and I speak the language."

"Yes. Well, I have been wanting a closer look at the place. I'll ride
out as soon as I clean up a few papers here and will stay
until . . . oh, three of the clock or so."

"Very good, sir," Robert said. "I'm sure that will suit Sir Arthur
very well, but if it should not, I'll be back before you leave."

In a sense Robert was delighted with the way things were going. If
he thought Wellesley a shade more brilliant in action than Moore, it
was only a shade, and Sir John was far easier to work for. Not to
mention the fact that he would finally get something decent to eat and
drink at mess for a change. But best of all, he would remain in
Portugal, where there was bound to be action even if Dalrymple did
hold command for a while. Boney wasn't going to take having his
army thrown out without a fight.

But that thought made nonsense of Robert's earlier rationalizations
that there would be no danger and hardship for Merry if she remained
in Portugal. Thus, it *was* wrong not to tell her about Sir Arthur's offer.
Well, it would have to wait until he had delivered Sir John's message,
Robert thought; duty came first. As soon as he had told Sir Arthur the
gist of his conversation with Sir John, he would go home and speak to

Merry. But Sir Arthur invited him to be present at his meeting with Moore, and, although that took only a few hours, Robert somehow found himself too busy all day long to get back to the elegant apartment he had rented until very late indeed.

In fact, Esmeralda was already in bed and alseep. She had had a very exhausting day finishing the packing and worrying about her reception by Robert's parents. A good reception would probably mean that Robert would leave her behind on his next campaign. A bad one would hurt him. Good or bad, Esmeralda did not like the prospects and, what was worse, it no longer seemed so simple to tell Robert that she had over half a million pounds. She had suddenly realized that it might seem to Robert that she had concealed her wealth for fear he might be greedy or dishonest.

The truth was that most of the time she had simply forgotten about the money. But he would never believe that. No one would ever believe one could forget half a million pounds. The thing was that Esmeralda had lived with that knowledge most of her life but had been forbidden to speak of it, and the money had been out of her reach. Silence on the subject had become second nature to Esmeralda. Besides, the things money could buy were not at all as interesting as the things that had been happening to her lately.

In the beginning, Esmeralda *had* shuddered at the thought that Robert might pretend devotion for the sake of her wealth. That fear had long passed, for she knew Robert now and could not believe money had such influence over him. It was far more likely that he would be indifferent to the money but very angry about her secrecy. Perhaps she could pretend that she had not known how much money there was? Only that would get her into still deeper trouble if Robert ever discovered that she had written most of the letters to the bankers. Esmeralda had finally fallen asleep without making any decision.

When he entered the apartment and realized Esmeralda was asleep, Robert had thought, with relief, that it would be unkind to wake her and tell her of Sir Arthur's offer. In the back of his mind was the notion that she might decide it was not worth the trouble to separate their belongings and repack if she had to hurry.

As always when she went to bed before Robert—for he had night duty sometimes—Esmeralda had left a lamp burning low. She had turned into the light while she slept, and with her bright, knowing eyes closed, her tumbled hair and stubby, indeterminate nose gave her face the unformed look of a little girl.

Robert's conscience stabbed him painfully. He remembered how she had gone to help the wounded during the battle of Vimeiro and how she had exhausted herself, and how sickened she had been by the unburied dead. She had had nightmares for a few days afterward, waking and clutching at him. And Robert knew Vimeiro had not been a great or desperate battle. How could he think of inflicting more horrors of war on her? Furious with himself for delaying, Robert crossed to the bed and shook Esmeralda by the shoulder.

"Merry. Merry, wake up."

Esmeralda started upright, her eyes wide and terrified. He had found out, she thought, mixing her worries and dreams into reality.

"Merry, I'm not going back to England," Robert said.

"What?" she whispered, still half asleep and thus half-convinced that he was angry because she had concealed her wealth and was punishing her by sending her away. "What do you mean?"

"It's nothing to do with you," he assured her, his heart sinking at what he believed to be her disappointment. "Sir Arthur has offered to escort you and to present you to my parents. I have transferred to Sir John Moore's staff."

"No!" Esmeralda cried, waking up and realizing this was no dream argument about money. "No! Don't send me to England alone, Robert. Everyone will hate me. They'll—"

"Don't be ridiculous," Robert said sharply, fighting the impulse to take advantage of her silly fears and keep her with him. "My parents aren't monsters, and it was not a matter left to my choice. Sir Arthur desired that I remain with Sir John because I know the language and might be of assistance to him in dealing with the Portuguese."

"But the war is over," Esmeralda pleaded. "I will be safe here. Please. I don't want to face your family alone."

"The war isn't over!" Robert exclaimed, growing more insistent because he was ashamed of his desire to grasp at any excuse to let her stay. "Don't talk like a silly goose. Do you think Boney is going to sit back and accept Junot's failure? We will be moving into Spain soon. You will be much safer with my mother and father in England, and if for some reason you cannot agree—although I cannot imagine that will be true—or if the life in Cornwall is too quiet, you can go to my brother and sister-in-law, Perce and Sabrina. They are young and very active socially."

"But I like Lisbon," Esmeralda cried, sobbing, "and it will soon be cold in England. And you told me that your brother is newly married. How can you think they would like to have me cluttering up their house?"

They didn't have a house, Robert thought, remembering that they were only taking over part of a floor in the Stour mansion. It *might* be inconvenient for Perce and Sabrina to house Merry. Worse yet, they wouldn't be in London in September, and it would be very dull for her in Cornwall since she didn't shoot or hunt or fish.

"Don't cry," he said, seating himself on the bed and taking her into his arms.

"I don't want to go to England alone," Esmeralda whispered, clinging to him. "I'm not afraid of staying, even if the war begins again. I like being with the army. Robert . . . please."

Her wisp of a nightgown had slipped off one shoulder, exposing most of one softly rounded breast. Her lovely eyes were magnified by unshed tears. At the moment to Robert she looked as beautiful as the most delectable of his images. Heat flashed across his groin and down his thighs, combining with a feeling of sensitivity and fullness that demanded a familiar but ever-new and ever-enthralling satisfaction.

"I don't know," Robert said uncertainly, his eyes straying from Esmeralda's face down her body.

"There will be many ships going to England now," Esmeralda murmured softly, running a finger gently over the curves of Robert's ear.

She had noticed the movement of his eyes and seen the small changes in expression—a sleepy lowering of the lids, a fulling of the perfect lips—that betrayed the onset of passion in him. Her lips caressed his cheek, nibbled at his chin. Robert's hand rose, tentatively stroked her shoulder, then slid down toward her breast, pushing her nightgown still lower. Esmeralda slid the arm that had been propping her erect around her husband's waist and leaned against him for support. She kissed his neck just under the ear, above his high collar. Robert stirred uneasily.

"But Sir Arthur is leaving tomorrow morning," he muttered, guilt giving him one last prod.

"I am sure Sir Arthur would honor his offer to help me at any time," Esmeralda whispered against Robert's mouth.

Robert bent his head to facilitate the meeting of their lips. "I am sure it is wrong for you to stay," he sighed when the kiss was over, but the words were meaningless, a phrase left over from an idea he had forgotten. Even as he spoke, one hand caressed Esmeralda while the other undid the buttons on his pantaloons.

Briefly the words hurt Esmeralda, and she wondered whether her long struggle to bind Robert was worthwhile. It seemed, from his reluctance to let her stay, that even his sexual desire for her was not strong enough to make her necessary to him. But he had his boots off by then, and her body was indifferent to the doubts in her mind, for her hands had unbuttoned his coat and shirt. He stood to push off his pants; Esmeralda forgot hurt and doubts. She leaned forward to embrace his hips, to run her lips and tongue over the male beauty displayed.

Robert groaned softly, then bent so that he could reach around her arms to caress her breasts. Esmeralda shuddered and after a moment uttered a sound deep in her throat. Sliding his hands up to her arms, Robert lifted her so that she could get her legs forward and around him. They fell back together, half on, half off, the bed, using the rubbing of their bodies as they wriggled to a safer position and as Robert lodged himself securely as a further stimulus to their excitement.

Neither knew at that moment whether this would be the last time they were together, for the question of Esmeralda's departure had not really been settled, and that, too, added height and depth to their passion. Both were unusually aware of each other so that every increase of feeling in one sparked an immediate reaction in the other, and Esmeralda's first cry of bursting pleasure was echoed by Robert's deep groan as his own culmination came.

Chapter 24

Of course, the question of Esmeralda's departure *had* been settled. Robert woke barely in time to throw on clothing and rush down to the dock to see Sir Arthur off. It would have been impossible to send Esmeralda to England with nothing but the gown she had prepared for boarding the ship and equally impossible to send all his clothing to England with her. In addition, Robert told himself, it would be ridiculous to annoy the ship's captain and Sir Arthur by asking them to wait just to exhaust Merry with hurried repacking when there was no emergency. It was true the war was not over, but, as Merry had pointed out, there would be no action for several weeks. During that time, many ships would come and go from England, carrying couriers and supplies and probably more men. Merry could leave on any ship.

When he returned from the dock, to ease his conscience Robert repeated his rationalizations to Esmeralda. She heard him out in silence and then merely repeated in essence—although with far less emotion—what she had said the preceding night. It was not, she assured Robert, enlarging on her theme, that she believed his parents to be monsters; however, to have thrust upon them a daughter-in-law of whom they had never heard and who could not prove her antecedents must be an unpleasant shock. But Robert's presence at the meeting, owing to their joy at their son's safe return, would considerably mitigate the shock and make acceptance easier.

Esmeralda did think of her money, but this was the wrong moment to confess. Robert might not care enough about her fortune to pretend love, but he was not a fool. He would know that such a dowry would insure her a warm welcome and the kindest consideration from his parents. As uneasy as she was about the secret, she did not dare give Robert any excuse to be rid of her. It seemed to her that, although

kindness prevented him from forcing her to leave, he was subtly
trying to convince her to do so in every way he could.

This reflection depressed Esmeralda considerably, but she was a
fighter. She had preserved her personality and even achieved most of
her purposes against years of pressure from a considerably more
unpleasant opponent than Robert. Moreover, she was sure that Robert
was not deliberately opposed to loving her. There could be no doubt
that he enjoyed her body just as much as she enjoyed his. Nor was he
ashamed of her or displeased with her company; he far more often
brought his friends to their quarters for an evening of talk and cards
than went out with them alone. Thus, Esmeralda reasoned, she must
simply have failed to ignite a particular spark in Robert.

Casting about in her mind for what had been lacking in their
relationship, Esmeralda realized that Robert had never courted her as
most men courted the women they hoped to marry. It was too late to
worry about that, but thinking about courtship brought another aspect
of difference to her mind. Robert thought of her as a "plain Jane" and
had never faced any competition for her favors as most men did
during courtship. And then she remembered the first few days at
Figueira when the other ADCs had found her a novelty and had acted
toward her with great courtliness. Robert hadn't liked it; he had been
more attentive whenever he noticed it.

Once the army was on the move and then facing the French in
battle, their attention had been diverted, of course. And by the time
they had moved into Lisbon, all Robert's friends were so accustomed
to her that they had treated her like a sister, with kindly affection but
no awareness of her as a woman. But now there would be a whole
new group of men, and there would be balls and rides to places of
interest—all sorts of entertainments. Perhaps if she flirted a little, just
a little, and got some response . . . But she *was* plain. Would she
arouse any new interest or would she just make herself ridiculous?

Esmeralda consulted the mirror on her dressing table. Well, she
was no beauty, but she was more attractive than she had been in India,
and there she had had partners at a dance or a man to ride beside her
on an outing—even though she usually was the last chosen. She had
known it was the lack of Englishwomen that provided most of her
company, and the same situation existed here in Lisbon. There were
several new factors, too.

First and foremost, she was married now, not a poor girl possibly on the lookout for a husband. Second, her gowns in India had been horrible; now she was quite fashionably dressed, owing to the fact that Robert had been able to get money and the Lisbon dressmakers had been very eager to oblige. Finally, in India most of her escorts had found her boring, owing to the curb her father had forced her to place on her tongue; now she was free to say what she liked, and steady application had given her both interest and expertise on the subject that would be of greatest interest to army men.

Esmeralda sighed. She did not really want to give her precious Robert a moment's uneasiness, and in addition, it would be a most delicate balancing act. If she were too bold, Robert might send her away because she was embarrassing him, or keep her out of the way of army officers. On the other hand, if she were too delicate, Robert would never notice.

In this judgment, Esmeralda underrated Robert's powers of perception. True, his attention was firmly fixed on military matters, but he had been growing increasingly responsive to her moods. Thus, although her eagerness to stay had pleased him, he had sensed her depression, too. His conclusion was that she was really disappointed at having to remain in Portugal with him, but her fear of facing his relatives without his support had been more powerful than her desire to go to England. This made him uneasy and stung his conscience so that, without discussing the matter again with Esmeralda, he wrote and announced his marriage to his parents.

Since Robert still felt unequal to explaining just how Merry had really become his wife after the initial marriage of convenience, and he did not wish to explain the delay between the fact and the letter, he sidestepped all these issues. He told his parents only that he had met Esmeralda Mary Louisa Talbot, a young woman of respectable family, whom he had known previously in India, and had married her. He would explain more fully, he said, when he came home, as the situation was rather too complex for a letter. And, in an attempt to accustom himself to the idea of losing her, since he was sure his letter would produce a demand from his mother and father to send his wife to England at once, Robert kept assuring Esmeralda she could go at any time and that his family would be happy to receive her.

These assurances merely fixed Esmeralda's intention of making Robert jealous if she could, and over the next few weeks, while Dalrymple's heavy hand lay over all military activity, she pursued this purpose. There was plenty of opportunity. All conversation might be directed to some aspect of the future—or nonfuture—of the war, but such mournful considerations did not deter the officers from enjoying to the full the amenities of Lisbon. Moreover, although the Portuguese were distressed and angered by the Convention of Cintra, they were also grateful to be rid of the French. In any case, they did not blame the English as a whole, and well-born officers were flooded with invitations to balls and suppers.

Esmeralda was careful, but soon Robert could hardly obtain a dance with his wife because her ball card was filled so quickly. As she had foreseen, the combination of a lack of Englishwomen and her deep interest in military affairs made her an enormous favorite with all British officers, especially Sir John's staff, to whom she was a novelty. Eventually she even became a favorite with Sir John himself, who had not originally been too happy when Robert informed him that he was married and his wife was following the drum.

Somehow Esmeralda managed to convince Sir John that, to a woman raised in India, the hardship endured by an officer's wife, particularly the wife of a staff officer, was minimal and that there was no need to feel uneasy about her comfort or safety. He found her so easy and delightful a companion, so eager a listener on any aspect of military life he felt suitable for discussion with a woman, that it became a custom for her to pour tea for his "family" of aides and other invited guests every evening she and Robert did not have another invitation.

Esmeralda could only hope that Robert would notice her popularity without perceiving the reasons for it, and her hopes were fulfilled. In fact, she very nearly played her game too well. Although he could not point a finger of blame at anything she did or said, Robert became so uneasy that he thought of sending her to England to remove her from the ardent attentions of his fellow officers. However, before he acted on the idea, it occurred to him that there would be many more men with even more insinuating manners in England and that he would not be there to recall Esmeralda's attention to himself. What was worse yet, he remembered that she had told him she had a competence to live on. She would not be dependent on his parents and therefore could not be controlled. It would be much better to keep her with him where he could keep an eye on her.

At this point Robert was struck by the oddity of his thoughts. Why should he feel it necessary to "keep an eye" on Merry, and why should he object to the attentions paid her? Did he feel she would dishonor him? Every instinct recoiled from such a notion, but Robert forced himself to examine her behavior objectively. His conclusion was that there was not a hint of any impropriety. In fact, now that he considered the matter he realized that Merry was careful never to be alone with any man other than himself. Then why should he care? What was troubling him? He felt a fool and resolved that, in fairness, there was nothing he could complain about to her. But he could not shake off his unhappiness.

Had the situation in Portugal been more satisfactory, Esmeralda might have attributed Robert's evident unevenness of temper to her activities. However, she was too convinced of her own lack of attractions and Robert's basic indifference to her. Thus, since he said nothing, even when he could not get a single dance with her or escort her to supper, she put his crossness down to his fury over the lack of progress in military operations. Moreover, there was good practical cause for Esmeralda's mistake. In his need to express his anger and confusion and at the same time avoid attacking Esmeralda, Robert spent all their time alone complaining about Dalrymple's political stupidity and military inertia.

Robert's complaints were justified. Despite the known intentions of the British government to send the army to the assistance of the Spanish rebels, Dalrymple had failed to institute any of the basic moves toward forwarding this purpose. He had made no effort to survey the roads and discover the best routes by which to move the army to Spain, nor had he made any arrangements to supply the troops with food, clothing, or even powder and shot as they moved inland where the navy could not land stores from England. He had, in fact, paid so little attention to the army that discipline had been neglected and troops were away from their companies, drunk, sick, and disorderly. Instead he had dabbled in Portuguese politics, offending the junta until they complained hysterically to London.

Thus, when Dalrymple's bubble burst and he and Sir Harry Burrard were angrily summoned home to answer for promulgating the Convention of Cintra, a totally unprepared army was thrown into Sir John Moore's hands. From that moment Robert's complaints stopped, which only reinforced Esmeralda's despairing opinion that Robert either had not noticed the attentions other men paid her or had not cared; certainly he gave no sign of jealousy.

With the dispatches Moore had received on October 6, giving him the command of the army, had been orders to make up for Dalrymple's delays. (When Esmeralda raised her brows at this statement, Robert admitted that was not what the orders said, but what they meant.) In any case, Sir John was to get the army into Spain immediately, before winter made any campaign impossible. The first necessity, of course, was to restore discipline and determine how much of an army they actually had. Sir John was a hard worker, rising before dawn to write letters and reports and to make plans. His ADCs were kept on the run from sunup, sometimes until late into the night.

Within a week, Moore had the reorganization of the army well underway and turned his attention to how to move and supply it. Since Robert spoke Portuguese, he was logically one of those chosen to interview people to discover what roads would be best and where the countryside was most likely to provide food for the troops. However, all Robert discovered was that the Portuguese in Lisbon were totally ignorant of the geography and agriculture of their own country.

This seemed so unlikely at first that Robert wondered whether it was his shaky command of the language that was causing misunderstandings. The doubt produced what Robert considered a brilliant idea. He asked permission from Sir John to use Esmeralda as a translator, since she was more fluent in Portuguese than he.

Ever since he had written to his parents, Robert had been living in dread of receiving a reply that demanded Merry be sent home. It had occurred to him that, if she were useful to British interests in Portugal, he would have a legitimate reason to delay her departure. In addition, Robert knew that Esmeralda had a fine patriotic fervor and was sincerely devoted to the welfare of the army. She would be delighted to be of use—as she had been that time she had translated for him about the use of boats in Porto Novo. Perhaps she would be sufficiently devoted to her task to overcome what he believed to be her disappointment at his transfer and protracted stay in Portugal.

In addition, Merry's work as a translator would mean they would be together much more. Busy as he had been, they had hardly seen each other since Sir John's appointment as commander. To Robert's mind, anything that forwarded the successful prosecution of the war was of greater importance than the inclinations and pleasures of any person.

Thus, although he was aware of his ulterior motives, Robert's conscience twinged only slightly.

Although Esmeralda's help did not really produce any better results than Robert had obtained on his own—the Portuguese *were* ignorant of the roads and available supplies in their countryside—she was so thrilled by being employed in a useful capacity that his remaining guilt was assuaged. Moreover, he found her infinitely capable in many other ways. He discovered that she had a remarkably good head for business—far better than his; she could keep accounts and would certainly have made a better commissariat officer than those presently employed by the British army. Sir John, learning of Esmeralda's expanding activities, was at first slightly shocked; however, her enthusiasm disarmed him and prevented him from reprimanding Robert, and he very soon became accustomed to, and even depended on, her efficiency.

Thus, at the end of October, when the army began to move, it took very little to convince Sir John not to oppose Esmeralda's stated intention of traveling with them.

To Robert's surprise, he had received no answer to his letter home. At first he had felt only relief, assuming that its arrival had been delayed and that he would have a reply in good time. Then, between the fact that he was busy and that Esmeralda seemed so content, he had almost forgotten having written. Finally it occurred to him that either his parents were showing their displeasure by refusing to answer him, or, what Robert preferred to believe, his letter had somehow been lost.

In either case, he was in a quandary. He could write again, giving a fuller explanation that would absolve Merry of anything other than misfortune, but it was really too late for an answer to his second letter to arrive before they moved. And without a direct invitation from his parents, Merry would be afraid to go alone to England. Perhaps since he did not speak Spanish or have any particular knowledge of Spain, it was his duty to ask for leave from Sir John to take his wife to safety, but Robert did not want to miss the campaign, and from day to day he delayed his request for leave.

Before Robert had come to a decision, Esmeralda had taken matters out of his hands. Quite casually on the day after the first units of the army had marched east, as if the question of whether she would be accompanying Sir John and his staff had long been settled, she had asked Sir John whether it would be necessary for her to hire servants or whether she could continue to use M'Guire and his wife. The phrasing of the question, implying as it did complete familiarity with an army on the move, did not invite expostulation on the difficulties and discomforts of the journey, and a few more exchanges settled everything. One man more or less in a unit could make little difference. Sir John wrote a request that M'Guire be detached to act as Robert's batman, and Esmeralda's continued presence became an accepted fact.

As the army struggled toward Spain, there were so many difficulties that the presence of a woman who made none sank into insignificance. Because of the insufficiency of the roads and supplies, Sir John was forced to divide his forces and send General Hope with five brigades of artillery and four regiments of infantry the long way around by Elvas to Badajoz and Espinar and so eventually to Salamanca, where Sir John and the remainder of the army would, hopefully, be waiting. Meanwhile, the British government had dispatched another fifteen thousand men under the command of Sir David Baird. These troops were to be put ashore at Corunna and would move south through Galicia also to rendezvous with Moore at Salamanca.

It was all very easy on paper. However, the contract to provision the troops was not honored and the Portuguese outside of Lisbon refused to take either British government promissory notes or even paper money in exchange for supplies. This put a serious strain on the British army's exchequer and nearly wiped out the fund of gold and silver coins with which Robert had provided himself. Still, the march through Portugal was not too difficult. For Esmeralda, in particular, it was actually pleasant. She suffered none of the doubts and uncertainties that had plagued her when she first accompanied the army. She knew how to find her quarters and how to make them comfortable most efficiently. Carlos, Molly, and M'Guire knew their duties and worked well as a team. There was a good deal of rain and cold, but Robert had had the foresight to buy her a very warm fur-lined cloak, and a broad hat and oiled silk overgarment kept her reasonably dry.

There was only one worry that prevented Esmeralda's contentment from being complete; Robert was not quite as happy as she. He was not overtly bad tempered or miserable, but there seemed to be a cloud over his sunny nature. Esmeralda tried to explain it away by attributing it to the difficulties in provisioning the army and news from

Spain, all of which was bad. The junta of Corunna was totally uncooperative about assisting the British in any way. Unfortunately, Esmeralda could not convince herself that Robert's trouble really had anything to do with his duties. Too often there was doubt in his eyes or a frown on his brow when he was looking at her and did not know she was watching him.

Actually, Robert was more puzzled than unhappy, but he was not accustomed to feeling any doubts about life. From childhood he had been sure of what he wanted to do and the right way to do it. Now his relationship with Esmeralda was making him uncomfortable. At first it had been right; he had done his duty to succor a distressed British gentlewoman, and Merry had responded in a sensible way. But since then everything had become very complicated.

Why in the world had he permitted her to come? Two words from him to Sir John would have prevented her accompanying them—but he had said nothing. Why? Well, he knew the answer to that. He had wanted Merry to be with him. But why? He had never felt that kind of need for any person before in his life. When he had gone to school and later into the army, he had missed his family, but he had never manufactured reasons to keep them near. Over and over Robert raised the same questions and found no answer, until the afternoon of November 13 when they had reached Salamanca.

Directly after arriving at his headquarters, Sir John had written a long letter to Sir William Bentinck in Madrid, who was acting as minister from the British Court. He had described the difficulties facing the British forces and, under the circumstances, the impossibility of their achieving what the Spaniards seemed to expect of them. Then, worn out with worry as well as work, he had dismissed all but two of his staff and had lain down to snatch a few hours' sleep. Robert and Major Colborne were thus alone in the staff room.

Having finished his copy of Moore's letter, Colborne sighed. "It's damned unfair," he said. "Every time they give Sir John a command, it's already a lost cause."

Robert shook his head. "I hope they shoot Burrard and Dalrymple."

"What, shoot the white-haired boys of the Horse Guards? The absolute proof that seniority is the one and only qualification for command? No, they won't do that," Colborne retorted sardonically.

"Besides, Sir Arthur is involved, and he doesn't deserve to be blackened. He should never have signed that thing."

"He was ordered to sign it," Robert pointed out. "Anyway, once the opportunity of catching Junot while he was trying to control a rout was lost, getting the French out by convention was really best."

"Not with the provisions agreed to," Colborne said dryly, to which Robert shrugged. "Besides," he went on, "the Convention has nothing to do with our troubles right now. It's the damned Spaniards. For them, everything can be done *mañana*. They want us to push ourselves between them and the French—but they won't supply us with food or transport, or tell us where the hell *they* are or what they plan to do."

Robert shrugged again. "I've told Sir John he can't trust a word they say. It's not only stupid, it's dangerous to lie to a military ally. The Portuguese are sometimes damned ignorant, but they mostly mean well and they'll tell you they don't know. The Spanish are liars—well, not the people—it's the government."

"But we've got to have information about what's going on in the country. . . ." Colborne let the words fade out. Robert knew what he was about to say as well as he did.

He rose a little stiffly, for they had been riding all morning, and moved to a more comfortable chair near the fire. A rather discouraged silence remained. Both men were very fond of Sir John and could see that he would be blamed if the army were defeated and forced to retreat. The Tory government, which disliked him on principle because he was a Whig, would not be willing to admit that they had been led down the garden path by Spanish lies. It would be politically expedient to make Sir John the scapegoat. Worse yet, he knew it, and it was draining his confidence.

After a few minutes Colborne yawned; naturally, Robert echoed. They were both tired, too. Colborne blinked his eyes exaggeratedly and screwed up his face, then yawned again. If it had been night, he would have allowed himself to drowse in the chair; however, since it was afternoon and they had only just arrived, there was a good chance that messages or visitors would appear despite their having gone through a formal welcoming. It would not do, Colborne thought, to have the Spanish discover only two sleeping men in Sir John's office.

"How does Mrs. Moreton like your quarters?" he asked Robert, more for something to say to keep them awake than for any other reason. To his surprise, a black frown spread over Robert's face. "If she is not comfortable, I am sure we could find something better for her," Colborne added anxiously. "We are likely to be here for some time, a week or two, at least."

"Oh, Merry never makes a fuss," Robert replied, but the frown only grew more marked.

Colborne looked at him uneasily and said tentatively, "You are very fortunate to have found a wife like Mrs. Moreton. She is a woman of the greatest intelligence and easiest temper and has been of considerable assistance to me." Then he smiled and, trying to lift Robert's spirits, said, "I wish I had met her first."

"Apparently so does every man in the British army," Robert riposted sourly.

"Good God," Colborne exclaimed, "you can't think Mrs. Moreton has ever given the slightest—"

"No, no," Robert interrupted. "Merry's good as gold."

There was a pause, and Colborne finally said, "We've known each other a long time, Moreton. I don't want to intrude, but if there's anything I can do to help . . ."

"God damn it!" Robert exploded. "How can I ask for help when I don't know what's wrong?"

But the very word "wrong" had been an admission, a confession of uneasiness and discomfort he had not openly avowed before now. The quiet intimacy of the situation and the knowledge of Colborne's complete trustworthiness were also inducements to the unburdening of Robert's heart. Before he knew what he was about to do, he had confessed the whole story—not only the actual events but his feelings and his confusion about the relationship.

Somewhere about the middle of the tale, Colborne had risen to his feet and walked over to lean on the mantelpiece and stare into the fire. When he moved, Robert hesitated, wondering if he was exposing overly personal matters and causing Colborne discomfort, but he needed desperately to talk to someone, and a single, rather muffled word of encouragement started him off again. He found himself able to talk even more freely now that his friend's eyes were not on his face and was grateful, believing, because he wanted to believe, that that had been Colborne's intention in moving away. In fact, although Colborne would gladly have spared Robert any embarrassment, he had not been considering his comfort; he was thinking only of hiding his own expression because he was trying hard not to laugh.

Like all of Robert's friends, he was familiar with Robert's struggle to avoid female entanglements. A young man who does not wish to be loved obviously is not likely to fancy himself in love. Moreover, Robert's single-minded preoccupation with military matters had precluded interest in novels describing the tender passions and the effects of love. All in all, Robert was totally ignorant of the subject. Having married as he did, without desire or even thinking of Esmeralda as other than "a distressed citizen," it had simply not occurred to him that he had fallen in love with her.

"So you see," Robert concluded, his voice both angry and exhausted, "I'm behaving in a completely irrational way. I can't imagine what's wrong with me."

"Nothing much," Colborne remarked after a little silence indicated that Robert had no more to say. "You're in love with your wife, that's all." His voice was quivering with suppressed mirth, but fortunately Robert was so stunned by this pronouncement that he did not notice.

"But she isn't even pretty!" he exclaimed, voicing the only idea he had ever had about love, which was that it was engendered by feminine beauty. Then he added doubtfully, "Is she?"

It was too much for Colborne, who gasped and choked, "Not beautiful, perhaps, but very attractive and charming."

"Are you laughing at me?" Robert asked, standing up abruptly.

"I am very sorry," Colborne exclaimed. "I assure you I do not find your . . . er . . . problems amusing. It is only your . . . ah . . ."

But fortunately Robert was not attending to Colborne's rather lame excuses. Although he had been offended and had reacted automatically, that was a minor matter in comparison with a revelation that grew momentarily more astounding. He was not really as ignorant about love as Colborne thought. No man can avoid the effusions of his friends on the subject, whether or not he is interested. Robert simply had never associated all the things he had been told with himself. However, stripped of the flowery language, which Robert still found embarrassing, what they had said about a desire to be with, talk to, possess, their beloveds applied very well to him and explained his reactions accurately.

"By God," Robert burst out, cutting across Colborne's flounder-

ings, "you're right! I'm in love with Merry!" And then, to Colborne's
great relief, he burst out laughing himself and sank back down into the
chair from which he had jumped. "How ridiculous not to have known
it," he went on, still chuckling, "but with one thing and another I've
been so busy and had so much on my mind, and she grew on me
slowly—"

"For God's sake!" Colborne gasped, struggling against renewed
mirth, for though a man may laugh at himself he does not like to have
others do so. "Will you please stop talking as if Mrs. Moreton is some
kind of loathsome disease? I understand that because of the reasons
for your marriage you would naturally avoid thinking of her in a
romantic light, and that might become a habit. And God knows,
we've got enough to keep our minds busy with a chance of French
reinforcements advancing and the Spaniards disappearing like smoke
in the wind. It's not really so very odd that you should misunderstand
a personal problem, but the expressions you use and the look on your
face *are* comical, Moreton."

"Then laugh," Robert said, but he was frowning again.

"Now what's the matter?" Colborne asked, returning to the chair
he had vacated and not laughing although he was still amused.

"Since you know so much, tell me how to get Merry to love *me*,"
Robert snapped.

"Don't be a fool," Colborne replied. "She must love you. I've
never seen a girl that wouldn't follow you around like a dog if you so
much as blinked an eye."

"Oh, yes," Robert snarled, "all the brainless little ninnies fresh out
of the schoolroom. Merry's not a fool. You just pointed out that a
pretty face isn't everything—and it's damned near all I've got."

"Don't underestimate yourself, Moreton. You aren't a fool
either—"

"Yes, I am," Robert interrupted, "about everything but the army.
And don't tell me I'm an earl's son and I have an easy competence
with which to support a wife. I don't want to hear the reasons why a
woman would marry. I know them, and they don't necessarily include
love. And I know that Merry will never cheat on me, that she'll be
loyal and agreeable, the best wife any man could ever have. But I
want her to love me. . . ."

"Why the devil do you think she *doesn't* love you?" Colborne asked, rather exasperated by Robert's doubts, considering his appearance and his advantages.

"She's too—too calm," Robert answered in a rather depressed voice, and went on to describe Esmeralda's seeming indifference to his going into action and to whether or not he spent his time with her.

"Well, she's a sensible woman," Colborne said, "and from the beginning she has known your profession."

But there was now a note of uncertainty in his voice. It did seem odd that a young woman in love should accept with so little protest the constant necessity of dining alone and, what was more, be so casual about the danger into which her husband was going.

"That's what I said," Robert rejoined, a little bitterly. "She's a sensible woman. What would she see in me?"

"Come, come, now you are talking nonsense," Colborne remonstrated, "and indulging, if you will forgive me for saying so, in self-pity." He hesitated, frowned, and then said, "You know, Moreton, I still think you are mistaken and that your wife does love you, but if she has resisted, does it not occur to you that it might be for her own protection?"

"Her own protection?" Robert echoed. "What the devil does that mean?"

"Simply that Mrs. Moreton is no less aware than you of the circumstances under which you married and . . . er . . . under which the marriage changed from one of convenience, to be dissolved as soon as possible, to a permanent arrangement. Might she not feel that *you* do not love *her* and might . . . er . . . give your affection elsewhere in the future? Under those circumstances, she would spare herself a great deal of pain if her own heart were not engaged."

"You mean Merry might expect me to be unfaithful to her?" Robert asked.

"Will you stop sounding like an idiot!" Colborne exclaimed, exasperated again. "You've got more brains than you want to admit. Use them. You married her out of pity. You consummated the marriage when you were drunk. You then did the honorable thing and offered permanence. What is there in that to imply more than a dutiful arrangement? Have you ever told her you loved her?"

"I must have," Robert said, but the truth was that he could not remember doing so. "After all, we—" He stopped abruptly as an officer entered to report that the first regiments were entering

Salamanca, and after that, he and Major Colborne were too busy to resume the discussion.

Neither really wished to do so anyway. What had been said had sprung naturally from the time and place and their own fatigue, which had stripped away their usual defenses. Now Colborne could only thank God that he had not mortally offended Robert by his interference and his levity—although he still burst out laughing each time he thought of Robert's amazement at discovering he was in love with his wife, but he did that in privacy. And Robert, who had stopped short just as he had been about to describe the frequency and intensity of his lovemaking, realized that that would, indeed, have been going too far.

Chapter 25

Robert was relieved when Major Colborne showed no inclination to return to the subject of his relationship with Merry. He did not believe he needed any more advice. Once the initial shock of feeling an absolute fool was over, he began to perceive the reasons for his blindness and to understand them. Understanding brought relief; he no longer felt such an insensitive ass, and he was able to apply his brains to the realities of the situation.

His first instinct was to rush to their quarters and tell Merry about the revelation that had come to him. He now thought it very possible that Colborne had been right and Merry had been guarding her heart against future hurt. Robert was well aware of the frequency with which husbands found women more to their taste than those they had married for money or family. Thus, if he told Merry he loved her, she would surely drop her defenses and love him. However, an ADC could not leave until dismissed, and once Sir John woke, Robert was fully employed until it was time to dress for dinner.

Naturally, since most of his employment required physical rather than mental activity, Robert continued to think of his own affairs while he carried out his superior officer's orders. It soon occurred to him that to make the announcement he had been considering would be more likely to induce contempt than love in Merry. What would she think of a man who did not even know when he was in love? And with his own wife, at that. Even Colborne had laughed, despite the fact that he understood that Robert had more important things on his mind than love. And to say that to Merry was impossible; it would more likely make her very angry than make her love him. Robert did not know much about women, but he knew that the majority of them regarded love as the most important thing in life.

This conclusion left him momentarily discouraged, but once Robert
started to use his brains, they worked very well. Besides, he soon
found a military analogy to help him. If you can't take a place by
assault and it is imperative that you take it, you besiege it. Since it
was too dangerous simply to tell Merry he already loved her and win
her by shock tactics, he could show her he was falling in love with her
and break down her resistance.

Robert was satisfied with this decision because it not only provided
for all eventualities but also because he could foresee a period of
relative inactivity during which he would have leisure to court his
wife. Once the divisions that had accompanied Sir John were
settled—a matter of a few days, he thought—there would be about a
week or ten days more to wait for Hope's and Baird's contingents.
During that time, he could ask for a few days' leave and devote
himself completely to Merry. The idea was extremely pleasant, but
when he began to plan *how* to court her, he realized he had a new
problem.

Although he'd never used them in the past, Robert did know the
correct moves. In addition to a distinguishing attention, one made
little gifts—flowers, for example, at first, then trinkets like a pretty
brooch or jeweled hair combs. But this was not London, where he
could order nosegays. Nor could he purchase jewels. There might be a
jeweler or two in Salamanca, but Robert doubted they would be
willing to give him credit or take English paper money in exchange
for gold and gems.

Now Robert blamed himself for accepting Merry's filled ball cards
so tamely. As her husband, he had a right to as many dances as he
wanted. In fact, if there were to be another ball, he would be sure to
write his name across the whole card at once; that would be a clear
way to demonstrate his feelings. However, there were not likely to be
any more balls.

Sir John, although sweeter tempered than Sir Arthur, was not
gregarious in the same way. Sir John was more prone to excellent
dinners in a select male company, followed by good talk over fine
wine. In any case, Sir John was scarcely in the mood for balls. Thus,
Robert was puzzled as to just how to go about showing Merry what he
felt, but it was a pleasant subject to ponder. Moreover, Merry seemed
even more than usually cheerful and content, so he was not impatient
about getting on with his wooing—after all, he was not being denied

the physical pleasures that accrued to an accepted lover. But those physical pleasures proved to Robert that he must, indeed, make an effort. Alert now to more than Merry's overt pleasure, he discovered that among all her sighs and little cries there was no word of love—at least, not while he was in a condition to listen. However, it was just as well that he was able to contain his eagerness to win Merry's love without real anguish because the military situation did not resolve itself as quickly as Robert had expected.

First, General Anstruther misunderstood his orders and detained some of the troops at Almeida. Then, General Baird, who had finally managed to get the head of his columns as far as Astorga, received the unpleasant news that there was no Spanish army between his mere nine thousand men and the tens of thousands of French under Soult and Lefebvre. To continue his march toward Salamanca would bring him right across the front of the French forces. Baird sent word of his situation to Moore and halted at Astorga, preparing to retreat to Corunna if Soult or Lefebvre moved in his direction.

Then, in the middle of the night of November 15, Sir John was wakened with an urgent message from General Pignatelli, the governor of the province. His hasty letter informed Sir John that the French army had entered Valladolid. Worse yet, Pignatelli had fled the province, leaving the people without leadership or even authority to resist the French. Nor could Sir John obtain any intelligence about the numbers or positions of the French in the vicinity.

Under the circumstances, Sir John felt he had no recourse but to warn the junta of Salamanca that if the French pushed forward, he would be forced to retreat to Ciudad Rodrigo. However, Sir John's staff and general officers protested these plans hotly. Encouraged by this support, Sir John sent out the senior members of his staff—Robert among them—with strong patrols to try to obtain some reliable information.

The result of these investigations set to rest the immediate alarm. It was not a French army that had entered Valladolid but only one corps of Lefebvre's hussars, and they had withdrawn to Palencia the very next day. This fact did not really diminish the seriousness of the situation; nonetheless, Moore sent orders to Hope to hurry forward if he could do so without danger and instructed Baird to assemble all his troops at Astorga while an attempt was made to find out more surely where the French were and what they intended.

By November 23 all the troops directly under Moore's command
were assembled in and around Salamanca, Hope's men were moving
with all the speed they could make, and Sir John had written to Baird
to urge him also to combine forces at Salamanca. At the moment,
there was little for the staff to do but run errands, and the weather
suddenly turned clear and unseasonably warm. On the morning of the
twenty-fourth Robert asked for five days' leave. Not only was his
request granted but, to his surprise, he was told he had better start that
very day.

Robert had been racking his brains for a method of courtship that
did not require balls—to show distinguishing attention—or gifts—to
show the attentions were serious. He had once or twice found a free
hour to spend with his wife and tried to change his ordinary manner to
one that he considered romantic. But when he sighed, Merry had
disconcertingly looked up from the accounts she was doing and asked
what disaster had now befallen them; and when he had managed to
catch her in an infrequent idle moment—actually she was mending his
socks—and attempted to look soulful, she had made him laugh by
asking whether she was undone somewhere.

It was also very difficult, Robert found, to be romantic when he
expected a knock on the door at any moment to call him to duty and
where the small apartment that had been assigned to them was full of
military paraphernalia, which somehow made him feel silly and a
little guilty when he tried to act like a lover. These minor irritations
brought to his mind the fact that, aside from the few days on the road
from Oporto to Figueira, he and Merry had never really been alone.
There had always been the pressure of his duties and the casual
interruptions of his fellow ADCs.

Suddenly Robert realized that what he needed to do was to go back
to the beginning. The ideal situation in which to court Merry was one
that would recall their first meeting, but this time he would display his
admiration for her instead of treating her like a scarcely endurable
burden. On his leave, they could stay in country inns, where he and
Merry would have only each other for company and entertainment;
they could picnic by the roadside as they did before, except that now
he would not be exhausted by his responsibilities. So when he was
told he could go, he rushed back to their quarters and asked Esmeralda
if she would like to spend five days exploring the attractive mountain
areas not far to the south of Salamanca.

"Oh, yes," Esmeralda cried. "I didn't think any country could be as dull as the plains in India, but really this part of Spain is."

"And do you think we could just forget the army for a while and pretend we're ordinary people doing a tour?" Robert asked.

This question astonished Esmeralda so much that she was incapable of replying to it aside from stammering a simple yes.

It was inconceivable to Esmeralda that Robert should deliberately put aside military concerns, and her amazement held her immovable for a little while after he advised her to provide a picnic lunch and pack only a few changes of clothing because they would be staying at very simple places. She racked her brains for a reason, but nothing logical came to mind, and she was forced back to her old device of enjoying while she could whatever came. Nor, after they were mounted, could she determine anything from Robert's manner when she asked where they were going.

"I don't know," he said lightly. "There aren't any French to the west or south, so we can take any road in those directions. Aside from Ciudad Rodrigo and Béjar, there's nothing but villages on the order of small, smaller, and minuscule. Maybe they aren't even large enough to have an inn, but I think Tamames might. Anyway, any big farm will give us supper and a bed—although there might be more than straw in the mattress."

Esmeralda laughed dutifully, acknowledging that the fleas in Spain were just as lively as those in Portugal. "As long as we don't go to Ciudad Rodrigo," she said. "It seems a shame to waste our time on a place we've already seen."

"Good," Robert acceded cheerfully. "I didn't intend to go there unless you wanted to particularly." He was delighted with Esmeralda's caveat, for he had wondered a little whether she might want to spend the time at an army base where there would be other officers to pay her attention. "Then let's ride toward Tamames."

Since Esmeralda had no idea where that village was, she agreed, and they set out on a road that ran almost due south of Salamanca. At first they talked about the countryside, which was obviously grazing land, but the land soon began to rise toward the mountains. Eventually they came to a village, but it was a poor tumbledown place, and they did not stop except to ask about the road, for it divided into two tracks ahead. The right-hand fork, a woman told them, went to Tamames; the left ran along the base of a long spur of the mountains, climbed a pass, and eventually joined the road that ran from Tamames to Guijuelo. There was a small village at the meeting of the roads, she said, and perhaps they could stay there.

"Shall we be sensible or adventurous?" Robert asked, laughing.

"Oh, adventurous," Esmeralda replied. "At the very worst, we have food enough for supper and sheets and blankets. I thought about the fleas, you see."

At which, Robert caught her hand and kissed it, saying, "You are a woman after my own heart, I think the only woman in the world I could ever live with in comfort."

For the second time in only a few hours, Esmeralda was rendered speechless by surprise. It was not so much the actual words Robert had spoken or the gesture—he had kissed her hand before and praised her before—but there was an intensity and deliberateness in his manner that added a deeper meaning. Was it possible, Esmeralda wondered, that Robert had begun to feel more than she had permitted herself to hope for? Her heart leapt, and she checked the emotion fiercely. *Do not hope too hard*, she cautioned herself, *or you will assume too much and startle or disgust him.*

For a mile or two the track they had chosen was clear enough; after that, however, it began to look as if, despite what the woman said, the way might become impassable. They began to climb right up the mountain, and the road, which had been little more than a rutted cart track to begin with, degenerated until there was no significant difference between it and the sheep or goat trails that meandered over the mountainside. Esmeralda glanced nervously at Robert, but he grinned at her cheerfully.

"We won't get lost, if that's what you're worried about," he assured her. "All we have to do is keep going up. At the top, we go down, keeping the main ridge to our right. The road—such as it is—will improve once we come to the valley." Then he laughed. "I cheated, you know. Sir John has fairly good maps of this area because we had patrols riding all over it for the past ten days."

"I can see that there are enormous advantages to being married to a staff officer," Esmeralda replied, laughing also.

"Do you mean that?" Robert asked.

This time Esmeralda was not so unprepared. "Indeed I do. I always—" But at that inconvenient moment Boa Viagem stumbled, and Esmeralda's full attention was taken up for a moment in steadying her mount.

She would gladly have finished her remark, but Robert had moved ahead, turning briefly to advise that they go single file and not talk until the path was less dangerous. The advice was too good to ignore. They were well up toward the crest now, and the track wound back and forth, sometimes threading its way between the shoulder of the mountain and a precipitous drop. More than once Esmeralda bitterly regretted choosing adventure over safety, but it was too late to change her mind; the way back—supposing they could find a place to turn back—was as bad as the way forward.

All Esmeralda could do was keep her eyes fixed on the path itself, praying that she would not disgrace herself by giving way to panic. Her endurance was not strained to the uttermost; fortunately, before long they came out on the crest, which was not, as she had feared, a sharp peak. The area was broad, and the downslope seemed to be more gentle. As she caught her breath she thanked God she had not complained. When Robert turned to gesture her forward and point out the magnificence of the scene, his eyes were glowing with pleasure. Not for the world would Esmeralda have dampened that enjoyment. If it killed her, she resolved, she would follow wherever he led.

Almost as if she were being rewarded for her resolution, Robert pointed downward and said, "Look. Isn't that lovely? Shall we eat there?"

Below them, the hillside became wooded, but at some time in the past either a tremor of the earth or a natural fault had caused part of the mountain to fall. The result was a small, flat valley, sheltered to the east and west by the remaining lower rises of the hillside. Catching the full force of the southern sun, the area was obviously warmer than its surroundings. The trees and brush on the nearby hillsides had not yet lost their leaves, while the valley, treeless itself except for a few saplings, was covered by a lush carpet of grasses studded with autumn wildflowers and watered by a sparkling stream that tumbled from the cliff behind it.

Esmeralda gasped with pleasure and agreed eagerly to Robert's suggestion. She was so delighted with the prospect that the downward path, which was in some ways more dangerous than the climb they had completed, held no terror for her. They found a place not far from

the stream, where several upstanding boulders would serve as
backrests to complete their comfort while they ate.

Robert released the food hamper and the blankets from their
fastenings on the saddles. Then while Esmeralda spread the blanket
and laid out the meal, he loosened the girths on Hermes and Boa
Viagem and fastened them lightly to some bushes nearby, where they
could graze. He was not much concerned about the horses even if they
should get loose. Both were well trained and would usually come if
called.

Robert seated himself on the blanket and examined the luncheon
Esmeralda had laid out. He had a passing thought that this was the
moment to continue the "distinguishing attentions" he meant to pay
his wife, but the ride had made him very hungry, and it seemed to him
that romantic compliments were better paid when one's mouth was
free of food. Thus, he addressed himself to eating and those brief
comments, such as "Please pass the salt" and "This is excellent
ham," natural to a picnic. He noted with pleasure and amusement that
Esmeralda, sensible and delightful woman that she was, was also
reserving her attention to what was on her plate.

Before they had finished, both heard a rustling in the wooded area
of the eastern hillside. Robert turned at once to look at the horses, but
they were where he had left them, innocently engaged with the nearby
herbage. Relieved of his concern that one of the animals had
wandered away, he took a sip of his wine and began to consider how
to introduce the subject of his growing admiration for his wife.

He did not give any conscious thought to the sound he had heard.
The immediate area was sparsely populated because it was unsuitable
for farming, but all around it was countryside that had been cultivated
and used as grazing land for many generations. At the back of
Robert's mind was the conviction that any large predators would have
been exterminated long ago. He assumed the rustling was caused by
deer that had been startled by their voices or scent.

Before he had put down his glass or really completed his thought,
the gentle rustling was replaced by a much louder disturbance—and
the sound was coming toward them, not moving away. Robert leapt to
his feet, suddenly remembering that it was not only sheep and goats
that were grazed in this region but also the fighting bulls of Spain.
Four long strides took him to Hermes, and he seized his pistol from
the saddle holster. The horse, startled by his rapid movement, threw

up his head and whinnied; behind Robert a snuffling grunt came in
reply.

Esmeralda had jumped to her feet a moment after Robert. She, too,
had ignored the rustling in the brush, not because she knew anything
about the area but because she was facing the horses and could see
they were undisturbed. She had passed through parts of India where
large predators roamed, but always the uneasiness of the horses had
warned her father and the rest of their party of the presence of
dangerous beasts. She had jumped up because of Robert's movement,
and her eyes were on him, but an instant later the violent crashing in
the brush caused her to whirl around.

Disbelief and terror froze Esmeralda into absolute stillness. A
huge, shaggy form had burst into the open and was advancing on her
with the speed of a runaway horse. She wanted to scream, but her
mouth would not open and her throat was sealed shut. Even her
breathing seemed suspended. And then the sight of the animal was
shut out by Robert's blue shoulder as he swept her behind him. If
anything, that was more terrifying. To be left alone facing the monster
after Robert had been struck down was worse than being struck down
first herself. Esmeralda fought for breath and took a faltering step
sideways, seeing for the first time that Robert had his pistol trained on
the animal. Relief brought air rushing into her lungs, but fear made
her hold her breath again when he did not press the trigger.

"Shoot!" Esmeralda whispered, terrified anew by the idea that
Robert, too, was frozen with fear. "Shoot!"

Robert did not even hiss for silence, so fixed was his concentration.
His first sight of their attacker had filled him with a despair almost
equal to Esmeralda's terror. A bull, he had been sure, would have been
startled away by the sound of the pistol. They were aggressive
animals, but not, after all, carnivores. And if the sound of the gun had
not diverted the bull, Robert had intended to try to hit it on the broad
head between the horns. Even if the pistol ball did not kill the beast—
which was possible, for they were thickheaded animals and Robert
did not intend to wait until the animal was very close—the blow in the
face would surely stop or turn it. Then he would have time to finish
the job or just let it go.

But it was no bull that was careening across the open ground toward
him. It was a bear!

Chapter 26

Robert's disbelief was almost equal to his horror. There should be no bears in this area. This was not a wilderness. It was many miles to the real mountains of the Sierra de Peña da Francia. Despair choked him. There was little chance that the sound of a pistol would frighten off a monster that charged with such determination. He had no choice but to try to kill the beast. But a pistol ball that struck anywhere except in the brain would be about as much deterrent as a rap with a lady's fan, and the narrow head of a bear, obscured by the heavy fur, was a much more difficult target than the broad head of a bull. Worse yet, the lolloping gait of a bear made its head bob irregularly.

Robert realized that he would have to fire at nearly point-blank range. He reached behind him to push Esmeralda away, but she had already moved aside and he dared not take his eyes from the bear. He prayed she was running—until he heard her whisper. He nearly did fire at that moment, but just as his finger tensed, the bear slowed and rose abruptly on its hind legs. Robert uttered a strangled oath. To shoot into the body was nearly useless, but if the animal was about to launch itself at them—

Robert's thought was abruptly shattered as Esmeralda shrieked, "No, don't! It's dancing, Robert. It's dancing."

For one long moment he stood with his arm extended and then allowed it to drop. Merry was right. The beast was dancing. Paws lifted and bent, the bear turned slowly in place, making little shuffling steps. As it came around, Robert could see the ring through its nose, and, as it lifted its head and uttered snuffling whines, he noticed that it also wore a broad collar. Obviously the animal was tame, but where was its keeper?

The same thought was in Esmeralda's mind, and she tore her eyes

from the slowly gyrating animal to scan the woods. But there was no
sound or movement other than—Esmeralda gasped—than the terrified
whinnying of the horses and the drumbeat of their hooves. "The
horses—" she began, and then gasped again as the bear dropped to all
fours and began to approach.

"Back away slowly," Robert said. "I'm pretty sure it's the lunch it
wants. Just don't startle it."

As he spoke, he reached out with his left hand and grasped
Esmeralda by the wrist. His touch reduced her anxiety enough so that
she was able to suppress her urge to run. It was all very well to know a
bear was supposed to be tame, but without its keeper she was
frightened by its approach. However, it did not rush them, but
shambled forward slowly, snuffling and whining. Strangely, when it
came to the blanket, it hesitated and looked up at them.

"Yes," Robert said, "eat."

Although it was improbable that the animal should understand
commands in English, it must have sensed assent or approval in
Robert's voice. It snapped up the half loaf of bread that had been left.
As this disappeared, Robert increased the pace at which he and
Esmeralda were moving away.

"Turn around," he said to her. "Look for the horses."

"I see them," she whispered a moment later. "Thank God horses
are so stupid. They've only run into the trees instead of dashing off
down the road. The brush must have caught them. They're still
moving, but slowly."

"Go after them," Robert ordered. "Go as fast as you can without
running. If the bear moves, I'll tell you what to do."

He released her wrist, and Esmeralda had to bite back a whimper of
protest. She would be moving farther from the bear, but that was small
comfort. Actually she felt safer where she was with Robert touching
her, but her panic was over, and her mind was in control. Obviously it
was necessary to catch the horses, and that was less dangerous than
facing the bear. Besides, Robert had a pistol.

By the time Esmeralda had caught her skittish mare, however,
Robert had determined that the bear offered little threat. Once shock
and fear no longer exaggerated what he saw, he realized that the
"huge" animal was not huge at all. As bears go, it was rather small.
There was further evidence that the bear had been raised by men.
When the bread was gone, it ate whatever was left on the plates and

then began to sniff the picnic basket, but although it pawed it experimentally and even turned it over, it made no attempt to tear the basket open. Finally it lifted its head, looked at Robert, and whined, almost like a dog.

With a shock, he realized that the poor creature had no claws. He had also noticed that if one discounted the thick fur, the bear was unnaturally thin. It occurred to Robert that without claws it could not dig for the roots and grubs that made up a good part of the diet of bears in the wild, nor could it catch fish. And then, when he did not respond to its whining and open the basket, the animal rose to its hind legs and began, pathetically, to dance again. Robert could not resist the appeal. He moved forward, eyeing the beast warily, but it only snuffled and shuffled about with more energy, as if realizing a reward was coming.

Having hurriedly dumped the contents of the picnic basket, Robert withdrew, chiding himself for taking such a chance. Nonetheless, now he felt no uneasiness at turning his head to see how Esmeralda was making out with the horses. To his relief, he saw that she already had Boa Viagem's reins in hand, but Hermes was proving more difficult to catch. The horse knew her, of course, but in his nervous state he was not prepared to allow anyone to approach too close. Moreover, Esmeralda was hindered by needing to hold Boa Viagem and pull her through the brush each time she moved toward Hermes.

Robert glanced back at the bear and saw it happily engaged in devouring every edible item. He moved slowly away, glancing back now and again, but his movement did not seem to arouse any interest. About halfway across the field, after a last glance, he uncocked his pistol, put it into his pocket, and called softly to Esmeralda that he would catch Hermes himself. However, no sooner were the words out of his mouth than Esmeralda uttered a cry of consternation as Boa Viagem almost tore loose from her grip and Hermes tried to bolt again.

Turning swiftly, Robert saw the bear hurrying after him. He growled an oath, but his irritation was mixed with amusement, and he did not reach for his gun. Half a chicken dangled from the animal's mouth, and without stopping, it was trying, by tossing its head and snapping, to get hold of the portion that was slipping away. The chicken dropped. The bear hesitated and whined anxiously and then,

when it saw Robert standing still, began to root around in the tall grass
for the tidbit it had dropped.

Boa Viagem had almost stopped struggling, and Hermes, whose
dangling reins had tangled in some bushes, was snorting nervously
but not fighting the restraint. Robert realized that although the size
and movements of the bear were alarming the horses, they were not as
terrified as he expected. He also noticed that the bear paid no attention
whatsoever to Hermes and Boa Viagem. Plainly it was accustomed to
horses, which would be a natural result of being part of a traveling
circus.

For the next few minutes they all remained in position as if they
were images in a tableau, the only movement being that of the bear's
jaws as it demolished the remains of the chicken. Then Esmeralda
asked softly, her voice trembling a little, "Why does it follow you?"

"Because, like a damned fool, I fed it," Robert replied. "Don't be
frightened of it, Merry. The poor thing hasn't any claws."

"But what are we to do?" The fear was gone from her voice, but
anxiety remained.

Before Robert could decide on an answer, the bear began to
advance again. It was impossible for Robert to retreat because that
would take the animal closer to Merry and the horses. He started to
reach for his pistol, but the movement was slow and uncertain. And
there was no threat in the casual, shambling advance. Plainly the bear
expected to be welcome. Robert could not shoot it.

Behind him, he heard Esmeralda gasp. And then the bear was upon
him, gently nudging him with its nose, pushing its head under
Robert's half-raised hand. Instinctively Robert scratched behind the
furry ear. The bear snuffled softly with pleasure, its eyes closing.

"Oh, my goodness," Esmeralda exclaimed, laughing shakily, "I
don't think you should do that. You'll have a friend for life."

"I know, damn it," Robert said, "but it's a nice creature. Look, I'll
try to lead it back to the food. See if you can find somewhere to secure
Boa Viagem and grab Hermes before he breaks loose."

"Robert—" Esmeralda began, but he had already grasped the
bear's collar and started off.

The beast grunted but followed him docilely, even quickening its
pace when it saw they were approaching the blanket, which was still
strewn with food. Robert stood beside the animal while it ate,
sufficiently relaxed now to pick up the basket to remove an item or

two that had stuck when he had hastily shaken out the contents previously and to replace in it the glasses, silver, and china they had been using. Significantly, the bear did not growl as Robert took items almost from under its nose, and even moved aside a trifle when he reached for a bottle that had rolled nearly to its feet.

"I have Hermes," Esmeralda called.

"Have a good time, old boy," Robert said, patting the animal's shoulders.

He experienced a twinge of guilt when he felt the way the bones protruded under the pelt. The bear had clearly almost been starved. It seemed cruel to leave it. Robert suppressed that thought. An army officer simply could not travel around with a dancing bear.

However, Robert soon discovered that it was not a matter about which he was to have much choice. Although the bear allowed him to get about twenty or thirty feet away, if he moved off farther, it snatched up what it could and followed. Twice Robert brought it back to the food and even ordered it to stay. Each time it went where he led it without protest; nonetheless, it would not let him get too far away. At last Robert decided it must have been trained, possibly by the tug of a long rope attached to its sensitive nose, to stay within a certain distance of its keeper.

Knowing that did not solve the immediate problem. Esmeralda needed Robert's assistance to mount; nor was she strong enough to hold both horses as they struggled to bolt while he lifted her to the saddle with the bear on his heels. Unfortunately, the brush and saplings available offered no place secure enough to tie either horse, and the branches of the trees that were strong enough were too high for Esmeralda to reach. At last Robert told Esmeralda to take the horses back into the woods, secure them as well as she could where they could not see the bear, and bring him one of the ropes that had been used to fasten the baggage to the saddles.

By then Esmeralda, too, was convinced the bear was completely harmless. She had been laughing at Robert's struggles to convince it that he was not its master, and she came right up to the animal. Not a scrap of food remained on the blanket, so the bear looked at her with hopeful interest, snuffled, and nuzzled her. She patted its head.

"I am very sorry," she said to it, "but I have nothing more to feed you, silly bear. Are you lost, poor thing?" And then, to Robert: "What are you going to do with the rope?"

"Tie the bear to a sapling by the ring in its nose," he replied. "It won't pull loose. The nose is very tender."

"Oh, no!" Esmeralda cried. "It will starve. Robert, don't."

He shook his head and smiled. "I won't leave it tied, Merry. I'd shoot it before I'd do that. Once you are mounted, I'll come back and untie it."

"But that won't work," she objected. "I don't think I would be able to hold Hermes for you, and you won't be able to mount if Bear follows you. Robert, the horses don't seem *very* frightened. I think I could have got Boa Viagem quiet if I hadn't been so frightened myself. I'm not frightened now. Could I bring her out of the wood and see if we cannot accustom her to Bear?"

"I see you've named the beast," Robert said, smiling.

Esmeralda was idly scratching the head still lifted toward her, and the bear was swaying slightly, its eyes half shut. Nothing could be more evident than the fact that the animal had not only been hungry but also very lonely. Whoever had owned it, Robert thought, must have treated it well. It seemed to be as much a pet as a performing animal.

Then he frowned thoughtfully. "You may have a better answer than mine, Merry. Although the horses were wary, they weren't really terrified. But if you aren't afraid to stay with"—he grinned briefly at the use of the name—"Bear, I think I had better deal with the horses. The only trouble is that it might take so long to get Hermes and Boa calmed down that we would be caught by the dark. Over this ridge, the road should run into a valley, but I'm not sure. I wouldn't care to climb another mountain at night, nor would I like to go back down the way we came up."

"No!" Esmeralda agreed with emphasis. "Well, the sooner started, the sooner we can judge how long it will take. I'm not afraid to stay with Bear, but I'm not sure it will stay with me. Go ahead and get Boa. She seemed to be the least affected."

Bear seemed content to remain with Esmeralda, who continued to scratch its ears and murmur soothingly. The animal clearly was not particular and would grant the favor of its company to anyone who would pet it. And, surprisingly, when Robert led the mare forward she did no more than jib a little. Very soon she seemed as willing to ignore Bear as it was willing to ignore her.

Finally Robert put Esmeralda in the saddle and was even able to fasten the empty picnic basket into position. When Robert brought the horse forward and Esmeralda stopped petting Bear, the creature moved aside to one of the boulders against which they had rested while they were eating and began to rub its back and sides against the stone. Robert watched it as he went to fetch Hermes, but this time the bear did not follow him. Although this made Robert's task easier since he could mount his horse at a distance and thereby control it more easily, he was oddly disappointed.

"I guess it realizes we have no more food," Esmeralda said, directing Boa Viagem toward Robert, who was now mounted and coming out of the wood.

He thought she sounded disappointed, too, but he made no comment on that, merely asking whether she wished to go down the track ahead of or behind him. She said behind, and Robert turned Hermes into the path, suppressing an urge to call out to the bear. Nor did he permit himself to look back to see if Esmeralda was following. Naturally she would be following; that would only be an excuse.

Although somewhat less steep than the upward route, the descending track was equally bad and full of sharp bends. Robert kept Hermes to a slow walk, and half the time he would not have known that Esmeralda was behind him if it had not been for the sound of Boa Viagem's hooves. He was not sorry the road was so narrow. Although he had missed any chance to woo Esmeralda as he had intended, he was not now, for some reason, in the mood for it and was glad of the excuse not to ride side by side. He thought sourly that the day had not even provided any useful military information. The path they were on could only be used by infantry and even then only in the direst of need.

However, they came at last to a flat area, and Robert forced his lips into a smile and turned to urge Esmeralda to come alongside. Instead he stared and then began to laugh most heartily. About thirty feet behind, down the last turn of the road, as if it had always patiently followed riders, came Bear.

"Merry, look!" Robert said.

"I know it's there," she replied.

"Why the devil didn't you tell me?" he asked.

"Because I thought you might not want it along," she said, somewhat guiltily.

Robert burst out laughing again. "I don't—I mean, I shouldn't."

But suddenly he was in a good mood again. "What the devil are we going to do with a bear? Good God, Merry, no commanding officer will ever let me loose again. First time off on my own I come back with a wife; the next time with a bear. What will people say?"

"That you have an extraordinary proclivity for picking up strays, owing to a very soft heart," Esmeralda said.

It was an excellent opening to say that the first stray he had found had brought him extraordinary happiness, but Robert could not follow it up. Down in the open valley, he could not pretend to himself that the sun was not a good deal lower than he had hoped, and it was getting cold. He knew that it was still a long way to the meeting of the roads and that there was another mountainous area to cross before they came to the village where the roads met. Despite his relief that Bear had followed, the creature would slow their pace now that they were out of the hills and could expect the track to improve. Furthermore, it had to be fed.

He said nothing of these concerns to Esmeralda beyond mentioning that they had better move on, but she knew he was troubled. And, in a little while when they came to a river, which the road forded, she pointed to a track that ran down the side they were on.

"Robert, do you think that might lead to a farm? Look out there." She pointed. "I think those are cultivated fields."

Esmeralda's guess was correct, but the warm welcome extended to Robert when he rode ahead and asked for shelter for the night was somewhat cooled when he mentioned the traveling companion they had acquired. In the end, it was necessary for Robert to walk the last half mile, leading Bear by a thong through its nose, but there was plenty to feed the animal and a shed in which to lock it. Robert had been worried that Bear might not be willing to stay alone, but he found that as soon as it was tied it settled down peacefully.

Then, over a plentiful if plain meal for themselves, they obtained an additional bonus. One of the farmer's sons thought he recognized Bear. He believed that he had seen the animal performing in Béjar, but that had been months ago, before the French left that part of Spain. The bear had been with a small group of foreign jugglers and acrobats.

This sounded right to Robert. Such a small group might well make a pet of their only performing animal. It was disappointing that they had been in Béjar so long ago, but Robert still thought it worthwhile to go there. He felt that the bear must have been valuable to the group and they might have remained in the vicinity or returned to it in hopes of getting news of their lost pet. Further questioning elicited the information that there was a way across the valley to the village of Belena, and from there a good road to Béjar. The farmer's son would guide them.

They reached Béjar in two days. Several people recognized Bear, and Robert learned, again to his disappointment, that the animal had been with the troupe when they left. One young man remembered hearing that the performers intended to go west, to Ciudad Rodrigo. Since Robert and Merry had found Bear wandering in an area somewhat to the north but roughly between Béjar and Ciudad Rodrigo, he could not help but feel that some accident had overtaken the group on the road. He would have liked to follow the route, but knew they would not have time enough before his leave was over. All he could do was leave word in each place they passed as they went back north to Salamanca that the lost performing bear should be inquired for at the headquarters of the British army.

Robert and Esmeralda had found that, aside from the excitement Bear generated, it was no trouble on the road, and once leashed it was completely docile. The chain Robert purchased seemed to give the bear a sense of security, and it would remain wherever it was fastened without attempting to get loose. Within two days the horses became quite accustomed, too, and Bear could be accommodated with them in a shed or a corner of a barn. All this was very well as long as Robert and Esmeralda were free agents, but there was a good chance that Robert would be ordered to get rid of the animal when they returned to headquarters in Salamanca. Although he would have been happy to restore it to its original owners, Robert had no intention of handing Bear over to those who might use it in one of the cruel sports so popular in Spain.

The hubbub when Robert and Esmeralda rode through the streets to the headquarters area leading the bear was quite as great as Robert had foreseen. It was even great enough to draw Sir John himself out to investigate the cause of the disturbance. Fortunately, stimulated by the crowd and the attention, which seemed to please the animal, Bear chose to give a spontaneous performance. After Esmeralda dismounted, Bear placed one clumsy paw on one of her shoulders and its

chin on the other, and it waltzed her solemnly around, whining and
grunting in a travesty of singing that was irresistibly funny.

Everyone roared with laughter and applauded. A few jokesters even
threw coins, which brought more laughter and applause when Bear
carefully picked them up with its mouth and dropped them into
Robert's hand. Later, when Robert reported for duty, Sir John told him
that it was the first time in months he had laughed so heartily. Then
Moore frowned slightly, as if he realized that he had trapped himself.
It would be ungracious after such a statement to order Robert to get rid
of the bear. But Robert knew it was only a suspended sentence.
Sooner or later, Bear would have to go.

He discussed this with Esmeralda as they were undressing for bed,
and she promised to make every effort to find some solution to the
problem, but it was only later, after they had made love, that Robert
realized that Bear had created quite another problem. So much time
and thought had been expended on the animal that he had quite
forgotten his original purpose for taking leave. Not one word of love
had been said to Esmeralda during the whole five days. Robert sighed
softly. He would have to find another way.

The next day, however, Bear and all other inessentials like love
were driven from Robert's mind. During the night of November 28,
Sir John received news of another great disaster for the Spanish
armies; there was now no organized force, aside from the fifteen
thousand men—and they were all infantry without either guns or
cavalry to support them—Sir John had to oppose more than eighty
thousand French. It was, in Moore's opinion, impossible that Baird
could possibly join him before he was confronted by the enemy.
Therefore, he wrote at once to Baird to retreat to Corunna. He wrote
also to General Hope to retreat, but by way of Ciudad Rodrigo. This
might still permit a conjunction of his men with Hope's.

The reaction of the general officers to the idea that they should
retreat without making a single attempt to confront the French was
such strong surprise and dismay that, uncharacteristically, Moore was
forced to inform them curtly that he had not called them together to
request their counsel. But even his own staff officers were appalled.
Robert found a free half hour to tell Esmeralda that she had better
pack any large items they had purchased to be sent back to Lisbon
with the heavy luggage.

Esmeralda's breath caught. "Are you going into action, Robert?" she asked.

"No, curse it!" he snarled. "We're going to back off like a bunch of whipped curs with our tails between our legs." And he stormed out of the apartment.

Grateful that he was gone, for she was not sure whether she could have concealed her relief even in the face of his rage and disappointment, Esmeralda considered what should be sent back. She was surprised, as she looked around, at how much she had accumulated over the period of the march and their stay in Salamanca. Then she smiled. It was Robert, really. Now that he had a little money, she had only to look at something and he would buy it for her. So different from her father. Could it be because Robert loved her and Papa had not?

That was a most seductive notion, but Esmeralda was too aware of Robert's general kindliness and generosity to allow herself to bank too much on it. Mentally she called herself to order. She had better send Carlos to get Molly to help her. Involuntarily she smiled as she thought of Carlos. He, of course, had been speechless with joy when the bear allowed him to pet it and lead it about. He had run all over town to find out what bears liked best to eat. Esmeralda had to remind him several times that Bear was only a visitor and that it would have to be returned to its owner as soon as the man was found.

"But a found thing, senhora, can belong to the finder," Carlos protested.

"Sometimes that is true," Esmeralda admitted. "But you know, Carlos, that Captain Moreton is a soldier. A bear is not a proper animal to have in an army. Luisa has her work, you have yours, I have mine. In an army all must be useful in some way. Bear only eats. While we are here, and there is plenty of food and no danger, Bear may stay. But if we should need to move quickly for any reason, Captain Moreton might be ordered to . . . to dispose of Bear. He would not wish to do it, but . . . but a soldier *must* obey orders."

Carlos's eyes had rounded in horror, and Esmeralda had hurried to point out that the reason Bear was so friendly and tame was surely because its original owners had been kind. Thus, it would be best if those owners should be found as soon as possible. And, she had added, if Carlos paid too much attention to Bear, Luisa would feel neglected and sad.

As she recalled the conversation, Esmeralda's smile faded. Would this retreat mean they had to be rid of Bear? She decided to say nothing to Carlos about the reason she wanted Molly and to warn Molly not to mention the packing to him. Perhaps if the retreat were leisurely, they could manage to keep Bear out of the way. She was sure that if no one mentioned the animal to Sir John, the general would not be likely to remember it in the midst of his other concerns.

It was necessary, of course, to explain the cautious retreat fully to Molly or she would not be able to help competently, but Esmeralda was surprised when Molly breathed a huge sigh of relief. Her maid seldom showed much emotion, even when she felt a good deal.

"Is there something wrong?" Esmeralda asked.

"Ah, weel," Molly said, smiling, " 'tis no bad thing, onny that Oi'm growin' a bit heavy fer long marches."

"Heavy?" Esmeralda repeated blankly.

Molly laughed. "Did ye no know Oi'm carryin' a child?" she asked incredulously.

Esmeralda's mouth dropped open and then worked wordlessly. Her eyes fixed on Molly's figure, but even knowing, she did not see what she expected to see. Esmeralda had chosen Molly as a servant partly because she was a big, strong woman. Now that she looked carefully it did seem that Molly was thicker than she had been, but she had naturally put on heavier clothing as the weather grew colder, and when working in the kitchen she enveloped herself in a loose outer garment to save her dress from splatters of grease and dirty water. Still, Esmeralda was appalled that she had not noticed.

"Oh, I am so sorry," she gasped, when she could speak. "How dreadful."

Molly looked indignant. " 'Tis no dreadful," she said angrily. "Bein' Oi'm no so young as Oi were, Oi'm glad t' give M'Guire a babe."

"No, no," Esmeralda cried. "Not the baby! I meant that it was dreadful I hadn't noticed. Oh, Molly, I'm so sorry. I shouldn't have let you—"

But Molly interrupted her with renewed laughter. "Ye're hardly more'n a babe yersel'," she said indulgently. "Th' fault's moine fer no sayin', but Oi thought ye were too leddylike t' 'see' sich a thing."

"No, just too stupid." Esmeralda sighed. "But don't you think it would be better for you to go back with the heavy baggage and the

sick to Lisbon? Robert thinks there will be a retreat, and those
marches may be dreadful."

"Oi'll think on 't," Molly said, "but fer now, let's git on wit' th'
packin'."

At first, Esmeralda did not want Molly to do anything, protesting
that she should not lift anything or stretch too far, which threw Molly
into such fits of laughter that she threatened she would have her baby
then and there if her mistress did not stop talking so silly. She pointed
out that she had been lifting and stretching up to that very morning
without any dire result and also that, at this stage of her pregnancy, it
was too late to worry. If the baby came a few weeks early, so much the
better. Esmeralda was all the more embarrassed when she realized that
Molly had been four or more months pregnant when she had hired her
in August, and she admitted she knew nothing about the subject other
than a few whispers overheard.

"Weel, if ye be wantin' t' know, Oi'll tell ye," Molly offered, "but
ye'll unnerstand it's a sojer's wife talkin', no foine leddy. Ye'll be
more delicatelike thin me, and need more cossetin'. Still, some things
is th' same fer all."

Thus, quite by accident, Esmeralda had a piece of the greatest good
fortune of her life: She learned about pregnancy and childbirth from a
woman who regarded them as both natural and joyful, who did not
shrink from the less delicate aspects of the experience or regard them
with disgust and horror. Such parts of the process as morning sickness
and the pain of bearing were simply part of it, to be endured with as
good humor as possible in the knowledge of the wonder to come.
Only at the end did Molly's expression change from eagerness to
sadness.

" 'Tis all nithin'," she said. "Whin ye hold th' little one, all thit's
been, it's nithin'. Th' pain—" Her eyes filled, then closed, and tears
rolled down her cheeks. "Th' pain is whin they die," she whispered.

Esmeralda's eyes were like saucers, and they, too, filled with tears.
"Oh, Molly," she sobbed. "I don't think I could bear *that*. I don't
think I could."

Molly dashed the tears from her eyes. "God willin' ye niver will,"
she said. "But ye bear what ye must. And silly the two of us are t' be
talkin' sorrow whin 'tis joy thit's comin'. Whist! Let's on wit oor
work, or th' master'll be comin' in t' a mess o' bundles over th'
floor."

Such a representation was the best way to shake Esmeralda out of the dismals. It was, of course, impossible to complete the packing in one day, particularly since Esmeralda had decided to send back everything, heavy or not, that was not absolutely essential. That meant all the summer clothing, her ball gowns, most of the linens and other household conveniences they had accumulated—anything, in fact, that Robert would not notice was missing. And, since he certainly would notice bags and boxes piled in the apartment, Esmeralda had the packed goods stored in the stable. With Bear there, she did not think that there was any danger of theft. Few people will approach a bear, even if it is known to be tame.

Chapter 27

Oddly enough, Esmeralda's assumption that no one would try to steal articles protected by a bear seemed mistaken. After two days it became apparent that someone was trying to get into the stable. Carlos, who slept with the animals, reported that twice on the night of December 1 Bear became very restless, even rising and going to the length of its chain to sniff and whine at the stable wall. The horses, too, had seemed briefly uneasy.

Esmeralda wondered whether to tell Robert, but she did not want him to think—because she was sending so many of their possessions to Portugal—that she was frightened. He might decide to send her with the convoy. Also, he was completely absorbed in the various efforts being made to induce Sir John to change his mind. Appeals were coming in from the English minister in Madrid and from the Spanish juntas that Moore not abandon the Spanish cause.

"And I wish to hell they would leave him alone," Robert snarled to Esmeralda. "The manner and attitude of the British minister toward him is most rude and improper, and the ignorance—or dishonesty—of the Spanish is appalling. All they do is infuriate him and confirm his opinion that they do not comprehend the situation."

"Do they not?" Esmeralda asked.

"Well, the Spanish do not. They continually write about huge armies, which they have created with their pens. But the worst of all, Merry, is that *we* are spread all over the place, and no one force is complete enough even to defend itself. Hope has all the artillery; Baird has nearly all the cavalry; and we have most of the infantry. Damn the Portuguese who don't know their own country, and damn that lazy idiot Dalrymple, who never sent out engineers to scout the roads."

"But Hope has nearly caught up with us, has he not?"

Esmeralda's question sounded anxious, and Robert looked at her gratefully, believing she shared his eagerness for a union of Hope's division with Moore's. Once that junction had taken place, Robert was convinced that Sir John would see the chances of the British army in a less despairing light. In fact, Esmeralda's anxiety was on the opposite side—she was praying that General Hope was far from union—but she knew well how to be sly about the phrasing of questions so that Robert believed her sentiments to be much the same as his own.

"Yes." Robert's eyes gleamed. There was no way he could see the expression in Esmeralda's since they were, as usual, fixed on some mending in her lap. "Bless Hope, he's only fifteen miles away. What's more, there's information that the French have no idea where we are. In fact, they seem to think we've already run back to Portugal."

"But didn't you tell me that they had some cavalry units at Valladolid? That's only about sixty miles. They must have heard—"

"Well, they didn't," Robert said triumphantly. "The damned Spanish officials may not be worth thruppence, but the people are with us all the way. It looks as if they were so closemouthed that not a hint of our being here was passed to the French. Besides which Romana insists he *does* have twenty thousand Spanish soldiers. He admits that they're half-starved and without shoes or other equipment but swears that if they were equipped, they would fight."

"Then . . . you think Sir John will change his mind about the retreat."

Robert sighed. "I don't know," he said.

Esmeralda went on hoping for one day that something would delay General Hope, but on December 3 Hope's division arrived in Salamanca. This gave Moore twenty thousand men, well trained and well equipped with adequate artillery, and changed the entire aspect of the situation. What was more, Hope brought information about the movement of the French: They were apparently ignorant of the English army and were moving southward, not toward Salamanca. On December 5 Sir John wrote to Baird again, canceling his previous orders for a retreat and requiring him to return to Astorga.

He knew the French were now determined to take Madrid, but the city was preparing to resist. The remains of the Spanish armies were converging on the capital, and the people were arming and barricad-

ing the streets. Sir John did not believe that they could hold out long,
but he might be able to do something to distract the French. If they
sent part of their army to combat him, Madrid might be saved. Of
course, if they sent the whole of the army after the British—and
Bonaparte might order that, urged by his monomania about England
and feeling that when they had finished the British army they could
return to take Madrid—then, Moore pointed out, they would have to
run for it.

A plan was made to join the British forces with the Spanish under
General Romana and attack the French lines of communication by
marching on Valladolid. Nonetheless, Sir John ordered the convoy
with the sick and the heavy baggage to leave. Esmeralda urged Molly
to go with it, but she would not, insisting that as a staff officer's
servant she was better off with the army. And when M'Guire was
asked to intervene, he only blushed and said, "But *you*'m goin',
mistress."

"*I* am not eight months' gone with child," Esmeralda protested.

"No, mistress," M'Guire agreed, blushing more than ever, "but
you'm a *leddy*." Then he shrugged. "Molly knows best. 'Tisn't her
first."

And then Molly pointed out that as a displaced wife she would be at
the mercy of a quartermaster sergeant, whereas with Esmeralda she
was assured of decent lodgings and food in plenty. Knowing about the
army and the treatment of the common soldiers' wives, Esmeralda
began to reconsider sending Molly back to Lisbon. Robert would give
her whatever money he could spare, but living in Lisbon was
expensive. Besides, without her husband and Robert's rank to protect
her, Molly could be preyed upon and might end up worse off in
Portugal than with the army. The reasoning was quite correct—but
neither Esmeralda nor Molly knew of the conversation taking place
around Sir John's dining table.

"What is hoped," he said to his staff as the wine went around after
dinner on December 5, "is that our attack will induce Bonaparte's
marshals to divide. Then, if we can defeat the portion of the army sent
against us, we will give the Spanish time to rearm, retrain, and
reorganize." Then he sighed. "Truthfully," he went on, "I have not
the slightest expectation that the Spanish will use the time we will buy
them with our blood to the smallest good purpose. I greatly fear we
will have to run, and I have already asked Lord Castlereagh to have

transports waiting for us at Corunna, but if the people of Madrid are ready to sacrifice their lives, we can do no less than give what aid is possible."

A murmur of agreement went around the table, and Robert said, "Is there any chance of arranging matters so that it seems the attack has been made solely by the Spanish? It is more likely that the French will send only a small force to quash them, whereas if it is known that we are involved . . ."

"That's a good idea," Colborne agreed, "but I don't think it would be possible. Some of the French are bound to get away, and many of them would notice the red uniforms or recognize and report that the men weren't speaking Spanish."

Sir John's lips twitched. "I am afraid, Moreton, that Colborne's objections are just. No, if we are successful and our men are still capable of it, we will try another strike near Burgos. Then we will have to look for a strong point that commands the roads to Corunna. If we can resist and settle into winter quarters, we will do so, but . . . I will speak my mind plainly, gentlemen. I believe we will need to run."

Oddly, it was while this discussion was taking place and after the baggage had been dispatched to Portugal that another attempt was made to enter the stabie in which Bear was kept. Carlos, who had been having his supper with Molly and M'Guire in their quarters, returned to the stable only to see a man about to unlatch the door. Carlos yelled, and the man ran off before M'Guire could come out of his quarters and see him. When Robert got home, Carlos told him that he thought the man was tall and fair.

"Do you think he's after the horses?" Esmeralda asked.

"He must be," Robert said. "But how the devil does the fool expect to get *my* horses out of Salamanca? They're thoroughbreds; any officer of the guard would start asking questions the minute he saw them."

"Yes, but the thief wouldn't necessarily know that, Robert."

"I suppose not." Robert shrugged. "At least he now believes that the stable is guarded and hopefully won't come back."

"Oh, Robert, he ran, but if that was only because he was startled and he saw that Carlos was a boy . . ."

"I can guard the horses, senhora," Carlos interrupted.

Robert blinked, realizing that Esmeralda was more worried about

Carlos than about the horses. "Not if the thief should come back with two or three to help him," Robert said tactfully. "I think for a night or two I will ask M'Guire to assist you. He has a gun."

To this Carlos made no objection. He was aware of the value of Captain Moreton's horses and did not wish to be responsible for their loss. Thus, M'Guire took over Carlos's bed near the horses. Molly offered to take Carlos in with her—over the months they had been in service together he had become like a son to her—but Carlos had no intention of missing the excitement if M'Guire should catch the thief.

M'Guire suggested that Carlos sleep with Bear. This was reassuring to Molly, who was certain no stranger would approach close enough to Bear to harm Carlos. And Carlos was happy to agree because he had been worried about being cold. M'Guire would have his blankets. Cuddled against Bear, however, he would be warm enough.

And, indeed, with no more than a low grunt, which might even have signified pleasure, Bear accepted Carlos's company in the clean straw. As Carlos had expected, the bear radiated considerable warmth. Moreover, Bear slept very quietly. The creature did snore, but it was a very regular noise, soothing once one became accustomed to it. Thus, although Carlos was determined to lie awake and watch for the thief—because he was sure M'Guire doubted the man would return and would fall asleep—he himself drifted off very soon.

Nonetheless, it *was* Carlos who caught the intruder. The boy was awakened abruptly when Bear suddenly stood up. For a moment he lay still, sleep-dazed and confused by his unusual surroundings. In that little time, he heard the clinking of Bear's chain. It was that sound that recalled to him where he was sleeping and why, and he jumped to his feet shouting, just as the man undid Bear's chain from the hook on the wall. The intruder was briefly paralyzed by surprise; he had not noticed Carlos sleeping in the straw. Then he pulled the chain, calling some incomprehensible gibberish. Bear moved forward, but slowly. The time of the long sleeping was approaching, and the animal was growing sluggish.

By then, of course, it was too late. Carlos launched himself at the intruder—again taking him by surprise because he had dismissed the boy as too young to do more than yell for help—knocking him off balance. The man staggered against the wall, crying out himself and attempting to fend off Carlos, who had drawn his knife. Then both of them were fixed in the beam of a lantern. M'Guire, wakened by

Carlos's shout, had unshuttered his dark lantern and was standing by the door, gun in hand.

"Ye be out o' the way, young Carlos," he ordered, "an' put away th' pig-sticker of yourn. Ye be a demmed sight too quick t' wave it aroond."

By then M'Guire had taken in the fact that the man had bypassed the horses, which were all in their proper stalls, and still had Bear's chain in his hand. Obviously he had come for the bear, not the horses. In the next moment, it became clear that he must be the bear's owner. Bear placidly accepted anyone who displayed affection or brought food, but as the animal's lethargy dissipated, it began to show excitement, snuffling and whining and rubbing its head against the man who stood absolutely still under the threat of M'Guire's gun.

M'Guire frowned. "If y' wanted th' demmed bear, whyn't ye jist come ask? The mistress's been half-woild tryin' t' find a safe place fer it."

The man shook his head and said something. M'Guire did not understand him at all. Carlos cocked his head and then said in broken English, "He speak maybe some Spanish, but no good."

"Weel, he don' speak anythin' I unnerstan'," M'Guire said. "An' I ain't about t' wake Capt'in Moreton at this hour. Git me a rope, Carlos. I'll jist fasten 'im down, gentle loike, and serve 'im up to the capt'in fer breakfast."

Ignoring the passionate protests, which neither could really understand, this program was put into action, so that Robert found the intruder waiting for him as soon as he had washed and dressed in the morning. After considerable fumbling with German, French, and Spanish, Robert determined that the bear keeper was a German named Joseph Grossmann and the reason he gave for trying to steal his pet, despite the messages that Robert had left along the road to Béjar, was that he and his companions had been mistreated by the French and consequently he was frightened. In fact, the other members of the troupe had been forcibly abducted by the soldiers they had been entertaining. Joseph had escaped only because he had taken the bear into a nearby wood to see if he could find some honey.

There was genuine anguish in Joseph's voice when he spoke of those abducted—and real hatred when he spoke of the French. However, Robert was not willing to take responsibility for giving Bear to the man and letting him go. There was a chance he was a spy, and

Robert did not trust his judgment completely in this case. He knew he was predisposed in Joseph's favor because of the evidence he had of his kindness to the animal.

Thus, he brought the man, under guard, to Sir John and related the story. Having added a few questions of his own, to determine from which principality in the Germanies Joseph had come, Sir John promptly sent to the King's Own German Legion to obtain a translator from the same area, if possible. Fortunately, a sergeant from a neighboring town was available. At hearing his own language, Joseph let loose a torrent of words, occasionally bursting into tears, but the story was essentially the same except for some details and the added information about his having fallen ill, during which time he had become separated from his beloved Bertha. Robert howled when he heard the name, "Bear-ta" as Joseph pronounced it. No wonder Bear had answered so happily to Esmeralda's designation. Sir John laughed too, and then ordered that Joseph be taken away by his compatriot and fed, but kept under guard.

When the man was gone, Sir John said to Robert, "I tend to agree with you. I think the fellow was telling the truth and does hate the French." Then he paused and added thoughtfully, "These roving performers are to be found everywhere. I wonder if the man might be useful to us. Let him stay in Sergeant Landsheit's company for a day or two. Then we need only see what the sergeant thinks and whether he can convince Joseph to serve us. We could give him some money and let him go, promising to return his animal to him if he will bring us information about the French. He wouldn't have to go near them, just transmit word of what the Spanish are saying. Probably it will be a waste of good money, but there is a chance. . . . And intelligence is so bad that even lies may help."

Robert nodded. It was, indeed, very difficult to obtain information. Town officials who should have passed along word of French foraging parties or units moving in their area either did not do so at all or sent word by couriers who seemed to think they were overworked if they traveled ten miles a day. However small the chance that Joseph would even try to spy for them, it was worth a few guineas and a few hours of Landsheit's time. Robert passed along the word to the sergeant and was not surprised to hear two days later that Joseph had agreed. What would surprise him was seeing the man return with anything but a string of lies and excuses.

What Robert had not expected was that Joseph would not return at
all. He might even have reported this to Sir John had his mind not
been taken up with more important matters. Even before they had
discussed what their action could do to assist those defending Madrid,
the city had fallen into French hands. The news was discussed with
groans of dismay, but to the ADCs' surprise, Sir John did not change
his plans or mention retreat again. Although it was the capital, it was
only a city, he said. No Spanish army had been inside it, and the
central junta had also escaped—except for those who had traitorously
opened the gates to the French. Spanish resistance was not entirely
dead, and he was determined to give it what assistance he could.

Thus, the army began to move. The cavalry, under Lord Paget, was
already out forming a screen behind which, on December 11, the
infantry marched. On December 13, Moore and his staff reached
Alaejos. Robert's contingent—now much increased from the single
baggage mule with which he had started—included M'Guire leading
Robert's horses, Carlos leading Luisa and Bear, and Molly leading a
second mule, which Esmeralda had purchased for her so she could
ride if she tired.

Nonetheless, this march had been less pleasant. The warm spell
that had briefly touched the end of November had given way not only
to cold but to heavy rain. Nor was Alaejos as large a town as
Salamanca, so that quarters were necessarily more cramped and less
elegant. Esmeralda valiantly did her best, but the room was still cold,
damp, and rather dirty when Robert came in. He was filthy himself,
soaked by the thin mud splashed up by his own and other horses'
hooves, but he did not complain when Esmeralda offered only a small
pot of hot water. It was the best their little hearth would do, and a
minor miracle at that, considering that the firewood was soaked.

However, when there was a knock on the door only moments after
he had stripped off his clothing and begun to wash, he did mutter
imprecations. Esmeralda ran down to tell the orderly that Robert
would come as soon as he had got some clothing on, but instead she
cried out, "Joseph!"

The guard, who had the juggler in an unkind grip, relaxed it
somewhat. "You *do* know the man, Mrs. Moreton?"

"Yes, he's Bear's owner," Esmeralda replied.

Involuntarily the guard smiled, and his grip relaxed even more.
Almost every man in the whole army knew Bear. Carlos, with the

excuse of exercising the animal, had shown her off all over the camp.
The guard shook Joseph, but not too hard, and asked why he didn't
explain himself instead of just saying Captain Moreton's name over
and over.

"He can't explain himself, Sergeant," Esmeralda interposed
quickly. "He can't even understand you. He only speaks German, and
a few words of Spanish and French. You can leave him with me." She
saw at once that the suggestion had made the guard uneasy, and
added, "Captain Moreton's above-stairs, and M'Guire is just behind
the stable, but come up if you wish. Yes, perhaps you had better.
Captain Moreton will want to know when and where Joseph
appeared."

Joseph had not understood a word of what had been said, except for
the various names, but he realized that he had been recognized and
accepted because of the difference in the way the sergeant was
gripping him. Thus, he went up the stairs most readily, and as soon as
he saw Robert, he tore open the hem of his ragged coat, fumbled
within, and withdrew a packet of papers, which he thrust into Robert's
hand. Robert glanced down at them, started to say something to
Joseph, and then drew his breath in sharply.

"Get the man something to eat and drink if he wants it," he said to
Esmeralda, "and try to explain to him that we will keep our word. He
may leave with Bear tomorrow if he wishes, or he may remain with
us. I wish I knew where the Second Dragoons were so we could get
hold of Landsheit. Sergeant, do you know anyone who can speak
German?"

The sergeant had seen Robert's reaction to the documents he held,
and he said, "I'll try to find someone, sir."

"If you do, bring him to headquarters. I'll be there."

"Yes, sir." The sergeant saluted, then sketched another salute, the
kind one comrade gives another, to Joseph, and added, "Sorry, mate,
I didn't know you was on our side," as he left.

Robert then tried to shrug into a dry coat, but he needed
Esmeralda's help because he refused to put down the packet he was
holding. His mind was so full of hopes of what it might contain that he
went out the door without another word and had to return to ask
Esmeralda if she was afraid to be left alone with Joseph. She smiled
and shook her head no and began by signs and a few words to suggest
that the man eat and try to dry his clothing in front of the small fire.

Joseph had begun to look alarmed when Robert was so obviously
startled by the documents he had brought, but he had relaxed again
when the sergeant left, and now he smiled at Esmeralda. He seemed
to understand that it was a mark of trust to have been left alone with
her, and he tried hard to show that he was respectful and would not
approach too near or threaten her. Esmeralda found it difficult to get
him to understand what Robert had said, but even though that took
considerable time Robert had not returned. It was growing very late,
and Esmeralda had not the faintest idea what to do with the man. She
had just about decided to take him to the stable and allow him to sleep
there with Bear, when there was a knocking at the door again.

It was the sergeant who had brought Joseph, this time accompanied
by the German translator Robert had sent him to find. They had come
to take Joseph to headquarters, the sergeant said, but he was smiling,
and the explanation offered Joseph in German seemed to satisfy him.
When they were gone, Esmeralda undressed slowly and went to bed,
but she could not sleep, and Robert found her, when he returned near
dawn, sitting beside the fire.

"What are you doing awake?" he asked, and then, without waiting
for a reply, went on, "Picking up Bear was the best day's work I've
ever done, I think. Do you know what Joseph brought? It was a
dispatch to Soult, and it contained all kinds of plans and orders and
details about men and guns—a gold mine of information. They *do*
think we're back in Portugal, and Soult was ordered to overrun Léon
with two infantry divisions and four cavalry regiments. Oh, Lord, this
is a piece of luck. We know pretty well where every part of the French
army is, how strong it is, and where it's going—and they don't even
know we exist."

"My goodness," Esmeralda exclaimed, "however did Joseph lay
his hands on such a thing?"

"By a miraculous accident. Oh, we would have gotten it anyway,
but probably three weeks from now when it would not have been the
slightest use. Let me tell it in order. Joseph was making his way—"

"What have you done with him, Robert?" Esmeralda interrupted.
"He seems like a very gentle, almost innocent person, perhaps not too
clever—"

Robert's laugh cut her off. "You're quite right. I would say he was
downright simple." Then he frowned. "In fact, I think the other

members of the troupe sort of took care of him. I tried to convince him to stay with us, but he refused."

"Couldn't you make him understand that it would be safer, that he wouldn't have to fight or anything like that?"

"Oh, he understood that, but he seems to be afraid of so large a concentration of armed men. You see, the troupe he was with was entertaining the French, and most of the soldiers were very good to them, paid them well, and enjoyed their performances. Then they ran into a group of bullies who teased Bear, mistreated the two women, beat up the men when they protested, and wouldn't let them go. My guess is that they let Joseph go into the woods only because they thought he wasn't bright enough to do anything on his own. He's afraid of running into the same thing in this army and, of course, he has been roughed up a bit twice. Braun and Landsheit tried to explain to him, but . . . he's just frightened."

"But what will happen to him and to Bear?"

"He has either friends or relatives not too far from here," Robert soothed. "He wouldn't say where. Maybe he's afraid we'll come and get him or . . . I don't know. Anyway, that's what the troupe he was with was doing in Spain, visiting these people and paying their way by traveling around and performing during the summer. I guess they didn't expect to get caught up in a war."

"Do you think it's true, Robert?" Esmeralda asked anxiously. "I mean, that he has somewhere to go? Could he have said it just so you'd allow him to leave?"

Robert shook his head. "It's true enough. We didn't really press him, of course. Why should we? Anyway, he can certainly take advantage of a situation—which was how he got the dispatches." He smiled into her worried eyes. "You'll feel better when I tell you."

"I hope so. Frankly, I don't feel Joseph is any more fit to be on his own than Carlos."

"Oh, yes he is," Robert insisted. "At least Joseph doesn't look for trouble unless it's forced on him." Then he grinned. "But he *is* simple. It never occurred to him to lie low and come back to us with a pack of lies that he could blame on bad information others had given him—which is what I expected. He went off toward, of all places, Madrid, to find something to tell us."

"Oh, my God," Esmeralda cried.

"Well, he apparently had been there before, and he had no way of

knowing the French had taken the city. After-all, we didn't know it
ourselves when he was here. He said it was the biggest city he had
ever seen, and he decided, logically enough, that it would be the best
place to get information." Robert paused and laughed. "I guess it's
true that God takes care of babes and idiots. Apparently he got rides
quite easily from people who pitied him. Anyway, he had been
dropped at a posthouse at Valdestillos just when a mob of peasants
recognized some poor French ADC, set on him, and murdered him.
Joseph seems to have understood that all right because he hung around
close by. The Spaniards put the dispatches aside while they were
arguing about what to do with the body and dividing up the money, so
Joseph just helped himself to them."

"But how did he know they were important?" Esmeralda asked in a
wondering voice.

Robert laughed again. "It was the seals. To him, any paper with
seals is important. My God, it could have been a deed to property or a
list of promotions. . . ." He sighed and stretched. "Can you make
some good strong tea for me, Merry? I've got to go out again.
Everything's been changed around, of course. Sir John and Colborne
are writing as fast as they can drive their pens, and the rest of us will
be riding all over the landscape with new orders."

On December 14, loaded with gifts of food, money, and a sturdy
mule, Joseph and Bear took their leave. Carlos wept bitterly into
Bear's fur, and Esmeralda sniffled a trifle herself, as she scratched
behind Bear's ears for the last time. However, she was as relieved as
she was worried. Bear had been growing more and more sluggish as
the year advanced into winter, and she knew it would not have been
long before they could not rouse the animal and induce her to travel
with them. Then they would have faced the agonizing choice of
killing her or leaving her to fend for herself, possibly to be found and
mistreated. All in all, letting Joseph go off seemed the least of the
evils, particularly since he appeared happy and confident.

The next day they themselves set out toward their new destination.
At first everything went very well. The weather had changed; the rain
had stopped, though it was bitterly cold. For the army, the drop in
temperature was mostly advantageous, as the roads, which had
previously been sloughs of mud, hardened to a good marching
surface. By December 20, they had gone as far north as Mayorga and
connected with Baird's column. In addition, the cavalry had a series

of minor successes, cutting off several detachments of French
dragoons, capturing a colonel and more than one hundred men, even
raiding into Valladolid itself, where a hundred hussars of the
Eighteenth carried off the intendant of the province and three hundred
thousand reals from the treasury.

The spirits of the whole army were high, but Robert was so busy
that he did not spend a single night with Esmeralda, barely managing
a flying visit or two along the route as he carried orders or messages.
This was just as well, because he would have been worried sick if he
had realized what his wife was enduring. Esmeralda was suffering
bitterly from the cold, to which she was not accustomed. Her misery
was increased by the fact that quarters on the road were dreadful and,
on two nights, nonexistent. She spent those in the open, huddling with
Molly and Carlos for warmth.

She managed not to complain, not so much from fear of being sent
away now as from the realization that Robert probably could no
longer arrange for her to be conveyed elsewhere. Again Molly was
her model and support.

"If ye're an army woife, ye must no expec' inny better," Molly
said with a wry grimace and a resigned shrug. "Fleas in summer 'nd
freezin' in winter 's ye're lot fer loife. Thit, or stay hoom."

Chapter 28

There was a hovel for them at Mayorga, with a shed at the back for the horses and mules. Esmeralda insisted that Molly and Carlos share it with her until Robert came in to sleep, if he did. And to Molly's argument that it was not proper, Esmeralda smiled wanly and retorted, "Perhaps not, but it's warm."

Under the circumstances the smell of the horses and mules might have been offensive, but Esmeralda's nose had ceased to function. Neither she nor any other member of the party had taken off the clothes they were wearing for a week. If Esmeralda gave the animals a thought, it was of gratitude that they added a mite of warmth to the back wall and stood buffer against the wind. Firewood was scarce, and it had begun to snow. That they had any firewood at all was owing to Carlos's enterprise, for he picked up every stick he saw and tucked it into Luisa's pack.

Robert had no more time for his wife at Mayorga than before. To Moore's disappointment, Soult had not yet begun the advance into Léon ordered by the intercepted dispatch. He could only assume that no copy of those orders had reached Soult or that the French marshal had other reasons for remaining in the position to which the dispatch had been addressed. However, a light cavalry brigade was stationed at Sahagun, only nine miles from the pickets guarding the extreme front of the English lines.

Lord Paget, a highly enterprising officer, sent for permission to attempt a surprise, and Robert rode back with the messenger to observe the action. Sir John knew Lord Paget to be in deep personal trouble. It was most unlikely that so responsible an officer would lead his men into a disaster because of a private death wish; however, Sir

John had a cautious streak and felt that Robert's presence might be a
reminder to Paget of his responsibilities.

Robert stopped at Esmeralda's quarters to change to his hussar
uniform and was horrified, but he had no time to do more than say,
"I'm sorry, Merry. If we stay, I'll see what I can do when I get back—
but I don't think we'll be here for more than the one night."

In this assumption, Robert was correct. Lord Paget's action was a
brilliant success—two lieutenant colonels, eleven other officers, and
one hundred and fifty-seven men were taken prisoner, twenty were
killed, and many were wounded at a cost of fourteen casualties for
Paget's troops. More important, Sahagun was cleared of Soult's
cavalry screen, and Moore's army moved forward on December 21.
Here Esmeralda's quarters were a little better, but that did nothing to
lift her spirits. Robert sent M'Guire to say that he was back safe, and,
strangely, Esmeralda was grateful that he did not come himself. It
saved her from the necessity of putting a good face on her misery. But
why she was so downspirited she had no idea. All she knew was that
she felt weepy and irritable and sometimes even slightly nauseated.

She did her best to control herself, but she snapped at Carlos so
often that he found duties to keep him in the stable despite the cold.
Molly also got the sharp edge of Esmeralda's tongue. At first Molly
assumed that the cold or the prospect of more fighting was upsetting
her mistress's usually equable temper, but several times she found
Esmeralda crying when she knew there could be no specific reason for
tears—and that was completely unnatural. Mrs. Moreton, Molly
thought, did not give way easily to tears.

Then a new idea occurred to her. Molly had not thought much about
the fact that Esmeralda had been married since late July and had not
conceived. Fine ladies, she understood, had their ways of preventing
such things. When she was free of the child she was carrying, if Mrs.
Moreton's mood improved, she might ask. . . . But Molly suddenly
recalled Esmeralda's failure to recognize her pregnancy and her
mistress's confession of complete ignorance concerning so vital a
female concern as childbearing. Molly wrinkled her brow in thought.
When was the last time she had washed rags bloodied with Mrs.
Moreton's "time"? It had not been recently. It had been . . . not
since they were in Lisbon. Could that be right? But on thinking it over,
Molly became certain. Not since Lisbon.

Once that was clear in her mind, Molly leaned back against the wall and looked speculatively at her mistress's back. Esmeralda was huddled near the fire, staring into the flames. Poor little creature, Molly thought, no wonder she was so interested in all the little details of carrying and bearing a child. And now she was frightened, poor little bird. Molly's eyes filled with tears, but not only for Esmeralda. She was worried herself. She was very near her time now, and although, in general, childbearing held no terrors for her, the circumstances were not good. She had hoped they would remain in Salamanca, where she had excellent quarters, until the baby was born.

Molly had considerable military experience, having followed the drum for over fifteen years. It had seemed to her, since she was ignorant of the real situation, that it was too late in the season to begin a campaign. She glanced again at Esmeralda, leaning forward a little, and saw her mistress was crying again. Molly sighed. If Mrs. Moreton hadn't spoken of her private fears, it wasn't her place to push in where she wasn't wanted, but it seemed that two women with the same burden should comfort each other.

Another few minutes passed in silence while Molly considered how very kind Mrs. Moreton had been. She had bought the mule and extra blankets and—Molly put up a hand to wipe the few drops from her cheeks—and even some special linen for the baby. It was true Mrs. Moreton knew her place and did not often invite familiarity, but she was not so high and mighty as some officers' wives. Molly watched the trembling shoulders. *Surely Oi owe her a word o' comfort*, she thought. *'Nd even if she doesno' wan' it, she will do no more thin not answer or tell me t' be quiet.*

"It'll be long till yer toime, ma'am," Molly said softly. "Ye'll no be brought t' bed till Juloy, mebbe. Weel be in a better place thin. There's naught t' fear."

Esmeralda jerked upright and turned so sharply on her chair that she nearly tipped over. "What?" she asked.

The question was puzzled, but not bad tempered. Molly thought her mistress had not heard her because she had spoken so softly, and she repeated herself, enlarging on the fact that Esmeralda's baby would not be born until the early summer, an excellent time owing to the warmth. And, she added, the time was at least seven months away. Since Esmeralda did not check her and encouraged her, if not with words, then by wiping away her tears, Molly continued to talk about the event, assuring her mistress that she would not be inconvenienced

by the child for a long time, that there would be plenty of time even to
go to England, if she should wish to do so, although Spain and
Portugal both seemed to have healthy climates.

Meanwhile, Esmeralda's mind had been racing wildly, not over
what Molly was now saying but over what she had said weeks before,
in Salamanca. Now Esmeralda realized that she had been so
concerned over many different things—Robert's inexplicable sadness,
which had, thank God, disappeared; Bear; the prospect of more
fighting; Molly's revelation of her pregnancy . . . A faint smile
appeared on Esmeralda's lips. Goodness, what an idiot she had been.
She had never noticed that her regular bleeding had stopped—of
course, she had never paid much attention to it since it caused her no
trouble—but she had not connected Molly's description of the early
stages of pregnancy with herself.

Hastily, while Molly was rambling on about what she had heard of
the dry, pleasant weather of the peninsula in the spring, Esmeralda
made the same calculations that had convinced Molly her mistress
was pregnant. Joy flooded her. She was carrying Robert's child! She
nearly choked, suppressing the laughter at her own foolishness, but
she would not admit that she had not recognized her condition. It
would be too embarrassing, after failing to recognize Molly's.

"So ye see," Molly was concluding, "there's no need t' fret
yerself, an' Oi've heerd 'tis bad fer the choild."

"Oh, dear," Esmeralda said, "then I must surely make an effort to
be more cheerful."

At that moment it did not seem to her that it would take much effort
at all. Molly had said nothing about feeling downhearted for the first
month or two, but Esmeralda connected her depression with the mild
nausea she had been experiencing. Now that she knew what it was,
she was sure she could combat it. And for the remainder of that day,
anyway, she was successful. She busied herself with their quarters,
although she had almost given up hope of Robert joining her.

But thinking of him gave her a double qualm of fear. The first sent
her to her baggage for a mirror, comb, and brush. Had she, in her
senseless sadness, allowed herself to deteriorate in appearance? She
was shocked at what she saw. Her face was dirty, and her hair looked
like a rat's nest. Was that why Robert no longer spent his nights with
her? She told herself it was ridiculous, that he and all the other ADCs

were frantically busy because they were the links of communication that held the strung-out chain of the army together.

Nonetheless, a seed of doubt remained. Robert had not been too busy to come back to her in the early days in Portugal. She felt tears rising again over his neglect—and then wondered whether she really felt neglected or if this was another part of her recent unevenness of spirits. She fought down the self-pity and tried to consider the situation calmly, which brought her to the conclusion that Sir Arthur's army had been smaller, and Sir Arthur did not seem to change his mind so often or communicate so frequently with his general officers so that the ADCs had much less to do. Perhaps Sir Arthur's situation had been less critical—she could not judge that.

But thinking about the military situation brought a new problem to mind. Esmeralda knew that as soon as Robert heard of her pregnancy, he would move heaven and earth to get her away to England. As she washed her face and straightened her hair, she considered her state with considerable satisfaction. Surely Robert would request leave and take her home himself. Then he would be spared whatever dreadful battle was coming.

The trouble was that it would only be the one battle, Esmeralda was sure. And then she began to wonder whether, if there was a battle in the offing, *would* Robert ask for leave? Would he not consider it his duty to remain? Sir John sent messengers to Lord Castlereagh with relative frequency. Would Robert send her off with one of those messengers to be delivered to his parents? No man who loved his wife would do that, she thought—and there were tears coming again, for she was not in the least sure that Robert loved her. A few times when they had started on his leave, before they had found Bear, it had seemed as if . . .

She was afraid to continue that line of thought, particularly in view of how little effort he had made these past few weeks to be with her. But how could any man be so cruel as to send her to strangers to bear his child? She would rather have Molly. And then it occurred to her that even if Robert took her to England, he would leave her there and himself return. And after the child was born—could she take an infant into a war zone? There was no question of it; the choice would not be hers. Robert would never permit it.

Esmeralda's emotions seesawed up and down, joy alternating with tears. At last, when heavy sobs began to shake her, she realized she

was pushing herself into hysterics. If Robert came by and found
her crying, she would have to confess. . . . Esmeralda's thought
checked, and so did her tears. There was no need to tell Robert of her
pregnancy—not for months. *He* would not notice any change in her
body—particularly, she thought wryly, if he did not share her bed.

Then she would not be sent to England. And who knew what would
happen in two or three months? The war would probably not be over,
but with the onset of really bad winter weather, there might be a
hiatus. If there was no prospect of action, Robert would surely come
to England with her. She rose briskly and washed her face once more
to remove all trace of tears, vowing she would not permit herself to
fall into the dismals again—and she did not, firmly controlling her
impulses to lapse into lachrymose self-pity over her dilemma.

She had a double reward—at least, she thought of it that way for
several days, although in the weeks ahead she had reason to change
her mind. Not long after she, Molly, and Carlos had eaten, Robert did
come in.

"It's all off," he said.

Esmeralda rose to her feet, putting aside the mending she had been
doing. "You mean that Soult has retreated?" she asked, and then
urged, "Come to the fire. You look frozen."

"Not half so frozen as I will be." His lips were thin with anger and
anxiety. "No, Soult hasn't retreated. The damned Spanish junta lied
to us again—or maybe they just didn't know. We've just had word that
Bonaparte himself is after us, not with eighty thousand troops, which
the junta kept swearing was the full count of French in Spain, but with
two hundred thousand. We have to run."

"We can be ready in half an hour," Esmeralda said calmly. Since
she was convinced that nothing could be worse than what she had
already endured—and survived—she was not frightened.

Robert looked at her blankly for just a moment, then his eyes
cleared, and he came forward to the fire, smiling and reaching for her.
"My dear," he sighed, "you never fail me. But there's no need to fly
this moment. Boney's army isn't at our door. We may have to make
some very long marches, but we are in no real danger."

Quite certain now that there was virtually no chance of a battle
taking place, Esmeralda felt free to express regret at the lost
opportunity. For this very false sentiment, she was fondly kissed and
praised.

"I'm damned sorry we couldn't smash Soult's division before we had to run, too," he said, sitting down on the chair opposite Esmeralda's and holding out his hands to the flames, but speaking much more cheerfully. "Still and all, in a way we've accomplished our purpose. With Bonaparte rushing north after us, it won't be possible for him to send any armies to southern Spain. The Spanish will be able—I hope—to train some troops so that they can fight, and equip them so that they have something to fight with, poor sods. Anyhow"—he smiled grimly—"I'll bet we've messed up Boney's plans. He won't be able to do much more until spring, and by then we'll be ready for him."

By spring . . . Esmeralda's throat tightened, but she managed to nod and ask steadily, "Will we retreat to Portugal?"

"No, there's no chance of that," Robert said, looking troubled again. "The French can too easily cut us off from the roads west. We will go north toward Corunna. There are magazines of supplies in various towns along those roads. I don't think it will be too difficult, but to tell the truth, Merry, I'm concerned about the men."

"The army, you mean? But if there are supplies, why should you worry about them?" She was considerably surprised. The men, she assumed, did what they were ordered to do, and it seemed to her they should be delighted with orders that would save them from a battle.

"They don't like to retreat," Robert explained. "I've seen this problem before."

"They don't like to retreat?" Esmeralda echoed, confused by what, to her, was irrational. "You mean they *like* the prospect of being killed or wounded?"

That drew a short laugh from Robert. "Not that, but they like the prospect of beating the French. No one else has done it, and *they* have. Those who were at Roliça and Vimeiro have been strutting around like heroes, and all the others are just burning to match or overmatch them." He shrugged. "And it will be worse this time because they don't understand why we are retreating. Had they fought and been beaten, they would have understood the need to withdraw to re-form, but we haven't been beaten. Even if they had a sight of the enemy and realized the odds were overwhelming—but all they've heard about is Lord Paget's cavalry exercise, and that was a flaming success."

"But surely the officers could pass the word about the new information."

"I don't know what Sir John will decide about that. But even if he decides to make the information public, it might not help." He shrugged. "I don't know why, but there's something about retreat that kills the men's spirits."

"I'm sorry," Esmeralda offered. There was sympathy in her voice, but it was for Robert's worry. She did not connect what he was saying with herself in any way.

"Well, it depends on the officers and the discipline, but sometimes there are disorders, and I don't want you caught up in anything like that, Merry."

"Me!" She was about to say that the men were always pleasant and respectful to her, but she suddenly remembered how they had become drunk and unruly during those early days in Portugal.

"There's nothing to worry about, my dear," Robert assured her quickly. "I just wanted to explain why I've changed your marching position. You will now ride with the Coldstream Guards. The first battalion's commanded by Lieutenant Colonel Cocks and the second by Wheatley. There won't be any trouble among the Guards, and you know Wheatley and Cocks, don't you?"

"I have met them, of course," Esmeralda said, controlling her voice with difficulty, "but I am sure they will not wish to be encumbered with—"

"I've spoken to them already. Both have said they would be delighted to have you join them. I'm sending M'Guire along with you, too."

Delighted to have her, indeed! What else could the poor men say, since they were gentlemen? Wasn't that what they called the Guards— "the Gentlemen's Sons"? Could they refuse to watch over a fellow gentleman's wife? A tide of fury rose in Esmeralda at the thought that she was to be thrust on two near-strangers, handed over like a parcel to be placed in storage. That was all she was to Robert, still—an inconvenient burden.

"And where will you be?" she asked icily. "Where will you be while Colonel Wheatley and Colonel Cocks see to my well-being?"

"I'm not altogether sure," Robert said.

He was aware that Esmeralda was upset by his answer, but he did not want to tell her that he had been detached to remain with Lord

Paget and the rear guard. She would guess there would be fighting and would worry—whether she loved him or not, he was necessary to her. He knew, too, that Esmeralda was having a hard time and that there was very little he could do for her. Sir John's accommodations were no better than hers.

Robert blamed himself bitterly for selfishly having allowed her to follow him just because he wanted her near, for letting himself forget what a winter campaign could be like. He thought Esmeralda might be angry for the same cause, but too just to accuse him because she herself had wanted to come. Each time he thought of that, of the clever way she had obtained tacit permission from Sir John without even raising the question, as if it had long been decided, it lifted his spirits. She could have stayed in Lisbon if she were afraid to go alone to England. It must be for his sake that she had arranged to follow him to Spain.

He looked across at her and sexual urgency swept him. How long had it been since they had slept together? More than a week, anyway. Damn Moore! He said, "Merry—" and reached toward her, but she did not look up from the mending, to which she had returned her attention, and he became aware of how pinched and pale she was. She must be exhausted. It would be unfair to thrust himself on her.

Besides, he was scarcely a sweet object to take into bed. He stank of horse and sweat and mud, and it was out of the question to bathe and change. Even if he had time, which he did not—in fact, he should be on his way right now—he would spend the afternoon riding all over with orders and getting himself filthy again. It made more sense to stay in the dirty clothes. He stood up abruptly, knowing that if he stayed a moment longer he would have her in his arms and be quite incapable of stopping.

"You'll leave tomorrow with whichever battalion marches first. I've arranged for Cocks or Wheatley to send a man for you. Stay with the Guards, Merry. That way, if the baggage train goes or the other corps start to straggle, I'll know where to find you."

"Very well, Robert," she replied, her depression making her nurse her resentment to hold back tears.

He stood a moment, irresolutely, duty fighting desire. If she had looked up, he would have been lost; but she did not, and duty won.

* * *

Resentment, however unhealthy, is a great stiffener of the spine, as
Esmeralda knew well. It was resentment against her father that had
permitted her to keep her soul intact and outwit him, too. Now
resentment preserved her from drooping, and she greeted with a smile
the young subaltern, one of Colonel Wheatley's ADCs, who came to
guide her to her place in General Baird's column.

He arrived at about ten o'clock in the morning, his boyish face
wearing an anxious expression, which cleared to astonishment when
he realized that everything was packed and ready to be loaded.
Obviously he had expected the worst, perhaps that there were no pack
animals or that he would have to supervise the packing himself, for he
explained, in some embarrassment, that he had actually come rather
too early. The column would not begin to move until noon.

"Well, then," Esmeralda said lightly, "we will have time for a
luncheon. We are experienced marchers, you know, and everything is
to hand."

They ate and chatted pleasantly, the young man growing more
relaxed by the moment as he became convinced that his task was not
nearly so onerous as he had originally thought. He looked anxious
again when he saw Molly, now unmistakably heavy with child, but he
shrugged off that worry. Molly was no business of his, particularly
since her husband was with her. His duty was to see that Mrs. Moreton
was safe and as comfortable as circumstances would permit.

It was an auspicious beginning, and from Esmeralda's point of
view, the weather cooperated at first. There was a thaw on Christmas
Eve, warm enough to melt much of the snow they had had. Since they
were accompanying infantry, Boa Viagem was not hard pressed, but it
was heavy going for those afoot. The roads were little better than
bogs. Christmas Day passed drearily as they slowly but steadily
progressed on their wet journey, but by the next day the thaw and the
continuous rain had made the passage of the Esla River, which they
crossed at Valencia de Don Juan, rather dangerous. However,
Esmeralda's party was ferried across without trouble, and fortunately
there were few accidents.

By this time Esmeralda, who had had a good deal of the young
subaltern's company and conversation, had begun to realize that
Robert was not simply trying to pass off the burden of protecting her
and knew what he was doing. Even among so well disciplined a group
as the Guards, the men were surly, and when they reached Astorga on

December 29, Esmeralda heard that the behavior in the other divisions
had been much worse. Men had broken ranks to seize food in towns
without waiting for the distribution of rations, which were available.
The countryside being virtually destitute of wood, the men had torn
down sheds and doors and even broken into houses to seize furniture
with which to build their bivouac fires. In Benavente, the castle of the
Duchess of Ossuna had been villainously damaged, the precious
medieval furniture broken up to burn, the priceless tapestries torn
down, and the porcelain friezes and alcoves wantonly destroyed.

Thus far, the subaltern remarked, trying to conceal his pride in the
superior behavior of his own unit, there had been few outrages against
persons, but if the officers did not control the troops better, that would
come, too. Had Robert appeared at Astorga, Esmeralda would have
greeted him with far more warmth than she had offered when they
parted. She thought often about him, sometimes worrying, sometimes
dwelling on how she would tell him, when it seemed safe to do so, of
the child she carried.

Robert, however, did not give Esmeralda a thought. He was
enjoying himself enormously, for he was in almost constant action
from the time he joined Lord Paget. The cavalry was having a far
more thrilling time than dully plodding through mud and rain. They
and the two light brigades that remained at Sahagun had so
successfully harassed Soult's advance forces that the marshal was left
in doubt on December 24 as to whether he was about to be attacked.
He hesitated until the twenty-sixth, and even after the pursuit began,
the cavalry and light divisions continued their rearguard action so
successfully that the main body of the army was completely
unmolested. And, on December 28, they pulled off a magnificent
coup, breaking a charge by about five or six hundred chasseurs of the
Guard and capturing their commander.

It had been rumored that Sir John would stand and fight at Astorga.
There were plentiful supplies at no great distance, the town itself was
walled, and although it could not be held long against forces so much
superior to their own, there was a formidable range of mountains
rising behind, cut only by two narrow and easily defensible passes.
The rumors were false. Not only was there no attempt to hold the
passes beyond Astorga, but the army did not even remain long enough
in that place to distribute the huge masses of stores accumulated there.
Part of the problem was the inevitable inefficiency of all armies, but a

great deal more was owing to the growing disorder among the troops.
M'Guire, having been out trying to get shoes for himself, Molly, and
Carlos, reported that hearing they were to retreat again had exasperated the men to the last degree. He warned Esmeralda to remain
indoors and stood guard at their door, gun in hand.

There was never any danger for Esmeralda. Before dark a
detachment of Guards was at her service, and both Colonel Cocks and
Colonel Wheatley came to bear her company at dinner and on into the
evening. Nonetheless, Esmeralda was distressed. She was bitterly
ashamed that British troops should misbehave in such a fashion.
Unfortunately, the little she saw and heard in Astorga was only the
beginning of a long nightmare.

Chapter 29

By December 30, when Esmeralda and the main body of the army left Astorga, the thaw was over. Rain had begun to change to snow, but on that day and the next, there was not enough to cause serious inconvenience. It was at Bembibre, on the evening of the thirty-first, when the trouble began. The village, unfortunately, was a local depot for the storage of wine, and marauders from the angry, disheartened troops found their way into the vaults and cellars.

On the morning of January 1, 1809, nearly a thousand men were drunk and incapable. A few companies of the Guards were called out to attempt to rouse the stragglers. Not one Guardsman was among the bodies strewn in the streets and the houses of the village. A combination of vigilant officers and a strong sense of pride kept them free of such excesses while on duty. Esmeralda's party was attached to one of the companies called out, not by chance but because it was one of the smartest and best disciplined. However, since she and her companions gave so little trouble, no one had remembered to order her on ahead in the emergency.

Thus, she watched with horror as men were lifted and shaken, beaten and dragged, in an effort to rouse them. Only a few responded. At last, the order was given to abandon those who could not or would not stir. If they could not be roused by the rear guard, which was a day behind, they would have to be abandoned to the French. As it was, the Guards companies that had been delayed in getting the stragglers moving had to step out smartly to catch up with their regiment.

Moving with them as they passed other regiments to overtake their own, Esmeralda saw further results of the breakdown in spirit that Robert had predicted. Many of the companies were preceded by a motley group who broke from the road whenever they were attracted by something they thought worth stealing. Behind came others, limping or sick or simply unwilling to keep pace.

But the disorders on the march were nothing compared with the scenes Esmeralda witnessed after they arrived in Villa Franca, Sir John's most important depot for military supplies. Sir John had ordered these to be burnt because there was no transport capable of carrying them off and because he had given up all notions of opposing the French. With the last hope of facing their enemies gone, most of the troops became openly mutinous at the idea of all the food and drink being wantonly destroyed. They broke into the magazines and began to load themselves with everything they could carry.

Hurrying through one square, Esmeralda saw a company break ranks despite their officers, who actually drew their swords and slashed at them. At the next crossing, M'Guire called out that Molly could go no farther. Esmeralda pulled Boa Viagem to a stop, and the entire group moved into the side street to be out of the way of the steadily marching Guards while Carlos and M'Guire rearranged the packs so that Molly could ride. Before M'Guire had lifted her to the saddle pad, two soldiers, already drunk on the rum that had been in the stores, staggered into the street demanding the two mules.

M'Guire's gun was slung on his shoulder, but the two drunks were in fact far less prepared to enforce their demand, since their arms were full of bottles and bags. Carlos slipped around under Luisa's nose and knocked the legs from under one, while M'Guire hit the other in the face. There was a roar of outrage from several other equally drunken men who were just turning the corner. By then, however, M'Guire had his gun at the ready, and Carlos had his knife out. The renegades paused, none of them quite drunk enough to want to take M'Guire's shot.

Esmeralda held her breath. It was an ugly situation. Once M'Guire fired, the gun was useless, except as a club, because the men were too close to give him time to reload or to fix his bayonet. But then she heard the regular tramp of marching feet. Uttering a shrill scream and simultaneously bringing her whip down on Boa Viagem's croup, Esmeralda drove her mare right through the group into the main road, knocking two men to the ground. A Guards officer was already turning toward the disturbance. In another two minutes the incident was over, but Esmeralda was terribly shaken.

It was not that she had been so very frightened; there had hardly been time enough for shock and surprise to turn to fear. However, she could not dismiss the incident from her mind as she had dismissed the attack of the French soldier at Roliça. He was an enemy, and it was natural that he should attack her to seize what he wanted. That English soldiers should do so turned her world upside down. She had not forgotten that Robert had warned her and had placed her in the care of the Guards battalions to avoid just such a situation, but she had never *really* believed it could happen.

Seeing how white and strained she was, the officer had remained with her, had seen her to her quarters, and had obviously reported the incident to his superior officer, for Colonel Wheatley himself had come not half an hour later. He had apologized for the failure of his men to protect her and assured her it would not occur again. He was most sincere; nonetheless, Esmeralda cried herself to sleep that night. No matter if a thousand Guards surrounded her, they could not give her security; she wanted Robert.

She was not to have him. Robert was only six miles away with Lord Paget, but the French were hard on their heels and Robert could not ask for leave, although he did think of Esmeralda. He had been thinking about her for the last few days. Several times in the past week he had escaped serious injury or death by very narrow margins, and it had occurred to him that, if he were killed, she would never know that he had loved her.

When the notion had first come to him, he thought that would be all for the best, not that he should be killed but that if he were, Merry should be completely free of him. But Robert found he could not bear the idea. He wanted Merry to remember him and to cherish that memory. And, as the French cavalry and dragoons came into sight, he cursed the fixation on military duty that had made him leave her that last night without a word or touch of love.

Esmeralda should have saved her tears. What she had seen and endured thus far was child's play to what was to come. For some reason unknown even to his closest associates, Sir John decided that forced marches were necessary. Since the draft animals were already on short rations—because it was impossible to obtain fodder in the barren, snow-covered country through which they were passing—they began to drop in their tracks from exhaustion. As soon as an animal failed, it was shot, partly to keep it out of the hands of the

French. Half the time Esmeralda rode with her eyes closed to escape
seeing the pathetic corpses.

But soon there were more pathetic ones. The women and children
who had been riding on the baggage wagons were the next to go.
Inadequately clad and shod, some clung to their refuges until they
froze to death. Others tried to follow the army, only to drop by the
wayside, victims of fatigue and cold. One day—later Esmeralda
calculated that it had been the afternoon of January 5, but at the time
she had no idea of the date—she saw a woman fall near the top of a
rise they were just beginning to ascend. More than half an hour later,
when they passed that spot, she was still there. Esmeralda told
M'Guire to see if a short rest, riding instead of walking, would help
her.

For her, it was too late. She had probably actually died on her feet,
still struggling onward. M'Guire brought the reason for her struggle to
Esmeralda with tears freezing on his cheeks.

" 'Twas tryin' to suck, mistress," he said, choking, "an' her
colder'n clay."

"Oh, my God," Esmeralda whimpered, taking the infant and
wrapping it in her furred cloak. "God have mercy on us all."

They did their best, although they dared not stop for more than a
minute or two at a time. They had no milk or bread, of course, but
Carlos cut a hunk of flesh from a still-quivering ox, and they pressed
the blood into snow that Esmeralda melted by holding a tin cup
between her breasts. To this they added sugar, and Esmeralda dribbled
the mixture into the baby's mouth; but its breathing was already very
bad, and it died a few hours later while they were still struggling along
the road. M'Guire did his best to bury it when the company of Guards
stopped for a half hour of rest, digging through the snow to the frozen
earth with his bayonet; the grave was very shallow, but at least the
little corpse was not exposed to the carrion eaters.

They had not plumbed the depths of horror yet. Just before the
dusk, Molly's mule failed. It had been the weakest of the three
animals, but all of them looked at Boa Viagem and Luisa and saw that
they, too, were nearing the end of their strength. M'Guire shot the
mule, and they went forward, all on foot now, even Esmeralda. An
hour later Carlos collapsed. Esmeralda dropped beside him with a cry
of despair, but he had only fainted.

When roused, Carlos denied emphatically that he was sick, and this

seemed true, for Esmeralda could feel no sign of fever, but she could
not be content, and continued to question him until he confessed that
he was nearly starving. He had been giving all his food, except the
meat, which she would not eat, to Luisa. Her tears over the mother
and baby barely dried, Esmeralda wept anew. What fodder they had
was doled out unevenly, the larger portion to Boa Viagem. No one had
questioned the division, not even Carlos, for it was known that mules
were hardier than horses and could stand deprivation better. The only
thing Esmeralda had forgotten was Carlos's devotion to Luisa and the
effect on him the shooting of the draft animals would have.

"How stupid I am." Esmeralda sobbed. "Why should Luisa carry
what we no longer need? M'Guire, get the packs off her. We can
discard the dishes and the water bottles and most of the pots.
Everything but the food, the blankets, and Captain Moreton's clothes
can go."

Molly had sunk to the ground, her face gray and her breathing
labored, but she began to push herself to her feet to help M'Guire,
whose hands were clumsy with cold. Esmeralda shook her head and
went to help him herself. She did not mind the work at all, but she was
worried by Molly's quiescence. It was not like her to allow Esmeralda
to work while she sat. Perhaps Molly, too, was nearing the end of her
endurance.

They had just about finished piling everything that could possibly
be discarded by the side of the road when a sergeant of the company
with which they traveled came plodding back.

"Ye must move on, ma'am," he said. "I'm sore sorry, but ye must
not stop to rest now. If yer servants canna keep up, they must stay."

"No, no," Esmeralda replied, "we are coming. I only stopped to
lighten the load on the mule."

They repacked in frantic haste, the sergeant standing by and
watching. It seemed to Esmeralda that if she had said Carlos or Molly
could go no farther, the man might have forced her on without them.
Carlos was no problem. With so much baggage discarded, he could
ride Luisa until his strength was a little restored, but Molly . . . Esmeralda glanced at her fearfully from the corner of her eye and tears
started to trickle down her face again. But all through the night,
somehow, with little rests riding on Boa Viagem and Luisa, Molly
managed to keep up. It was already faintly light when she moaned

through gritted teeth and said, "Oi must stop. Oi'm sorry, ma'am.
Ye've done yer best, but ye must leave me now."

Esmeralda, placing one foot in front of the other like a puppet
without conscious volition, stopped and turned to look at her.
Esmeralda was not crying anymore, not because there were no tears
left but because her mind was so numb. There is a point beyond which
horrors cannot be absorbed, and the scenes they had passed, unable to
help, had equaled and outdone the dead mother and child left behind.
Even the Guardsmen were failing now, steady old soldiers falling out,
some of them literally dropping dead on their feet.

"Put her up on Boa," she said dully.

It was not a good time for it, as she had dismounted only ten
minutes before when the mare had stopped and stood trembling,
obviously near foundering. Esmeralda had pulled Boa forward, and
the horse had managed to walk with no weight on her, but she was still
shaking and swaying. Luisa was in little better condition and was
already carrying Carlos, who had fallen again and was obviously
incapable of walking.

"'Tis not thit," Molly gasped. "'Tis th' baby comin'."

"No!" Esmeralda cried, jerked out of her numbness by a more
personal horror. "Not here! Not now!"

But Molly had sunk to her knees and did not answer. M'Guire knelt
beside her, tears running down his face. Wildly, Esmeralda stared
around, but all she saw were splotches of dirty red on the clean white
snow, marking the places where men lay exhausted, dying, or dead.
There could be no help for them in this desolation, yet these were her
people. Somehow she must find something, but she was so tired
herself that she did not know for what to look. And a rising sense of
horror and despair was making her even less capable because, no
matter how dreadful the things were that she had seen and heard up to
this point, she did not know the people who lay dead or too exhausted
to move, slowly freezing. This was different. This was Molly. Could
she even think of leaving Molly to bear her child in the freezing snow,
to die with the infant in her arms?

The horror of that thought made Esmeralda's mind whirl. She
would not willingly leave Molly, no, but she might be forced away.
The Guards had their orders. Mrs. Moreton was to be brought safely
to Corunna. As long as she kept up, no one questioned how, but if she
dropped out someone would come seeking her. She had already been

told she would not be permitted to wait for her servants, and she was sure that if she said her horse had failed, another would be found for her even if one of the officers had to walk. Molly groaned again, and M'Guire put his arms around her, crying, "Whut'll I do for ye?"

Again Esmeralda's eyes searched the landscape. The panic in M'Guire's voice was catching, and desperation focused her previously unseeing eyes. Down the slope, not far from the road, were the remains of a small house. Hide. The word came with sensible meaning. They could conceal themselves in the house until Molly's baby was born. Esmeralda was sorry for the anxiety she would cause the officers responsible for her, but that was insignificant compared with Molly being left behind.

"Can you carry her, M'Guire?" Esmeralda asked. "Look, down there, the house. I'll help if I can—"

But M'Guire had already picked up Molly and was staggering toward the haven Esmeralda had indicated. She followed, dragging Boa Viagem, fearing each step would be M'Guire's last. Although he was the strongest of them, he was also the only one who had walked every foot of the way. And he had put out the most effort of any of them, for in addition to walking, he had lifted each of the others on and off the horse and mule innumerable times.

He just barely made it, sinking exhausted on the doorstep, but with Esmeralda's help, Molly managed the few steps through the gaping doorway into the interior. The marauders had been there before them. Not a stick of furniture nor a door remained. Even the floorboards had been ripped up in some places, whether for firewood or in search of hidden valuables, Esmeralda did not know or care. She only noticed because the floor sagged crazily so that she and Molly nearly fell.

Having managed to ease Molly down without disaster, Esmeralda ran out again. M'Guire was lying where he had dropped, sobbing with effort and fear, for he loved his wife. Seeing his helplessness, Esmeralda hesitated, panic rising in her again. She pressed her hands to her mouth, trembling on the edge of collapse herself, but was saved by the sight of Carlos staggering toward her with his arms full of blankets, topped with a small white package—the baby linen.

The whirling world steadied. With the blankets to keep her warm, perhaps Molly and the baby would live. They were not starved. Molly would have milk. Hope renewed Esmeralda's strength, and she ran forward and seized the blankets and bundle from Carlos.

"Take Luisa and Boa around to the back where they cannot be seen from the road," she said to Carlos. "Then, if you can, help M'Guire inside—but it is more important that you keep yourself and the animals out of sight."

She did not take the time to explain. The need to hide Luisa and Boa Viagem was obvious. They might be seized by stragglers or even by legitimate authority to draw supply carts, not that they really would be of much use, owing to their condition. In any case, their presence would draw unwelcome attention to the house, and Carlos might even be recognized by a Guards officer searching for Esmeralda. M'Guire lying on the doorstep was less important. So many men littered the roadside that another body, seemingly collapsed seeking shelter, would hardly be noticed.

As she made her way past M'Guire into the house again, a new fear shook Esmeralda. Aside from helping her onto the blankets, she had not the faintest idea of what to do for Molly. But as it turned out, she had no time to do even what she intended. As she entered the room, Molly screamed, "Take the baby! Take it! 'Tis out!"

Esmeralda dropped everything and threw herself forward onto her knees. Molly had turned up her skirts, under which she was naked, and between her wide-spread thighs Esmeralda saw a tiny black head and narrow shoulders. Before she could think, her hands had gone out to support the little body. Even as she grasped it, the rest of it slithered out as Molly gave one last push, gasping with pain and effort and relief. For a moment, Esmeralda simply knelt where she was, paralyzed between wonder and terror and not knowing what to do, for the baby was still attached to its mother by a long slippery cord.

"Turn 't over," Molly whispered. "Turn 't over, head doon, 'n give 't a slap."

Fortunately Esmeralda was so numb that she obeyed. She was far too afraid of dropping the slippery little creature to think of much else, and it was just as well she was concentrating so hard on holding it, for she might have dropped it in disgust when it gagged up a mess of slime or in astonishment when after that it suddenly let out a lusty squall.

" 'Tis aloive," Molly breathed.

"Oh, it certainly is," Esmeralda assured her. "It's squirming like anything."

"Lay 't on me belly," Molly instructed, her voice growing stronger,

" 'nd pull me skirts over't. Thin ye'll need t' foind a knife t' cut th' cord."

With mingled relief and regret, Esmeralda placed the baby as Molly had instructed and rose to her feet. It was a horribly ugly creature, red and wrinkled, with spidery limbs and a misshapen head, but it pulled at Esmeralda's heartstrings nonetheless. She felt dazed, and repeated to herself, "A knife. A knife," until the words suddenly took on meaning. "A knife," she said aloud, frightened again. "Where will I find a knife? We left all the cutlery by the road."

"For what do you want a knife, senhora?" Carlos asked in a trembling voice, staring at Esmeralda's hands.

"To cut the cord of Molly's baby," she said, smiling for the first time since they had begun this nightmare trek. "Don't be frightened by the blood, Carlos. Molly and the little boy are both alive."

"Thank God! Oh, thank God," came M'Guire's voice from behind her. "God bless ye, mistress, God bless ye. For whut ye done this day, I'll die for ye, so I will, I swear it."

"I would prefer it if you would stay alive for me, and for Molly, too," Esmeralda replied, still smiling, but even as she was speaking, a frown replaced the smile. "Do you have a knife?" she asked anxiously. "I think it is very important to cut the cord."

M'Guire shook his head and started to struggle to his feet. "Me bayonet—" he began, but Carlos was already holding out his knife.

Esmeralda took it almost reluctantly, alarmed again about being responsible for something which, if done wrong, would have dire consequences, she was sure. However, on returning to Molly, she found that the cord no longer trailed inside the new mother. There was a horrible mess on the floor to which it was attached. Esmeralda recoiled.

" 'Tis th' afterbearing," Molly said. She sounded almost normal and had recovered sufficient strength to push herself a little distance from the worst soiled part of the floor. "Ye need not touch it. Jist pick up th' cord 'n cut it. Now toy a knot in it. Thin turn th' little un over 'n toy anither close 's iver ye can t' his belly. Whin ye're sure that's toight 'n sound, cut th' cord agin not far from it. Soon 's Oi cin find a bit o' silk threat, Oi'll toy 't off closer."

The instructions were easier to give than to follow. Esmeralda found tying knots in the resilient, slimy cord no easy thing, and cutting it, even with Carlos's sharp knife, was not simple, either. The

baby, who had quieted when placed on Molly's belly, began to squall
again when Esmeralda handled him. Nonetheless, she could not help
smiling once more as she struggled to follow Molly's directions.
There was something very wonderful about the arrival of the new little
creature in the world, despite the mess that surrounded it.

Molly had fallen asleep with the baby at her breast the moment
Esmeralda handed him to her when she finished cutting the cord. For a
minute or two, Esmeralda stood looking at her, knowing she should
try to rouse her so that they would not fall too far behind and become
stragglers themselves. But she could not find the strength. Her last
reserves had been expended in acting as midwife. Orders or no orders,
she could go no farther. She dragged two blankets over Molly,
wrapped another around herself, and sank down into a blessed
unconsciousness. Her last thought was that she would probably freeze
to death, like the pathetic women and children they had seen, but she
no longer cared.

Fortunately, despite his temporary collapse, M'Guire was not as
exhausted as his wife or Esmeralda. He moved both women together
and wrapped them up, brought Luisa and Boa Viagem into the house
to add the heat of their bodies, and took up the broken floorboards
with which he made a fire. Then he and Carlos huddled together under
the remaining blanket, but M'Guire propped himself against the wall
so that discomfort roused him as soon as the worst of his exhaustion
had passed.

It was late afternoon when he woke and shook the others awake. By
then they were far behind their escort. Esmeralda should have been in
despair, but the enforced rest had done her good, and she was able to
think. The rear guard, she knew, was a full day behind the main body
of the army. Thus, they were in no danger from the French until the
rear guard passed. The worst danger they would have to face were the
renegades from their own army, but that might be reduced by
attaching themselves to any company that was marching in reasonably
good order. She handed Carlos his portion of food and sent him out to
watch for such a group and, in the meantime, suggested that M'Guire
make another fire. They would eat and give all the remaining fodder
to the animals.

"Wherever we are going cannot be far," she said. "Even Sir John
cannot expect men to march for much more than twenty-four hours
without rest."

This conclusion, reached more out of hope than out of reason, was quite correct. Before M'Guire had got his fire going, Carlos came running back to tell Esmeralda that he had seen a file of men in good order just coming over the rise. There was little to pack. M'Guire lifted Molly to Luisa's back, Esmeralda mounted Boa Viagem, and they came out to the side of the road and waited. When the company was close, Esmeralda rode forward and explained who she was and what had happened. The captain was courteous, but not enthusiastic. If they could keep up, he said, he would do his best for them.

Had any of them known how close they were to Lugo, where Sir John had halted the army, Esmeralda would not have bothered to wait for a company in good order and the captain would have been warmly welcoming in the hope of making a friend in high places. Still, they were all satisfied with the outcome when they arrived about an hour later. One more unpleasant task lay before Esmeralda—reporting herself to Colonel Wheatley. However, he was so glad to see her alive and well that his strictures on her foolishness were minimal.

Relieved of immediate problems and shrinking from any contemplation of the horrors she had seen, Esmeralda's mind reverted to its lodestar. Now she grieved at having parted from Robert in anger. She knew, wryly, that he probably had not realized she was angry, but she had a vague feeling that his hesitation before he left had been a silent appeal that she had not answered. She was worried about him, too, although she had no idea that he had been in great danger. From the vagueness of his answer when she had asked where he would be, she assumed that he was detailed to do observation or possibly act as liaison with the Spanish.

She knew, too, that it was pointless to ask for information about Robert at headquarters. Major Colborne was doubtless aware of where she had been quartered, or could find out, and Esmeralda trusted him to send her any news he had. Thus, to occupy her mind and also to accustom herself to an experience she expected to have, she offered to bathe Molly's little son that evening. The fire had warmed the room reasonably well, and she took the infant on her lap, dipped a cloth into a bowl of warm water, and started to uncover the child.

Esmeralda was aware, of course, of the impropriety of becoming involved too personally with servants, but she and Molly had been through too much together to worry about that. Thus, she did not hesitate to ask a question that handling the baby had brought to her mind. As she exposed one and then another small portion of the infant and cleaned it, she said, "Is it always so quick, Molly?"

"Quick?" Molly repeated, looking up from the supper she was preparing.

"The birthing," Esmeralda explained. "It could not have been fifteen or twenty minutes between the time you told us the baby was coming and when it was born."

Molly laughed. "No, ma'am, 'twasn't so quick as 't seemed. Th' pains started whin th' mule fell, but loight they were, 'n Oi kept hopin' they'd stop, as sometoimes happens, or thit we'd git where we was goin' before 't came."

Esmeralda's eyes were round with astonishment. "You mean you walked all night while—you were in labor? Oh, Molly, I'm sorry I didn't notice. I was—" Suddenly the horrors she had deliberately excluded from her mind surfaced. "All those people," she whispered, "the soldiers, the women—" Unconsciously, she wrapped the linen protectively around the infant in her lap and caught him up in her arms. "The children." A sob caught her voice. "The poor little children . . ."

" 'Tis no use thinkin' o' thit," Molly said sharply. " 'Twas noon o' yoor doin' nor o' moine. 'Nd walkin's good fer birthin'." Then her lips tightened. "But from whut wuz we runnin'? We niver saw iny inimy. Oh, as Oi have th' hope o' hivin, so Oi hope thit th' giniral rode up 'n doon th' road 'nd saw whut we saw—'nd Oi hope he roides thit road feriver in hell, seein' those babe's froze 'nd th' little 'uns limpin', leavin' bloody tracks 'n th' snow." Her voice began to shake, and she stopped abruptly.

There was nothing Esmeralda could say. She liked Sir John, who had been very kind to her personally, and up until now Robert respected his military ability, but she had seen too much to utter platitudes about necessity.

"Oi big yer pardon, ma'am," Molly said softly. " 'Tisn't me place t' say sich things t' ye, but 't would've bin me lyin' there if no fer ye."

"And if not for you," Esmeralda said, forcing a smile, "I would be very frightened and very ignorant about many things I need to know. And I would not have had the pleasure of meeting—good gracious, Molly, have you decided what to call him?"

"Kivin, 'tis his father's name." Molly turned from the fire and smiled as the infant, who had been making little whimpering sounds despite Esmeralda's rocking him in her arms, began to squall loudly again. She held out one arm for him while she bared a breast, then sat down and offered it to the blindly seeking mouth. The babe suckled eagerly, strongly, and Molly smiled again. "He's strong," she said. Then the smile faded and her eyes shadowed. "Whoile ye were wit th' colonel, we had 'im baptized—jist . . . jist in case."

"Nothing will happen to Kevin," Esmeralda said firmly. "Colonel Wheatley told me that we will be here for several days. We have plenty of food now, and blankets, and Luisa and Boa will be rested. We will—"

Her voice cut off, and her breath drew in sharply as a fist pounded on the door and a voice called, "Are these Mrs. Moreton's quarters?"

Chapter 30

"Robert!" Esmeralda shrieked, leaping up and rushing to the door. "Robert, is that you?"

The door flung open, and they fell into each other's arms, Robert saying thickly, "Oh, Merry, Merry, I never meant you to suffer so. I never meant you to see—"

While Esmeralda, not paying the slightest attention, cried, "Oh, you're safe, you're safe. You must be so tired—"

The disjointed ejaculations went on for a little while until Robert said, "Merry, I love you. I love you so. I've tried to find a sensible way of telling you, but there's no time."

Both statements shocked Esmeralda into silence. She stood staring up into Robert's face, her big eyes wide, incapable of any reply because joy and despair were struggling so violently inside her. She had been given the crowning perfection of her life in one phrase and what amounted, in her opinion, to a death sentence in the next. Robert loved her—it was more than she had ever dreamed; but if there was no time and they must continue the march that night, she really did not expect that any of them would survive.

"It's all right, my dear," Robert said, pulling her tight against him. "I know I've probably shocked you. I always seem to burst out with things that should be introduced slowly and carefully. I don't expect you to be in love with me this moment—"

Molly had done the best she could by moving into a dark corner and turning her back. She knew she should not be present, witnessing this nakedly emotional moment, but there was nowhere for her to go except out into the stable shed at the back. Had she been alone, she would have slipped out gladly, but she would not take her infant into the cold unless she were actually ordered to do so.

She had also tried not to hear, but it was impossible. Thus, though she did her best to concentrate on suckling her baby, Robert's ringing declaration of love forced itself on her. She missed the end of the sentence, spoken more softly, but she also heard his last statement, which was so silly that a hiccup of laughter escaped her before she could stifle it.

The sound checked Robert's speech, and he turned affronted eyes in its direction. "It must be the baby," Esmeralda said quickly. "Molly had a baby, a little son, early this morning."

Robert stared at her, forgetting in his amazement even the delicate matter of his passion and Esmeralda's reaction to it. "How? Where? A *baby*? You mean she . . . er . . . produced a *baby*? On the *road*?"

Desperately Esmeralda bit her lips. This was no time to laugh. "Come upstairs, Robert," she gabbled. "Molly must watch the supper. I am sure you must be starved as well as soaking wet. I have your clothes. Do come up."

He followed docilely, still too stunned to protest, and as soon as they were in the loft room, Esmeralda insured further silence by throwing her arms around his neck and kissing him, murmuring when their lips finally parted, "Oh, Robert, I do love you. I have always loved you."

"Have you?" he asked delightedly. "That's what Colborne said, but I thought you would have too much sense to love a fool like me."

Rendered speechless again by another violent urge to laugh simultaneous with a desire to weep over Robert's modesty, Esmeralda bent her head and pressed her face against his chest.

He kissed the top of her head, and then said, "I don't think you ought to stand with your nose buried in my coat. I can't imagine how I smell, I'm too used to it, but it must be awful."

That remark released Esmeralda's pent-up mirth, and she kissed him again. "I cannot believe I smell any better. We can only heat water in very small quantities because I discarded all the large pots to lighten Luisa's . . ." Her voice faded, as reference to the deadly trek they had just finished reminded her that Robert had said there was no time.

Robert's arms went around her protectively. "I'm sorry," he murmured, "I'm sorry, my love. I could kill myself for being so stupidly selfish, for keeping you with me at such a cost. You must hate me for exposing you to—"

"I will never hate you for anything, Robert, never, but . . ."
Tears rose in her eyes. "Must we go on tonight? Must we really? Is
there no way—?"

"Tonight! Of course not. Whatever put that into your head?"

"You said there was no time."

He touched her face, running an index finger along the hollow that
had not been in her cheek when they left Salamanca. "I meant there
was no time for me to court you, to show what I feel instead of just
saying it. But I do love you, Merry. You've become the center of my
whole life. I hope you don't mind if the flowers and pretty things
come after the declaration rather than before. I swear, you won't be
cheated of them."

Esmeralda laughed again. "I never cared for that and never will. I
can—"

She stopped. She had been about to say she could buy all the pretty
things she wanted, but realized that this was still not the right time to
mention that she was very, very rich. Robert had had enough shocks
for one day. He must be even more physically exhausted than she
was—he certainly looked it. And to confess about the money right
after he said he loved her would make it sound as if she had been
deliberately concealing the information all this time out of lack of
trust.

"But that's all nonsense," she went on hurriedly. "How long can
you stay? Can you eat with me? Will you have time to sleep for a
while?"

Robert had been looking slightly puzzled. He felt there was
something more to that aborted "I can—" that Merry's quick change
of subject was a cover over something she was hiding. He was about
to revert to the words, more interested in those than in inessentials like
eating, but her last question diverted him. A slow smile curved his
lips.

"I am a bit short on sleep," he admitted, "but that isn't what I want
time in bed for."

"There isn't any bed," Esmeralda murmured, burying her face in
his coat again.

She felt ridiculously shy, far more like a virgin bride on her
wedding night than an experienced married woman. Robert's confession of love had somehow made a tremendous difference. He held

her against him, feeling her tremble, and then lifted her face and
kissed her very gently.

"No, and it's cold, and we're both filthy and tired," he said. "I
want you very much, but not this way, my darling, not in a dirty
huddle where we can't even take off our clothes."

"Oh, Robert—" she began to protest.

He put his fingers gently over her lips. "No. I'm sending you on
ahead of the army tomorrow, Merry. I don't often pull rank and
influence, but I've done it. It's less than sixty miles to Corunna, and
I've got a carriage and horses—"

"No," she interrupted him, pushing herself out of his arms. "I
don't want to go. I can't leave you. I can't."

"Don't fight me, Merry," Robert said tiredly. "Whatever you fear
in England can't happen. The worst—"

"I was never afraid to go to England," she cried. "I only wanted to
stay with you. It was all an excuse, only an excuse so you wouldn't
send me away."

His face lighted. "Oh, my darling, my sweet, sweet Merry. How
glad I am. But it doesn't change anything. You must go." He saw her
expression and shook his head; then, made perceptive by his own
feeling for her, said the only thing that could have silenced her. "You
are a danger to me, my love. I can't concentrate on what is going on
around me because all I can think about is you and whether you are
falling by the wayside, about to become one of those pitiful
bodies. . . ."

She stared at him, realizing that it was useless to tell him that she
would be protected, that the Guards would have carried her if
necessary. He knew it as well as she. Fear for a loved one cannot be
cured by reason.

"But what about Molly and the baby?" she whispered. "And
Carlos."

"They can go with you. And don't tell me that Carlos will not go
without Luisa—I know it. Luisa and Boa Viagem can follow the
carriage. The only one who must remain is M'Guire, and, frankly, I
can use him."

Tears welled into her eyes and then ran over, streaking her hollow
cheeks. "Let me wait at Corunna for you," she pleaded brokenly.
"Oh, please. I will be in no danger there. I will be warm and safe. Let
me wait at Corunna."

Robert could not resist this plea, and he agreed without argument that she should wait. On thinking it over after he had seen the carriage off, he did not regret it. Merry would be safe, and there was another, more practical reason for allowing her to wait until he arrived. He intended to pull rank and influence once more to be sure that she went on the best and safest ship and that the captain of the vessel was properly impressed with his father's connections in the Royal Navy.

Robert realized that he, personally, might not make it to Corunna, but that would make no difference to the pressure exerted on Merry's behalf. Colborne would see to it, or any of Sir John's other ADCs, or even Sir John himself. Robert's mouth hardened. He was not quite so fond of Sir John as he had been. There were aspects of this retreat that he was unable to understand or even excuse. There had been no need for such haste. The French could have been held for days at Astorga while the army left, one detachment at a time, properly supplied with the stores that had been burnt. But it was useless to think about that now.

Robert knew that he would be exposed to a second dose of resistance when he arranged Merry's passage at Corunna, but he was armored against that now. The French were closing in.

Sir John allowed the army to wait at Lugo for three days, drawn up to resist an attack, and during that time the men, although still sullen, were better behaved. But Soult did not move. Sir John's general officers urged him to initiate the action, saying that a good drubbing of the French would insure that the remainder of the retreat would be carried out in better order. It would make Soult less eager to pursue closely and put heart into the Spanish, who felt they were being abandoned; most important of all, it would restore the pride of the men.

But Moore would neither attack nor, as a suggested alternative, await Soult's attack, which everyone agreed must come very soon, as the French were worse supplied than the English and would soon starve if they were not doing so already. Instead, at midnight on January 8–9, leaving the bivouac fires burning to fool the enemy, the army resumed its retreat.

This notion might have been a good one on a clear night in an open area. Near a town in a mountainous countryside where there were walls and fences and many small byroads to farms and in a pouring rain, it was a disaster. The troops, even more surly and mutinous,

feeling their commanding officers were fools and cowards, became
little more than a disorderly mob. Coming along with the rear guard,
Robert was disgusted by the scenes of pillage, worse now than ever
before.

On January 11 the army, such as it was, reached Corunna. M'Guire
came in the next day, leading Mars, who had lost a shoe and was
already limping. Had they not been so close to their destination, he
would have had to be destroyed, like Apollo, whom Robert had been
forced to shoot outside Villa Franca. Quite innocently, M'Guire gave
Esmeralda a terrible shock when he came to her room in the hotel to
deliver a note from Robert. The note said little—that he was well but
held by duty at El Burgo and did not wish to stress his one remaining
horse by riding back and forth for short visits. Esmeralda smiled,
thinking how those words would have hurt her before Robert's
confession of love and how easily she could accept them now.

Happy herself, she asked M'Guire how he liked his son, and he
beamed proudly and told her that if they all lived long enough, the
captain had promised to be Kevin's sponsor.

"He couldn't have a better," M'Guire said. "A divil th' capt'in is
in action."

"Action? What action?" Esmeralda gasped.

"Ach, the Frenchies needed a lissin t' keep thim frum gettin' too
boold."

But then, equally unwitting, M'Guire withdrew the sting of fear, for
when Esmeralda asked fearfully if there was now fighting, he
laughed.

"No, nor wull be. They've blowed the bridges."

On January 13, Robert himself came. The French had discovered a
passage of the river, and Sir John had ordered his rear guard back into
the heights in front of Corunna. When Robert rode in to report, he was
recalled to ordinary staff duty, the rear guard now being close enough
for Moore to oversee it himself. Sir John was busy writing a long
report of the present situation to Castlereagh, and Robert asked
Colborne who was going to carry it.

"Sir Charles Stewart. And Moreton—"

"Castlereagh's brother," Robert interrupted. "Good. Where is
he?"

"I don't know," Colborne said and then, shocked at the expression
on Robert's usually good-humored face, added hastily, "but he'll be

here soon. Take it easy, Robert. What the devil is the matter with you?"

"If you don't already know, you won't want to hear," Robert snapped. "I'm sending Merry home, out of this mess. I want Stewart to escort her, and I've got to speak to him. My family won't be in London at this time of the year. Stewart will have to—"

"Robert, calm down. I'm sure Sir Charles will do everything necessary to assist Mrs. Moreton, but not much may be necessary. There are letters for you. I've sent them out three times, and they've missed you. What have you been doing?"

"Trying to herd together the disaster that once was an army," Robert snarled.

Colborne made no reply to that, and Robert took the letters—an enormously fat one in his mother's delicate hand, a relatively plump one from his father, and a single, thin sheet from Perce. He opened the third one. It contained three sentences:

"You damned lunatic! Send your wife home at once. Sabrina and I are coming in from Cornwall and will wait at Stour House in London until she arrives."

A little of the tension eased out of Robert's face. He stuffed the two unopened letters into his coat pocket. He was not in the mood to read raptures or bewailings from his mother and carefully phrased suggestions from his father. But Perce's letter had solved most of his problems. Although he had been determined to do it, it did seem the outside of enough to saddle Sir Charles with finding Merry a decent hotel, guaranteeing the bill, seeing that she had money, and arranging all the other details entailed in protecting a young woman who had no friends. Now all Sir Charles had to do was drop her at Stour House in London, and he was going to London anyway.

All Robert had to do in addition to insure Esmeralda's comfort was write a draft on his banker, which Perce would have cashed, so that Merry could buy what she wanted without the embarrassment of asking for money. He sighed with relief, then frowned again. Merry was going to get stubborn as a mule if she had to leave Molly and Carlos behind. Robert's mind checked and backed up to the word "mule." He groaned audibly.

Colborne looked up from what he was writing. "Now what's the matter?"

"Is the ship that will take Stewart in the harbor now?"

"Yes. Why?"

"I have to speak to the commander. Is he bribable, do you think?"

"What?" Colborne asked, unbelievingly.

Robert smiled wryly. "I want to see if I can get him to take a horse and a mule as well as my wife, her maid, her maid's infant, and her boy servant."

Colborne just stared at him, his mouth slightly ajar. "A horse and a mule on a courier ship?" he got out at last.

"Well, I think Merry will trust me to bring Boa Viagem if there isn't room for both," Robert said thoughtfully, "but Carlos will not go without Luisa. If we force him, he'll probably jump overboard and try to swim back. And I'm going to have enough trouble with Merry without suggesting that she leave Carlos, so the mule *must* go."

Colborne closed his eyes and shuddered. Then, faintly, he gave the name of the vessel and the name of the naval officer commanding her. Robert smiled grimly and set out for the docks. There he was fortunate enough to encounter not only the naval officer but Sir Charles also. It was not exactly easy to arrange matters, and Stewart's guffaws of laughter did not help much; however, when he stopped laughing, Sir Charles gallantly added his own request to Robert's, and the thing was done. No poor naval commander was going to oppose the Earl of Moreton's son and Lord Castlereagh's brother.

All this took so long that, when Robert at last went to Merry, he had to tell her that she and all her dependents must be ready within the hour. In one way he regretted it; there was time for nothing but one hungry kiss. In every other way, he was devoutly glad. The suddenness of her departure was such a shock that her emotions were numbed; he did not have to see the fear and grief in her eyes. He knew she would worry about him—he was worried about her traveling the wintry seas—but it was less painful to know something if one did not see the stark evidence of it.

But Esmeralda would not have argued in any case. To weep and plead could only make Robert miserable; his expression told her it would not change his mind. Knowing that, it was best to make everything easy for him, as she had always done—and his gratitude was thanks enough. She did not even ask what she was to do when she came to London. She knew his parents had a residence there, and she intended to send a note to Moreton House with the name of the hotel at which she would stay. That way Robert would know where to find her. They were actually all on board ship before Robert said that she was to go not to Moreton House but to Stour House, where his brother and sister-in-law, Sabrina, would be expecting her.

"Oh, no," Esmeralda cried. "I could not—"

"Perce is the best of good fellows," Robert assured her, and thrust into her hands Perce's letter and the draft on his banker, "and you will like Sabrina. She looks like a candy doll, all silver tinsel, but she's just as tough as you are, my love, and has most excellent good sense. And if you're safe with Perce and Sabrina, I'll not worry about you."

So she agreed to that, too, thinking in the back of her mind that she would convince Sir Charles to leave her in a hotel. She could tell him that she wished to wash off the soil of her journey and change her dress—not that she had a dress to change into, since all had been abandoned to lighten Luisa's load—and that she would go to Stour House when she was presentable. She did not begin to cry until after the boat had taken Robert back to the docks, not until they set sail and she could no longer see him—a tiny blue and white speck—watching the ship recede.

For the remainder of that day, Robert felt very strange. There was a large hole in his life. It was not only that he missed Merry in a physical sense. These past weeks he had actually seen very little of her, but until this day he had always been conscious that she was *there,* a certain number of miles away, that he could get to her if it was really necessary. Now she was no longer there, and he did not like the feeling at all.

The next day, January 14, was busy. The transports had finally arrived and embarkation of the sick, wounded, and dependents began. In addition, the French were now heavily massed. Colonel MacKenzie of the Fifth reported that another division and a multitude of stragglers had swelled the force with which Soult had been advancing cautiously. Moore seemed to throw off his depression at this news and went out to examine the ground himself.

There were three ridges of hills, the first two more formidable than the third and far more extensive. Moore had no more than fifteen thousand men. He resolved to set his defense on the third ridge, called the Monte Moro, and for the first time since they had left Sahagun, Robert recognized the commander under whom he had begun his career. By the morning of January 15 the British were in position, braced for an attack by a force considerably larger than their own, but in surprisingly good spirits.

The first part of the day was a grave disappointment. The French could be seen moving on the higher ridges, but nothing happened. As the day advanced to noon, Sir John became convinced that Soult would not attack after all and ordered General Edward Paget to march his troops down to the harbor, since they were to be the first to embark. About a quarter to two in the afternoon, however, there was a crash of artillery fire from the top of the westernmost crest.

Sir John at once galloped up behind General Baird's division and saw columns of French pouring down into the valley and cavalry regiments pushing out from behind the Penasquedo Heights. The first smile Robert had seen since the retreat had begun lightened Moore's face. Although the excitement that Robert always felt at the prospect of action stirred in him, one part of his mind remained very cold.

He knew Sir John welcomed this battle because a victory that would permit him to embark his troops under the very noses of the French would do much to soften the bitter criticisms that would be launched at him. But Robert could not forget that if Moore had permitted the army to stand its ground at Astorga and had managed the retreat in a less hysterical fashion, there would be fewer frozen bodies along the road. Thus, the satisfaction Robert felt at seeing his old mentor enthusiastically discussing the coming action with Baird had a tinge of bitterness in it.

Not more than fifteen minutes later, another dose of gall was added. The artillery barrage grew more intense. Even Hermes, hardened old trooper that he was, danced and curveted, and Robert reined him hard and backed him, suddenly aware that one stirrup seemed loose. He bent to check and then jerked the horse farther aside as a muffled scream sounded ahead of him and an angry whoosh seemed to go right by his left leg. When he came erect he saw a crowd surrounding General Baird, lifting him from his horse and working over him.

"What—" he said to Colborne.

"Ball shattered his left arm. It missed you by a hair."

Robert gritted his teeth. He liked General Baird.

"Moreton," Sir John called. "The Fiftieth is coming up from Elvina. See that it re-forms on the Forty-second. They are to make ready to charge down when the French come up the slope."

The Fiftieth was retiring under heavy fire. Robert knew that Sir John had intended him to wait with the Forty-second, but his anger and frustration needed an outlet. He passed Sir John's order to Lieutenant Colonel Stirling, left Hermes with the reserve mounts of Stirling's ADCs, and ran down toward the action. It was just as well that he had decided to go down, for Major Charles Napier was trying to rally his men already, and Robert's instructions eased his conscience about not holding the village.

The regiment had fallen back in good order, however, and were quite ready to come down on the French again. With the support of the Forty-second, they drove in the *tirailleurs* with a crushing fire, but the supporting columns held out against them, and they took shelter behind a line of stone walls. Not far from the major, Robert took aim with a musket snatched from a wounded soldier. He swore in disgust as his target remained standing. But a man to that soldier's right cried out and fell, and Robert wondered whether it was his bullet that had struck him. He cursed the inaccuracy of the weapon in his hands and threw it down, drawing his pistol.

Before Robert could fire, he saw Sir John coming down the slope, calling out that they must advance. He expected next to hear his name and a scathing remark on his self-indulgence, but either the general did not see him or he was too busy to concern himself with the erratic behavior of one of his usually reliable aides. The regiments, encouraged by their officers, climbed or leapt the walls and pressed forward, Robert with them.

The head of the French formation melted before their volleys, and the battle rolled downhill toward Elvina again. At the closer range of a pursuit, Robert's pistol took its toll, and he blessed it and its maker because it did not jam. Just above the village, the Forty-second halted, but Major Napier was determined to take back what he had lost and led his men in among the houses. The French were not making a determined stand, but even so, clearing them out of the place was dangerous work.

One of the *tirailleurs* who had survived the initial charge suddenly stepped around the corner of a house and fired at Robert from about ten feet. Obviously he had been confused for just a moment by Robert's blue coat and had not lifted his gun until he saw Robert raise his own, which gave him no time to aim. His bullet took off Robert's

cocked hat, but Robert's shattered the man's head. Robert leapt for the
shelter of the wall while he drew his saber, for his pistol was empty.
He suspected that where there was one Frenchman, there might be
others. Shouts made him turn to look, relieved to see red coats only a
few yards behind—and the world exploded. . . . And then there
was nothing.

Chapter 31

There are many things that can be said about a winter sea voyage, most of them bad, particularly on a very small ship not intended for passengers. However, if the wind is right, it is usually strong, and the one good thing about Esmeralda's trip to England was that it was quickly over. Moreover, the sour, silent moods of the commander of the vessel, whose quarters Esmeralda and Molly occupied, and of Sir Charles Stewart, who carried less than exhilarating news for his brother and in addition was having serious trouble with his eyes, suited Esmeralda very well. All of them hardly exchanged a hundred words, although they saw each other every day.

Even Esmeralda's attempt to avoid being pushed on Robert's family was settled in very few words. She asked to be settled in a hotel, and Sir Charles said, very simply, "No." When she gave her reasons, he shrugged. Then he uttered a full sentence. He allowed that she could walk out of Stour House one minute after he brought her into it, but that was where he said he would take her, and he would do it.

Esmeralda did not really fight very hard. Naturally she had read Perce's note, and there was something very warm and comforting in it. When she considered that aspect of it, she felt a thrill of hope that she might, after so many years of isolation, again find the tender concern of fond relatives, which she had lost when her mother died.

Then at other times she found herself enraged at the notion that Perce should call Robert a damned lunatic. She was not personally offended. Somehow she was sure that the words did not have to do with Robert's sudden marriage but with the fact that he had allowed his wife to follow the army. She resolved firmly to defend her husband's decision even if that defense did not please Robert's brother, and she further intended to make clear that in the future she would go right on following her husband and she would not thank anyone for trying to interfere.

But then the question of her baby would arise. Now that they were on the ship, Molly confessed that she had been surprised Esmeralda had not lost the child, owing to the hardships she had endured. Esmeralda had exclaimed in horror. It had never occurred to her that she would miscarry; Molly had had the same experiences or worse. But Molly soothed her by assuring her she had only mentioned the matter because it was the best of good signs. The baby was sure to be strong and healthy.

New hopes flickered in Esmeralda's heart. If Perce and Sabrina accepted her and if she could convince them that it was *her* desire to follow the army, could she induce them to believe it was not wrong? Then would they act as surrogate parents for a few months at a time so that she could be with Robert? This hope was so enticing that it did more harm than good because it made Esmeralda nervous about the impression she would make on her new relatives.

Fortunately, this idea did not occur to her until she was so exhausted by being shaken and banged about in the post chaise racing toward London that she soon fell asleep. Just as her eyes closed, Esmeralda gave a dizzy thought to Molly and Carlos, traveling with Luisa by slow stages. She would have much preferred to go with them, but Sir Charles would not hear of it. He had promised his escort, and his escort she would have, even if it meant she must travel at courier speed.

In the end, she had no time for nervousness before arrival because she was not aware of having arrived until Sir Charles shook her gently and said, "Here we are, Mrs. Moreton."

He lifted her out of the carriage and supported her up the steps. Esmeralda's lips trembled. Among the many reasons she had been relieved at going to Stour House rather than Moreton House was that she thought a Mr. St. Eyre's home would be less grand than an earl's residence, but the building into which she was being shepherded seemed more magnificent than the governor's house in Bombay. She was shaking so hard that Sir Charles kept his arm around her as he sounded the knocker. Esmeralda shuddered. There was something strange about the house, a blank, empty look that was forbidding.

"I don't think there's anyone here," she said faintly, crushed by disappointment despite her initial reluctance to come.

However, the door opened just as Sir Charles began to answer, and he turned to the footman instead, saying, "This is Mrs. Moreton. I believe Lord and Lady Kevern are expecting her."

The footman's eyes first widened in shock and then narrowed in disbelief. His glance flickered over Sir Charles's arm, which still supported Esmeralda, then over her stained, ragged riding dress and Sir Charles's uniform, which was in even worse condition, torn and blackened with powder stains, mud, and dried blood.

"If you will give me your card," he said coldly, "I will present it to—"

Upon which Sir Charles put a hand on the footman's chest and shoved him back into the house with considerable force, following him in and dragging Esmeralda with him.

"You bloody nodcock!" he roared. "D'you think I carry visiting cards on the battlefield?"

Almost simultaneous with Sir Charles's outraged bellow came the sounds of footsteps—several heavy pairs from the back of the house and the brief click of high-heeled slippers as a woman crossed a piece of polished flooring between two carpet runners. But Esmeralda did not notice that. In fact, she had hardly taken in Sir Charles's enraged roar because what she saw on entering had confirmed her original fear. There was no one to meet her. The house was empty. All the furniture was dust sheeted.

"Sir Charles—" she began in a shaking voice, intending to urge him to leave and take her to a hotel. She got no further, being interrupted by a firm feminine voice.

"Whatever is the—" Sabrina began, and then she, too, took in the condition of her visitors' clothing. However, she was much less impressed with the external marks of status than her footman, and she came immediately to the correct conclusion. Of course, she also recognized Sir Charles Stewart, which was helpful, so she finished with an exclamation. "Sir Charles! Oh, have you brought my brother's wife home? Oh, thank you."

"Yes," he said as Sabrina came down the stairs, "this is Mrs. Moreton."

But Sabrina did not acknowledge the introduction. All her attention was focused on Sir Charles. She remembered with horror similar stains on a uniform her husband had worn. "Are you hurt, Sir Charles?" she asked breathlessly, and then when he shook his head,

"Is there anything I can do for you? I see you have come directly from the field. Would you like to bathe? A change of clothes?"

"I thank you, no," he replied. "I am going directly to my brother's house and will be accommodated there." Then his voice softened. "Mrs. Moreton has had rather a bad time," he said.

"Oh, my God!" Sabrina cried, "Robert? Has—"

"No, no," Sir Charles said hastily. "Captain Moreton was perfectly well when we left him. I only meant . . . Well, Mrs. Moreton will explain, I am sure. My business with my brother is very urgent, so if you will pardon me, I will take my leave at once."

Esmeralda stood quite frozen through this exchange. She heard it, of course, but it made little impression on her mind. All she knew was that Sabrina's eyes had flicked over her once, and from that moment all of her attention had been given to Sir Charles. It seemed Robert was wrong. She was not welcome to Lady Kevern. She heard Sabrina say something about sending the footman out with Sir Charles for the baggage.

"I have no baggage," Esmeralda said.

Sabrina had started to accompany Sir Charles to the door, but something in Esmeralda's voice stopped her. She turned, and her eyes met Esmeralda's. "My dear," she cried, "I didn't mean to overlook you. I thought he was hurt. Perce was with the Russian army at Eylau. . . . Oh, that can't mean anything to you, but when I saw the blood on his coat . . . But Mrs. Moreton—Esmeralda—you are welcome. I cannot tell you how welcome you are."

"Robert calls me Merry," Esmeralda said, her voice shaking.

"My darling Merry," Sabrina murmured, putting her arms around her. "My darling Merry, you have come home."

Those words were the last thing Esmeralda remembered. When she opened her eyes, she was totally bewildered. She was in the middle of a huge bed hung with the most elaborate curtains she had ever seen. She lay for a while looking at them, but no amount of staring brought the slightest familiarity. Nor was there anything else, when she began to examine the remainder of her surroundings, that was in the least familiar. Never in her life had she slept on silk sheets, nor been covered by so intricately embroidered a feather quilt, nor worn a nightgown of sinfully expensive lace, tucked and pleated to display the body beneath it so provocatively.

Eventually she remembered arriving at Stour House, and the

amenities explained themselves. She remembered, too, the oddly erratic greeting, so seemingly cold in the beginning and then so warm. Vaguely it seemed to her that she had been given a reason, but she could not remember what. In any case, she thought, she had better get up at once. She realized she must have fainted. It would never do to confirm the impression that she was weak and sickly. Someone might tell Robert. She reached for the bedcurtains.

They were instantly pulled back, and a pleasant-looking woman smiled at her warmly and said, "Dinna ye move a bit. Brina'll be here in a minnit, and yer breakfast on her heels. Ach, ye'll be wonderin' who'm I. I'm Katy."

The manner indicated a very privileged old servant, probably Lady Kevern's nurse, although she did not call herself "Nanny," as most of them did. Esmeralda smiled in response, feeling more confident. If Lady Kevern had sent her own nurse rather than just any maid to watch by her, it must mean that those arms around her had not been an impulse that soon passed.

"There isn't anything wrong with me," Esmeralda said. "I'm so sorry to have made such a dramatic entrance. It was the post chaise. We only stopped to change horses, and that was done so quickly there was no time to get out—"

"Of course there isn't anything *wrong* with you," Sabrina's voice interrupted, "but why didn't you tell Sir Charles you couldn't travel at such a pace?"

"I couldn't do that," Esmeralda protested, her eyes large. "He was a courier on army business. It was only that I am not accustomed to riding in a carriage—" She stopped abruptly, realizing she had made a faux pas from the astonishment on Sabrina's face. Ladies always traveled in carriages. But, Esmeralda thought, not army wives who followed the drum, and she pushed herself upright and went on defiantly, "I have always ridden Boa Viagem and accompanied the army on its marches." Then her mare's name reminded her of the carriage following. "My servants," she said, "are also suitable to the wife of a military man. Molly is a soldier's wife, not refined, perhaps, but strong and willing, and Carlos, though young, is clever."

"My dear," Sabrina said softly with tears in her eyes, "you do not need to defend yourself. I admire you more than I can say. You are a heroine. You must love Robert very much to have given up so much, to have endured so much, to be with him."

"Well, I do adore him," Esmeralda admitted, her spirits rising mercurially at the evidence of Sabrina's sympathy and understanding, "but I'm no heroine. I was quite accustomed to riding horseback because Papa was such a nip cheese—"

She stopped again, this time putting her hands to her mouth. It was "not done" to say such things, and she would not have slipped up except that she was so accustomed to speaking freely to Robert about her father and, of course, there had never been any occasion to speak of him to anyone else. However, Sabrina laughed heartily.

"You are a refreshment to the spirit, Merry. I wondered whether it would be necessary to avoid discussing your father. Papa Moreton was appalled—now don't start to look like a lost waif again; I assure you he does not associate you with your father's peculiarities, and Mama Moreton does not even know about them. In fact, if you feel strong enough, they are very, very eager to meet you."

Esmeralda drew a deep breath. "Of course, but I cannot go to Cornwall at this moment. Please. I must wait for Robert." Her voice started to shake, but she added another, "I must," appealingly.

"Naturally you must wait for Robert," Sabrina said. "Dear Merry, there's no question of you going to Cornwall. The Moretons are here. Perce didn't know they were coming when he wrote to Robert. You were equally invited to Moreton House, and I thought you would go there, which is why I was just a little surprised—"

"Oh, gracious, I hope the Earl and Countess of Moreton won't be offended," Esmeralda exclaimed. "I just did what Robert told me. I didn't even know Robert had written to them—or to your husband."

"Oh, that Robert!" Sabrina exclaimed, laughing. "If I know him, he never read his father's or mother's letters. Anything longer than five lines is too much bother for him. Perce was perfectly right, and I should not have scolded him about the note he wrote."

"No," Esmeralda protested, ready to leap to Robert's defense, but she paused as a maid carried in a tray, which she prepared to set over Esmeralda's thighs. Esmeralda shook her head. "I would prefer to get up," she said firmly.

Sabrina waved the maid toward a table, and Katy brought an exquisite peignoir, which fit Esmeralda very well. "I thought Meg's things would fit her," Sabrina said to Katy with satisfaction. "What a relief. That means we can shop at leisure." And when Esmeralda protested faintly at the notion of borrowing some unknown person's clothing without permission, Sabrina laughed, said, "It's only tit for tat," and explained how Megaera had also arrived without a stitch except what she was wearing and had worn Sabrina's clothes. "And, you know, Leonie came to England without any clothing, too. Well, neither had I any, but I was only nine. Still, it's becoming a family tradition. Really, I begin to think one of us will have to write a book. We seem to be very adventurous females.* How did you happen to be all alone in Lisbon when Robert married you?"

Esmeralda almost dropped the cup she was lifting to her lips and stared at Sabrina. "Robert did not marry me in Lisbon," she said. "Did he not explain. . . . Oh, heaven, what did he say?"

"Merry—" Sabrina put her hand over Esmeralda's and squeezed it gently. "Don't be so frightened. We are all very eager to love you, and I can see that you well deserve that love for yourself. I will not deny that Perce and I were a little concerned when we first heard about it. It seemed so unlike Robert to marry for money—"

"Money?" Esmeralda squeaked. "How do you know about the money?"

Sabrina looked a trifle self-conscious. "Well, of course, when Robert simply announced that he had married a woman named Esmeralda Mary Louisa Talbot whom he had met in India, Papa Moreton began to move heaven and earth to discover who you were, and when the Earl of Moreton and Roger St. Eyre start to move heaven and earth, believe me, it moves. Your bankers were as clay in their hands. Merry, what *is* wrong?"

"Robert doesn't *know,*" Esmeralda wailed. "Oh, he will be so angry. He will never understand why I did not tell him."

"No one can be angry about half a million pounds," Sabrina said, laughing, and then the first sentence Esmeralda had said hit her. "Robert doesn't know!" she repeated, stunned. "But why . . . Oh, Merry, forgive me, I don't mean to offend you, but I *know* Robert did not carry a broken heart home from India, and he was always *so* determined not to marry. So why—"

Esmeralda picked up her cup, sipped her tea, took a deep breath, and said, "Because he is the kindest, most chivalrous man in the

* Sabrina's story is told in *The Kent Heiress*, Megaera's in *The Cornish Heiress*, and Leonie's in *The English Heiress*.

entire world," and began at the beginning and told the story of her life.

Naturally, it did not take five minutes. There were questions, and pauses while Sabrina whooped with laughter, and other pauses when both women wept, and there were interruptions when emotions became too intense and Katy insisted Esmeralda must dress to give her a chance to calm down. However, before noon the whole tale was told—all of it, even including Esmeralda's pregnancy, at which Sabrina exclaimed with intense joy and reported she was in the same condition herself.

"And I was growing afraid that I never would be," Sabrina said. "Because, you know, Perce and I have been lovers for more than a year, but right after we were married—in September because William was killed a year ago August and it seemed wrong to marry virtually the day the official mourning was over—" Sabrina stopped, aware from Esmeralda's stunned expression that she had heard nothing of this before. "Robert never told you," she said, and then asked, "What in the world do you talk about?"

"The army," Esmeralda said simply.

Sabrina whooped with laughter again. "I should have known," she gasped, and embarked on the story of her life, which brought in Leonie and Megaera and their experiences.

By the time Sabrina was finished, Esmeralda was as lighthearted as she could be, considering that Robert was still in Spain and might be in danger. She was no longer in the least troubled by any irregularity in her background. "I'm awfully glad to know I am not the only one who has seduced an innocent husband," she said laughing.

Nor did her meeting with Robert's parents later in the day do anything to dampen her happiness. It was clear that the countess was utterly delighted with her new daughter-in-law. She was as kind as her son and would have loved any woman Robert was willing to marry. That Esmeralda was also gentle and most eager to be loved filled her cup of joy. She had never believed that Robert married for the money and now put it out of her mind. The earl was less simplistic in his response, but he knew Esmeralda was from a decent family. The earl had, naturally, applied to Robert's commanding officer for information and had received rather more than he expected, but it was good news.

Thus it was her father-in-law who told Esmeralda that Sir Arthur

had not forgotten his promise to try to discover her relatives in
Ireland. He had been successful and had traced both her Connor and
her Talbot relations. Both had immediately offered her a home or any
other help they could give her. And this, the earl said dryly, must be
out of disinterested kindness, because Sir Arthur had no idea she was
an heiress and could not have passed the information to them.

All the while he had been talking and listening, the earl had also
been judging, and before he parted from Esmeralda, he made it plain
that he would have approved Robert's choice even without what
Esmeralda brought.

"Not that I have any objection to an Indian heiress as a daughter,"
he said, bending down to kiss her brow, "but I am very glad to know
that my opinion that Robert is an idiot need not be revised. I hate to
revise an opinion."

"Robert is *not* an idiot," Esmeralda protested, smiling impishly.
"After all, he did not marry me for love, either."

"That is what I said," the earl pointed out, with a teasing grin.
"Any man who did not love you on sight *is* an idiot, my dear."

Thus Esmeralda's homecoming was truly a homecoming. She
remained with Sabrina, not because she was not pressed most lovingly
to live at Moreton House but, she explained, because Robert had told
her to go to Stour House and would expect to find her there. However,
she saw almost as much of the occupants of Moreton House as if she
had lived there. Her days were very busy: There were arrangements to
make with her bankers; there were long letters to write to her relatives
in Ireland; there was an apartment in a neighboring mews to fit out for
Molly and Carlos, above the stable where Boa Viagem and Luisa
would live; there was her own shopping to do, for when the Season
began, all of the Moretons' and the St. Eyres' social connections
would wish to meet her.

However, despite the steady and absorbing occupation and the
kindness of her new relations, Esmeralda's eyes grew more and more
haunted as each day passed. No one remarked on her growing fear;
they were all afraid themselves. Perce spent half his time at the Horse
Guards prying for information, but no one had any news more recent
than that brought by Sir Charles. Roger St. Eyre came down from
Stour himself to speak to Lord Castlereagh, but even Roger could not
obtain information that was not available. They did learn, from Philip
via the smuggler Pierre Restoir, that Bonaparte himself had left Spain

before the English had reached Corunna, but that gave no assurance that the embarkation had been successful.

Esmeralda cried herself to sleep every night, and the only thing that could make her smile by January 26 was little Kevin, who was growing like a weed in summer. At teatime the next afternoon, the whole family had gathered in Sabrina's parlor. The conversation was strained and disjointed, and there were frequent silences. The last of these was broken by the sound of horses trotting down the street. Everyone burst into talk at once, frantically denying the need to listen in the hope that the carriage would stop, but Esmeralda could not pretend. She rose to her feet with a gasp and ran to the window. Silence fell again like a pall until she turned and ran out of the room.

Into that silence, her voice came, high and terrified. "Major Colborne, oh, no!"

And then a man's voice, but no one heard what he said because there was a concerted rush to the door. Naturally, the jam there prevented anyone from getting out for a minute. Chivalry was forgotten; the stronger males pushed out in front of the women and went racing down the stairs then out the open door, but there they all stopped, effectively blocking the view of their anxious womenfolk so that the countess began to weep aloud until her husband turned and said joyfully, "It's all right, Emma. He's just getting out of the carriage slowly."

Then Robert was shaking off Colborne's steadying grip, catching Esmeralda to him, and saying, "Don't cry love, don't. I'm quite all right."

"You would be," Colborne snapped, "if you hadn't insisted on driving at such a pace." And then to Esmeralda: "He's had a nasty knock on the head and lost a bit of skin on his ribs, that's all. When he's had some sleep, he'll be fine."

"I'm fine now," Robert insisted. "You're all making a fuss."

"I never make a fuss," Esmeralda said firmly, "but you are not fit to be seen or smelled, Robert. Your appearance is frightening your mother. She is not accustomed to filthy rags. Come to my room, and I will make you decent."

She did no such thing, of course. He barely made it up the stairs, although he stubbornly refused any assistance, and when Esmeralda tumbled him into bed, boots, and all, he fell asleep in the middle of a mumbled protest. Tactfully, no one disturbed them. Truthfully, no one wished to do so. Now that his family knew Robert was alive and not seriously hurt or ill, everyone was more interested in Colborne's news than in Robert himself; even Robert's mother was content to leave him to Esmeralda. Robert was not easy to nurse.

Fortunately, he did not need nursing. He had been suffering from no more than a recurrence of the dizziness and raging headache, caused originally by his concussion and brought on again by the jostling of the carriage. About ten o'clock Robert sighed and opened his eyes. He, too, looked at the elaborate bedcurtains, but he guessed at once where he was and said, "Merry?"

She was there before the sound died, bending over the bed, kissing him, murmuring disjointed ejaculations of love and joy, and then pulling away a little to say, "You must be starved. I'll ring for the maid to bring up some supper."

"A bath first," he said, smiling. "We did get food along the road." Then he frowned. "What happened to M'Guire?"

"Oh, I am so glad he is safe, too. I didn't see him. I didn't know he was with you. But don't worry about him. I'm sure someone will have taken him to Molly's rooms."

"I hope you've done well by her," Robert said soberly. "I owe M'Guire my life."

Esmeralda's breath caught. "What happened?" she whispered.

"I haven't the faintest idea." Robert shrugged, but his voice was cheerful. "You know M'Guire isn't the greatest of talkers. From what I made out, I must have been hit on the head during the action and left for dead. When the French were rolled back and I didn't show up, M'Guire started to ask questions, found Hermes, and came looking for me."

"You mean no one else noticed you were missing?" Esmeralda said in a tight voice.

"Well, they had a lot to think about," Robert replied, the lightness gone from his voice. "Sir John's dead. He was struck by a cannon-ball." He blinked back tears. "It took him such a long time to die." But then he sighed and said, "Maybe it was worth it to him. He knew that we had beaten the French before he died. We buried him there, at Corunna."

"Oh, I am so sorry, Robert."

He looked at her steadily for a minute and then dropped his eyes. "I am, too—I think. But you know, Merry, the government would have made him a scapegoat. They would have torn him apart for this campaign, even with the victory at Corunna and despite the fact that I believe he *has* saved Spain. He was a sensitive man. He never had the resilience Sir Arthur has. I think that partly caused the mistakes he made; he felt he couldn't take a chance, that they'd be down on him like dogs on a rat if he was defeated."

There was nothing she could say, and she kissed him wordlessly and when he lay quietly, unresponding, she pulled the bell cord and went to the door to wait for the maid. When she had instructed her to arrange for a bath, Robert was sitting up. He put out a hand to her, and she took it and kissed it and then began to help him take off his clothes. She shuddered a little at the raw patch on his ribs, but she could see it was healing well, and she made no remark, merely handing him one of Perce's dressing gowns. He stood belting it, looking down at her.

"How beautiful you are, Merry," he said, smiling again. "I'm glad you grabbed me and were screeching 'Robert, oh, Robert.' I might not have recognized you. And then I would have made my bow to you as if you were a stranger."

She laughed. "I hope it's love that has changed my appearance and not that your eyes have gone funny because of that knock on the head."

"There's nothing wrong with my eyes. But maybe it's all the finery." Suddenly he frowned. The word "finery" had brought to mind the cost of such ornaments for a woman and that reminded him of money and a statement in his father's letter that had shocked and hurt him—and the truth of which he could scarcely believe. "Damn it, Merry," he exclaimed, "do you have some secret you don't want to tell me?"

"Not now, Robert," she said eagerly. "I've been waiting to tell you. You'll be happy. In July you'll be a father."

"A—a what?"

She laughed aloud at his stunned expression, unaware that he was thinking along other lines. In the ship on the way home, Robert had come across his parents' letters and for want of other occupation had read them. His mother's was simply full of joy at his having taken a wife and concern for him—motherly nonsense. But his father's had been read several times over in stunned disbelief. It had informed him that Merry was worth over £500,000 and had inquired delicately why he felt the need to marry for money.

"A father," Esmeralda repeated distinctly, enjoying herself. "It is a natural consequence of . . . of consummating a marriage, you know."

His mouth opened, closed. "Me?" he said, still not really absorbing her meaning. "Me? A father?"

"I swear to you that I have been faithful." Esmeralda giggled. "Unless this is another immaculate conception, you must be the father."

"Oh, my God," he gasped. "Sit down. Or should you lie down? Can I—"

"Robert"—she choked, almost unable to speak for laughing—"stop. I am not ill. Honestly, you must not coddle me or worry about me. I have been with child since we left Lisbon."

He sat down so hard he almost bounced off the bed. "Since Lisbon? You could have killed yourself! You might have died on that retreat! Merry, for God's sake, why didn't you tell me? Why?"

"I didn't know myself," she assured him. "I wasn't sure until we were at Sahagun. One doesn't know right away, Robert. There are so many things that can cause a woman to . . . to be irregular. And after Sahagun . . . oh, Robert, my love, what could you have done for me? What good would it have done to tell you? If I had lost the child, you would have blamed yourself for what was not your fault."

"But it was. I never should have let you come. I should have sent you home from Lisbon. I will never—"

She put a hand over his mouth. "Don't say it, Robert. Don't. There is no need. I did *not* lose the baby. I do not think I will ever live through a worse experience than that retreat. I survived, and I still have our child. Don't you see? I *want* to follow the drum, Robert. I love it."

He pulled her close and buried his head in her breast. "I don't know what to say, Merry. I missed you. I can't tell you how different everything was when you were gone. I felt empty inside. But . . . but it isn't right. I don't want you to endure—"

"Oh, Robert!" She kissed the top of his head, which was all she could reach. "When we're on the march together, even the fleas are fun. The retreat . . . That isn't likely ever to happen again. You know it. And you told me yourself that the worst of it was—was not necessary. It's not because *you* want me to do it but that *I* want to do it."

"What about the baby?" he asked, without looking up.

"Your mama will be delighted to keep it, or Sabrina would. She expects a baby a month or two before ours should come, and Katy can nanny both of them with a nurserymaid to help her. Robert, this war can't go on forever. And when it's over we can have our son or daughter with us wherever you are stationed."

He looked up then and smiled at her. "I think I am being led down the primrose path again," he said. "It can't all be this easy. I've known other men who had children, and it was all very complicated— fetching peaches in January and tears over the nanny's misbehavior. Is life really going to be a bed of roses?" He bent his head again to the breasts exposed by Esmeralda's low-cut gown. "You smell like roses," he murmured, and then suddenly turned his head aside. "I'd better leave you alone, I guess."

"Leave me alone?" she repeated. "What do you mean?"

"Well, if you're . . . er . . ."

Esmeralda was laughing again. "*Enceinte* is the polite word, I think. My book of etiquette had that—although why it is more polite to say pregnant in French than in English, I have no idea. But I assure you, having a child is no reason to stop being married. My goodness, you would end up hating the poor little creature—and so would I."

"But I thought—"

He left that unfinished and pulled her between his legs, standing up at the same time so that his hard shaft slid up her body. Esmeralda gasped with surprise. She had not had the least suspicion of the side effect their discussion was having. Before she could react in any way, however, Robert was kissing her, pulling at her dress, running his lips down the side of her neck and then around to the top of her breasts.

"Robert," she whispered, "Robert, wait."

But he was not willing to wait, and when the maid most inopportunely scratched at the door, just as he was removing her pantalets, he roared, "Go away, and don't come back," reducing Esmeralda to embarrassed giggles. When he had her naked on the bed, however, he did not mount her immediately but bent over her, gently stroking her body, placing featherlight kisses on her breasts and belly, and finally lying down beside her, still stroking her, running his fingers between her thighs, just barely touching and touching again the most sensitive spot in her whole body. She shuddered, lifted herself toward his hand in a mute appeal.

"Why did you want me to wait, Merry?" he whispered.

"There's no reason now, my love," she sighed, pulling at him urgently. "Come now. Come to me."

Later, when they were both content, she started to laugh. Robert lifted his brows. "It was the maid." She giggled. "That was why I said wait. I knew the maid would arrive right in the middle. Everyone in the house will know. . . ."

"Everyone in this house would have assumed the worst, even if we were innocent as saints," he said, and then sat up. "But you are *not* a saint, and not innocent. I'd almost forgotten. Do you have half a million pounds, Merry?"

"Oh . . . yes."

"Why the hell didn't you tell me?"

Her eyes were wide and apprehensive. "Because in the beginning I knew you would send me away if you found out I didn't need your help. And after . . . oh, Robert, I just forgot. It was so unimportant compared with all the exciting things that were happening in Portugal and Spain. . . . I just forgot."

He was silent for a moment, staring down at her, wondering if any woman could "forget" half a million pounds. And then he smiled. Merry wasn't "any" woman. She was Merry, the only perfect woman in the world.

"All right," he said, grinning from ear to ear, "you win. If you think riding all day, sleeping in flea-ridden hovels, and serving endless cups of tea to a bunch of loudmouthed army officers is more interesting than half a million pounds, I guess following the drum *is* the life for you."